The
Continuity
Girl

The Continuity Girl

Leah McLaren

HarperCollins*Publishers*Ltd

For Mum and Dad

The Continuity Girl
© 2006 Leah McLaren. All rights reserved.

Published by HarperCollins Publishers Ltd

Originally published in trade paperback by
HarperCollins Publishers Ltd: 2006.
This mass market paperback edition: 2007

HarperCollins books may be purchased for educational,
business, or sales promotional use through our
Special Markets Department.

HarperCollins Publishers Ltd
2 Bloor Street East, 20th Floor
Toronto, Ontario, Canada
M4W 1A8

www.harpercollins.ca

Library and Archives Canada Cataloguing in
Publication

McLaren, Leah
The continuity girl / Leah McLaren.

ISBN-13: 978-0-00-639130-2
ISBN-10: 0-00-639130-3

I. Title.
PS8625.L37C65 2007   c813'.6   c2007-900623-X
HC 9 8 7 6 5 4 3 2 1

Printed and bound in the United States
Set in Electra
Text design by Sharon Kish

1

A long night staggered into day. It was four a.m., the witching hour of the daily production schedule, and the crew was divided. They'd been shooting for fourteen hours and were now well into triple time. Tempers were either ready to break or soothed by mental calculations of the next pay stub. The collective energy was out of sync. It had been one of *those* days.

Dan Felsted, the director, was jogging back and forth between the set—a soggy card table and a couple of folding chairs arranged at the end of a rainy, wind-whipped pier in front of a swivelling camera and a floodlight mounted on a cherry picker—and the monitor tent, where Meredith Moore had been living like a gypsy in her caravan for the better part of the past three weeks.

Felsted was wearing a blue oilskin coat from Australia (for the Outback wildman look) and a baseball cap (for the Spielberg-at-work look), and chomping on an unlit cigar—an affectation he had taken to since quitting smoking six months ago. To Meredith he looked absurd, but only in the way that half the people on movie sets look absurd.

The lighting technician looked on, slack faced, as Felsted pointed at imaginary objects in the sky and on the ground. Beside him, the sound operator stood screwing the handle of his boom together like an assassin assembling his gun.

"Okay? Guys?" Felsted shouted to no one particular in his folksiest Little League–coach voice. He clapped his hands. "This is going to be wicked. It's going to be awesome. Best scene in the whole thing, I'm telling you. This is going to look better than anything we've done so far. You'll love it. *They'll* love it. Everyone will love it!"

He said something to the first assistant, then walked over, crunched his forehead against Meredith's Gore-Tex hood and whispered inside it. "We're going to do this all in one take, just to make it nice and easy for you."

"Great."

"Continuity girls need their beauty sleep."

"Do we?"

"Yup. And you know what actresses need?"

Meredith's blood redirected its flow toward the middle of her face, into the area beauticians call the "T-zone." Without moving her head, she shifted her gaze toward Helene, the twenty-two-year-old Québécoise model-turned-TV-star. Helene was wrapped in a blanket, shivering and blue-lipped after

2

having jumped off the pier seventeen times that evening. Beneath her mackintosh, Meredith felt the first pinpricks of sweat.

"What *do* actresses need?"

"To be controlled. But that's not what you thought I was going to say, was it."

Meredith looked down at her binder and noted the act, scene, shot and take number in a strict horizontal line. "For scene six you wanted to print takes four and eleven."

"Right you are. As always." Dan smiled his vulgar, handsome smile.

He was such an unapologetic and total bastard, you couldn't help but love him. At least Meredith couldn't. She'd had sex with him once, in the storage locker of a producer's condo during a wrap party. That was over two years ago.

***

Everybody said Meredith was the perfect continuity girl. She wasn't just good at her job, she looked the part. From the crown of her glossy brown bob to her six pairs of identical flats, Meredith Moore was as eerily tidy and well composed as an Edward Hopper painting. It was her job to sit in front of the monitor during shooting and watch every single take of every single scene to make sure every last detail was consistent with that in the take before. She was the error-catcher. The needle-in-the-haystack finder.

While Meredith's co-workers were busy worrying about halfway-creative things like lenses and lights and line delivery, she watched for the tiny narrative aberrations everyone else was either too technically skilled or famous to worry about. It was her role to fret and nag the director like a dissatisfied wife. Her days were spent snapping and comparing a thousand Polaroids, smoothing the narrative and perspective into fictional consistency. A cigarette in the left hand when it should be in the right, a prematurely melted ice cube in a half-empty glass of Scotch, a stray lock of an actor's hair—these were the details by which Meredith measured her working life.

After a full day and night of shooting a publicly funded, narratively troubled TV movie of the week, Dan, the darling auteur who had been given creative carte blanche by a public broadcaster known mainly for funding historical dramas set in drizzly mining towns, decided what he needed was a surrealist poker game, at the end of the city pier, in the rain, between the main character (a cynical rogue much like the director himself and played by the director himself) and the father of the main character, a retired postal worker played by a septuagenarian summer-stock theatre veteran with a prostate condition that had him shuffling to the Porta Potti on the quarter-hour. This incomprehensible fantasy sequence was not in the script, but had occurred to Felsted while they were shooting the suicide scene in which the protagonist

4

fails to prevent his heartbroken mistress (Helene) from throwing herself off the pier into the frigid black waters of the city harbour.

Felsted was generally pleased with himself, but he was especially proud of his half-cocked late-night flights of postmodernist fancy. Like that of some bloody minded First World War general, his own exhilaration for the job at hand grew in inverse proportion to the enthusiasm of the people around him. He sucked energy from his crew like a desert fugitive wringing out a dishrag over cracked lips. He was forty-two and had recently taken a Korean bride on the recommendation of his film school mentor.

The idea for the poker scene had emerged a couple of hours ago. "It'll be like Banquo's ghost storming the set of *Vertigo*," he'd shouted, emerging from his trailer mussy-capped after taking Helene up on her shyly lisped offer of an "East Indian head massage" during the dinner break.

The props mistress waddled out of her trailer and produced a deck of cards and a whisky bottle filled with flat, watered-down Coca-Cola. She divested Dan of his director props—the raincoat, ball cap and cigar—and replaced them with his character props—a different ball cap (this one New York Yankees instead of Boston Red Sox), a wine-coloured oilskin jacket (this one from Scotland) and an unlit cigarillo to allow better enunciation. Several floodlights combusted to life. The actors were powdered. Reels began to roll.

Meredith scrutinized the action. Not the actual action, but the eight-by-eight-inch video feed before her face. She was beyond tired. It was as if her right eyeball was winding itself up in its socket and untwisting in a brain-gouging whirl. She watched the pint-sized Dan Felsted through the monitor, acting up a hurricane, improvising every second line, slapping down the playing cards, dealing hands with the arrogance (if not dexterity) of a Vegas shark. Meanwhile, Glen, the theatre veteran playing his dead father, did everything in his power to react to Dan's impassioned tour de force without making use of the adult diaper lurking below his blue mailman's uniform. When Dan laid down his hand (a full house) and scooped the pot against his chest, he waited a triumphant beat before shouting his second favourite word in the English language: "Cut!"

"Unfuckingbelievable, was that not?" He stuck his head under the tarpaulin and beamed at Meredith. "Now, on second thought, maybe we *could* use a few close-ups after all."

An hour and a half later, when the first assistant director barked things a wrap, half the crew was silently crying while the other functioned in a waking coma. Dan, in a moment of touchdown glory, ran up to the camera and pretended to hump the lens.

From where she sat in front of the monitor, Meredith saw something bad.

"Sir?"

"Yeah, baby, yeah!"

"Seriously, Dan. Could you please come over here now. Please?"

The crew was already packing up, coiling wires and disassembling metal rods into black trunks. In their minds they were already on the highway and halfway home to the warm bums of their sleeping girlfriends, boyfriends, husbands and wives.

Dan's disembodied head poked around the edge of the tarp.

"What."

"Your pants."

He made a sooky-baby face. "You don't like my pants? I got them at Banana Republic. I mean, maybe they're not the most stylish thing in the world, but really, Meredith, I think you're being a bit harsh—"

"No, Dan. Before, you were wearing cords. Now you're in khakis. They're not the same pants you were wearing in the earlier scenes, the ones we shot before dinner, which means—You know what it means. Nothing will match. We have to reshoot."

Dan looked down at his drizzle-splattered khakis and when he slowly lifted his face he was the other him—the bully.

"Are you admitting to the fact that you personally wasted three hours of triple time? Do you have any idea how many tax dollars you just pissed away, sweetheart?"

"Me?" Meredith sputtered. Unfortunately, she was a sputterer. "But, but—*you.*"

"No, honey—you. You did this on purpose."

Without taking his reptile eyes off her, Dan Felsted called out for the crew to halt packing. The set froze in tableau. "Fucked-up sabotaging bitch," he hissed.

"You think I let you screw up for fun?"

Felsted rolled his eyes theatrically. "Not think. Know. I *know* you did."

"Fuck you," Meredith said quietly.

"Actually, doll, I wish I never had." He turned to stride back to his trailer. "Let's do it again!"

For the first time in weeks a cold tide rose over Meredith. She swivelled her indented bottom around on the milk crate that functioned as her desk chair and began gathering the things she could reach from under the tarpaulin: two empty notebooks, one swollen paperback collection of Mavis Gallant short stories, a woolly hairbrush, half a bag of organic baby carrots. She gathered the meagre detritus of her life as a continuity girl and dumped it in her bag. Then Meredith walked off the set and down the pier toward the deserted taxi stand. Behind her, the wind off the lake distorted Dan Felsted's shouts. He was, she knew, threatening the worst thing he could imagine, which was to fire her. She would never have lunch in this town again, blah, blah, blah. Which was fine with her. She could stand to lose a couple of pounds anyway.

Meredith opened her eyes and spoke aloud a terrible, startling confession: "Today is my thirty-fifth birthday." The words froze her where she lay, her muscles rigid. She'd heard of a tropical fish—was it blowfish?—that contained a poison that could do this to you. And, Christ, she *had* eaten takeout sushi for dinner last night. No blowfish, though, as far as she could recall. The toxic shock of being thirty-five was enough to immobilize her.

She studied the fine network of cracks in the slab of raw concrete suspended twelve feet above her bed. As on every other morning, she experienced a sweet flush of relief that the ceiling had not crumbled to dust while she slept. After a time she managed to raise her head on one hand and, in a sweeping glance, assess the entirety of her living quarters. While most people would look at the room and see a clean, ordered space decorated in Swedish pine and stainless steel finishings, Meredith saw nothing but disorder and grit—a progressive deterioration back to the mud of the original construction site from which her building had sprung, fully formed, two years prior. A cashmere throw-blanket grown nubbly, half falling off the side of her Bauhaus-style armless sofa. Her book smushed open on the coffee table where she'd left it the day before. A single white ceramic coffee mug on the counter beside the sink from the morning before that. She knows that when she looks into it she will see a thin film of baked-on brown tar at the bottom. She will fill it with water to soak before she leaves for yoga class. She hates to admit it—she would never tell a soul—but the soaking coffee mug will nag her thoughts all day.

Try as she might to think of her place in the soothing, advertorial terms she had in mind when she moved in ("home," "loft," "lifestyle") she has never been able to see it as anything other than a wall-less ("open-concept") condo with exposed ductwork the developers were too cheap to cover up. Meredith felt about this place, which she bought three years ago from a drawing in a model suite for the same price as a four-bedroom house on a leafy street a half-hour drive in any direction out of the downtown core, the way most people feel about a misguided purchase of a bit of spangled nightclub stretch-gear—specifically, *For what sinister hidden purpose did an alien enter my body and buy this thing?* All the same, for the past two and a half years, these eight hundred square feet in the howling industrial wind tunnel just west of the city's business district had been her home. As a matter of principle, she was attached to the place. The more the cheap new construction deteriorated, the more secretly at home she felt. Deterioration made her anxious. Anxious was normal. Normal was home.

Thirty-five, she thought. *My eggs are thirty-five today.*

Having once heard the gynecologist on a morning talk show impart the following facts, Meredith has never been without them: A woman is born with all the eggs she will ever have in her life. With each menstrual cycle, an egg is discarded, never to be replaced. At the age of twenty-seven a woman's fertility begins to decline. After thirty-five things deteriorate rapidly. By forty she has half the chance of getting pregnant that she had a decade before. Beyond forty, the odds approach the hopeless ones of winning a lottery jackpot.

Meredith felt a great yawn in her belly and a flush through her veins that fizzed and came out salt water at the corners of her eyes. Her small breasts ached with expectation.

***

Saturday morning prenatal yoga class was packed. Expecting mums wielded their bellies around the room like competing cigarette girls. They handed off toddlers and toddler-related equipment to nannies who whisked their wards into a government-safety-code-approved play area in the next room. The instructor, a beaming blonde, switched on the lute music as the women found their places. Meredith and the instructor were the only non-pregnant women present. They smiled at each other.

Meredith had been coming to the class for more than three months now with her friend Mish. At the age of thirty-seven, after months of turkey basters and technological intervention, Mish had finally succeeded in getting pregnant by the seed of her roommate, Shane, a gay interior decorator and Chinese pug collector with a strong male biological clock. While Mish had conceived only two months ago, she had started dragging Meredith along at least six weeks earlier than that, in the hope of "good fertility juju" rubbing off on her during her prenatal sun salutations. Apparently it had worked.

After a while, Meredith came to enjoy the class for reasons of her own. It was close to her place and at a convenient time, but more than that, it afforded her a chance to eavesdrop on the Yummies.

The Yummies were the women who, next to the Starlets and Professional Have-It-Alls, Meredith envied most, and therefore half-despised. You could see them at the latte bars, drinking green tea smoothies, hoisting their fat-cheeked offspring from one hip to the other, comparing notes on washable diapers and baby-friendly resorts. But here in prenatal yoga you could truly study the Yummy in her entire evolution—from initial bump to stroller-wielding mother of three. Eventually, every Yummy ended up at Saturday morning prenatal yoga.

Here the hierarchy of the outside world did not apply. Second- and third-time Yummies were the gurus, wise lionesses licking their young and calmly answering the anxious questions of the younger, inexperienced first-timers. Listening in on their queries in the change room (Is it all right to have soy milk with my cereal? Drink decaf? Smoke a bit of pot?), Meredith could not believe how much more she knew about managing the modern pregnancy than most of the pregnant Yummies around her. Had they *never* read baby books in their spare time? Spent time with their mummy friends? Still, they must know something she didn't—they were Yummy while she was UnYummy, thirty-five, her Fallopian tubes like a pair of half-empty Pez dispensers.

Her project was to study the Yummies in the hope that she might one day learn the secret of their effortless perfection. That is: how to get knocked up.

She assumed the lotus position, placing one hand palm-up on her knee, the other cupping her belly just above her pubic bone, and in unison with the Yummies, commenced her first set of cleansing breaths.

Halfway through her second toe stand, Meredith heard a familiar hiss. She turned and saw Mish standing in the doorway, dressed in pajama bottoms and a sweatshirt, her face raw and unfamiliar without its usual makeup. Meredith disentangled her limbs and scurried to the door. Mish pulled her into the hall.

"I tried to call you all night but your phone was turned off," Mish whispered. "I couldn't—I didn't know where you were."

"I was shooting. What's wrong?"

Her friend's face squashed in on itself. "Shane was away at a design show in Philadelphia. I called my doula and she was away too. The doctor said . . ."

Meredith put her arms around her friend as the last of Mish's words twisted in a sob. ". . . she said—just to ride it out."

"You need a drink."

"No," said Mish, wiping her nose with the heel of her hand. "I need six."

Forty-five minutes and two Bloody Caesars later Mish and Meredith were huddled outside a crowded brunch spot. Mish was smoking hungrily, lighting each new cigarette from the smouldering butt of the last.

"Turkey fuck," said Meredith.

Mish's head bobbed up and down at the end of her neck like a marionette's. "Huh?"

"That's what my mum used to call it when you light one cigarette from another. Some sixties term. She thought it was so hilarious. Made me want to die of embarrassment."

This got a snort out of Mish. "Do you think I would have made an even more embarrassing mother than yours?"

"I'm sure you will yet."

"Fuck it. I'm done. This in vitro thing's a come-on. These fertility doctors make real estate agents looks like straight shooters. Pun intended."

"But, hon, you were *so close*. I'm sure next time."

Mish looked at Meredith and sucked so hard on her smoke it crackled.

"Fuck next time. I can't go through this again. I'd rather die."

"Maybe you shouldn't, then."

"I wish I'd never even tried in the first place."

This was not the first lost baby for Mish. In her twenties, she'd had two abortions—the first, ten weeks after a one-night stand with the former bassist in a semi-famous Detroit thrash band, the second, the result of a desperate year-long love affair with a married psychotherapist whom her girlfriends had disapprovingly nicknamed "Herr Doktor." Like most of the women in her postal code (thirty-odd, unmarried, urban-dwelling, career focused in an aesthetic rather than hard-nosed way), Mish had never pondered, even for a millisecond, the thought of having a baby until she was thirty-five. In her case, the hunger came on suddenly in the middle of being dumped, for the third and definitive time, by an Israeli merchant banker whom she had been faithfully dating for two years but in whose company she had probably collectively spent only a week and a half.

"It was as if I woke up one day and my leg was hollow," she had told Meredith.

In the two years since, while taking time out from her job as a freelance wardrobe stylist, Mish had tried to get pregnant, finally employing the sympathetic sperm of Shane, the man with a pompadour whom she referred to (somewhat depressingly, Meredith thought) as her "gay husband."

Now, seven months, six thousand dollars, five botched inseminations and two miscarriages later, Mish—a gal famous for her ability to chug a bottle of tequila only to get up the next morning and run a half-marathon—was finally exhausted. Meredith could see it in her eyes: she looked beaten.

"Guess we better head out," Mish said.

It was their friend Elle's daughter's fifth birthday party this morning. The party, which was being thrown at Elle and her husband Andrew's house uptown, had started off as a birthday dinner party for Meredith but had evolved into a daytime reception with hired magicians and a Barbie ice-cream cake for Elle's daughter. Zoe and Meredith shared a birthday—a coincidence Meredith had thought mystical when Elle called her from the hospital in the midst of her thirtieth birthday celebration and asked Meredith (happily stoned off a mother lode of birthday Moroccan Gold Seal) to be godmother of her firstborn. Meredith had cried sisterly tears and reminisced about the days when the three of them—Mish, Elle and Mere—were kids at school, sneaking smokes in the furnace room at lunch hour. She went on in this slightly embarrassing but unstoppable vein until Elle, exhausted after twenty-six hours of labour and an emergency Caesarian, said she loved her too, and hung up.

Since that moment, Meredith's birthday had become a shadow of its former self. Gone were the dope and hired DJs, replaced by goody bags and glasses of supportive sangria for Elle (now a mother of two).

"You sure you want to go?" asked Meredith.

"We can't miss your birthday party." Mish managed a small, wet smile. "Mommy would kill us."

Elle and Andrew lived in Summerhill, an enclave of pointy-peaked toy houses whose modest, post-war facades belied the opulent salaries of their occupants. The neighbourhood, though average in every outward way, was one of the most sought-after in the city. The reason for this was purely practical: it happened to be located six subway stops away from the financial district. Four stops away from the place where Andrew, like many of his fellow Summerhill residents, toiled in a tower seventy hours a week arranging the smooth transfer of vast millions from one multinational conglomerate to the next.

Elle and Andrew's house was a solid place. A house constructed as much with the false memory of a bygone era when men were men and women wore a-line skirts and red-checked oven mittens as with mortar and bricks. Just the sight of it made Meredith feel nostalgic for a past she had never known, a vision of a time of domestic balance that, she knew, probably never existed in the first place.

As she pulled into the driveway and shifted the car into park, Meredith reached over and patted her friend on the knee.

"I'm fine. Really." Mish emptied her lungs of smoke with a whistle. "Let's do it."

Elle appeared on the front stoop, waving, in a cotton sundress. It was an unseasonably warm day in April and everyone except Mish was dressing hopefully. Elle mouthed the words *New car*! (Meredith had recently traded in her old black Volkswagen for a new black Volkswagen) and made a wide, fingers-splayed Broadway chorus-line gesture with both hands.

Mish began to unbuckle her seat belt. She tried the door but it was locked. "Fuck-a-duck," she muttered. Then she noticed Meredith sitting stiffly in her seat.

"What is it?"

"I think I quit my job yesterday. I mean, this morning."

"Seriously? Aren't you freelance?"

Meredith thought this over. The lack of sleep and the two Bloodies were beginning to take their toll on her cognitive abilities. "I am, but I had a fight with Felsted—not *even* a fight really—and I just walked off the set."

"In the middle of shooting?"

"It was sort of at the end but, yeah, pretty much."

Mish hooted. "Right on!" She punched her friend on the shoulder before prying up the door lock with her fingers and hoisting herself out of the car. "It's about time. That guy's an asshole. I'm just sorry you didn't do it sooner."

Meredith removed her key from the ignition. Elle was now clipping down the driveway with a puzzled expression, pulling on her fingers with a dishcloth. A Jack Russell terrier bounced around her ankles emitting a series of high-pitched barks.

Mish leaned back into the car and pinched Meredith on the thigh.

"Let's not mention it to her today, okay? I can't deal."

"No prob." Meredith got out of the car and took a deep breath.

"Down, Starsky. I said *down*! Don't—I told you NO. Guys—" Elle pulled her friends together and hugged them both at the same time. "Welcome to bourgeois hell. Don't worry, I've got spiked punch for the grown-ups. And pregnancy punch *pour vous*." She bumped her hip against Mish's and began clicking her way along the flagstones back to the house. "How sick are you of cranberry soda? By my second trimester I couldn't even stand the sight of the stuff."

Meredith took her cue. "Where are the brats?"

Elle sighed. She often pretended (though not very convincingly) to be bored by motherhood for the sake of her as-yet-childless girlfriends. "In the backyard being molested by Krusty the Clown. You should see this guy—talks like a thug and charges a mortgage payment an hour—but the kids are absolutely bonkers for him. He's like the pied piper of Summerhill."

The kitchen was at the back of the house, a half-renovated addition that Elle and Andrew had started before getting pregnant for the second time. The stainless steel appliances, imported from a restaurant supply shop on the boulevard St-Germain in Paris, were already covered in a lifetime's worth of tiny fingerprints. The floor was plywood covered in blue plastic. The tarp snagged on Elle's kitten heel as she led Mish and Meredith into the room, trilling the praises of white wine sangria.

"Oh hell," she said, bending down to detach herself. "I was afraid the kids would get splinters. Half their fathers are lawyers and Andrew is completely paranoid. You know he kept saying we should just have the party at Chuck E. Cheese's instead? As if."

She poured pale cloudy liquid into tumblers as she spoke, clawing extra chopped berries out of the pitcher and plopping them in each glass with her fingers. Elle shook her head and smiled, seeming to marvel for a moment at the vast stupidity of it all, the excess of poor taste and misjudgment that she alone had to put up with. Her facial expression was one Meredith recognized from wives in television sitcoms, usually adopted after their husbands had returned home with something laughably out of place, like a Christmas tree too big to fit in the front door.

Mish took a glass of sangria from Elle's hand, and her friends watched as she drained it in a single swallow.

"What's Chuckie Cheese's?" Meredith asked, hoping to distract Elle.

The other two women looked at each other and snorted. This was a joke they shared among the three of them: Meredith's astonishing ignorance of mainstream popular culture. What she did know had been gleaned through movies and television as an adult. Meredith had retained the overly literal, slightly alien quality of a child who had grown up in an institution. In this case, as a boarder at the girls' school where the three of them had met. Mish and Elle had attended the same school, but as day students. Meredith had spent her summers and Christmases with her mother at artists' retreats and friends' vacation houses in Arizona, Ibiza and Banff.

"Chuck E. Cheese's is a kiddie trough in the 'burbs owned by a rodent in a red hat by the name of Chuck," Mish said. "Imagine a lot of horrible people and their screaming, puking offspring eating greasy pizza and swimming in vats of coloured balls. It's enough to make you run to the bathroom and tie your own fucking tubes."

As she spoke, Mish began walking around the kitchen with her face parallel to the floor, scanning flat surfaces for food, probably hoping for some sort of dairy product—the orange, processed, high-sodium kind. Meredith thought she seemed to be making a comeback. Either that or she was falling apart.

"Right," Elle continued. "So *obviously* I'm not taking the offspring of the Audi brigade to Chuck E.

Cheese's for a birthday party. I haven't given up *completely*, you know."

"So where is he?" Meredith asked, keen to draw Elle's attention away from Mish, who was now rummaging through the fridge's crisper with a bagel between her teeth.

"Upstairs napping." Elle smiled and motioned to the baby monitor leaning cockeyed against the windowsill.

"Your *husband*?"

"Oh God, not *him*, I meant the baby." Elle laughed dismissively. "He's gone into the office for a couple of hours. Big deal, you know. Super important. Couldn't bear to miss a second of it. All those exciting tax loopholes to negotiate."

From the backyard came an enormous *thud* followed by a screeching chorus. Meredith ran to the window then turned to look at her friend. Elle cleared a spot on the counter between a bag of silver sugar-balls and a water-swollen copy of *Vanity Fair* and set her drink down. Hers was the reaction of a soldier with acute post-traumatic stress disorder reacting to a grenade going off in the next trench. That is, no reaction at all.

"What is it?" she asked Meredith, searching for a strawberry trapped beneath the ice at the bottom of her glass.

Elle was clearly happy to have someone else analyze the crime scene before she rolled up her sleeves and stepped in to do the dirty work.

"The kids are all right but the clown guy appears to be dead. Or dying. It's unclear."

"Shall we?"

They walked out onto the back deck, leaving Mish with the fridge.

The scene outside looked like the aftermath of a tornado touchdown in the land of Oz. Mud-smeared children ran in all directions, clutching whatever scraps of party trash they could hold in their jammy hands. The weak hid under peony bushes or crouched behind faux seventeenth-century cement garden ornaments, waiting for it to be over. In the centre of the lawn was a half-collapsed picnic table, three of its four legs splintered to bits, and on top of that, a blue ice-cream cake, flattened and oozing out from beneath the twitching body of a grown man in a pink gingham jumpsuit. Starsky lavished hind-pumping love on the clown's left oversized shoe, ears pinned down in amorous concentration. Detached streamers and balloons floated through the air. In the corner, two boys in matching overalls squirted green Silly String into a bowl of blue Jell-O and taste-tested their creation.

At the centre of the melee, the birthday girl—five-year-old Zoe—presided with queenly authority. She stood over the man's body in a gold lamé fairy dress and rhinestone-encrusted tiara. In her hand was a wooden spoon with a tinfoil star glued to one end. When she saw her mother and Meredith emerge from the house, she shrugged sweetly, gave a pageant-winning smile, and returned to her task of beating the clown with her wand.

"Bad! Bad! Ucky!" Zoe scolded, increasing her volume as the women approached. She beamed at her mother. "He stood on the table, Mummy. He made a bad mess. My cake—" Her small face collapsed into a coursing river of snot.

Elle crouched and hugged her daughter, murmuring mummy-ish things in her wet ear. "Don't cry. The clown didn't mean it. He was just trying to be funny. Remember the time when you were trying to do a cartwheel and you fell and hit your face on the rock? It's like that."

"That was different."

"No, it wasn't, honey. The clown was just trying to be funny."

"It was *different*."

"Why?"

"*Because*, Mummy. It was *me*."

Elle and Meredith paused. Zoe raised her wand to clinch the argument.

"And *I* didn't wreck the cake."

Elle nudged the clown's thigh with her heel. He groaned. "Uh, sir? Mr. Clown? Assuming you're okay, do you mind getting up? You're scaring the kids."

"Bad clown! Scary!" Zoe whacked him once more on the back of his head for good measure.

"Don't be evil, Zoe. Mr. Clown is in pain."

The clown rolled his head to the side and revealed one watery eye that he trained on Meredith.

"Are you okay?" she asked.

"Urrghyehfinkso."

"You sure?"

"Yeah." He paused to spit a handful of disintegrated gummi worms from his mouth. They lay glistening on the grass, the punchline of a forgotten magic trick. Starsky began slurping them up.

"I hate you."

"Zoe!"

The clown struggled to his feet, pulled off his wig and rubbed the damp, sandy hair underneath until it stood on end. His torso was plastered in blue, black and white icing. If you looked closely, the vague silhouette of Cookie Monster was discernable.

Under the makeup, the clown looked to be in his early twenties. The kind of young man who wore wraparound sunglasses and reversed ball caps and made the "hang loose" hand sign to his friends from the window of his yellow Jeep.

Meredith whispered, "Why don't you take him inside and see if he's okay? I'll deal with the kids."

Elle looked relieved to be receiving an order rather than issuing one for once. She led the clown inside. Meredith looked down at Zoe. She had finished crying and was chewing the top of her tinfoil wand. She turned her tear-streaked face up and glared at the sky.

"I hate my birthday," she said.

Meredith silently agreed.

Looking around the garden, she felt like an insecure Mary Poppins recently dropped from above. Faces peeked out from behind clay pots and shrubbery. After ascertaining the coast was clear they began to emerge. Dirty fingers attached to doughy arms attached to stout bodies, punctuated with outie belly buttons. A couple of the children still had diapers popping out from the waistline of their Gap Kids corduroys, which Meredith found slightly frightening. She stayed put in the centre of the yard, waiting for them to come to her. She wanted so much for them to like her that she became paralyzed with the need. More than men, or figures of professional authority, Meredith desired the approval of dogs and children. She sensed it was best not to try too hard—she had noticed that when it came to getting other people to feel the way you wanted them to feel, the head-on approach never worked. So Meredith did with kids what she did with all people whose attention she craved. She hung back quietly and pretended to have other things on her mind.

"Mer-dith?" Zoe looked up at her.

"Yes?"

"Can we do bobbing for apples?"

And so they bobbed.

After the boiled wieners, veggie patties and McDonald's rental cooler of "orange drink" were laid to rest, along with great scoops of smushed cake on paper plates, the mothers arrived to collect their broods. They came all at once in a gypsy caravan of Saabs and Subarus, rushing in, accepting glasses of mineral water in lieu of sangria (they were driving), collecting their goody bags and swirling out.

These Yummies of the Backyards, Meredith observed, were of a different order than the downtown soy-latte-sippers in her prenatal yoga class. In their fleecy weekend-warrior wear and brutalist haircuts, the uptown Yummies were more weather-beaten, less sexy but far more efficient. Children aged you—that much was evident. But maybe they aged you for the better. Meredith envied their matronly *gravitas*. These women lacked the starry-eyed wonder of the new Yummies but had developed other skills—such as the ability to break down a baby jogger and pack it into the back seat of an SUV in six and a quarter seconds flat. They hitched their kids on hips and made intense small talk about kitchen renovations, real estate and private versus public education. They pulled wash-cloths out of thin air, spit and rubbed infant faces with just enough abrasion to buff without eliciting complaint. Smacking their lips to each other's cheeks and fishing around for car keys in handbags the size of small arms carriers, the uptown Yummies were galva-nized by the reality of life. Watching them, Meredith felt light as helium.

When the last guest was gone, Elle walked back

into the kitchen, slipped off her apron and collapsed on the floor in a convincing stage faint that Meredith recognized from their grade-seven production of *Gone With the Wind*. Starsky speedboated into the kitchen and began slathering his mistress's face with goober. Zoe snorted at her mother's performance. Meredith could see it was a game they often played.

Elle opened one eye. "I'm glad *that's* over."

"Me *too*," Zoe said, with a stamp of her sequined slipper.

"Thanks a lot, Zoe. Time for bed."

Elle lifted herself from the floor and scooped up her daughter in one movement.

"But, Mummy, where'd he go?"

"Who?"

"You know. The *clown*."

Elle looked at Meredith. Zoe was right. The clown had disappeared. Also conspicuously unaccounted for was Mish.

"I doubt he'd leave without his money," Elle said, not without suspicion.

Then they heard it. A female giggle followed by an unmistakable mouth-to-mouth slurp. It came through the speaker of the pink plastic Fisher-Price baby monitor sitting on the kitchen windowsill.

"Oh God." Meredith looked at Elle.

"Gross. I mean, for a *pregnant* woman," said Elle.

"It's a long story," said Meredith.

"Should we interrupt?"

"It's your house, but . . ."

"In the *baby's* room. You'd think they'd have the decency to go to the bathroom, at least. I did notice she was getting a bit sloshed. I was going to say something, but you never know with Mish. I just got the vibe, you know? And anyway, the next thing I knew she went into this Florence Nightingale routine— dabbing the guy with iodine where he scraped his chest on the picnic table. Anyway, he had his shirt off and she offered to go up and help him wash it in the sink . . ." Elle looked at the kitchen clock and lowered Zoe to the floor. "That was about forty minutes ago."

"Where's your nanny?"

"Night off." Elle stared at Meredith meaningfully. "What's up with Mish?"

Meredith opened her eyes wide and grimaced.

Elle left the room with Starsky and her daughter in tow. As usual, she was bent on truth and justice. Meredith shrugged. Whatever the circumstances, the continuity girl never calls "Cut."

***

When she returned home that evening Meredith found a chartreuse envelope in her mailbox. As far as she knew, only one person on the planet regularly used chartreuse writing paper. She poured herself a glass of wine and made a dinner of organic peanut butter spread on a celery stick before opening the letter.

Dear Moo,

    It's time you came for a visit. I may be a
wretched old cunt, but I'm still your mother.
Everything here is very nice. The forsythia is
out and I have a new lover called Jose. He is a
Colombian political refugee and poet I met on the
jury of the Diaspora Prize—absolutely gorgeous.
The drizzle has given him a bad case of psoriasis,
which puts the poor boy in a cranky mood much of
the time. Luckily I am treating him with the Crème
de la Mer you sent me for Christmas. Now don't be
jealous. Enclosed is a one-way ticket. You can get
your own way home.

Love, Mums

P.S. No need to worry about ££ as I have arranged
a job for you doing whatever it is you do.

Meredith set down her celery stick and dabbed the
corners of her mouth with a cloth napkin. Picking
up the letter from her lap, she folded it into quarters
and placed it back in its envelope. After a moment of
silent deliberation she got up from the sofa, crossed
the room and tucked the envelope into a slim file in
her bottom desk drawer labelled CORRESPONDENCE—
THAT WOMAN.

The green voice-mail light was blinking so she picked up her phone and dialed. The phone company fembot informed her she had three new messages. She pressed one and was not surprised to hear the voice of her agent, a warm, fat mother of four named Fran.

"Meredith, it's me. Happy birthday, honey. Listen, I just got a message from someone in Felsted's production office at the studio and they sound pretty ticked off. I just wanted to talk to you before I called them back. Could you call me? Thanks."

Meredith pressed seven to delete, and then one to hear the next message. Fran again. This time more distressed.

"Meredith. Fran here. Your cell seems to be turned off. The production office called again and I told them I'm waiting to hear from you. I know it's your birthday but let's get this sorted out."

Next: the same voice, but cooler and clipped. "Meredith, listen. This is important. Felsted's people are saying you walked off his set. Is this true? I need to hear from you. It's your *agent* speaking."

Meredith was about to hang up when the fembot announced, "One new message has been added to your mailbox. To listen to your message, press one." Crunching on her celery stick, Meredith hit one. It was Fran again, but this time frothing with delight.

"Hi, sweetie, it's me. Sounds like you're on the other line. Listen, forget about Felsted for now. I just got a call from Osmond Crouch's people in

London. *Osmond Crouch!* They're shooting a big feature in England and they want you on the set next week. You've got British citizenship, right? That's what I told them, anyway. Called completely out of the blue—they got my home number somehow. I had Viia and Ashton in the tub at the time—there's water everywhere! I hope you're excited, sweetheart. They're faxing over the contract tomorrow. I hope your passport's up to date 'cause you're on your way to jolly old . . ."

Meredith hung up. Across the room on the granite kitchen island sat the white ceramic coffee mug she had set out to soak that morning. She flicked on the kitchen halogens, lifted the mug and peered inside. Impressively, the coffee sludge, which only a few hours ago had hardened into a charcoal-coloured resin at the bottom, had dislodged and redistributed itself throughout the liquid, tinting the remaining soap suds brown. Meredith emptied the mug, wiped, rinsed, dried and re-placed it on the specially designated hanging hooks in the cupboard. She returned to the sofa and resumed rabbiting down her celery sticks. Eating seemed to take forever. It was more work than working.

She did not turn on the television. Instead, she stared at the coffee table in front of her. There was nothing on it but half a glass of red wine, a stack of magazines (*Us, Vanity Fair, The New Yorker, American Cinematographer*) and the plane ticket her mother had sent her. She examined the airline (BA), the class (economy), and finally, the date (Thursday). The day before Osmond Crouch's people wanted her in London.

Meredith picked up the phone and, even though it was past midnight, dialed her agent's number.

4

She was often early but never late to her annual Pap appointment. It was a superstitious thing.

"Afternoon, hon," said Hyacinth, the receptionist, fiddling with the radio dial to find her preferred easy rock station.

Meredith snapped her health card on the counter.

As Whitney Houston's warbling filled the waiting room, she felt her shoulder blades unlock. For some reason she found it strangely relaxing here. Hyacinth typed her numbers into the computer.

"You're aware Dr. Stein is on stress leave, so Dr. Veil will be filling in?"

"Is she . . . okay?"

"Oh, fine. Just needs some time with her boys. And don't worry—you'll like Dr. Veil. You'll be in the hands of an internationally renowned specialist." Hyacinth winked. "Dr. Veil's on TV."

Meredith lowered her bum into the waiting-room chair gingerly, like a schoolteacher afraid of tacks. She failed to take her usual pleasure in the room's finishings: the raw-silk seat covers, the fake lilies, the tidy stacks of magazines dating back to medieval times (Sharon Stone smiled on the cover of one). She didn't do her favourite waiting room experiment, the one where she flipped open a magazine from the top of the pile and one from the bottom to confirm that, even over a five-year span, the advice inside was exactly the same. ("Wash your hair in vinegar to make it soft." "Drink cranberry juice for bladder infections." "Place cucumber slices over the eyes to erase dark circles." "Give your man blow jobs to stop his wandering eye.") Usually these dribs of common wisdom delighted her, but not today. She was deeply suspicious of change where gynecological practices were concerned.

Dr. Stein had been a figure in her life ever since high school. As a teen, Meredith would take the subway here, bare-kneed and itchy under her kilt, and ask quavery questions about boys and fluids. Once, she came in certain she was dying of syphilis (caught, she reasoned, from a short boy's groping paw at a school dance), but it turned out only to be her first yeast infection. She had waited in this very room for her first morning-after pill, her first breast exam, her first of many STD tests (the truth was, Meredith had had more STD tests in her adult life than she'd had unprotected sex). The only hope was that the new doctor would be as compassionate and rigorous as Dr. Stein.

Hyacinth ushered her into the examination room and told her the doctor would be with her in a moment. Meredith noticed certain details had been altered since she was last here. The broken cuckoo clock had been taken off the wall, replaced by a Nicolas de Staël calendar. The small metal-frame desk was messier than usual, jumbled with pamphlets and script pads. Propped on the corner was a framed snapshot of an almond-eyed toddler peeking over the rim of a giant white teacup. Meredith recognized the setting as the Mad Hatter's Tea Party ride at Disney World—

"Ever been there?"

A man in a lab coat was leaning in the doorway. He looked too happy and sharply focused to be a doctor. Not in real life, Meredith thought, figuring him for a student. Meredith half-coughed, half-laughed, focused intently on the photograph and wished he would go away. Who wanted to make small talk before a Pap smear?

"My mother believed amusement parks were a religious conspiracy," she said, gaze cemented on the photo of the child. There was a gap between the little girl's front teeth. "She took me to nude beaches in Norway instead."

"Sounds like a racy gal."

"She is. Completely nuts. Lives in London. England."

"You don't sound English."

"I grew up in Canada. Boarding school was cheaper overseas, not to mention farther away."

Meredith wished someone would duct-tape her mouth shut. There was a silence and when she peeked back she noticed the man was smiling and had extended his left hand toward her. What an odd thing—to shake with the left, Meredith thought, applying her palm to his. She wondered if he was allowed to do that. Shake hands. It seemed somehow inappropriate.

"Hello, uh"—he glanced down at the chart— "Meredith. I'm Joe Veil. I'm filling in for Dr. Stein."

There was an awkward pause.

"Is that all right?" he asked.

Meredith picked at some grit trapped under her right thumbnail. "I wasn't expecting a man," she said finally.

"That's fine," he said. "I can refer you to someone else. You may have to wait a couple of weeks."

"I can't," Meredith said. "I'm going out of town and I need to do this now. There's no other time."

"So do you want to proceed with the appointment then?"

"Not particularly."

He tossed the chart on the desk and looked at her. "So what are you saying?"

"Whatever." She glowered. "Let's get this over with."

"All right," he said, closing the door behind him. "I'm both a gynecologist and fertility specialist. I haven't done much clinic work in recent years, so this is a bit of an anomaly for me too. Now," he said, sitting down, crossing his legs and checking the chart again, "you're here for a Pap smear?"

Meredith corrected her posture and smiled as if to say, Ah, of course, you are the handsome stranger who is preparing to scrape my cervix with a Popsicle stick—and I am *completely* comfortable with that.

He continued to leaf through his papers without looking at her. Meredith noticed his wedding band— white gold, fine, a little loose. She always checked.

"First off, I have the results of your G-test," he said.

Meredith nodded tightly.

The GnRH analogue test (commonly known as the G-test) was a new procedure that gauged female fecundity by measuring both ovarian function and the state of the ovarian reserve. Meredith had asked Dr. Stein about it after reading a magazine article on the high incidence of perimenopause (prematurely aged eggs) in professional females in their mid-thirties. It was the results of a G-test that had kicked off Mish's two-year insemination obsession, and Meredith (who was a couple of years younger) was determined not to get stuck with an abdomen of raisins at the age of thirty-nine. She knew it was a pragmatic, preliminary investigation—but what was so romantic about fertility anyway? What, after all, was responsible for the desire to have children other than an involuntary biological twitch? What separated it from hunger or the urge to draw breath? On the other hand, what made it any less important? Why fight it, Meredith thought, when you can *do it right* instead? And so she convinced Dr. Stein to administer the G-test, a non-invasive procedure involving one blood test and two inhalers of gaseous hormones meant to stimulate the pituitary gland and measure rate of ovulation. The whole thing seemed like a pretty good deal in the end: Meredith endured a bit of dizziness and paid a thousand bucks in order to count how many eggs were left in her basket. This information, in turn, promised to give a rough picture of her window of fertility in coming years (she thought of it as the "pre-premenopausal period" and sometimes before sleep would say it aloud three times fast).

Meredith closed her eyes and quickly opened them again. As she had suspected, Dr. Joe was just as male and married as he had been three-quarters of a second before.

"Okay, lay it on me."

"First of all I want to make sure you're aware of how the G-test works. You know we give you hormone treatments in order to stimulate your pituitary gland, which controls the ovulation function in your reproductive system, and this way we are able to determine both rate of ovulation and—"

"Yes, I'm familiar with how it works, Dr. Veil. Just the results, please." Meredith noticed yet again how she sounded unintentionally bitchy when she was nervous.

"All right." He lifted the clipboard closer to read what was written there. "It seems that your ovulation rate is somewhat depleted, which is not unusual for a woman of your age. You're thirty-four?"

"Thirty-five."

The doctor flipped back to the questionnaire portion of the test.

"A smoker?"

"Never."

"Right. Well, that's good. Smoking decreases ovulation rate dramatically."

"But you thought I *might* be a smoker. Isn't that bad?"

"Not necessarily. Your results show that your ovulation rate is lower than it probably was a decade ago. But what I'm saying is, this is normal. How long have you been trying?"

"I haven't yet. I was just wondering for when I *do* try. I mean, I've been thinking a lot lately about how I should *start* trying. Or at least *trying* to try."

"So you've been thinking about trying to try to conceive?"

"That's right."

"Do you mind if I level with you?"

"Absolutely not."

"As I mentioned, I'm a fertility specialist at Women's College, which means I spend most of my waking hours trying to get women pregnant," he paused, looking slightly perplexed. "In a manner of speaking."

Meredith smiled, then she thought of Mish, of the ribbon of blood unfurling down her inner thigh.

"Most women who come to me are not as forward-thinking as you," Dr. Veil went on. "They end up in my office at the age of forty or later, after they've been trying with their partners off and on for five years. We do everything we can, but by that time, more often than not, it's too late."

"So what are you saying?"

"I'm saying that if you really want a baby, you should start trying as soon as you can. Within the year is my advice."

"This year!" she shouted (she couldn't help it). "How am I supposed to fit in having a baby this year? You talk about it as if it's just a matter of putting in the effort, like 'Don't forget to clean out those eavestroughs before winter comes.' It's crazy. I don't even have a boyfriend. I haven't been on a date in months. I work all the time. I barely have time to take care of myself, let alone someone else. I have no family here. My friends are either turning into their parents or are completely fucked up."

He waited for her to finish before starting to speak. "Meredith, you seem pretty pulled together—"

She interrupted him with a sharp laugh. "You know, that's what everyone always says about me. I seem so together. So on top of everything. So under control. But you know what I feel like inside? A bomb site. A disaster area." She opened her eyes wide and pointed to her chest. "I am Beirut."

"That's how everybody feels," he said.

"That's not true."

"I assure you," he said, "it is."

"Then why is everything so well timed in other people's lives?" she said, glancing at the photo of the little girl on his desk. "It's like I've been off schedule from day one. I think I was born out of sync."

His eyes smiled. "If you're talking about children, I can tell you, there is never a convenient time—for anyone. Children are not convenient. They require . . . a leap of faith."

Meredith shook her head. "I'm sorry, Doctor, but it's hard for me to take advice from someone like you."

"What do you mean?" He looked surprised.

Meredith looked at his shoes—perfectly safe. "You just don't seem like someone who's taken many leaps of faith."

"I don't?"

"Not to me."

He folded his clipboard and stood up. Meredith remained seated. Her face felt tingly, like she had been smacked.

"I'm sorry if my bluntness offends you," the doctor said quickly. "It's just that I see this sort of thing every day. It's really discouraging to watch healthy young women become infertility statistics just because they waited too long and didn't have the facts."

Meredith nodded and reached for her bag to leave.

"Don't forget," said Dr. Joe.

"Forget what?"

"Your Pap test."

"Oh, right. That."

"I'll just step out for a moment so you can put on your gown. Please take everything off including your underwear, lie on the examination table face-up and place your heels in the stirrups." He paused in the doorway and turned back. "I hope my advice didn't upset you."

"Not at all," Meredith said abruptly. "Really. Thanks for being honest."

When the metal door clicked shut behind him, she looked around the room. It was one of those moments when everything suddenly appears shifted from where it was a second before, a skipped beat in the time–space continuum. She looked at the hospital gown folded on top of the examination table's waxed paper sheet. It was pink. Meredith liked pink, but this shade reminded her of a dog's inner ear. She stared at the gown and thought of what a strange couple of days it had been. Walking off set, consoling Mish, being told by a man she'd just met she'd better get pregnant soon and fast . . . And now this same man was preparing to scrape cells from inside her body so someone else could examine them under a microscope. Meredith looked at the oven mitts at the end of the table and imagined the cold metal stirrups beneath them.

For the second time in seventy-two hours, Meredith bolted.

***

The day before Meredith left for London, she and Mish met for brunch at a French bistro in Kensington Market. Mish chose the place for its fried cheese, homemade hollandaise and indignant ban on all American products since the war in Iraq. Not having to eat folic-rich greens every five seconds was, she assured Meredith, one of the major bonuses of not being pregnant. That and smoking. And drinking. Meredith arrived exactly on time. Mish was already there, at a corner table, sitting behind a two-thirds-empty bottle of rosé, nose in a copy of *Us*.

"Okay," Mish demanded when she saw Meredith. "How is it possible that every single celebrity in the history of the world is currently engaged? I mean, don't these people ever just date? And their engagements are so weird. They don't announce it or anything like normal people—instead they just go around wearing gigantic rings and publicly denying everything. What's the fucking point?"

She pointed to a photo of a pop star and an actress crossing the street. Over top of the image the magazine art directors had added a large yellow arrow pointing to the third finger of the actress's left hand, which was wrapped around a takeout latte the size of a construction worker's lunch Thermos. Lower on the page, the same image of her hand had been blown up to twice its size and framed in the outline of a church bell. "Wedding bells for Carrie and Ben?" read the headline, followed by a caption: "After a walk along the beach in Malibu, Carrie and Ben grab a coffee at their local Starbucks. Back in action after a brief winter hiatus (during which time Ben was spotted canoodling with his former publicity agent), the golden couple are looking more serious than ever. If you don't believe *Us*, check out the diamond-encrusted emerald on Carrie's left hand! According to friends, this could be it. 'I've never seen them happier,' says one close acquaintance. 'They can't keep their hands off each other. The chemistry is explosive!'"

Meredith looked for other words to read on the page but there were none. Mish poured her a glass of wine, but Meredith murmured something about wine in the daytime and poured most of hers into her friend's glass.

"You okay?" she said.

"Yes and no. You?" asked Mish.

Meredith shrugged. She wanted badly to tell her friend about the handsome gynecologist and the G-test and the Pap smear that never was, but felt it was perhaps better not to mention anything fertility related for now. She was worried Mish might break down. Actually she was more worried *she* might break down, but worrying about other people breaking down helped her to not break down herself.

46

For two hours they spoke of every amusing thing they could think of that didn't particularly matter and ate eggs and butter and cheese and pastry. Afterwards, Meredith ordered decaf coffee, explaining her new theory that caffeine was the devil, and Mish teased her for being such a priss.

After lunch, Mish wanted to stop by a pharmacy to pick up cold sore ointment (the clown had left her with that special tingling) and Meredith said she would come with. Wandering around drugstores was something they did very well together. It was just like high school, except that Meredith no longer worried about Mish stealing cosmetics.

"Hey, remember the summer you stayed at my house and we put this in our hair?" Mish was standing in aisle three holding up a box of Flirt.

"Totally." Meredith smiled. "It was meant to be burgundy but it turned our hair pink."

"Mine was more fuchsia. It matched my fluorescent bikini."

"Clit pink. That was what my mother called it when she met me at the airport."

"Didn't she think it was so cool she copied it or something?"

"Yup." Meredith took the box from Mish's hand and placed it back on the shelf. As she did, she saw something flash in the corner of her eye. A big diamond ring—like the one in *Us* magazine—on the very small, slender hand of a very young girl. Meredith tried not to stare but it was hard—the girl was so pretty. She was indeterminately Asian, or possibly Middle Eastern—with the sort of fine boned, sloe-eyed darkness that politically incorrect casting directors described as "exotic." In a wife-beater tank and grubby, frayed jeans, she was doing the rich-hippie thing. The look was one Meredith had always admired but had never been able to pull off.

"Hello? Fashion moment," said Mish, who always talked to strangers after a couple of glasses of wine. She winked at the girl and pointed approvingly at her outfit.

"Uh, thanks," said the girl, grabbing a tube of organic lemon-verbena toothpaste—not, Meredith sensed, because she wanted it but because she wanted to get away from the weirdly complimentary gawking women.

Meredith wondered if they looked middle-aged to her. She was just about to say this to Mish, when she noticed him. The handsome gynecologist. Farther down the aisle, choosing conditioners. As Mish wandered away, Meredith watched surreptitiously while the rich young hippie sidled up to him. Dr. Veil smiled and said something to her. She giggled, took the bottle of conditioner from his hand and exchanged it for another. Then confidently, almost cockily, she walked away. He waited a dignified amount of time before following her out of the aisle, an adoring expression on his face. He did not seem to notice Meredith at all.

Meredith found Mish in the contraceptives aisle, looking at a box of condoms. "Who do you suppose the ribs are actually *for*, anyway?"

"Listen, can we go? There's someone here I can't really run into."

Mish paused, but Meredith was already halfway out of the store.

When they were outside and a full block away, Mish put her arm around her friend's waist. "One-night stand?" she asked. "High school enemy? Shrink? The host of a party you got totally wasted at and ended up dancing topless on top of the freezer? Or wait—that wasn't you. That was me."

Meredith laughed. "Worse," she said. "That modelly looking Asian chick? The one with the diamond? Did you see that guy she was with? The tall, good-looking one about twice her age? That's my gynecologist."

Mish wrinkled her nose. "I hate people," she said. "Don't you hate people?"

Irma Moore feasted her eyes on the buffet of horror laid out before her. Terminal Four, Heathrow International, at seven a.m. was, she decided, a magnificent contemporary re-staging of Dante's lowest circle of hell, or perhaps, if she closed her eyes to freeze its last image in her mind, Picasso's *Guernica*. Trails of human sausage-links tangled and writhed across the industrial-tiled floor, and Irma was one of them, bravely navigating her small form through the seething mass. The din was dampened only by a faint misting of perspiration. The weight of this respirated atmosphere pressed down on Irma's head like a dumbwaiter. Everyone took a place in line: queues of the paranoid waiting to have their old suitcases wrapped in cellophane. Mothers and infants in rows outside a metal door bearing a sign of a grinning cartoon elephant and the words BABY PIT STOP. A whole generation of smartly swaddled Saudi ladies waiting in line to get their VAT tax-back forms signed after their vodka-and-Prada sprees in Knightsbridge.

Irma paused to watch a customs official, his nose decorated with gin blossoms, glare over the counter at a small Muslim woman shrouded in a Gucci-logo-print head scarf. He pointed at the woman's bag on the floor. The woman bent down wordlessly and hoisted it onto the counter, spilling its contents before him. He held up a flimsy pile of paper and made a dismissive, uncooperative gesture. The woman stamped her foot and raised her hand in frustration. They stared at each other for a moment before the woman — perhaps because of a language barrier, perhaps sheer annoyance — swept up her purchases and her carry-on bag in two arms and clopped away, burka swishing out behind her.

More than any other version of hell, Irma Moore preferred the hell of other people. As someone who had rarely behaved normally — let alone well — in her life, Irma thought it was lovely to watch otherwise polite people lose it. This was especially true in public. For this reason, she had a soft spot for airports. She cruised over to the arrivals board but couldn't get a view for the mobs of people standing in front of her.

"Ucchh," she said. The Ulsterwoman's trademark articulation of frustration. An involuntary, guttural reflex that she often made, and the only discernible trace of her middle-class upbringing in Belfast.

"A poor-bog Irish peasant girl" is how Irma liked to describe herself, though in fact she grew up in a tidy Protestant suburb. Her father was an eye surgeon, not a potato farmer, as she sometimes passively led people to believe. But Irma had never been much of a fan of unadorned facts—the truth, in her mind, was too barren and plain. She preferred a more cluttered version of reality.

Being a poet, Irma was big on metaphors. She rarely thought of things as they were, but instead imagined them as what they represented in the larger scheme of things. Human existence, in her mind's eye, was a vast, messy castle with high turrets and secret passages, crocodile moats and magic suits of armour that might spring to life at any moment. Life was loud, animated and bloated with waste, not unlike Heathrow's Terminal Four. But in the case of the great metaphoric castle, she mused, while craning her neck to read the flight numbers on the screen, there was one crucial difference: the castle contained only one royal personage. And that was Irma.

Ah-*ha*. BA flight from Toronto due to arrive at 7:05 a.m. Just minutes ago, Irma noted, checking the pocket watch she carried in her handbag. For once, her daughter was late. Even if it wasn't Meredith's fault, Irma couldn't help but take a bit of pleasure in this uncharacteristic tardiness.

She pushed on, towards the arrivals gate at the other end of the terminal. When she got there a man in uniform informed her this was the arrivals gate for domestic flights only. She would have to go back and check the message board to find the right gate. Irma reached through her batwing sleeve and scratched at a spot under the restrictive cummerbund of her traditional geisha's kimono. (What had possessed her to put on this wretched thing anyway? She really should have worn the rabbit-fur poncho instead.) Another message board, with more encoded messages. She flung her head up like a garbage can with a spring lid, and her red velvet beret came loose from its bobby pin and Frisbeed off her head.

Ucchh.

She bent down with some effort and, after a couple of lunging steps, caught the hat mid-air by its peacock feather. She had taken to wearing hats after noticing a bald spot at her crown reflected in a restaurant mirror she had made the mistake of sitting in front of during a recent gallery board-members' luncheon in Soho. Getting old was a bugger—a point she planned to impress upon her daughter. The young should be grateful, if only for the fact that they are not yet old.

The only thing that delighted Irma Moore about being a mother was the tyrannical irreversibility of it. She was a fatalist.

While dismally ill-equipped at empathy, nurturing and polite conversation, Irma excelled in other departments. Smuggling exotic and dangerous house pets into Britain via Heathrow, for instance, and consuming large quantities of sweet Italian liqueurs. To date, Irma had concealed six snakes, twenty spiders, two lizards and four rare birds in her battered crocodile carry-on bag. Each night before bed she chugged a half pint of Limoncello. She claimed it kept her young.

In her youth, Irma had littered the English-speaking world with a great deal of bad poetry. Highly acclaimed bad poetry in the vein of Sexton and Plath, except, as Irma famously pointed out in her *Paris Review* interview, "without all the depressing bits." All that left, naturally, were the sexy bits, and Irma tore into the burgeoning sixties literary market of women "taking control of their own sexuality" like a horny priest at a boy-band convention. Her expertly timed 1969 collection, *Dirty Girls on Acid*, launched Irma as a sort of English poetess counterpart of Erica Jong. For one perfect summer the international literary world couldn't get enough of her. She toured North America doing readings in every city and college town from Dartmouth to Denver. Accompanied by a smack-addled vanload of jazz musicians from Cornwall, bird-boned Irma had been a vision of threatening feminine liberation—a *vagina dentata* for a new era.

It was on her trip through New Mexico that she established her signature look of live jewellery (she often turned up at parties with a tarantula on her scarf or a defanged asp coiled around her throat). It was on the California leg of that trip that her daughter was conceived.

Righting herself slowly, Irma was stopped dead by a word.

"Mom!"

She looked up and spotted her daughter jogging toward her in a velour leisure suit. Clearly some kind of awful Canadian trend.

"Hello, dear. Lovely to see you."

They kissed apprehensively and began to push through the crowd.

Meredith's luggage cart jammed in the exit door and she stumbled over the hem of her pants.

"Mom! For God's sake, what's the hurry?"

Irma put her hand to her pumping heart and glowered at her daughter. They'd been together less than a minute and already Irma felt misunderstood. Much as she enjoyed the anticipation of going to a place, as soon as she had reached her destination, she was filled with a compulsion to leave. She wanted out of this airport. Now. She was well known for disappearing between courses at dinner parties and fleeing the theatre at intermission. As a quitter, Irma never quit. Just the day before, in fact, she had coolly broken it off with Jose, the South American refugee poet. Her reasoning had been simple: it could never last, and anyway, this was probably her last chance to make a man under the age of forty weep. And weep he did.

Irma took in the whole of her daughter with a glance, noting with relief that while Meredith's style remained grimly conservative, she had not yet grown fat.

"Well . . ." Irma said conclusively. She smiled and placed a hand on each of Meredith's cool cheeks.

"I thought we could take a taxi into town this time, Mom. On me."

"Oh dear, would you mind terribly if we don't?" Irma winced. "I just loathe making chitchat with the drivers. And besides, the tube is *so* good for you."

"Good for you? How?"

"Lots of novelty bacteria for your body to absorb. A real workout for your immune system."

Meredith looked too tired to argue.

"Come along now, don't get scratchy just yet. Wait till we're back at the flat." Irma grimly hauled a knapsack from Meredith's luggage carrier and wriggled it onto her back. "There's a brave old sausage."

With that, they stepped aboard the escalator that would take them down deep, hundreds of feet below the teeming city, the buzzing, ancient catacomb of laughter, conniving and stink that is London.

* * *

The flat on Coleville Terrace was located on the third and fourth floor of an ivy-strangled townhouse. The building had originally been intended as an upscale single-family dwelling, but had been chopped up into several apartments sometime during the post-war boom.

Dragging her luggage uphill from the tube, Meredith listened to her mother's rant about the neighbourhood. Over the past couple of centuries the area had risen and fallen in its fortunes, and risen and fallen again. In the four decades since Irma moved in, the area had changed dramatically, and in her view, for the worse. The West Indian flophouses had been bought at a pittance and renovated into gleaming mausoleums by the offspring of ailing rock legends. She could barely leave the house to buy a can of sardines without running into one of these trustafarian twits, on the way to the salon to have their hair matted or tuning up their vintage kit cars. They put her in a bad mood, the bohemians of today. Such pretenders. So *rich*. The village was nothing like in the old days when drugged gypsies flopped for the night in doorways playing bongo drums and everyone pretended not to mind. Back then, Coleville Terrace was dirty and uncomfortable and *real*. Now it was a movie set inhabited by upscale squatters.

Of course Meredith didn't remember it this way. Her early recollections of life here were hazy. Literally. A film of smoke permeated the inner atmosphere of the flat from morning to night—cherry tobacco fumes emanating from a hookah pipe Irma kept smouldering in the corner of the living room. There were visitors—hundreds of them, coming and going, sleeping and dancing, eating and throwing up in the loo. These happy wanderers lit fires in the sink and sang campfire songs, pinched Meredith's ears and knees, and roared through the night at jokes she didn't understand.

Early childhood—pre–boarding school, pre-Canada— was murky territory for Meredith. She had been back to Coleville Terrace only once in the twelve years since graduating (on a layover flight to Croatia where she was working on a sci-fi vampire Canadian–European co-production).

Now, standing outside the chipped front door, Meredith was suddenly starving. This was unusual. Like her mother, she ate little and was particular about what she did eat. Unlike Irma, she abstained for reasons of health and vanity, rather than defiance of social conventions.

She watched Irma fumble, muttering, in her hand-bag and, after a minute or so, withdraw a Hello Kitty key ring from which hung two brass keys. One of them she detached and handed to Meredith with a ceremonial air. The other she slipped into the lock.

"Mom?"

"Yes, dear? Oh, and before I forget, if you must call me that, could you at least pronounce it in a way that doesn't make you sound like a cashier at Wal-Mart?"

Irma rammed the key into the keyhole, withdrew it and rammed it in again.

"All right, then. *Irma*."

"Yes?"

"Do you have anything in the fridge?"

The door swung open with a *thud*.

"To eat?" said Irma, as if her daughter had just suggested they spend the afternoon inline skating to Brighton. "I'll pour you a nice glass of London tap and that should curb it. They say eighty percent of hunger spells are actually caused by dehydration. Particularly after a long flight. Murder on the skin. You look parched."

Meredith began to drag her roller suitcase up to the flat. She remembered her prenatal yoga instructor's words: "Be mindful of your body, and the bodies of others." She translated the words into a mantra of her own: "Try not to smack your mother, no matter how much she tempts you."

The flat was not so much dirty as decimated. Whole pieces of furniture were simply lost—buried beneath the heap of abandoned human implements: paper, cloth, metal, plastic. The odour of wet wood shavings was overlaid with the suggestion of long-forgotten fruit. For a moment Meredith considered the hopeful possibility she might be hallucinating from exhaustion. She gave her head a shake. No luck.

The front hall opened onto the third floor of Irma's building and served, illogically, as the upper floor of the flat: it housed the two bedrooms and the bathroom. Immediately to the right of the front door was a largish bathroom, the walls covered with crumbly tiles. To the right was the master bedroom, discernible by the piles of books, board games and discarded bottles of Limoncello. Under a huge heap of velvet and a Cossack coat hulked Irma's single bed. Beside it was a tea tray bearing half a honeyed crumpet. Somewhere, from under something, a transistor radio brayed yesterday's football scores.

Irma opened a door that led to her daughter's child-hood room. Meredith was relieved, and even touched, to see that it was tidy compared to the rest of the place, even if it was barely the size of a pantry. The only furniture was a narrow military-issue sleeping cot pushed against the far wall and made up neatly with a yellowed, but quite possibly clean, eyelet bedspread. The walls were bare except for a framed and yellowed fingerpainting of a flesh-toned blob on a grassy expanse under a teal sky. Meredith had no memory of executing this work, but figured she must have done it during one of her summer holidays spent with her mother's artist colony in the south of Spain.

"So what do you think?" Irma said.

"It's very nice. But is there somewhere for me to work? I need to prep for tomorrow."

"Hold your horses."

Meredith dumped her suitcase and followed her mother up the stairs. At the top, she surveyed the main room.

"Hasn't changed a bit, has it," said Irma.

She walked into the kitchen (really just the south-east corner of the room), refilled the prehistoric electric kettle and set it to boil with a flick of the switch. Meredith's heart did not sink, it plummeted.

The room—a postage stamp of living area tacked onto a narrow galley kitchen—had the look of a well-loved bomb shelter. There were books and papers and china teacups and strange swaths of gauze and feathers and tree bark and fur and antique hospital equipment. Scraps of fabric that had once been ladies' undergarments had been left to disintegrate on every open space. Piles of human consumer waste—records, shoes, cutlery, ornamental gourds, dried-up potted plants, decorative papier mâché party place-setting cards left over from a long-forgotten dinner party, discarded auto parts, socks—were scattered about the place.

Meredith longed for a cheap hotel room but had to concede the truth. She was broke.

"Where, then?"

"Over there." Irma pointed to a heap of books on top of an old steamer trunk.

"A trunk? You want me to work on a trunk?"

"No, dingbat, beyond it. In Jose's old spot."

Irma crossed the room, turned on a standing lamp and pulled away a saddle blanket to reveal a child's school desk, the kind with a plastic chair attached by a curved metal bar.

"You aren't serious." Meredith rubbed her face and reopened her eyes.

"Ucchh, of course I am." Irma took her daughter's hand and held it to her chest. "This is where Jose wrote his best poem." Her eyes shone with emotion. "It was only six lines long and it was about my hands. He called it 'The Digits of Experience.'"

She fanned her fingers out for Meredith to see. The knuckles on her third and fourth fingers were thick with arthritis. A liver spot on the back of her left palm looked like a tiny map of Africa cut adrift.

"What did it say?"

"I'm not sure. It was in Spanish. But it was beautiful. Poets communicate in a universal language." Irma retreated across the room toward the whining kettle.

As her mother puttered over the tea, Meredith fell asleep on the leaky bean-bag chair in the corner of the flat. She awoke several minutes later and wandered into the kitchenette.

"What is it, dear?" Irma had been reading a story in a tabloid newspaper about an eleven-year-old single mother of twins living in Yorkshire.

"Nothing."

Meredith was overcome by a sudden need to tidy. To organize and itemize. She felt weightless, as though she were floating just outside her own body. Forget food—instead she would clean. If she could do something to introduce order, that would make her feel better. She would start with something small, a surmountable task at the core of the chaos.

Irma vanished down the stairs to her bath (she had one every Sunday). Meredith observed her go as if from a great distance. She searched the room for where to start. Of course! She would defrost the freezer.

Her mother's icebox was a stout Frigidaire from the 1960s, a barrel-chested soldier of an appliance.

Meredith held her breath, gripped the stainless steel handle, pulled down hard and felt the latch give and the door swing out towards her. Inside, the fridge was startlingly bare and bright. She sniffed. Nothing but the faint chemical smell of working electrical machinery. The appliance hummed a meditative *om* and Meredith exhaled in unison. She reached up and flicked open the smaller blue plastic freezer door—and was blinded by a glittering flash. There was a loud *crack*, a stab of pain and then, nothing.

When she came to she was staring into a house of glinting mirrors.

"Silly goose!" her mother called from somewhere above her head. "Wake up and stop this nonsense, would you? There'll be no dying on my kitchen floor."

She felt a hand on her forehead, but still the prisms glittered. In desperation she dragged herself a few inches along the floor, until her mother pulled her up by the shoulders and propped her against the cupboard like a doll. Oh, poor, poor head.

"What were you doing in the freezer? You know I only use it to store the chandelier."

"The *what*?"

"It must have fallen out and hit you on the head. It's very valuable, you know. Edwardian."

Meredith noticed the dangling topaz crystals, now scattered over the floor. She opened her mouth to say something, but before she could do so, a longing moved through her. All the familiar sensations were there: the gaping belly yawn, the arterial fizz, the hardening of her nipples . . .

"Mummy."

"Yes."

"Can you help me with something?"

"What's that?"

"I want to have a baby of my own."

Irma pressed a damp, dirty J Cloth over the bump on Meredith's forehead. "Is that all?" She laughed and patted her daughter on the cheek. "Easy-peasy."

* * *

That night Meredith's eyes snapped open in the dark. She raised herself from the bed and removed the plastic bite-plate she wore to bed each night in an effort to "deprogram" her from grinding her teeth. There would be no more sleep for now.

Fumbling around in the dim chaos of her mother's flat, she managed to open her binder-sized laptop and dial up a modem connection. Cross-legged on the floor, Meredith logged onto the server and opened her account. There were eighty-six new messages, the predictable bulk of them advertisements for penis enlargement, mail-order college degrees, discount Viagra and urgent salutations from African despots in need of a temporary overseas loan. Meredith scrolled through her in-box, deleting whole screens at a time, until suddenly she came upon a message that froze her thumb in mid-click.

To: *Meredith Moore*
From: *Dr. Joe Veil*
Subject: *Your disappearance*

Dear Meredith,

    I hope you don't mind that I have taken the liberty to contact you via the e-mail address provided in your file, but after your exit yesterday I found myself at a loss for what to think. I hope my advice was not overly blunt. If that was what made you leave my office so abruptly, I apologize. As your doctor I felt it important to take the time to check in and make sure you are not in any kind of distress.
    I hope you are well and taking good care.

Yours sincerely,
Dr. Joe Veil

Meredith read the note twice before even attempting to compose a reply. What to make of it? Professional obligation? Fatherly concern? Flirtation? No, Meredith did not detect of hint of that in his tone. Though, how strange that a busy gynecologist should go so far out of his way to contact a skittish patient. For all he knew she was simply a nut. What to make of this sudden interest in her behaviour? She clicked on "reply" and began to type.

To: *Dr. Joe Veil*
From: *Meredith Moore*
Subject: *Re: Your disappearance*

Dear Doctor,

Thank you for the kind note, but I can't accept
your apology. I did not leave your examination
room because of any offensiveness on your part—
quite the opposite. You were professional and direct,
and I thank you for your concern. I am currently
away on business but will make an appointment
with one of your colleagues upon my return.

Sorry if I alarmed you by leaving so abruptly. It
wasn't like me to run away. I guess I haven't been
myself lately. Perhaps it's the biological twitch
twitching. You'd probably know better than me.
You're the doctor.

Sorry again,
Meredith

6

Meredith didn't mind being called the continuity girl. Over the past year or so, however, she had begun to wonder whether she ought to be slightly embarrassed by the title. Like so many otherwise driven women, her greatest fear was not having a lack of authority but having a surplus of it. Too much power (she had to admit it) made her feel less . . . *feminine*. She waited anxiously for the terrible day some third-assistant-director film school grad would turn around and unthinkingly call her "the script lady." That would be the day she'd quit.

In recent years, the industry had been called to task for its use of outdated terminology, particularly when describing jobs traditionally occupied by women or gay men (this being show business, there were lots of both). Since Meredith had started working on set, producers had been forced, in official contexts at least, to hire makeup artists instead of "pretties," actors instead of "talent," and background artists instead of "extras." It wasn't that anyone on set actually talked any differently than they used to, just that everybody now had two job titles instead of one. Meredith's twin title was script supervisor, but thankfully no one called her that. She was still performing what the trade considered a young woman's job, and she wanted to keep it that way.

Of course, in a way, she *had* quit. Walked off Felsted's set with the bleary intention of getting out of show business altogether. (There had been the occasional intention of enrolling in cooking school, until she remembered nearly fainting the time she had to "dress" the turkey giblets at Elle's house one Christmas, and the thought passed.)

But here she was in London, back on set and in the thick of it all. Toughing it out with a bunch of men who in all likelihood resented her presence more than they appreciated it.

But that was where the similarities to any previous job ended. Richard Glass was an altogether different sort of director from those she had worked with in Toronto. For one thing, he was slender and almost girlish looking. And he wore suits—unhemmed pants and monogrammed shirts so worn you could see his flat penny-sized nipples through the fabric.

While most directors tended to be brusque and proud of their macho to-the-pointness, Richard seemed to have all the time in the world for silly small talk and pranks. Like others in his position, he spent a lot of time flirting with the actresses (whispering in their ears, placing a supportive hand on the small of their backs), but unlike most, he flirted with everyone else on set as well. He slipped and slithered about the set all day, offering every individual the unexpected treat of his undivided, if momentary, attention. In this way he managed to charm every member of the crew into carrying out his orders without ever raising his voice.

Meredith had been on the set for eight days of the forty-day shoot and was coping well enough so far. The film was a Victorian period murder-mystery/romantic-comedy starring Kathleen Swain, an American starlet coming to the end of her bankable period. In it, she played a spinster pathologist who falls in love with a brooding detective while performing autopsies on the bodies of the prostitute victims of a Jack-the-Ripper-like murderer. The film was financed on the slope of Swain's cheekbones.

The project's backer was the mysterious and never-present Osmond Crouch, who, it was widely rumoured, was a former lover of Swain's. In his place, Mr. Crouch (as everyone called him on set) had sent a line producer to oversee the shoot. Dan Button, an overgrown Scottish goth boy, minced about in a black trench coat and skull boots, looking terrified to talk to anyone. He couldn't be more than thirty, Meredith thought, and yet Crouch had for some reason sent him here to oversee the production of a twenty-million-dollar movie. Twenty million! That's what this pimply monkey of a boy, this wannabe vampire, was in charge of. It boggled the mind. While most of the hands-on crew generally ignored Button, the director would occasionally slip off with him for a little chat. Button would invariably emerge from Richard's trailer flushed with pleasure, and for the rest of the day would skulk more happily around the set, occasionally tap-tap-tapping his walking staff to the tune of some dark, internal symphony.

The crew was setting up in a large empty warehouse space on the third floor of a nearly condemned East End building when Meredith arrived for her call time of seven-thirty a.m. She grabbed a juice from the "tea cart" (funny Brits) and unfolded her tiny portable camp stool in a quiet corner, then began her day's logging. Hauling a binder out of her bag and wiping the crumbs from its surface (a packet of airplane pretzels had somehow escaped its packaging), she examined the day's pages for the third time that morning. The script had been changed so many times by Glass and the writer that it was now an unruly rainbow of candy-coloured revision pages. Every revised page in the script was dated and printed on a different-coloured page from the one before. The rotation, according to protocol, began with white and was followed by blue, pink, yellow, green and goldenrod (Meredith had never understood why they didn't just call it orange). The scene they were shooting today (which involved a fight, a kiss and a bad guy being set on fire and thrown out of a fifth-story window) was printed out on white paper—double white—which meant it had been rewritten exactly six times so far. Meredith would not be the least bit surprised if handwritten blue revisions—double blues—appeared and had to be stapled into her binder. Usually, by the time shooting began, Meredith knew the script so well, had read it and made so many detailed notes on it, divided it into eighths (for scheduling purposes, all scripts were organized this way—Meredith's job was to keep track of the shooting times of each eighth of a page), and numbered all the scenes and shots that she felt she could recite the thing by heart. Nevertheless, she now studied the scene once more.

Act 1, Scene 6
Int. Empty Victorian garment factory—
the scene of the crime.
The voices of Celia and David can be
heard off camera as they make their
way up the stairs.

           CELIA (OFF SCREEN)
  Once again, Inspector, I'm not
  sure what you think you're going
  to find here that the police
  already haven't.

Int. stairwell.
David is helping Celia up the rickety
steps. She struggles a bit and tears
her petticoat on a nail.

CELIA

Good heavens.

DAVID

Are you all right, Miss?

CELIA

(irritated) Yes, yes, fine. To be
perfectly honest, Inspector, I'd
be a great deal better if I was
back at the morgue doing some
useful work.

DAVID

My dear Miss Hornby, thank you
again for your skepticism, but
surely as a doctor you must agree
that no hair can be left unturned,
particularly when lives are at
stake.

Just this snippet, Meredith knew, would take most of
the morning to get on film. First a camera set-up for
the interior of the factory, then another for the stairwell. They would shoot the interior scenes of the factory first, and likely get to the stairwell segment later.
Meredith made a mental note to ensure the wardrobe
people had provided a visibly ripped petticoat for
Celia in the interior garment factory scenes.

The truth was, for all her copious work and attention to detail, few directors or editors even looked at
the continuity notes anymore. Schedules could be

generated by computer. The log was kept more out of tradition and protocol than genuine need. The bulk of Meredith's job was to record the difference between what was on the page and what was shot. If dialogue was added or cut, Meredith made note. If an actor strayed into an unscripted moment of genius or folly, she noted that too. If anything changed from the original plan, she was on it. Her first loyalty, as continuity girl, was to the script.

She removed a ruler from her case and darkened the dividing lines of eighths using her sharpest pencil. Then she flipped forward in her binder to the Daily Continuity Log sheet, on which she would take careful note of the set-up, scene and slate (the clappy board) number, as well as shot time, pages shot and, most important, which take of which shots the director wanted the lab to print and send out to the editor. With her Polaroid camera, digital stopwatch, binder and sharpened pencil, Meredith would record and keep track of even the most seemingly unimportant detail on the set, from the exact time (down to a quarter of a second) when the crew broke for lunch, to precise measurement of the rip on the hem of the actress's petticoat. She would keep notes for the assistant editor in a daily log, recording the scene, slate, time and print numbers for him to note when he looked over the rushes in the following days.

As continuity girl, Meredith's job was to be the editor's eye on set. They were in it together, she and he (in this case, a grumpy little Glaswegian named Rowan who lived and worked in a dark suite deep in the Hammersmith riverbed). As the rest of the crew busily manufactured random narrative fragments out of time and out of context, Meredith kept the order in her daily log books so that the editor could put the story back together again.

The grips were setting up a camera across the room, wheeling around dollies, taping down wires and trading lame jokes. No sign of Richard. Meredith took the moment of calm to take stock of her kit—opened her black, nylon pack and accounted for its contents by touch.

Script in script binder—*check*. Book-light for night scenes—*check*. White-out—*check*. Victorian slang dictionary—*check*. Polaroid camera and extra film—*check*. Pencils and sharpener—*check*. Hat, mitts, scarf for outdoor shooting—*check*. Envelopes: legal size—*check*. Eraser—*check*. Organic yogourt and Fuji apple for lunch—*check*. Waterproof felt pens—*check*. Reinforced three-hole paper—*check*. One-hole punch—*check*. Paper clips—*check*. Ruler—*check*. Self-stick three-hole-paper reinforcements . . . self-stick three-hole-paper reinforcements . . . no! *Where* were the freaking self-stick three-hole-paper reinforcements?

Meredith took in air and closed her eyes. Yes, she was sure she had noted them the first time she completed the checklist that day, just before leaving the flat at dawn. The self-stick three-hole-paper reinforcements were a small but essential tool for her job. Without them, she would have to punch holes in her blank paper, clip them into the binder and simply trust that they would stay secure. If a careless technician bumped against her while she was working, or if her binder slid off her knees onto the floor (as it often did if she was absorbed in watching the monitor or talking to the director and forgot to steady it with her elbow), then carefully compiled pages of log sheets would be in danger of detaching at their weakest, unprotected spots. Columns of painstakingly listed shot details could be damaged or, worse yet, lost completely. What if she wasn't looking when a page ripped off and got stuck on the second A.D.'s boot as he walked by, barking call times into his walkie-talkie? By the time Meredith noticed the missing log sheet it could be six hours and two set-ups later. The page could have been swept up by the cleaners, dumped into the dustbin, bagged and ready for the afternoon pickup. It would be too late to get the page back, impossible to remember all the relevant details, a disservice to the editor and the director—and she would be fired. *Again.* And all because her brand-new packet of self-stick paper reinforcements had probably slipped beneath her dusty little bed.

Meredith felt her guts constrict. There was a pounding in her ears. It was not impossible she would die. People died all the time. Cells exploded in their brains or their throats just swelled shut. She reached deep into her pack and found the inner pocket containing a small bottle containing a dozen or so dissolvable half-doses of Ativan from a prescription she had filled four years ago after a particularly bad break-up. She wrapped her hand around the bottle and the imminent-death feeling gradually faded.

She'd spent enough time in therapy to know her anxiety was likely brought on by the sudden close proximity to her mother. But Irma was trying her best. She had somehow arranged this job, hadn't she? And she was supportive of the donor quest—devoting herself to the task of setting Meredith up with a suitable specimen using every connection available to her.

And Irma's connections were considerable. In spite (or perhaps because of) her immutable eccentricity, she had compiled a network of friends and ex-lovers who ranged across London society. She belonged to half the clubs in the city and was well known in the others. There were dinners and book launches and pub quizzes to attend several times a week. Irma sat on a number of boards and governing committees of art galleries, a library and a major literary prize. While she never contributed anything in the way of actual work in these postings, she amused her fellow artocrats by telling animated stories of the old days of Notting Hill—hanging out with the arty crowd, dropping liquid acid and sipping Campari on the rooftops. She was, and always had been, a hit wherever she went. And now, for the first time ever, Irma finally had something to offer her daughter: a rich and varied social life.

On Wednesday, Meredith was to attend a dinner at the Chelsea Arts Club with her mother. Perhaps he would be there: the father of her child.

Meredith pushed these thoughts from her mind and forced herself to concentrate on the job at hand. Richard was striding across the set, right hand pitchforked deep into his bale of brown hair. He obviously needed something big from her, and Meredith resolved to make herself useful.

"Meredith. Heavenly to see you. Turns out you're *just* the person I was looking for." Richard covered his heart with ten long white fingers and bowed like a courtier. There was a slightly sarcastic inflection to everything he said or did, as if his entire life was one elaborate adolescent boarding-school prank. Meredith felt very slow and cement-witted whenever he was around. She stood up.

"Sir?"

"Listen." He lowered his voice to a clamp-toothed whisper. "We have a rather serious crisis on our hands—one that I think you could help to diffuse by employing your . . ." He searched. "*Womanly charms.*"

"I'm sorry?"

"I'm afraid it's Miss Swain." He winced and looked around to make sure none of the crew members were in earshot. "She's—how to put this delicately?—

having a bit of a hissy fit at the moment. A sort of a does-my-ass-look-fat-in-this-dress tantrum. In her trailer. Won't come out. It's all quite ridiculous, but she's utterly inconsolable—by *me* at any rate. She's already scared the wardrobe stylist off set, and if she doesn't calm down shortly I'm afraid Dan could be next in line." He glanced across the warehouse to where Dan Button sat dejectedly polishing the carved ivory knob on his walking stick with a shammy.

"That's awful," said Meredith, feeling confused. Swain's diva antics were hardly surprising, but Richard's confidence in her was. Continuity supervisors had little contact with the actors, apart from annoying them by taking Polaroids of their costumes or reminding them to back-match their lines to their actions. Meredith preferred it this way. Actors were unpredictable, self-obsessed and invariably unstable. No good could come of befriending them. She worked around them like a stable hand sweeping out a thoroughbred's stall.

"You see, Meredith, what I was wondering was—and no pressure, by the way, although to be perfectly honest, at this point the entire balance of the show does depend upon it—if you wouldn't mind *talking* to her, American woman to American woman."

"But I'm Canadian."

Richard corrected his stoop and looked over Meredith's shoulder towards a team of grips assembling weights on the back of a crane. "Ms. Swain's trailer is the third on the left. The first set-up should be complete in half an hour." The conversation was over.

As she made her way to the line of trailers (affectionately referred to as "the circus") Meredith often marvelled at how archaic the average film set was. In an era when computers could be chess champions and compose original symphonies, cinema was clunky up close. The makeup artist applied blue lipstick to the mouth of the girl playing the corpse; and fake blood—a mixture of gelatin, water and purple food colouring—was splattered at the scene by a propsmaster wielding a child's plastic squirt gun. Cameras were still laboriously rigged on the outside of cars, fastened to the top of cranes or mounted Snugli-style on the chest of the Steadicam operator.

As continuity girl, Meredith felt more of an affinity with the camera than with any of her breathing colleagues on set. She and the lens had certain things in common. They were both dispassionate observers valued for their ability to meticulously record details without judgment or embellishment. Immovable in their pedantry, both were utterly indispensable to the process.

The door of Kathleen Swain's trailer was slightly ajar. Meredith tapped twice and stood frozen on the floating stainless steel stoop, listening for signs of life. After a half a minute or so, she knocked again.

"Oh, *what* now?" That unmistakable sandpaper drawl.

The words sounded scripted to Meredith. *What now, is right*, she thought. Her hands were trembling. Maybe she should have taken that Ativan.

Meredith spoke—but did not look—into the crack in the aluminum door frame. "Ms. Swain, my name is Meredith Moore. I supervise continuity on the set and I was just wondering if I could maybe help you with anything."

A stocking-clad toe appeared around the edge of the door and tugged it open. Inside, the trailer smelled mysteriously of baby powder and Chardonnay (or was it cat pee?). In a far corner a makeup girl was crumpled on a stool, sniffling into the industrial-sized cosmetic kit on her lap. Swain lay on the daybed beside the door, wrapped like a California roll in what appeared to be a velvet curtain, complete with rod. Her face was covered with what Meredith thought were bandages, but on closer inspection turned out to be a pair of white cotton gloves.

"Continuity, huh?" she said, peering out from between her fingers. "Courtney, you're free to go."

The makeup girl clamped her kit shut and shuffled out, giving Meredith a miserable glance as she passed.

Only when the door was shut tight did the actress take her hands away from her face. Meredith saw what she had already known: that in spite of age, stress, a slightly overzealous collagen injection artist and a layer of trowelled-on camera makeup, Swain was still very beautiful.

"You're not English," Swain said. "But you're not American either. That makes you Canadian."

"How'd you know?"

"I've been to Toronto a bunch of times." She stretched her arms above her head and yawned like a bored housecat. "In 1982 for *The Taste of Honey*, then in '87 for *The Sorceress*, then '91 for *Mr. Smith and Mrs. Jones*. I got a Golden Globe nom for that one, you know. A complete surprise. And then I was there in 1998 for the opening of *Blue Orchid*. Oh God, Valentino sent me this dress the night before and it didn't fit so I had to get it pinned. Terrible picture. Anyway, Toronto's not such a bad town. Do you ever go to Bistro 990?"

"Sometimes," Meredith lied.

"Well, good. You're practically American, then. I just get sick of all these English people all the time. They're so . . . shifty. You can never tell if they're joking. And the men all smell funny. Sort of sad and sweet—"

"It's the detergent."

"What?" Swain had removed one cotton glove and was peeling a coating of pink paraffin wax from her previously concealed hand.

"It's the cheap laundry detergent they use. I forget the brand name. It smells like a dead marriage."

"Yes, exactly! It's awful. Oh *God*, I'm so glad you noticed it too. I honestly thought I was going crazy." Swain laughed long and hard, and after a little while Meredith joined in.

"Have a seat." Swain motioned to the kitchenette table across the room, a whole two feet away. "Welcome to my movie star trailer," she said, pronouncing the term "moovee schtaa" in her best mid-Atlantic lockjaw.

Meredith wasn't sure if she was joking.

"You see, Meredith, the thing about acting, the truly rotten, vicious thing about it, is not the scrutiny, the superficiality, the endless rounds of boring interviews. Most of my colleagues have got it all wrong. They're complaining about the *good* things. The really *rotten* thing is the people. The people are awful. I mean, most people are. But show people? The *worst*. And the higher up the food chain you go, the worse it gets. Me? *I* am a Hollywood movie star. In other words, a monster. As bad as it gets. You know what they say?"

Meredith shook her head.

"People in drama like drama."

"I've heard that."

"You know I made Courtney cry."

"I assumed."

"Do you know why?"

"No."

"I said some very nasty things to her because a moment before, I'd looked down at my cleavage and noticed that it was wrinkly. My famous tits, wizening into a couple of floppy papayas. There's no operation for that, you know."

"No?"

"Not that there'd be much point even if there was. I mean, you can only put off the inevitable for so long."

Swain threw off her curtain in one swoop. Underneath she was wearing Victorian ladies' underwear—a pair of bloomers, wool stockings and a corset. Her body was, it had to be said, not what it used to be. She was still slim, but her skin was loose under her upper-arms and on her chest. Meredith correctly judged her to be about forty-five. Draped over the kitchenette table to the right was Swain's costume, a heavy blue velvet dress with thousands of complicated-looking lacings and hooks and eyes. It would take at least twenty minutes to get her into it, and given the situation with wardrobe, Meredith realized the job would probably fall to her.

"Listen," Meredith began, "I know this isn't a great time, and that you seem preoccupied with other things. But they're out there setting up for the first shot, and you're in it. So it might be a good idea to get dressed. You know, to save time."

Swain laughed. "Time is of no concern to me. The cliché is true—in the movies, time is money. And the money, in this case, belongs to Osmond Crouch. And guess what? Osmond Crouch owes me—not money, but something far more precious. He owes me my youth."

A knock at the door and the second A.D.'s voice announced Swain's call time.

"FUCK OFF!" she roared.

"I hope you don't mind listening to me for a bit. It's

just that I get so lonely for female company, and these English women, they don't really count. They're all so cold. They don't really have the same body image anxiety we do. It's hard to relate." Swain looked directly at Meredith for the first time.

"No children," she pronounced.

Meredith shook her head, unsure where this was going. She suddenly wanted to leave. Just when she was about to gather her binder, Swain stood up, stepped into the layers of velvet and began pulling up her dress. She did not talk about this, just did it. Meredith began the painstaking work of slipping each little hook into its intended eye.

Swain sighed. "I was married three times, but no babies. I even miscarried twice, like Marilyn Monroe. That was during my second marriage, to Peter, the entertainment lawyer. The normal one. I didn't realize it in my twenties and thirties, but husbands are really not the issue at all. They're basically disposable. You can always find a better one at some point." She giggled cruelly. "But babies . . . you only get one chance for those."

Meredith continued hooking and eyeing.

"People tell me I should adopt. A little girl from China or a foundling from Guatemala or wherever. But I've never been one for rescuing people. I haven't got much of a martyr complex. I don't think that's what parenthood is about. For me it's about the flesh. My own flesh. Flesh of my flesh, to love and care for, for the rest of my life, you know? That's what I long for. But you know, on the bright side, there are operations for that."

"For what?"

"For having babies later in life. At my age. Not operations, I mean, but procedures. New technologies, drugs and that sort of thing. So sad old hags like me can have a hope—"

Meredith felt Swain's ribcage release beneath the layers of velvet. She hoped that Swain was not about to cry, because if she did, she would have to have her makeup redone. The actress straightened her back and looked in the mirror. She was, Meredith saw now, very controlled. Swain breathed out with a *whoosh* and patted her face, then grimaced, remembering something.

"Good Lord, what am I going to do?"

"About what?"

"About the wardrobe stylist. I can't get into these horrendous things on my own, and I don't suppose we can convince her to come back after I burned her with my curling iron, can we?"

Meredith hid her smile in the folds of Swain's bustle. She stood up and smoothed down the back of her dress.

Swain was moaning, "Oh God, oh God, what am I going to do?"

Meredith had an idea. She felt her face brighten. "Actually, Ms. Swain, I may have just the woman for the job."

The actress raised one eyebrow, intrigued. "Is she American?"

"Almost," Meredith said. "She's Canadian."

"Close enough," Swain winked. "She's hired."

Mish arrived in London the following day. Meredith had arranged to meet her at a new sushi lounge in Knightsbridge, kitty-corner from Harrods on a tiny street called Raphael. The place was one of those sprawling subterranean London nightspots that gave Meredith the feeling the city might be a grim facade built over-top a buzzing underworld populated by demons. The very young and the very rich mingled around the bar, balancing jewel-toned saketinis between their thumbs and middle fingers. Despite her best efforts to look bored, Meredith could hardly breathe. She had never seen such people—dusky and decadent. Men in dark suits sliced from such fine silk Meredith felt soothed just looking at it. The women were like fancy desserts—skin and hair polished in glossy shades, fine bones weighted with crocodile, gem stones, precious metals and swatches of sheared sable. In addition to Arabic, Meredith heard snippets of French, German, Russian and Italian in the air as she made her way through the throng and scanned the human layers for Mish.

Slate trays of raw eel, squid, tuna and sea bass slid by with waitresses in orange coveralls and black stilettos. Watching them, Meredith noted her own simple outfit—sleeveless black sweater and jeans. She worked behind the camera for a reason.

"Mere bear!" Mish enveloped her in a mango-conditioner-scented embrace.

Bangles clattered in her ears. Mish drew back and clapped Meredith's grinning face between her hands.

"Thank you, thank you, thank you! Can you believe I'm even here? I mean, can you actually? And we get to work together again? In London? I mean: How. Fucking. Great. Is. That? Eh?" Mish squeezed Meredith's face vertically for emphasis.

"Get this girl a dragon-fruit saketini on the double! Extra poppy seeds! Make that *two* doubles!" Mish bullhorned across the bar to no one in particular. She was wearing a lace-up lavender bustier over a pair of glitter-flecked leggings and thigh-high white vinyl go-go boots. Meredith noticed she had lost weight. Under normal circumstances she would have said so.

"Do I not looking completely fucking awesome?" Mish passed over a brimming glass with a twig and berries sticking out of it and kissed Meredith on the forehead. "Can you *believe* this shit?"

"It's so great to see you."

"Is this town even aware? Does it even *know* what it is in for? Have you even *warned* these people?" Mish waved an elbow-length kid glove around the room and leaned in to Meredith's hair. "We are going to tear it up, sister. You and me. Tear it to pieces and eat it raw." She threw back her head and honked like a goose.

They clinked and began to fill in the gaps of the past couple of weeks. Mish told her the story of the party clown she had met at Elle's. She had ended up having what she deemed a "highly therapeutic eight-and-a-half-night make-out session" with him, which had started the day Meredith had seen her last and ended shorty before she got the call to come work on the Crouch movie as Kathleen Swain's personal wardrobe stylist.

"So the thing is," Mish was saying, "I've finally realized what I was put on this earth to do." Her eyes gleamed. "It's to *amuse myself*. Completely, fully, ad nauseum and without guilt. What do you think? It's my new trip."

"Sounds like a plan," Meredith said.

"Done."

Three rounds later, Meredith was sloshed and feeling guilty. She still hadn't told Mish about the Quest. And she wasn't quite sure how this new improved and biologically defiant Mish would take it.

"Oh, and Shane," Mish went on, "did I even *tell* you? What he *did*? Do you even know what he did the day he, you know, heard? He went out and bought a pug puppy—another one! And guess what we called it? *Junior!* I mean, isn't that the sickest thing you've ever heard? He came in a giant Tiffany box with a hole cut in the top and the little farter's head poking through with a ribbon on it. Oh my God, the box stank so badly when I took the lid off, I nearly fucking died. It was the cutest thing in the whole history of cute things ever. That *guy*." She reached over and squeezed Meredith's arm. "So what about you? What's up? How goes the London head-trip thus far?"

Meredith bit her lip and looked at the ceiling. There was an equatorial constellation painted on a dome. "Well, let's see," she began. "My mother just broke up with a man half her age, I'm completely single and working all the time on a set that's being funded by the Wizard of Oz and supervised by a teenage vampire. It rains constantly and everything costs twice as much and the men smell funny. Other than that, I can't really complain."

Mish cocked her head and made a sympathetic face. "Is it really that bad? I mean like bad-bad?"

"Not bad-bad, more bad-weird."

"If it's any consolation, everyone in Toronto is saying how great it is that you told Felsted to go fuck himself. And apparently the studio is threatening to withdraw his post-production funding because he went so insanely overbudget on the shoot."

Meredith managed a detached smile. She waited for a rush of pleasure, but felt nothing. Felsted, Toronto, her whole life at home—it was all an emotional galaxy away.

"Listen, Mish, I have to tell you something. The reason I really came here."

Mish narrowed her eyes. "You're in love."

"No, not that. Completely not."

"In lust."

"Sadly, no."

"You've had your heart broken by a famous married guy you couldn't tell me about because his lawyers swore you to secrecy. Don't worry, I totally understand."

Meredith blinked.

"So what, then?"

She opened her mouth, but Mish shushed her.

"No, wait, I want to guess. Now, let's see . . . what else makes a girl drop everything and fly away—and then call her best friend for transatlantic backup? I don't geddit—" she clapped a sake-soaked glove over her mouth. Her next words were muffled. "Oh—you *caaan't* be." She patted her stomach meaningfully. "With whose?"

"Jesus, Mish, no! Would you just let me talk for two seconds?"

Mish shoved her hands under her bum like a child trying to behave. "You *are*."

"I'm *not*," Meredith said slowly. "Not yet. But I want to be. I *intend* to be. And by the right man. I just figured I had to expand my pool, you know, in order to broaden the search. For the perfect one."

"Oh, I get it—" Mish's face darkened. "Big Daddy."

"The donor of my dreams."

"Prince Charming in a tadpole suit."

"Exactly."

Above her smile, Mish's eyes were glassy and far away.

"Are you okay with this?" asked Meredith. "I didn't want to tell you. I was afraid it would make you sad."

"Why would it make me sad?" A tear slid down the bridge of her nose and hung quivering at the tip. "Seriously. I'm beyond that baby shit at this point. I'm done with it. I want you to have one so I can corrupt it with cigarettes and beer."

"So you're okay?" Meredith looked at her carefully.

"I'm fine. It's just coming off the hormones." Mish blew her nose on a cocktail napkin.

"Do you think I'm crazy?"

"No, honey, I think you're brilliant." Mish grabbed her knee and squeezed it tight. "Absofuckinglutely brilliant. Oh!" She remembered something and began digging in her handbag like a crazed terrier. "In that case I have a present for you . . . I'm sure it's still in here . . . ha!" She stiffened, her hand still deep in the bag, and made Meredith close her eyes.

"Why?"

"It's a surprise, for Chrissake. Now, hold still. You're so squirmy."

Meredith flinched as something cold poked her ear.

"What are you doing?"

"Just keep your eyes closed, okay? Just a second."

Beeping sounded in her ear. "Okay, open!" In Mish's hand was a small device that appeared to be an electric toothbrush without the bristle. She flipped it over and revealed a small digital screen with numbers on it.

Meredith took the device from Mish's hand and brought the screen close to her face.

"Amazing thing—takes your temperature and tells you exactly where you are in your cycle. Cool, eh? Have it. It's yours."

Meredith examined the cylindrical appliance and imagined herself as an ovum, a gelatinous micro-scopic dot floating through the dark tunnel of her Fallopian tube to—where? To meet a force who had not yet revealed himself. The elusive biological stand-up artist. How many blind dates had been made and broken? How many eggs had showed up on time, checked the reservation, taken a table, ordered a glass of champagne and waited . . . fifteen minutes, twenty, half an hour, staring at the bread basket, wishing they had brought a magazine, toying with their cell phone, avoiding the pitying glance of the waiter, until finally skulking out, burning with shame and rejection at the hands of a lover they had never met.

Meredith thanked Mish, then placed the ovulation measuring device in her handbag and snapped it shut.

"More libations, please!" Mish shouted.

Meredith excused herself.

The bathroom was a world of frosted glass urinals (for women!) and a mossy waterfall down one wall for handwashing. In the powder room, half a dozen Arabian Hilton-sisters look-alikes sprawled on love seats playing with one another's hair and reapplying makeup. Meredith did something she never did sober: she looked in the mirror. Not just for a quick check to make sure her clothes weren't on inside out, but for a close and critical personal inspection.

Standing before her was a slight young woman, eyes peeking out from under dark bangs. She pushed her hair from her forehead and looked more carefully at the face—small, heart-shaped, with a straight nose and clear, if pale, skin. The chin, with its witchy prominence, kept her from being typically pretty. But Meredith had never minded. Pretty girls, she had noticed at school, tended to be much more unhappy and markedly less sane than *almost*-pretty girls. The world had a way of raising the expectations of the pretty perilously high and, in the vast majority of cases, dashing them on the rocks. She did not envy the Cleopatras, the Princess Dianas or the Marilyn Monroes. Much safer to be the girl with the pointy chin whom Misery (that shameless social climber) snobbishly overlooks. Satisfied, she removed a tube of clear gloss from her handbag and applied a modest daub to her lips.

When she returned, Mish was deep in conversation with a yellow-haired man in a sleeveless leather vest whom Meredith automatically took to be gay. He said something and Mish slapped his chest and erupted into one of her noisy, throat-pumping honks.

"Mere! C'mere!" Mish grabbed her hand and squashed it between her palms. She turned to the leather vest and grinned. "I want you to meet my very best girl—Meredith Moore. She's doing continuity on the new Osmond Crouch picture and she got me a job too."

On top of the vest was a head. Not a bad head, either. Possibly a little over-gooped in the hair department, but even featured and straight toothed.

"Charming to meet you both. Gunther," said the head.

He had a faint German inflection on top of his London accent that made him sound slightly formal. Meredith liked it.

"I hope you don't mind my being so forward, but when I saw your friend here at the bar I could not resist the opportunity to bother her."

Mish slapped his chest again and laughed. "What a load of cack—he was asking about you the whole time."

"Me?" Meredith asked.

"Who *me*?" Mish teased. She turned to Gunther. "Isn't she adorable?"

Gunther turned his well-made features to face Meredith and slid his eyes over the whole of her in a way that made her cheeks burn. "Indeed." He paused, took a deep breath and broke out of his trance only at the sound of his own voice. "Listen, I was wondering if you two would like to join my friends and me for dinner.

We have a private room in the back and there is more than enough food and drink to go round. I expect you will find it a . . . unique experience, if nothing else."

Meredith winced apologetically and began to explain about the problem of their catching the last tube home and tomorrow morning's seven a.m. call to set. But it was funny, because none of her words seemed to come out, or if they did, they were drowned beneath the sound of Mish's cries of acquiescence.

In a blink, they were squeezed together on a love-seat in a backroom, making slurry small talk with a group of four tall blond men in black business suits. Gunther introduced the men as his "patrons." More trays of drinks appeared, and one of the men—a tall, hawk-faced banker named Benedict—stood up and raised his glass.

"To our good friend Gunther, on the cusp of his great success. Cheers to a true artist among all the other contemporary rubbish. Hah!"

The men banged glasses and shouted things in German. Gunther went around the room slapping shoulders, heads and buttocks like an American football coach.

Meredith glanced at Mish hoping to share a quizzical look, but her friend was already deep in conversation with a pair of black lapels to her left.

"In Canada, we don't have castles," Mish was saying, popping the tip of a Silk Cut into the corner of her mouth. "We have cottages instead."

"And where exactly are these cottages located?" The man produced a gold lighter and offered her the flame.

"On lakes, or sometimes islands. In Georgian Bay, for instance, you can buy an entire island for like less than fifty grand."

"A whole island you can purchase? With trees on it as well? For the price of a used car?"

"Oh, yes, plenty of trees. And bushes. And rocks. And everything."

Meredith felt a nudge. Gunther appeared on the loveseat beside her. He inclined his head and smiled like a bashful boy.

"I apologize for my friends. Men in money are inexcusably boorish. But they are mandatory, don't you think?"

"What do you mean?"

"That they are a necessary evil."

"I understand, but for what?"

"For art."

Meredith thought this over. "I guess in another era you'd be having an affair with some duchess or other."

"Stealing in the servant's entrance and ravishing her on the drawing room sofa when the duke is away. This I would prefer."

"She would expect you to compose works in her honour."

"Which I would, most dutifully. Pay homage to her everlasting beauty, despite the fact that she is fat and old."

"And bald."

"Yes, that too."

There was a loud collective whoop from the bankers that made Meredith and Gunther look up. A Japanese girl in a blue kimono, who looked to be only slightly older than a child, had entered the room. She did not smile, but bowed and took her place beside a potted bamboo tree in the corner. Soon a waitress followed, bearing a large platter of sushi, and another after her, who cleared the glasses and ashtrays from the low glass table in the centre. The kimonoed girl bowed again and in one practised and elaborate motion untied her sash and let her garment drop to the floor. She was naked and in perfect minuscule proportion, pubic hair trimmed into a tidy little Valentine's heart. The song on the sound system was that big hit by Coldplay. An odd choice for a stripper, Meredith thought, waiting rigidly for the girl to begin grinding her hips in the familiar pot-stirring peeler fashion. But instead of dancing, the naked girl took two steps forward, arched her back and draped herself backward over the glass table, stomach to the ceiling, feet and head dangling over the side, her throat exposed and quivering slightly. She lay there like a flank steak on a butcher's block. The room was silent as the waitresses began to arrange fish in fans and swirls over the girl's flesh. Hamachi sashimi around the left nipple, unagimaki around the right, raw lobster in between the collarbones, a knob of green wasabi in the belly button, pickled ginger palate-cleanser in each smooth armpit.

"The super deluxe," Gunther whispered into the nape of Meredith's neck. "A popular delicacy in Japan. I hope you will forgive my friends' political incorrectness. I understand you Americans can be a bit . . . unamused by such spectacle."

Meredith and Mish exchanged uncertain, bug-eyed smiles. One of the waitresses began passing around ivory chopsticks. The men laughed and elbowed one another, making cracks in German. They spread their napkins on their laps. The naked girl giggled and goosebumps rose up under their food.

There was a pause. And it became clear that, for all of their noisy jostling, none of the men was willing to be first.

"I'm hungry," Meredith announced. Clicking a pair of chopsticks, she reached down, plucked a sea scallop from the point of the girl's left hipbone, popped it in her mouth and swallowed it whole.

8

Waking up with a hangover was one thing, but waking up hungover two hours from the time you'd gone to bed by a grinning woman in a half-slip was quite another. Meredith pushed her face deeper into the satin throw cushion that was doubling as her pillow.

"Good morrow, Moo," Irma said. "Thought you might like a persimmon before work. I found it at the back of the fridge. How 'bout it, my little corker?"

Meredith raised herself on one elbow and fell back again. Her brain rustled in her skull like a bloated pigeon.

"Time?"

Irma consulted her locket. "Five thirty-eight on the dot—you'd better hustle if you want to make it out there by seven."

Meredith scowled but managed to retain the bitchy remark that pressed itself against the inside of her teeth. She waved her mother away and staggered towards the bathroom.

Half an hour later Meredith scrambled downstairs,

late for work. "Don't forget!" Irma called from the door.

"What?"

"Tonight."

"What's tonight?"

Irma poked her head over the landing, and her blue kerchief floated from her head and landed on the stairs.

"Blast. Dinner at the club at nine-thirty, darling. I've arranged some specimens for you to examine. Bring your little Canadian friend along. Unless, of course, you'd rather not have the competition."

Meredith stumped down the four flights of stairs two at a time, hurrying to make it before the light timer went out and left her stranded in the lightless stairwell. This country! Timers on lights, cold-water flats, coin-operated heaters, pay-as-you-go public washrooms, the absence of paper towels, napkins or paper products of virtually any kind. Somewhere along the line this great empire had taught its people to live without Kleenex, and its children to bathe in two inches of tepid water. Why? The English must *enjoy* physical discomfort on some level that North Americans do not. Meredith wondered if the grottiness—the chilly, unheated, unpampered misery among the privileged people was the English way of keeping a connection to history alive. For North Americans it was different. If it was good enough for our ancestors, it *couldn't* be good enough for us.

Meredith made her way through the urban dawn toward Notting Hill Gate. The pastel-painted townhouses seemed dull and two-dimensional. It was the tail end of spring and the sidewalks were covered in fetid brown blossoms, glued to the pavement by rain and fixed there by feet.

She felt surprisingly okay, despite her lack of sleep, and realized it was possible she was still drunk.

The tube rumbled towards Piccadilly, roiling Meredith's stomach inside her. The previous night returned to her in strobe-lit glimpses. Mish slurping a sliver of barbequed eel directly off the thigh of the nude girl. Both of them dancing on top of a single chair until it cracked and gave way. Some commotion involving a car. An over-lit flat somewhere in South Kensington with polished concrete floors and hardly any furniture. Dancing again, but this time to something terrible—UB40? The smell of kebab sauce. Talking intensely with Gunther on the couch about his photography while Mish locked herself in the bathroom (to throw up?). A blurry bit. Then home.

She couldn't remember if she had kissed Gunther goodbye, whether they had exchanged phone numbers or even affectionate words. She did recall him begging her stay, pinning her to the sofa in a half-playful way. She had resisted—though now she was not sure why. What was it with the Pollyanna routine? If she wanted a baby, she was going to have to get tactical.

Travelling east into the city, the car filled up. Across

from Meredith a hot-dog-shaped man in a three-piece suit was reading the *Times* folded meticulously into eighths. Watching him, Meredith suddenly wondered how her own father had read the newspaper. Was he a spreader or a folder?

The train surged aboveground into the daylight and suddenly the car was loud with the sound of cell phones ringing, beeping messages from loved ones and colleagues who'd been momentarily out of contact. All around Meredith, people dove for their bags and coat pockets. Just then her own phone, which she kept in the special compartment on the outside of her knapsack, began to play *Ode to Joy* at an intense volume (one of the Germans must have switched it from the usual ring last night for a joke). A message she hadn't noticed earlier. Meredith plucked the handset out of her bag, flipped it open. The voice-mail had been left from the night before, a Toronto number. She pressed one and entered her password: SCRIPT.

"Hello, this is a message for Meredith. It's Joe Veil calling—the doctor. I got this number from your file. I hope you don't mind my checking up on you. I just, well, I just wanted to call in person to see that everything is okay. I'm not sure if you've rescheduled your appointment, but if you haven't, call the office anytime, or even if you just want to come in and talk. Or talk on the phone. I'd be glad to answer any . . . anything. Okay, so I hope you're well."

Without pausing to consider, Meredith pressed the call-back key. Within four seconds a phone was ringing somewhere in Toronto.

"Hel-lo?" A man's groggy voice.

"Is that Dr. Veil? It's Meredith Moore. Calling from London. I guess I kind of forgot about the time change—God, sorry. What time is it there, anyway?"

Muffled pillow noises, followed by a phlegmy grunt. "Uh, 1:37."

"I'm sorry to wake you. I should let you sleep. This is so rude of me—I completely forgot. I'll let you go back to sleep."

"Don't be sorry. I'm used to it. I actually feel neglected if the phone doesn't ring at least once in the night." Another cough. "How's London?"

"It's okay. Super busy." The train pulled into an outdoor station. Beyond the outdoor platform Meredith could see a woman on the balcony of her high-rise building hanging a flowered bedsheet out to dry. "To be honest? Not so great. I'm pretty mixed up."

"Mixed up how?"

"I've decided I want to have a baby."

"Congratulations."

"No, wait—which is crazy because I'm not even in love or in lust or *anything*. I mean, isn't that wrong? Shouldn't a baby like—I don't know—grow out of love?"

"Meredith, babies grow out of stem cells. The love part comes later." She could hear his head shift against a pillow.

"Do you think I could do it on my own?"

"I don't know you well enough to say one way or the other, but let me ask you this. Of all the other things in your life you've set out to do on your own, which ones have you failed at?"

The train rocked her from side to side. "None, I guess," she whispered. "But sometimes I wonder—"

"Daddy?" A girl's voice in the background. Muffled noises, then Joe's voice saying gently, *Go back to sleep*. "Hi. Sorry, you were saying?"

Meredith lowered the phone and stared at the digital mini-screen on her handset. She watched a timer ticking off the seconds of contact.

"Hello?" came his voice from somewhere on the other side of the ocean. "Meredith? Meredith, I think I'm losing—"

The windows went black as the train was sucked underground again.

Hello? Hello? said the passengers on the train, as Meredith stared at her screen. A new message flashed on it: SEARCHING FOR SIGNAL.

9

Barnaby Shakespeare stood at the bar drinking his second pint of lager and vowing to pace himself. Tomorrow morning he was driving back to the Cotswolds and he didn't want a hangover. On the last trip back from London his hands had been so shaky on the wheel he had nearly swerved into oncoming traffic while changing gears on the motorway.

Overall, he was a much better driver the night before than the morning after. Although he tried not to make a habit of driving pissed in the city (he'd been done twice for operating a motor vehicle under the influence already—the next time they would take away his licence and throw him in the hole), in the countryside it seemed unavoidable. Everybody simply *did*.

Barnaby was not one of those lushes whom no amount of liquor seems to slow or sicken. He invariably woke up shattered the morning after. The trick was predicting when the devil was coming to visit so he could clear off the calendar for the following day. Not that he generally had anything much to do—living, as he did, in the country, without an occupation or a wife. Unfortunately there never seemed to be any rhyme or reason for his benders. Unlike other people, he did not drink to celebrate his triumphs or kill his woes. He simply drank. And on some days, for reasons that remained a complete mystery to himself, Barnaby drank significantly more than on others. The problem of predicting his own behaviour was getting worse as he got older (he turned thirty-three last December).

He vowed to begin keeping a diary of his daily movements starting tomorrow. His father, Nigel Shakespeare, a non-practising barrister, had kept a diary religiously his entire adult life. After brushing his teeth and before turning off the light in the evenings, Dad would jot down exactly what had happened that day in point form. The outcome, Barnaby discovered when he unlocked his father's nightstand the day after his funeral and flipped through the small leather-bound books (there were stacks and stacks of them), was impressive. Mundane details of daily chores or digestive complications were given equal weight to events of massive personal significance. The result, Barnaby thought, was a terrible, inadvertent joke. One entry in particular stayed with him: "June 15th, 1975. Kippers for breakfast. Popped in at the motor shop. Rosa in labour upon my return. Girl—stillborn. Cook's half day—scrambled egg for dinner."

Barnaby, however, planned to keep quite a different sort of diary, one with far more colourful anecdotes and jokes and even the odd sexy bit. His diary would be read aloud at his funeral, and everyone would laugh and say what a bright, jolly fellow he had been. How he had lived life to its fullest despite his flaws. Possibly (and this was an especially private thought) someone would want to publish it.

While Barnaby knew he drank too much, he wasn't particularly worried about being an alcoholic. He had read somewhere that real alcoholics don't get hangovers. He knew this to be true, since his own father had consumed at least twenty ounces of Famous Grouse with soda every single day of his life and yet bounced out of bed each morning at five-thirty on the dot. Barnaby, however, was reduced to a quivering, wretching muck. The more he drank, the more he found himself perversely reassured each morning when he woke up to find the old symptoms were still there (if anything, they were getting worse!): rolling thunder claps of nausea, jitters, a crushing head and a mysterious acrid peppermint smell everywhere he went. What he secretly feared most was the morning he would wake up to find his hangover gone.

That morning, he conceded now while ordering his third pint, would probably not be tomorrow. It was not yet six, and he had the whole night ahead of him. Soon people would start arriving at the club for cocktails, and then there would be dinner in the dining room with more wine, and who knows what sort of nonsense after that. Part of him wished he could stay on in London an extra day. And he would too. If only he didn't miss the birds so much.

***

It had been Mish's idea to take a taxi to dinner in the first place, so she couldn't reasonably complain. Meredith had tried to warn her about rush hour in London, but Mish hadn't listened. Even worse, Mish had insisted on paying for it. Now they were sitting in the back of a black cab stuck in a roundabout in central London wondering if they would have to camp for the night. In the past twenty minutes, the cab had moved a total of one car length. The driver, a thin, bald, mean-looking youth in a Manchester United jersey, alternately swore and leaned on the horn. Every few minutes he turned around and gave Meredith and Mish a look of irritated surprise, as though he'd never seen a traffic jam before in his life. Meanwhile the meter ticked away all the cash in Mish's handbag, plus her per diem, and half tomorrow's pay as well. So far, the fare was roughly what it cost to fly to Paris, and they were only halfway across town.

"I rather fancy a drive," she'd said (pretentiously, Meredith thought) while they were still back on set packing up after a long day's shoot. "And besides," she added, applying extra body-glow to her throat in front of the full-length mirror of the wardrobe trailer, "there's no way I'd be caught dead on the tube in this outfit."

When it came to clothing, Mish had a penchant for the inappropriate. Her personal style was a blend of the most outrageous, unseasonable and (all too often) unsightly trends of the moment. Today, for her first day of work on set, she had shown up in an acid-wash denim miniskirt, suede stiletto boots and a large yellow sweater knitted out of feathers that looked as if they'd been plucked from some unfortunate cousin of Big Bird.

Now, in addition to being hungover and under-slept, Mish was sinking into a terrible sulk. This was just two steps away from a tantrum, Meredith knew, and it made her twitchy with apprehension. They sat in a grump, stomachs lurching as the car crept forward another few inches and came to a halt, nearly rear-ending a girl on a Vespa in front of them.

"Wanka!" the driver hollered at the girl in the helmet, and then wagged his tongue in the rearview mirror.

Mish hissed softly into her feathers, and Meredith was afraid her friend might be about to chuck. The only thing that ever made Meredith ill was the sight of other people throwing up.

"So what did you think of Kathleen?" Meredith hoped to distract Mish from any vomit-related thoughts.

Mish shrugged, still facing forward. "She's okay."

"Okay-bitchy or okay-nice?"

"Just *okay*."

"Yeah, but do you mean—"

"Meredith, sometimes an 'okay' is just an 'okay.' Okay?"

The driver, seeing an opportunity to move a few paces ahead, changed lanes, causing the rear end of the car to swing violently to the side. Mish gripped the armrest with one hand and felt for the window button with the other. It was locked. Her face paled beneath its layer of makeup, and pearls of sweat appeared on her upper lip.

"Excuse me, sir? Could you please roll down the window?" Meredith used her most officious voice with the driver.

"Wassat, luv?" the driver squawked through the intercom.

"The window!" Meredith was shouting and it felt good. Felt right. "Please open the window before my friend pukes all over your cab."

Both windows lowered completely and the cab was filled with rush-hour fog. Meredith was relieved to see the blood rushing back into Mish's cheeks. They waited a few moments before picking up the conversation they had cut off.

"She was nice enough, I guess," said Mish, "but in a dangerous way. Like she was just waiting for something to lose it over. You can tell all the rumours are true—I bet she can be a total cunt."

"Mish!"

"What? People say that here. It's no big deal."

"How do you know?"

"I saw it in a movie."

"What movie?"

"*Trainspotting.*"

"Hello? That was about heroin addicts, and besides, it was set in Scotland."

"Same difference." Mish rolled her eyes like an exasperated teenager. "The point is, I wouldn't want to catch the woman in the wrong mood."

Meredith hadn't bothered to tell Mish about the incident involving Swain's last stylist and the curling iron.

"And you can immediately tell she's one of those women who's super touchy about her age," Mish went on, "not to mention her weight. One of the wardrobe assistants was telling me they had to rip all the size-eight labels out of her dresses and sew on new ones that said size six."

"No."

"Supposedly."

Somehow the driver had managed to manoeuvre the car out of the clogged roundabout and they were now moving over a bridge with the rest of the traffic flow at the pace of corn syrup being poured from a pitcher. Meredith looked out the window at the river and Westminster Abbey. She marvelled at how truly enormous the clock tower was. Unlike most things in life, Meredith thought, Big Ben actually lived up to the promise of its name. The thought of that comforted her.

"You know she's desperate to have a baby," said Mish.

"She told you that?"

"I can smell it."

"Really." Meredith was suddenly uncomfortable. Not just with this conversation but with the whole topic of babies in general. She thought about pregnancy so much these days that talking about it had become embarrassing. Funny how the things that obsessed you privately became a matter of public shame. She felt like a person carrying a secret torch so large she could hardly bear to mention the name of her crush out loud.

"Good luck to her, I guess."

"Yeah." Meredith nodded, looking straight ahead. "Good luck."

***

"It's been ages!" cried the barman.

To Irma he looked as tasty as sardines on toast.

In fact it had been only a fortnight, but usually Irma had dinner in the club at least two—if not three—times a week.

"You know my heart, darling," she said, giving him a wink. She searched for his name but could not find it in the clutter of her brain. Perhaps she was starting to lose her marbles. Then again, it was possible she had never known the name in the first place.

Without a pause, the young man reached under the counter and produced a bottle of Strega—the one with the label written in fancy curlicue Italian—

which they kept at the club just for her. She had developed a taste for Italian liqueurs one summer while visiting her old friend Osmond Crouch at his villa near Florence. That was years ago (decades, possibly), but since then she had been religious about taking it before and after her evening meal as both aperitif and digestif. She looked at the bartender's forearms as he poured. They were smooth but textured with fine blond hair, the veins visible just below the skin. Coursing with blood, Irma thought, and felt a pang in her navel. Even now. Amazing.

She looked around the half-full barroom and nodded at several acquaintances. There was silly old Lady Viola in her dirty dungarees. Apparently she had once spent a summer in Spain shagging Picasso. That's what she told anyone who would listen, but Irma didn't believe it. Anyone who knew Picasso knew he wasn't keen on redheads. Across the bar was young Barnaby Shakespeare, lost in thought and looking carelessly handsome, if second-son-ish. Poor boy, thought Irma, though she wasn't sure why.

While not the most fashionable destination in town, Irma's club was still considered one of the most venerable and exclusive in all of London. This was largely due to the reputation it had established for being a hub of creativity and scandal between the wars, when a group of semi-insane, semi-famous sculptors had hung out here and made the place known by hosting a series of parties, in which all the guests stripped off their clothing and molested one another with plaster. Since then, occasional nudity had become a tradition. Once or twice a year, toward closing time, some member or other would get drunk enough to take off their kit and end up posing for impromptu life drawing sessions on the billiards table. In recent years it had become a half-hearted exercise—to tell the truth, no one much enjoyed getting naked anymore—but it was a point of pride at the club, definitive proof of its status as a bohemian institution, and so the members dutifully kept up the tradition.

The place itself was a sprawling and shabby white-brick cottage just off the King's Road. Since Irma had first joined in the sixties, the club had expanded to include a large new bar, skylights and French doors leading out onto the back garden. The barroom atmosphere was more pub than posh—plywood floor covered in squashed cigarette butts, cheap chrome-and-vinyl chairs of the sort you might find in any legion hall, ashtrays bearing the logo of the local football team.

Dinner was served every night at nine at a great oval table in the older, grander part. The walls of the communal dining room were hung exclusively with paintings of past members dining in the same room, creating a ghostly reflective effect that Irma approved of. If ever you forgot where and who you were, you could just look at the walls and be reminded—without having to look in a mirror.

"Well, if it isn't our fair Irish poetess."

Irma offered up her cheek to be kissed by a fat man upholstered in navy blue pinstripes.

"Henry. How goes public life?"

"Dull as ever," he said, grinning in a way that suggested he thought it was anything but. "What about you? Still mad as a hatter?"

Irma bit the inside of her lip and forced a smile. She hated jokes at her own expense but had always pretended the opposite. "I prefer to think of it as a form of *alternative sanity*," she said.

Henry roared and slapped her so heartily on the shoulder that her drink sloshed onto her shoe. Irma wished Meredith would get here so she could fob Henry off on her. He was the man she had in mind for her daughter's purposes. A prime candidate, she thought: he was handsome enough, and charming in a boorish sort of way. Not *her* type at all, of course—far too earnest, even though he tried to pretend to be jaded (Irma could see through it). A Tory MP, for heaven's sake. Not to mention the author of several historical biographies and father to countless illegitimate children. He was one of those men who seemed able to do the work of six, without ever appearing any the worse for wear. Yes, Irma thought, Henry would almost certainly be up for a romp with her daughter. He didn't have a reputation for being terribly picky, and there was no question about his fertility. He would do.

"Mother, you'll have a heart attack!"

"Oh, don't be such a prude, darling."

Irma held the straw up to her nose and sniffed a line of fine white powder off her pocket mirror before handing it over. Meredith took it gingerly and frowned. Irma didn't wait for her daughter's reaction. She turned around and beetled across the room to get the attention of the barman.

"Fantastic," Mish said with the kind of hysterical admiration that people often showed after experiencing Irma for the first time. "Aren't you going to do some?"

"I don't know." Meredith stared at the row of tiny ridges in her palm. The outside of the mirror, she knew, was inlaid with Irma's initials in mother-of-pearl. She had an early childhood flashback of watching her mother use it to reapply her lipstick in a restaurant.

Once again, she was shocked. How could she possibly be the offspring of this reckless cougar? Irma had taken one look at Mish and Meredith when they arrived at the club (under-slept, cranky and still reeling from the cab fare) and pulled them over to the corner table for what she called "a little pick-me-up." Now Meredith was trying to contend with two things: a) the realization that her elderly mother was quite possibly a cokehead, as well as b) the fact that she had never in her life encountered the stuff up close.

"What does it *do*?" Meredith wrinkled her nose, feigning disgust to mask her fear. She had been offered coke exactly twice before. Once at the fateful Felsted wrap party and another time by a rocker boyfriend of Mish's. Both times she had refused it on the grounds that she had a tendency toward nosebleeds. The truth was, as did all drugs that you couldn't grow in a clay pot in the backyard, coke scared the wits out of her. What if she had a heart attack? Or a stroke? Or got one of those bubbles in her vein that travelled through your arteries and then exploded in your cerebral cortex? Or did that only come from needles?

Mish glanced around to see if anyone was watching. Then she extended her hand. "Give it here," she said. "I don't know about you, but I'm wiped."

"So am I!" Meredith jerked the mirror away and nearly dropped the whole thing on the floor, her hands were quivering so badly.

"Careful," Mish hissed. "Now, are you going to do one or not? It'll perk you up. It's like the best cup of coffee you've ever had. Hold the straw like this."

Mish mimed the action and Meredith copied it, hoovering up a thin line. She immediately felt like a morally bankrupt teenager in a movie. If anything, her mouth felt sort of numb, like after a dentist's freezing. A funny Javex taste dripped down the back of her throat.

"I don't think it works." She shrugged. "I mean, I don't feel any different."

"Just wait," Mish said, reapplying her lipstick in the mirror and brushing off her upper lip.

She closed the compact. Taking Meredith's chin in one hand, Mish assessed her friend's face like the fussy mother of a toddler. Meredith was afraid Mish was going to lick a thumb and start wiping the corners of her mouth. Instead she fluffed Meredith's bangs and smiled.

"Your mother is exactly the way you described her."

"How so?"

"Completely bonkers."

Meredith sighed, and Mish jumped up from the table and led her over to where Irma was standing, talking to a fattish, middle-aged man in a suit with a mop of dark hair.

"Girls! I want you to meet Henry Cazalet. Henry, this is my daughter Meredith and her charming friend from Toronto."

"Mish."

"Right. So sorry. I'm awful with names. And faces. But in all my years, I've never forgotten an arse!"

Everyone roared.

"So what exactly brings you two to London?" Henry asked, taking a sip of his whisky and looking around the room, probably to see if any of his colleagues had arrived for dinner.

"Work, actually," said Meredith. "We're both on the new Osmond Crouch film."

"Right, Crouch. How is the old bugger? I haven't seen him in years. Is he still collecting vintage Fiats?"

"I wouldn't know, I've never met him. And he never comes to set."

"We hear stories, though," Mish said, rolling her feathered shoulder and angling her head in a coy way.

"Like what?" Cazalet leaned in.

This was the first Meredith had heard of any "story."

"Well, I shouldn't be telling tales out of school, but . . ." Mish paused and looked around like a secret agent in a spy movie. "I was talking to one of the stars in the wardrobe trailer today, and she was telling me that apparently Crouch has completely lost his mind. He hasn't left his villa in Italy for years and the place is completely falling apart around him, and all the while he's making this strange film . . ."

"You mean the one you're working on?"

"Oh no, that's just a money project. Supposedly he's been directing his own thing. Some sort of monolithic art movie. No one actually knows anything about it. He's been shooting it for years and it never gets anywhere closer to being finished. It must be costing him a fortune. Once a year he has a dinner party and invites people to watch some of the rushes. But that could be just a rumour. I wasn't exactly hearing it first-hand, if you know what I mean."

"Really." Cazalet's eyes were wide with interest. He held up a finger indicating they should wait a moment and then turned to the bar for another round of drinks.

Meredith was continually amazed at Mish's ability to wander into any social or professional situation and come away with the most scintillating gossip in record time. It was, she thought, one of the great things about having Mish for a best friend.

"So what do you think?" Irma was upon them.

"It's good," said Meredith, who had just begun to realize she felt much more awake and hopeful about the evening than she had as recently as ten minutes ago. "My chest feels sort of *fluttery*."

"Not *that*, silly goose." Irma waved her hand in front of her face irritably. "What do you think of Henry? He's very bright and successful. A Tory MP, you know."

Meredith shrugged. "Yes, but isn't he married?" She had noticed the gold band strangling one of his fat fingers when he handed her a drink.

"Yes, exactly." Irma smiled, nodded with satisfaction and tossed her silk scarf over her shoulder.

"Exactly . . . what?"

"Exactly the sort of man you ought to be looking for, darling. I should think a married man would offer far fewer complications in your situation than an unmarried one."

"And why is that?" Meredith raised an eyebrow at Mish, who gave a theatrical cough. The drugs made her mother seem amusing. She wasn't sure whether this was an actuality or just a perception, but for once she felt she could see what everybody else saw.

"Well, it just seems quite obvious if you want total independence," said Irma.

Meredith began to tell her mother that she had absolutely no intention whatsoever of giving birth to the unloved bastard of a philandering politician, but before she could, a bell was ringing and Henry Cazalet was herding them all toward the dining room for dinner. It was unfortunate, because suddenly Meredith didn't feel the least bit hungry, but she supposed it would be nice to sit down anyway. Her appetite had been replaced by *a lot of things to say*, and a dinner table was a much better venue for conversation, all things considered.

Dinner was a choice between salmon or pheasant, although the bird, they were informed by a maid in a floppy white lace cap, had "a fair bit of lead shot in it." Everyone except Meredith ordered the salmon. She figured it would give her a good excuse not to eat, and besides, she was curious to see what lead shot actually looked like.

There were just over two dozen people at the dinner table including Mish, Meredith and Irma. Meredith, of course, was made to sit beside Henry Cazalet, who bored her all through the soup with his theory on how the Tories could take the country if they were able to grab the inner-city single-mother vote. Meredith thought this sounded about as likely as Labour taking the rural retired-colonel vote. She was feeling restless and full of mischief and in order to amuse herself, she began asking Cazalet all about his wife. What was her name? (Margaret.) How had he met her? (At a cricket luncheon in Chichester.) How old were they when they married? (Twenty-five and nineteen, respectively.) How many children did they have? (Four: two girls and two boys.) Was she beautiful? (She had been very pretty, but people do change, you know.) Were they still in love? (In what sense of the word?) And on and on until Cazalet, after the soup bowls were cleared, announced he was "terribly sorry," but one of his constituents was at the other end of the table and he must go over and say hello. And off he buggered, to Meredith's considerable relief.

Mish, by this point, was deeply entrenched in conversation with Irma. She demanded (between honking fits of laughter) one story after another about Meredith's mother's days as wandering hippie poetess. Meredith listened to the one about the time her mother had snuck into an orgy at a San Francisco men's bathhouse by pretending she'd had a sex-change operation. It was a decent yarn, but one Meredith had heard about five dozen times. She swivelled around and assessed the room. Across the table was a famous interior designer Meredith recognized from TV. The woman was wearing the most amazing jewellery—dangling diamond chandelier earrings and a great aquamarine dinner ring on her right hand. Meredith remembered (from reading it in the Wicked Whispers column of the *Daily*

Mail around the tea trolley on set) that this was the woman who had left her husband on his sickbed for a married Saudi billionaire oil tycoon. The husband eventually died of colon cancer and the billionaire ditched his long-suffering wife and three children in favour of shacking up with the interior designer and her twin boys. The designer was now flanked by two pearl-laden blond women friends with identical layered hairstyles that Meredith always thought of as the "mummy-cut." They were hanging on the designer's every word, and kept touching her arms and shoulders in a competitive show of sisterly support. Although she couldn't hear the words, Meredith could tell from the designer's brow that she was telling a story that centred around her own unjust persecution at the hands of some faceless Goliath.

Just then, the designer arrived at some salient point in her story and looked up at Meredith. The flat, almost challenging expression in her eyes conveyed that the woman had known she was being watched. Meredith looked away, embarrassed at having been caught gawking. Terribly uncool. Fiddling in her handbag, she reflected, as she often had while discreetly observing famous actors on set, how strange it must be for celebrities to go about their lives being recognized by complete strangers—a constant reminder that they existed for people who did not exist for them.

Meredith was lost in this thought when she felt a lukewarm splash across her left shoulder and lap. She jumped up, but too late. Her outfit—a white dress shirt and camel trousers—was completely soaked with red wine.

"Oh God. How stupid of me. How utterly, unforgivably rude. You must think I'm awful. And here I was, trying to come to your rescue. Not that you needed rescuing, I mean, but just that, what I mean to say is—" The young man searched for a napkin as he spoke. The longer he searched, the more rapid his babbling became. "What I was going to say to you was, well, I hadn't actually thought of an opening chat-up line. I'm afraid I'm rather bad at those. And then I end up spilling a drink on you instead. How typical."

He pulled a napkin out of a glass from an empty place setting two seats down and, in his flustered state, pressed it against the wet red blotch on Meredith's left breast. She gasped and pulled away. And then laughed.

"Oh God, I've done it again, haven't I." The man dropped his face into his hands. "You must think I'm such an idiot."

"No, just a klutz and a lech." Meredith smiled to show she wasn't angry, and his face lit up like that of a little boy presented with a puppy.

"Barnaby Shakespeare." He offered his hand and Meredith shook it.

"Meredith Moore."

"More wine?" He had already reached for the bottle of Côtes du Rhône and was refilling his glass.

Meredith shook her head. She wasn't sure how alcohol mixed with drugs, and besides, she felt so perfectly relaxed and confident, she didn't really crave any. The waiter placed their main courses in front of them. Meredith looked down at her pheasant and saw that it still had a bit of unplucked down sprouting from its tiny breastbone. Barnaby, like everyone else at the table, was having salmon. He picked up his fish knife and began to eat.

"You probably get asked this all the time, but are you any relation to *the* Shakespeare?"

"I might be," said Barnaby, cocking his head as though this was the first time he had ever considered such a possibility. "There was a rumour he was a distant cousin on my father's side. Mind you, there are a lot of Shakespeares in Britain, and I suppose we're all related to one another somehow."

"Neat," Meredith said, and elbowed Mish, who failed to turn around. Irma was halfway through the story of how she had given a reading at the original Woodstock.

"The problem of course is that everyone thinks I ought to be a good writer, and the truth is, I don't have a literary bone in my body."

"What do you do instead?"

"Do?" Barnaby looked bewildered as a forkful of peas tumbled into his lap. "You mean with my time or for money?"

"For most people it's both, isn't it?"

Barnaby frowned. His hair, which was fine and golden brown, hung in his eyes like a schoolboy's at the end of a summer holiday of growth. He adjusted his spectacles, which were sliding down his nose. "I suppose it is. The fact is, though, I don't do much of anything. I mean, obviously I have a few things I *like* to do, but as for a job, the truth is, I don't really have one. I guess you could say I'm unemployed."

"Where I come from we call that being 'between jobs,'" said Meredith. She noticed there was a cigarette burn through his lapel and felt a funny urge to stick her finger through it.

"Really?" He had an endearing amazement at everyday banalities. "So what is it you do, then, Miss Moore?"

"I'm a continuity supervisor. On a film set."

"And what exactly does a continuity supervisor do on a film set?"

"I'm glad you asked—most people just pretend they know all about it and then try to change the subject. In fact, it's pretty boring. I sit by the monitor during shooting and check the script for errors and inconsistencies."

"And do you ever find them?"

"All the time."

"And what sort of errors do you find?"

"Well, for instance, sometimes an actor might be doing a scene in which he's drinking wine and eating salmon. In that case, each time you do a take it's important that the actor takes a bite of his salmon and a sip from his glass of wine at exactly the same moment he did in the take before—otherwise it won't match with previous takes. If he starts sipping and biting all over the place, the scene will look strange in the final cut—with the portion of the level of the liquid in the glass going up and down indiscriminately and the actor sipping too often or not all. Do you see what I mean? It's my job to make sure the director tells the actor to sip and bite at the right times."

"Fascinating," Barnaby said, taking a bite of his salmon and dribbling a bit of dressing on his chin. "And how do you make sure they're getting it right?"

"I take notes."

"Is that all?"

"And I keep track of other things, like the axis the camera is shooting from, which is a complicated way of saying angle. For instance, if you shoot a conversation between two people, you have to place the camera looking over one person's shoulder, then the other person's shoulder. It has to be the same shoulder consistently. If you switched from left to right you'd be changing the axis, which doesn't sound like much but is actually very disorienting to the viewer. Directors do it all the time. It's my job to tell them not to cross over."

"So you keep them in line?"

"That's right."

"And—and so, they actually pay you to do this?"

"It's not like I'd do it for free." The dressing glob was

now threatening to drip onto his tie. Meredith rubbed her napkin all over the lower half of her face, hoping the gesture would be contagious.

"And do you find it helps you in your own life?"

"Being paid? Well, obviously—"

"No, no." Barnaby narrowed his eyes and leaned in slightly. "I mean, moving the story forward smoothly. Without flipping back and forth or making mistakes. Does your job help you do that in your own life?"

Meredith licked her thumb and gently wiped the drip off Barnaby's chin. He didn't pull away the way most men would have done. Instead he smiled.

"Not so far," she said, "but I'm hoping to change all that."

They were locked in a sort of moment, one that Mish interrupted by turning around and extending her hand.

"Why, darling, you haven't even introduced your friend."

"Mish, this is Barnaby Shakespeare."

"Pleased to meet you." Barnaby extended his hand for a shake, but Mish raised the back of her hand to be kissed, smacking Barnaby in the face and causing his glasses to fall to the floor. He bent down, searching with one arm under his chair and apologizing profusely, as Mish collapsed into giggles.

"Why, you two haven't even touched your dinners!" he said when he sat up, glasses replaced, indicating their cooling plates.

"Mine has lead shot in it." Meredith abruptly excused herself and stumbled out of the dining room.

She felt funny. The giddy confidence was gone, replaced by a worrisome knot just below her ribcage. Meredith found a small wooden bench in a narrow hallway and sat down. With two fingers, she massaged the cramp in her diaphragm and practised a few square breaths she had learned to do in prenatal yoga class. Ten counts of inhaling, ten counts of holding, ten counts of exhaling, ten counts of holding. She checked her watch—nearly midnight. People ate so late here, dinner was rarely finished before the next day began. She wasn't sure how they did it, as everyone seemed to get up early and rush off to work as well. London was exhausting her. She wondered what bearing this would have on her eggs.

Just as she was about to get up, Meredith heard a faint *tweet* from the direction of her handbag. There were no cell phones allowed in the club (they aggressively confiscated them at the door), but Mish had convinced Meredith to smuggle hers in. Meredith had forgotten to turn the thing off, and now there was a message. She looked around the hallway to make sure the coast was clear before checking. It was a text from a number she didn't recognize.

R U coming 2 my Xibit? Pls do. xo G.

Meredith felt a little thrill. She had an acute sense of smell and had always used it to suss out potential lovers. She was never wrong. Gunther had smelled of calfskin and burnt pepper, which she found encouraging, if odd.

Meredith was stabbing at the keypad on the phone with her index finger, trying to figure out how to save the message, when she heard someone approaching from the darkened hallway behind her. She grabbed for her handbag and threw in the phone. Lucky thing too, because the snooty club doorman appeared and stooped over her. He was a dead ringer for Riff Raff from *The Rocky Horror Picture Show*, all caved-in cheeks and purple eye sockets rising up out of a threadbare undertaker's suit.

"Hallo, Miss," he said, bowing slightly in a way that made Meredith certain he felt superior to her. "Are we enjoying our evening or may I be of any assistance?"

"Oh, no, I'm fine."

He had straightened and was turning to walk away when there was a rogue *tweet* from her handbag. The doorman froze in mid-step.

Meredith closed her eyes.

When he turned he was no longer smiling.

"Now, Miss," he began, taking a step forward, "when you arrived here with your friend tonight I remember clearly that we discussed the rules and regulations of the club, one of which—indeed, perhaps the most important of all—is that there are absolutely no mobile telephones allowed on the premises under any circumstances. It is *quite* forbidden."

He took another step towards her.

Meredith began to quiver. Her hands fluttered and her teeth ached.

"Oh, sir, I—uh, I don't know how—" She scrambled over to the other side of the bench and slipped her hand into her bag to root out the offending device.

"I'm afraid, Miss, if you don't hand over your mobile right this instant, I will have to ask you to leave the club."

Meredith felt around for her phone desperately. She plunged her entire arm into her bag and searched around for anything she could grab. There was her lipstick, her hairbrush, an extra belt, a DVD copy of *The Singing Detective* that she had bought at lunch, an old bag of sticky dried apricots, a nail file, the ovulation detection device, a calculator, a highlighter and two pens, her keys to the flat on Coleville Terrace along with her Toronto car keys, an Elizabeth Jane Howard novel, her wallet stuffed with receipts and two kinds of currency, a change purse, sunglasses. . . . Ack! Where the fuck?

"Honestly, I just had my hand on it." She winced at the doorman and pushed down farther, until she was up to her armpit. It was as if her handbag kept growing deeper and deeper. She wished she could jump inside it and disappear.

"I'm afraid that's not good enough, Miss."

The doorman smiled his awful smile and placed a bony digit on Meredith's elbow. Her heart skittered.

"I'm going to have to ask you to step outside the club

until you have sorted yourself out, and once you have, you are quite welcome to return. Lydia at the door will be happy to check your phone when you find it." He tapped her elbow, indicating that she should rise. "Chop-chop."

Just then, Barnaby appeared. His tie was half undone and he had an unlit cigarette dangling from his mouth. "Good evening, m'lord," said the doorman, straightening slightly but keeping a frigid grip on Meredith's elbow.

Barnaby coughed. "Hullo there, Mr. Tonbridge. May I ask what you are doing with my Canadian friend?"

"I was just escorting her out. The lady had a mobile in her handbag, and as you well know, the rules of the club clearly dictate—"

"Really, Tonbridge. Do leave her alone, would you?"

"Well, sir, I—"

"With all due respect, my good man, you ought to chill out." Barnaby turned to Meredith. "Would you mind terribly giving me your phone, Meredith?"

At that moment the phone seemed to leap from its hiding spot into her hand. She gave it to Barnaby, who turned the phone off and slipped it into Tonbridge's breast pocket.

"Very good, sir," said the doorman. He gave a shallow bow and shuffled away.

Barnaby waited until Tonbridge turned the corner before he laughed. "I do apologize about Tonbridge.

He's a bit of a bore. Not his fault really. The poor bloke has been working here for centuries." He produced a monogrammed gold lighter, rolled it on his pants and lit his smoke. "Care for a cig?"

"No, I'm fine. Thanks. I mean, not just for that, but for the other thing as well."

"Not at all." He smiled. "Now, after all that, do you mind if we do go outside? My sister-in-law's uncle is here tonight and I don't want him to know I smoke."

Outside it was drizzling and chilly, so they stood under the front awning. Without a word, Barnaby took off his jacket and slipped it over Meredith's shoulders. She could feel the tattered silk lining on the back of her arms.

"Listen," he said. "I was thinking about our conversation inside, about me not doing anything. And I was thinking you must assume I'm such a ridiculous layabout, and I really don't want to give you that impression. I mean, I do have interests. Honestly."

"Oh, really?"

"Well, for one thing, my birds. I'm a great falconer."

"A *falconer*?"

"As in, one who falcons. Hunting with birds of prey. Not just falcons either. I keep owls and hawks as well."

"What do you hunt?"

"Oh, you know, depends on the time of year. Pheasants and rabbits, the occasional small dog."

Meredith looked stricken.

"Kidding."

She shook her head. "I'm so gullible. The gullible Canadian."

"Anyway, I'd love you to come and meet them—my birds. Perhaps one weekend you could come? They really are the most marvellous creatures."

"I'd be honoured."

He leaned in and kissed Meredith quickly on the mouth. No hands or anything, just enough for her to get a scent. Turkish cigarettes, lemon rind and furniture polish. Lovely.

10

The day before the gallery opening, Gunther called and suggested a picnic on Hampstead Heath. She rode the tube up to North London. Rocketing up the line in the un-ventilated subway car, "Dancing Queen" looped through her head. It was all she could do not to hum. Meredith never hummed.

Before leaving the house, she'd put on a dress and stuck Mish's thermometer in her ear: it had greeted her with an enthusiastic *beep*. She was ovulating.

Gunther picked her up in a battered Volvo station wagon and drove to the Heath. Soon they were sitting halfway up the grassy slope on a flannel sheet, unwrapping waxed paper from tongue sandwiches he had purchased at the local butcher shop.

He was different than he'd been the other night. Softer spoken and full of apologies. Tongue was all they had left, he explained. All the curried chicken and pulled pork were gone. Meredith shrugged and smiled and sipped red wine from a small plastic cup. Wind washed over her shoulders and tickled the hair on the backs of her arms. She felt this might be The Day, and was soon lost in fantasies of what her life would be like, back in Toronto, with a small tow-headed half-German child.

"His father was a famous London photographer," she would say to the other Yummies in the park. "We had one perfect picnic together and that was it. I never saw him again."

Gunther placed his hand over hers.

"Where are you?" he said.

"What?"

"Where did you go to? You seemed so far away. I want to know where you'd gone to in your mind."

Meredith laughed with discomfort. "I was just thinking what a perfect day it is." Then she remembered her manners and asked about his childhood.

"My mother moved here from Munich after my parents divorced when I was fourteen. She wanted to change me into a little Englishman." He laughed.

Meredith asked about his work.

"I make my money as a carpenter," he said, "but photography is my real love. Here." He pulled something from his wallet.

It was a pamphlet showing photos of frames. Not just implements to put pictures in, but frames carved from exotic woods, some covered in tangled vein patterns that made Meredith think of medical diagrams. They were sculpted like wreaths, some tangled, some smooth. To Meredith's eye, they appeared almost human.

"These are beautiful," she said.

He waved his hand, snatched back the pamphlet and tossed it aside with the waxed paper. "Bourgeois pap for Notting Hill craft shops, nothing more."

Meredith couldn't tell whether he was just being modest or whether she should push the compliment. "Well," she said, "I like them anyway."

He asked if she enjoyed her work. Meredith shrugged.

"It's okay. It's not a calling, but I think it suits my personality."

"How so?"

"It's very precise and technical. The thing I like is the mystery of it. Hardly anyone really understands what a script supervisor does. It has its own secret language. It's like the opposite of being an actor or a writer, where what you're doing is so out there and obvious. It's not the kind of job that many people think they could do." Meredith picked a piece of grass and ripped it in two neat strips. "Not that they'd want to. Most people would find it boring."

"I don't find it boring."

"You might if you had to be me for a day."

"I doubt that."

Meredith studied the ground and felt him looking at her. Being stared at made her uncomfortable, but she did nothing to stop it. She'd read in a magazine once that you shouldn't interrupt a man's gaze by talking. Men, apparently, like to stare.

"I want," he said finally, "to get to know you very well."

So do I, Meredith thought, and was about to say, but he kissed her. A perfect kiss. Velvety, tentative, but with just the right pressure.

Meredith could barely contain her excitement. She felt like dragging him into the bushes, but she knew that wouldn't do. He was wearing all white. She folded her hands in her lap and waited for the picnic to be over.

After the sandwiches and wine, they went for a walk on the Heath. The grass was squelchy and her kitten heels sank into the muck.

By the time they started back, it was verging on nine o'clock, but the sun was only beginning to drop behind the hill.

"I can't believe how bright it is," she said.

Gunther reminded her that London was farther north than Toronto. She asked about the climate in Munich, and as he was talking Meredith reached for his hand. By the time she had woven her fingers into his, they were nearly back at the parking lot.

As they approached the car, she had a vision of Gunther grabbing her by the waist, leaning her back against the Volvo and kissing her hungrily. Her interest was purely pragmatic. Kissing led to sex. Sex led to pregnancy. Her pelvis throbbed with anticipation. She would tell him she was on the pill.

She looked at Gunther, rooting through his leather

man-bag for a misplaced set of car keys. Good jaw line, she thought. Then he opened the door for her and he motioned for her to get in, but Meredith stood her ground.

"You want *me* to drive?" (She didn't have a licence—a fact she would have to remedy once the baby came along.)

"Wrong side," said Gunther. "Welcome to Britain."

Meredith smiled at her mistake and walked around to the left side of the car. "So where to now?" she asked as they got in.

He said he would drive her back to Notting Hill. Obviously this was the first stage of seduction. Everything was coming together nicely. Her mother was out for dinner with some drunken poet friends and wouldn't be home for hours. Time, Meredith knew, was of the essence.

"Come up for a drink?" she said when they reached Coleville Terrace.

Gunther put the car into park but kept the key in the ignition. His head swung and he fixed her in his sights. Abruptly, the mood between them went from buoyant to intense. Meredith had no idea why.

"I need to say something to you." He grasped her forearm and held it in both hands like a baseball bat.

"Okay." She nodded encouragingly.

"The first night we met I was very drunk and I didn't . . . I feel I didn't represent myself well."

"We had fun," Meredith offered, and then, feeling

she ought to say something slightly more suggestive, "*serious* fun."

She leaned over and kissed him again. He returned it, but only for a moment and with barely parted lips. It was exactly the sort of kiss Meredith normally liked—but tonight she had a mission. Kissing would not do. She undid her seat belt and hurled herself over the gearshift in the hope of falling seductively into Gunther's lap. She landed awkwardly, with one knee between his legs and the other foot jammed against the emergency break.

"I want to be with you," she breathed into his hair, as she had seen actresses do in movies. With one hand she braced herself against the windshield and with the other she grabbed Gunther's fingers and pushed them under her skirt.

"Whoa, whoa," he said, and in one fluid motion lifted her over the gearshift and back into the passenger seat. Meredith smoothed her clothes and coughed.

"We did have a lot of fun," Gunther began, "but I don't want you to think that's all I'm after. The other night, I was drunk. I'm sorry for that. I want you to think better of me. And after tonight, the way we were talking . . . I think we should take some time to get to know each other . . . don't you?"

Meredith looked down. "So come upstairs and have a drink with me."

"That's what I'm trying to tell you," he said. "I don't think it's a good idea for me to come inside tonight."

"But I *want* you to," she heard herself whine.

141

He reached forward and stroked her face. "Like I said, I think we should take some time. I don't want to screw this up."

Meredith opened her mouth to argue, but he pressed a finger to her upper lip.

"I'm kissing you good night now, Miss Moore."

***

"He's the one. I'm sure of it," Meredith said into the phone.

"Well, that didn't take you very long."

Meredith stopped and squinted at the ground. "Look, I just found a penny. Hang on a sec." She located a tissue in her bag, wiped off the mouldy copper and slipped it into the pocket of her hoodie.

"Well, that confirms it," Mish was saying when she pressed the phone back to her ear.

"Don't laugh in the face of fate." Meredith stepped out onto a zebra crossing, causing six cars to slam to a halt. She was on her way to the tube, which would take her to work.

"What's your call time?" Mish asked, yawning.

"Revoltingly soon. You?"

"Not till later. Her highness has the morning off."

"So you're coming with me to this opening tonight, right? It's in the East End, not far from your place." Mish was staying with friends across town in Hoxton.

"Of course. But what happened last night? You still haven't told me."

Meredith smiled to herself and did an involuntary little skip along the sidewalk. "We had a really nice picnic, and then he drove me home and that was it."

"He didn't try to get some?" Mish sounded skeptical.

"No, that's just it. We were making out and then he stopped. He says we need to get to know each other better."

"Really?"

"Isn't that cute?"

"I guess." Mish was silent.

"Not all guys are total sluts, you know," Meredith said.

"I know, it's just unusual behaviour," Mish said.

"Well, this was an unusual night," Meredith sniffed. "Besides, I thought it was kind of old school."

"But you think he'll be up for it tonight?"

Meredith hummed into the phone. A closed-mouth giggle.

"He might be a gentleman," she said, "but he's still a guy."

***

When Meredith arrived at the gallery that night, Mish was standing outside having a cigarette.

Meredith gave her a sticky lip-gloss smack on the cheek.

"C'mon," she said, dipping her head towards the door.

"I'm not sure you want to go in there," said Mish.

"Why wouldn't I?"

"I'm just warning you."

"About what?"

Mish shrugged and raised her eyebrows until they nearly touched her hairline. "I don't want you to freak," said Mish.

"Why are you being so weird?" Meredith hated it when Mish guarded information.

"See for yourself," Mish said.

Meredith turned to enter the gallery alone.

His work, she imagined, would be a porthole into his mind. Through his pictures she would be able to see not just his character, but the character of her unborn child. The child she was meant to conceive tonight. She was sure of it.

And what a gift it was that she would be able to understand Gunther's inner workings by looking at his artwork. This way they could skip the relationship part and get right to the important business of making a baby.

What luck they had met when they did.

Everything was set: her hair, her outfit, her pretty lingerie. Even her cycle was co-operating. If biology was on side, surely it was a sign. Stepping over the threshold, she was filled with warmth and certainty. Yes, the universe was a beneficent place after all. It had listened to her calls and answered them in turn.

Gunther was standing near the back door, deep in conversation with a woman in a purple caftan. Meredith took a glass of champagne from a thin man with a tray, and consumed half in two consecutive gulps. The small, overlit room was mobbed with people, most of them, she noticed, wearing glasses with architecturally complicated frames. Another tray appeared before her, this one bearing chopped-egg finger sandwiches with the crusts cut off. *Ironic snacks*, she thought, and took two.

She eagerly elbowed her way through the throng towards the wall. If she looked at Gunther's pictures now she hoped she could come up with something extra-insightful to say about them when he found her.

But when she finally reached the front of the scrum, the sight brought her up short. Before her was a largish photograph in black and white depicting a young girl of maybe thirteen or fourteen, nude and heavily pregnant. Some sort of ball or sock was shoved in her mouth, making it impossible to discern whether she was enjoying herself. Meredith guessed not.

She quickly moved on: a decapitated dog (maybe a collie?) being fellated by an old man. Hard to tell exactly how old, because he wore a leather face mask like the one Hannibal Lecter wore in *The Silence of the Lambs*, only without the little cage over his mouth to prevent him from eating people. Meredith moved around the gallery in a mounting state of unease. The more she looked, the more shocked she was, and the more shocked she became, the more deflated she felt.

How could she have been so naïve? It was humiliating. Who were these people anyway? And what was wrong with her that she could be attracted to someone who took photos of people in pain? The exhibit was a porthole all right, one that led directly into Gunther's twisted, rotten brain. Maybe it was fashionable or some kind of sick joke—Meredith didn't care. She also didn't care if he thought she was a tasteless bourgeois provincial for loathing him for it. She simply wanted out of there.

In a quick, ten-minute lap of the gallery, she observed a young girl being penetrated by broomsticks while a snake slithered out of her open mouth, an elderly man in various positions of coitus with a horse, and two nude little boys in ski masks smoking cigarettes. The funny thing was, none of the people around her seemed the least bit unnerved. Meredith eavesdropped on their commentary, which consisted mainly of observations on composition and shadow, rather than the subjects of the photographs themselves.

A young woman and a man dressed in identical black V-necks and shapeless army jackets stood to her left, looking at a photograph of a topless old woman wearing a nose clip and a bathing cap shoving a handful of baby mice into her mouth like popcorn.

"Hilarious," said the girl.

"Yes." Her date's head moved vigorously up and down. "I love the way he submerges his humour in the corporeal anxiety of significance. *Enormously* funny."

Neither of them laughed.

When Meredith went to the bar for more much-needed champagne, Mish was standing by with a concerned look on her face.

"So," she said.

"Oh, don't *even*."

They tried to make a break for it, but found themselves blocked. Gunther was in a corner near the coat check, chatting closely to a young man in a Greek fisherman's cap. He started when he saw Meredith. (Mish disappeared to the bathroom.)

"Ah," he said, kissing her on each cheek and drawing her forward. "Meredith, I'd like you to meet my friend Perry. He is a member of my group."

"Nice to meet you," she said, fists clenched in her pockets. "And are you a photographer as well?"

The young man pushed his hands deep into his pockets and coughed, obviously uncomfortable with female scrutiny. Meredith judged by the smear of angry red pimples across his cheeks that he must be very young.

"Nah. Jus sculpcha." He spoke with the accent and cadence Meredith could only identify in her mind as "cab driver."

"So what exactly do you sculpt?"

"Dicks mosely. Black dicks at the moment, but oy've done Oriental and whites as well."

Meredith chewed her lip.

Gunther jumped in. "Perry is doing a racial study of male sexual organs around the world—isn't that right?"

"At's it, guv," said Perry. He drained his pint glass and, without another word, abandoned company for the comforts of the open bar.

Gunther smiled. "So what do you think?"

"About what?" Meredith asked, hoping to stall him.

"About the art!" He laughed harshly, and then came in close and whispered in her ear. "Before you answer, I think you should know I can't take criticism."

Meredith nodded brightly.

"I was *joking*," he said. "I want an honest Canadian perspective. What do you think?"

The smile on her face congealed. "To be honest—" She paused. How to put it? She panicked. "I love the way you submerge your humour in the corporeal anxiety of significance."

Gunther cocked his head. "An astute observation."

She had no idea whether he was joking or not.

"Listen," Meredith said, "my friend isn't feeling well, so I'd better take her home, but it was really nice to see you. Thanks for inviting us."

"What?" His features returned to their stern equilibrium. "You're leaving already?"

"I'd love to stay, but Mish—she's really exhausted. I'm afraid she might have SARS or something and I wouldn't want her spreading it around the party."

He nodded solemnly. "That would be bad."

"Yes. Yes, well."

He grabbed her by the arm without warning, pulled her towards him and inhaled her hair.

"You look wunderbar."

"Thanks."

He bent down and began to kiss her throat. "You must come to Munich."

Meredith muttered something about work.

Gunther drew back and looked at her. "You don't approve of my work, do you."

Meredith shifted from foot to foot, wishing she were a better liar.

"I've felt misunderstood for most of my life—don't you see that's what these photographs are about?" he said.

Meredith could barely bring herself to nod. "But those people . . ." she said.

Gunther looked exasperated. "They are not people. They are *subjects*."

"I have to go," she said.

"So go."

***

Two hours later Mish and Meredith sat draining a bottle of pinot grigio at a booth in a wine bar around the corner from the flat on Coleville Terrace.

Mish put down her glass and threw her head back. "Sitting around, getting tipsy, moaning about men. Isn't it all just so *London*?"

"I guess so."

"Oh, I know what we should do! Let's go to Sainsbury's and get a box of those Quality Sweets and go back to your flat and watch *Big Brother*!"

"My mother doesn't have digital. And, by the way, it's Quality *Street*, not Sweet."

"C'mon, Mere, buck up," Mish said, pinching her friend's chin and wiggling it like a faulty light switch. "So Gunther wasn't the one. You can't expect to find *him* at the first party you go to."

"I know." Meredith stuck out her tongue and looked towards the ceiling. It was an expression she only ever used around Mish.

"So you didn't tell him what you really thought?"

"No way." Meredith pushed away her glass. "Why would I? I mean he's essentially a pornographer. No — worse than a pornographer, he's a pornographer who's also cruel to animals."

"I thought he was good looking."

"So did I, but that's not enough in this case. I mean, *come on*. I'm not looking for a one-night stand here, I'm searching for the father of my firstborn child. In all likelihood my *only* child. It's probably the biggest decision I'll ever make in my whole entire life. Anyway, who knows if it even would have worked. At my age . . ."

Mish lowered her face into her hands and rocked her head from side to side. "So much pressure."

"What do you mean?"

"Why do you always have to make sure everything is perfect? Maybe if you'd just let things unfold . . ."

Meredith looked at her nails and noticed the pale pink polish she'd applied just yesterday was already starting to grey. Something about the newsprint over here. It rubbed off too easily. Maybe Mish was right. That was what everybody always said, wasn't it? That you only ever find the thing you're looking for when you stop searching altogether and let things happen for themselves. But how to stop trying to control the story? It was the only way she knew.

Meredith's previous relationships had all been variations on a theme. She started off distant, a little cool, remote. This seemed to spur men on, and it was easy because the chill was something she came by quite naturally—at first. There was a lovely period while they wooed her: phoning half a dozen times in a single night, sending flowers with only the flimsiest excuse, showing up in places where they knew she would be. It was when she was keen on someone that things went wrong. Eventually, if she liked the guy enough, Meredith would submit to the chase. Go to bed with him a few times. Insist on splitting the bill here and there, so he wouldn't think she was cheap. Then the day would come when she realized that now she was calling him more than he called her. She would find herself acting out a kind of reverse courtship—using all the tactics he had used early on, except that now her actions took on a slightly paranoid edge. She sent anxious, mushy e-mails and showed up at his office. She insisted that they *talk about us*. Finally one day, more often than not in a crowded restaurant over lunch, he would reach across the table and take her hand and mutter something about "not being ready." "Ready for *what*?" she would always demand—for she had never, ever, not even at her weakest point, brought up the subject of marriage or children. But she knew what these men meant, and that such serious topics had been in the air, uncontainable, ever since the first date.

"What did your doctor say?" Mish asked.

"Him? It doesn't matter—he's not available."

"Sheesh, Mere, when did you become such a man-eater?" Mish leaned across the table and shoved her. "I meant, what did he say about your *health*. Like in terms of your, you know, baby-making capacity."

"He said I'd better stop messing around. Shit or get off the pot. You know, time is of the essence. That kind of thing. He said . . ." Meredith trailed off, thinking of Joe's voice on the other end of the crackly telephone line. "I haven't spoken to him in a few days."

Mish set down her wineglass with a clatter. "Are you saying you've spoken to your gynecologist on the phone since you arrived here?"

"So?"

"Does that not strike you as just a little weird?"

"Not really. I mean, okay, maybe a bit. But it makes sense."

"How?"

"For one thing, *I* am a little weird. And besides, is it so strange for a doctor to take interest in his patient's welfare? I mean, is there anything against that in the

Hippocratic oath? And for your information, he's not a regular gynecologist, he's also an internationally recognized fertility specialist."

"Really." Mish's eyes narrowed, zoning in on Meredith's face. She paused. "Is he hot?"

Meredith covered a grin with both hands. "Maybe."

"I can't *believe* you're flirting with your gyno." Mish wrinkled her nose. "That is so David Cronenberg or something."

"I never actually . . ." Meredith began, and then thought better of it. "This is gross. Can we talk about something else?"

They sat for a few moments listening to Kylie panting over the stereo backbeat.

"There's still that Shakespeare guy," said Mish, upending the wine bottle in its cooler. "He seemed pretty into you."

Meredith smiled. "I think he was drunk."

"Most people in this city are—haven't you noticed? I don't think it's worth holding against him."

"He invited me to the country to see his pet birds."

"Really?" Mish stabbed out her cigarette and made a circle in the ashes. "I had a parrot once. My brother taught it to say 'Fuck you,' so my mother got rid of it."

"These are totally different. I think he hunts with them. To be honest, I don't really understand it."

"Killer birds." Mish rocked back in her chair and honked. "That is so medieval. You *have* to go."

"Well, we'll see if he even calls."

"You gave him your number?"

Meredith shrugged and looked at the ceiling.

"You little slut!" Mish cried, and with an involuntary push of her boot, tipped her chair over backwards.

***

The following morning was Sunday. Instead of succumbing to a hangover, Meredith got up early and went for a run. She took a random route, jogging along street after street of pastel-painted brownstones, indistinguishable except for their exotic names: Cheapstow Villas, Ladbroke Grove, Arundel Gardens, Penzance Place, Hippodrome Mews. To her surprise, she found she still knew the neighbourhood by feel—as if a map of its curvy crescents and private gated garden squares had been imprinted on her DNA. She ran up the hill, past grand, six-storey mansion blocks with whitewashed wrought-iron Juliet balconies and potted palms sprouting in their front courtyards. At the summit she stopped and raised her face to the sky, letting the moisture gather on her face. She closed her eyes and opened them again, noticing, for the first time, the way the chimneys poked up from the rooftops like rows of stubby fingers. It was not raining so much as dewing, as though the atmosphere was being spritzed from the nozzle of an enormous spray bottle.

When the blood-thump in her ears quieted, Meredith continued down the other side of the hill. The streets were full of discarded blossoms—the last foliage of spring, blown from the trees by an early morning wind. The street cleaners hadn't been around yet to clear away the debris and the pavement was coated in a layer of this sweetly rotting snow.

Meredith trailed her hand through the waxy shrubs that pressed out through the fences. A holly bush pricked. She stuck her finger in her mouth.

When she came to Clarendon Cross she paused to stare in through the windows of the little shops with their painted signs and ruffled awnings. A store window crammed with beaded lampshades and lace table shawls filled Meredith with a toothachy claustrophobia. Beside it was a linen boutique with nothing but shelves of folded sheets in neutral colours. A kitchen store advertised a sale on wicker picnic baskets. A gallery specialized in religious icons—sacred gilt antiquities stripped from European churches now being sold off as bathroom and foyer chachkas for the grand homes of the London haute bourgeois.

In the window was a glittering brass etching of the Madonna and baby Jesus. The mother's eyes were downcast in an expression of milky shyness. Her infant son, by contrast, was improbably alert. In one tiny hand he held his mother's naked breast like a piece of fruit he was saving for later; the other hand was raised in the air as though he was just coming to the punchline of a complicated anecdote.

Meredith turned and saw two little girls in duffle coats and pirate hats returning from church or brunch with their parents. The adults—slim, tweedy bohemians in their mid-thirties—bickered gently over something. The children amused themselves in the square by jumping up and down on a bench they had found with a loosened board.

"My turn!" the smaller girl demanded, outraged when her sister refused to yield her place on the sproingy surface. The wood groaned and threatened to snap under the older girl's weight. Meredith felt a twinge of panic. She had a mental vision of the crack, the little girl falling backwards, head hitting the cement, a tiny stocking-clad leg rammed into a splintery crevice. The parents, however, seemed oblivious to danger. They looked back and continued their half-hearted dispute (the wife was obviously winning). The girls switched places.

She continued on her run, heading south towards the river, through Ladbrook Grove, across Holland Park Road and into the land of million-pound urban manor homes, with their splendid glass awnings and great bowed front windows. Here was one of the few areas in London where residents reserved the right to live in much the same way as their recent ancestors had. Domestics in uniform threw open shutters and gardeners swept stray twigs off flagstones and dumped them into mulch buckets. Meredith ran on, inhaling the expensive perfume of other people's lives.

Eventually she came to an ivy-covered wall with a small door in it. Meredith darted through and ran up a crooked set of log stairs embedded in the mud. She remembered Holland Park from the haze of early childhood; only then it had seemed less like a park and more like an enchanted forest. She continued through the cultivated glades and garden paths, past the man-made pond with the statue of grumpy Lord Holland in the middle, down the laurel walk, and through the Kyoto Garden with its tinkly waterfall and tiny Japanese houses made out of stone. She cut across the periwinkle ground cover and ran through a gap in the hibiscus shrub, and when she emerged she found herself in a topiary maze surrounded by low walls. Women were pushing carriages—perambulators—with plastic tents draped overtop to keep out the mist.

Meredith jogged on the spot for a moment, trying to decide where to go next. Through a spray of willow branches, she glimpsed a swish of peacock feathers, tempting her back farther, around the bend in the path to where the gardens opened up to the rest of the green.

When she turned the corner, Meredith felt almost physically assaulted by the view before her. In the centre of the path was an island of grass fenced off by a series of knee-high iron arches. The animal sanctuary was a sort of cageless zoo populated by terminally bored peacocks and tamed rabbits snacking on compost. It was not the scene that shocked her, but the memory. Meredith knew exactly what it felt like to reach her hands out in front of her chest and feel those very iron arches in her fists. Looking at their height, he couldn't have been more than four or five at the time.

Yes, it was all bleeding through, like one screen image dissolving into another. A day much brighter than this one, and cooler too, judging by the bite of the metal in her grip. A scratchy wool beret on her head she wished she could take off but didn't dare. They had come here to feed the rabbits. Or one particular rabbit, who Meredith believed was Peter *the* Rabbit despite the fact that he was black.

This was the memory: The hand of a man reaching down towards her. Skin like soft, worn leather and hairy at the knuckles. On the pinky finger was a ring. A thick gold band. A flash of jade. In her memory, the hand unfolded before her eyes to reveal—what was it? Something pale green and waxy. A wedge of cabbage? Of course! To feed the bunny. And then herself, a small child, still wobbly on her feet, taking the cabbage and throwing it over the fence, giggling, waiting for the black bunny to come and fetch his treat. Meredith could see the bunny, the cabbage, the big hand that she reached for, but try as she might she could not bring the whole man into focus.

11

If only they wouldn't touch her so much.

After autograph hounds and those nude photos on the Internet, the touching was definitely the worst thing about Kathleen Swain's job. The poking, the prodding, the fiddling with laces and clips and zippers. The powdering and re-powdering and pincurling and plucking of follicles. In her twenty-five years as a working actress, Kathleen had been groomed within an inch of her life, and she was sick of it. But the more the preening annoyed her, the more she needed it. The vicious cycle of aging. And so she submitted to the ever-burgeoning hours of adjustments. Some days she felt that if one more smiling lady came at her with a daub of liquid foundation, or a yawning eyelash curler, she would simply disappear —*poof!*—having been primped to death.

Not to mention the misery of small talk. Day after day, hour upon hour of sitting in an overheated trailer trying to turn the conversation around to what the hairstylist did for *her* summer holidays. (As if she cared! And yet, one obviously couldn't talk about oneself. She'd learned her lesson on that score after she showed up for makeup one morning several years ago with an unstoppable nosebleed, then spotted the following week's tabloid headline: "Kay Swain Drugs Hell"—accompanied by a paparazzo shot of her stumbling out of the gym without makeup.) No, these people, as chatty and folksy as they might seem, were not to be trusted. And the only way to get them to stop asking questions about you was to ask them questions about themselves, their families and their grim little Wal-Mart–furnished lives. This, however, required *feigning an interest*. And while Kathleen Swain was paid millions to pretend emotions she did not feel in front of the camera, she found doing the same thing in real life to be a chore.

Luckily Vicky from Essex, the new makeup artist on the Crouch show, seemed to need absolutely no prompting when it came to pouring out the details of her personal life. As she put the final touches on Kathleen's eyeliner, she continued the monologue she'd launched into forty-five minutes earlier when she began sponging beige foundation on her subject's forehead.

"An' I told 'im the last time I saw 'im, I did. I said, darling, I love you too, but I ain't putting up wif no more of this nonsense wiffout a ring. I'm a traditional girl, see? Not one a fese old slappers who jes goes 'round shagging everyfing that moves fer the bloody fun of it. If 'e wants a good time, 'e can go down the road and get 'iself some of that, 'e can."

Kathleen's gaze slid over to the portable television in the corner. The volume was turned down on an episode of a soap opera, one of those grim dramas that followed the lives of a group of depressed and unattractive poor people living in a hard-luck town—the sort of show that could have been made only in Britain. Or Canada. On the screen a teenage girl was spoon-feeding mashed banana to an infant. An old man in a shopkeeper's apron walked into the frame and they began to shout at each other, jaws chomping noiselessly at the air.

Just as Vicky was about to launch into the story of her sister's recent divorce ("Di'int trust 'im as far as I could throw 'im. And was I right?"), the trailer door swung open and the new costume girl staggered in carrying a bale of petticoats, purple taffeta and corsetry that made Kathleen's lower back spasm just looking at it.

"Morning ladies," said Mish, dumping the garments on the nearest daybed. "Another frock for the return rack. Our dear Director has decided he doesn't like taffeta—apparently it interferes with the light."

Vicky acknowledged Mish with only the slightest nod. As she applied a final dusting of powder to the plasticized tip of Kathleen's nose, Vicky continued with her story. "As I was saying, Miss Swain, my sister Abbie, she gets 'itched up to this bloke and wiffin a two months the police is called in 'cause 'ees—"

Kathleen turned her cheek and Vicky hovered above her face with the powder puff. "Vicky, I think that's enough for now. It's time I got into my costume. You're free to go."

As Vicky packed up her case and huffed out of the room, Kathleen turned her attention to Mish. The girl had her back to Kathleen and was anxiously sorting through a rack of vintage undergarments, which, with their array of laces and stays and hooks, resembled torture devices. Even more painful to look at was Mish's own outfit, Kathleen thought. How could she bend over—let alone walk—in that skirt and those ridiculous clogs? And that black lace top—it was simply beyond the beyond. A one-way ticket to the back pages of *Us* magazine, if worn on a red carpet—which, thank God for this girl, it never would be. She watched without lifting herself from the makeup chair as Mish dropped an ancient garter belt between two hat boxes.

"Fuckbugger. Sorry, Ms. Swain, I'll be with you in just a moment."

Kathleen felt a rare but not-unfamiliar wave of self-disgust wash over her. *When did I become such a complete bitch?* she wondered. *Was it before or after wardrobe girls started having better bodies than me?* She vowed to try to be nicer to her inferiors, more folksy and down to earth, like Julia Roberts, who was said to always be chumming around with the crew and who had actually ended up marrying that handsome second-camera assistant.

Mish handed Kathleen a piece of stretchy flesh-toned undergarment that looked, to Kathleen's eye, like a linebacker's jock strap.

"What's this for?"

"It's for under your corset. To keep everything . . . smooth."

"And who requested this, may I ask?"

Mish seemed to stiffen. Smiled. "No one requested it. The company sent it to me and I just thought you might want to try it. Apparently Nicole Kidman wore one all the way through *Cold Mountain*."

"Nicole?" Kathleen wrinkled her nose and looked down at the support garment, held gingerly between her thumb and forefinger. "But she's a stick."

"Exactly." Mish nodded.

"Well, okay. I guess it can't hurt, can it?" Kathleen smiled. On second thought there was something about this new girl she liked. Trusted, even. In fact, she seemed to recall having had a conversation with her earlier in the shoot. Or was that the other one with the dark hair? Anyway, she felt unusually relaxed with these Canadians. English accents made her tense. She slipped off her robe and began struggling into the girdle, rotating her hips like a novice belly dancer while hoisting the elastic up over her thighs. Mish stepped behind her and began to help.

"I've become such a disgusting pig ever since I started trying for a baby," Kathleen laughed, feeling proud of herself for employing self-deprecating humour (very endearing and down-to-earth). "It's all the folic acid I have to eat now. Bowls and bowls of peanuts all day long. I mean, really you're only supposed to have a small handful, but I haven't allowed myself nuts in decades. Once I get started I can't stop. It's like . . ."

"A free-for-all?"

"Exactly! A nut orgy. Oh—ow." Kathleen winced as Mish tugged the corset strings in another quarter of an inch.

"Sorry, almost done." Mish double-knotted the string and began rummaging through the rack for the matching petticoat. "How's that going, then?" Kathleen exhaled to make her rib cage as narrow as possible.

"Oh, fine. You know."

***

Actually Mish didn't. Nor did she bother to say so.

The digital trill from a tiny silver cell phone distracted Swain. She pressed the phone to her ear with one hand and waved the other like a flipper. "Just a second. Where's that converter?"

Mish dropped the laces and began searching the trailer until she found it under a copy of HEAT magazine.

"Oprah," said Swain, and then, directing her attention into the phone, "She's just getting it. What channel again? Twenty-four? Okay. I'll call you after."

Mish turned on the TV and there was the Most Loved Woman in the World. The studio audience applauded hysterically until Winfrey shushed them with four papal sweeps of her arms.

"And on today's show we'll be talking about the issue of late-in-life fertility," Oprah was teleprompted. "Specifically, how late is too late? When should a woman start to worry and when is it too late to try? We'll be talking to a group of women who have succeeded in conceiving later in life—one of our guests had her first baby at the age of fifty-two! Can you believe that, y'all? And a couple of other women who have not succeeded in making their dreams of motherhood come true, despite the best medical efforts. Some of these women felt they waited too long, and they are here to tell other women who want to conceive not to make the same mistake they did by putting things off until it's just too late."

Mish, who had been searching for a needle and thread to repair a hem, fell still. "Do you want me to come back later?" she asked.

"No, no, stay," said Swain. "That was my assistant calling. My fertility doctor in L.A. is going on maternity leave, so we have to find another specialist and apparently there's this guy on *Oprah* who's written some book. Can you believe what a coincidence this is? I mean, we were just talking about this and now it's on *Oprah*—it must be a sign."

Swain motioned for silence as the commercials

finished and the *Oprah* theme music introduced the next segment.

"Our expert today is Dr. Joe Veil, a fertility specialist and the author of *Baby Love: The New Battle for Motherhood*. He's here to give us the straight goods on what women trying to get pregnant later in life can realistically expect. Now tell us, Dr. Veil, what kind of odds is an average woman facing who's decided she wants to get pregnant at, say, the age of forty? We see it all the time on television, or in the tabloids. Seems every established middle-aged movie star and pop singer is walkin' around with a bump these days. Is it really as easy as they make it look?"

The camera swivelled over to Dr. Joe Veil. He loosened his collar as he spoke. "Actually, Oprah, it's *not* as easy as it looks." Dr. Veil launched into a litany of the risks and difficulties involved in late-in-life pregnancies. Swain, however, was too busy swooning to listen.

"He's a *dish*, isn't he? Did she say he's a practising fertility specialist?"

"I hink ho." Mish's mouth was full of pins.

Swain stabbed a finger into her phone keypad and began talking almost immediately. "I think he could be the one. Yeah—yeah. That's him. Find out for me as soon as you can. I don't care if we have to fly him over here and put him up at the Ritz. Get him yesterday. Me *want*."

She got off the phone and let out a significant *whoosh*. Mish was doing up the final buttons of her collar.

"Do you have children?" Swain asked.

"I haven't got a maternal bone in my body." Mish grabbed Swain's dress off the rack so fiercely she felt the shoulder seam rip. "We'd better get you on set. You're already late for your call."

***

"Oh, for Chrissake, where is she?"

Richard was agitated and talking to himself. Meredith, who was sitting in her usual spot to the left, pretended not to hear. Instead, she focused on her notes for the next scene.

The shoot had moved locations to Kewkesbury Park, a sprawling Edwardian country house located at the end of the Northern tube line, and the crew had just finished setting up for one of the film's most complicated and expensive segments—the ballroom dancing scene. Dozens of extras from the London Ballet Academy milled around the set waiting to take their places for the waltz sequence. They held their heads self-consciously high (even for dancers) as a result of the rustling vintage silks they wore, the women in bustles and the men in tails and top hats. The crew members moved among them adjusting lights and lenses in militaristic form.

Kathleen Swain was late for her call and things were behind schedule as usual. Meredith had spent much of the morning wandering from room to room, exploring the corridors and back stairwells, each one leading to another set of rooms that opened onto another set of rooms. The place was damp and drafty, the ancient plaster striped with water marks from the rain that had seeped its way indoors over the years. Everything reeked of mould. And yet, to Meredith (who had a fondness for the ancient and austere), the place was beautiful.

The house, after all, was very nearly a celebrity in and of itself. In the past couple of years alone, it had appeared in dozens of BBC Agatha Christie dramas, and a reality-TV series in which middle-class Brits re-enacted the life of Edwardian aristocrats and their servants, as well as doubling as the interior of Windsor Castle in the TV version of *Diana: Her True Story*. So much production went on here, in fact, that the owner, an impoverished duke who bred dorgis (a demented-looking cross between dachshunds and corgis), had confined his living quarters to three rooms above the garage at the end of the lane. While production companies and tourists overran the grand house of his ancestors, the duke lived the cramped, frugal existence of an inner-city welfare recipient.

The crew had been waiting for Swain for most of the morning and now Richard was becoming visibly agitated. He had already sent the first assistant around to her trailer twice, to no avail. Meredith pulled a chair over to a corner of the room, not far from the monitor where Richard was pacing and tossing out commands to his crew, and began to scribble down the complicated set of shot descriptions they had discussed the day before in rehearsal. *Start MS angle toward ballroom door. Inspector enters. Pan his walk X-L-R across room past waltzing dancers. Hold Full 4/should over Inspector to Miss Celia seated on the sidelines* . . . And so on, describing the entire scene through the unblinking eye of the camera in her secret continuity girl language. Meredith spent so much time at work translating, in cryptic point-form and code, what things looked like from the outside, that she often amused herself by doing the same thing in real life. Bored on the subway or over dinner, she would find herself making shot descriptions of scenes as they were playing themselves out.

Tite to Continuity Girl scribbling
notes in a binder. RL angle toward
door of room. The Movie Star enters.
Pan her walk across the room toward
the Director's chair. Hold Full 4/
shot over Movie Star's R-should to
Director seated on chair.

                    DIRECTOR
  Kathleen, how sweet of you to
  show up for work. And looking
  ravishing as usual.
            MOVIE STAR (*HUSHED*)
  Thank you for being patient, darling. So sorry about the delay.

I'm afraid I was having a bit of
a woman's problem.
                    DIRECTOR
A nasty affliction, that. Now,
where were we? Oh, yes, we were
in the middle of making a movie.

Wide shot of the room. The crew
and extras wait for the Director's
command.

                    DIRECTOR
    Places!
                    FIRST A.D.
    Let's have a bell!

Angle on the Sound Mixer pressing a
button on his panel. A buzz is heard.
New angle on the red light outside
the stage door.

                    FIRST A.D.
    Quiet!

Silence engulfs the room.

                    CONTINUITY GIRL
    Scene 26, Take 1.

FIRST A.D.
Roll sound.

A beat as the Sound Mixer waits for
the recorder to stabilize at the correct speed. Tite of the Sound Mixer
whispering the slate number into the
recorder.

SOUND MIXER
Scene 26, Take 1. (*Beat of
silence*) Speed.

Tite on the Camera Operator peering through the lens to make sure the
picture is in perfect frame and focus.
Angle over R-should of Operator as
he snaps the camera switch on. P.O.V.
camera. A slate appears in front of
the lens.

CAMERA OPERATOR
Mark it.
Tite on the clapsticks snapping shut.
Timecode on slate freezes, indicating
the picture and sound are now in sync.
Angle on the Slate Operator dashing
out of set.

CAMERA OPERATOR

Rolling.

Pan across the room, the dancers
stand in pairs, poised to begin.
Tite on Director.

DIRECTOR

Action!

When Meredith got home that night her mother was
reclined on the living room sofa smoking a pipe and
listening to a vinyl recording of Leonard Cohen recit-
ing a poem about a girl on a beach. Meredith came
up the stairs, dropped her knapsack and exhaled. Her
mother, who was wrapped in a black satin dressing
gown, acknowledged her with a nod.

Meredith looked around for somewhere to sit, but
as usual every surface was piled high with rubbish. Not
the *same* rubbish, however, as everything seemed to
have been shifted around as the result of some invisible tidal pull since she'd last surveyed the room. She
lifted a long-dead potted fern and discovered a perfectly
serviceable footstool beneath it. Pulling her cardigan
sleeve over her hand, she dusted it off and sat down.

"Brilliant!" Irma said, opening her eyes. "I've been
looking for that footstool since the eighties. I remember the night it went missing. I had a very large dinner party. Full of journalists. Everyone got frightfully

pissed and a few of them stayed over. In the morning the footstool had vanished. Naturally I always assumed one of them had filched it. Don't ever date a journalist, darling. They're dreadful people. Cheap. Unhygienic."

Meredith said nothing. She placed her chin in her upturned palms and rested one elbow on each knee. Leonard Cohen continued his droning description of a nude girl's bottom. If you tuned out the words, he sounded like a man delivering a eulogy for a person he didn't particularly like.

"Care for a nip?" Irma indicated the bottle of Limoncello balanced on the sofa near her gnarled and naked feet.

"I'll have water." Meredith rose and wove her way around the stacks of magazines and books towards the kitchenette sink. "Want some?"

Irma's eyes fluttered open again. "Ucch. Silly Moo, you know I loathe water."

Irma was always reminding Meredith of things she supposedly knew, but didn't actually know at all. Had no way of knowing.

Meredith searched for a glass (there were mugs, but she had an aversion to drinking anything cold out of an opaque vessel) and eventually found one at the back of the oven. She rinsed it out with the last bit of dish soap and dried it with a tea towel. Filling it took ages. When the water from the faucet finally did pour steadily, it came out warm and full of suspicious-looking white clouds, which her mother assured her was only gas. Unconvinced, Meredith poured the water down the sink. The drain belched in protest. Tomorrow she would have to go buy some Evian.

"You know, *he* was the reason why I sent you to boarding school in Canada," Irma said.

"Who?"

"Leonard, of course." Irma seemed suddenly exasperated. "I met him in Montreal at a reading in the early seventies. You were just a wee thing. He was so charming, just like the young Dustin Hoffman, only with more sexual confidence. He had a son about your age and the two of you played together. Don't you remember?"

"No."

"Anyway, we had such a nice time, I thought it would be lovely for you to grow up Canadian. Icicles, snowball fights, that sort of thing."

"You sent me to school in Canada because you flirted with Leonard Cohen?"

"I did a great deal more than flirt with him, my duck."

Meredith pushed her hands through her hair and tugged on the ends. "Please — don't. I really don't want to hear about it. Just, why Toronto?"

"Fewer French people. You know I detest the French. Completely humourless."

Meredith picked up the bottle of Limoncello and poured some into her empty water glass.

"That's an awful lot, darling. Are you sure you need that much?"

Meredith brought the drink to her lips. It was almost unbearably sweet but somehow tart at the same time, like those sour gobstoppers you bought as a kid that were meant to give you a funny face from sucking them.

Meredith sat down on the footstool again and balanced her drink on her knee.

"Listen, I have something to ask you. Remember when we used to go and feed the rabbits in Holland Park?"

"Of course! You named the black one Peter, and you thought there was only one—of course there were probably thousands, but I didn't have the heart to tell you. It was terribly cute."

"What I was wondering was, did you ever let anyone else take me? To feed the rabbits, I mean? Like maybe a boyfriend of yours, or another man?"

Irma raised herself up on a throw cushion and turned her head towards Meredith. "Why would you ask such a thing?"

"It's just that I have this memory of a man. He's holding my hand, in the park. It's not a bad memory or anything. That's the thing. It's actually quite a nice memory. The only problem is, I can't remember who the man is, and I was wondering . . ."

"No."

"What do you mean, 'no'?"

"I mean, I told you—your father is dead. If you choose not to believe me, that's your problem. But don't expect me to reinforce your delusions."

"Who was he, then?"

"I told you. He was a dashing American film director. We had a drunken shag in his pool house during a party. I left around three a.m. and the next thing I heard he was found floating face-down in his pool. Bloody idiot."

"No, Mother, I mean the man I remember from the park."

Irma shrugged, settled back into the sofa and closed her eyes. "It was such a long time ago, darling, I've no idea. There were so many men around then. To tell you the truth it could have been anyone."

Meredith drained her glass and stared at her mother. Bones poked out of her dressing gown like concealed weapons. Meredith ran her tongue over her teeth and found they were sticky. She vowed to brush them for a full five minutes before bed, instead of the usual two.

Meredith spent most of the train trip to Gloucester
looking out the window at the mist-blurred fields
while Mish snored in the seat beside her, slumping
onto her shoulder with each sideways lurch of the car.
The train was already forty minutes behind schedule.
It kept stopping, inexplicably, for rests between sta-
tions. Meredith tried to imagine the possible reasons
for a train to stop in the middle of the countryside and
couldn't come up with any good ones apart from life
threatening technical problems. She worried about
Barnaby, who was meeting them at the station.

Squirming in her seat, Meredith smoothed her
new chocolate corduroys (bought at Selfridges the
weekend before, specifically in anticipation of the
weekend), and adjusted the laces on her hiking boots
to make sure the bows were evenly tied.

Ever since pulling out of Waterloo she had been
considering, for the first time, the real ramifications
of bringing up a child on her own, without a man. It
was not the image of destitute single motherhood that

bothered Meredith (she earned a decent wage and had saved up enough over the years to tide her over for a year if not longer), but the issue of denying her child a father. It was the same thing her mother had done, after all. And while she had always convinced herself she didn't particularly care about not having a father (one crazy, ill-equipped parent was enough, thank you very much), the question of paternity had lately started to bother her. Not having had a male parent on site introduced certain problems into the issue of rearing a child. She had been thinking more and more about genes. For instance, what if her father had a genetic deformity that had skipped her generation (or was only carried through the male line) and that would now affect her baby? How could she be sure that the father of her child didn't come from a family with a history of madness, premature baldness or some other inherited defect? Above all, though, Meredith had begun to consider the moral ramifications. It had all started this morning when Mish met her at the train station waving a copy of the *Times*. On the front page was a story about how there was a movement afoot to make British sperm donors untraceable, so that future sperm-bank recipients could have complete parental rights over their anonymously fathered children.

"Forget the sex part," Mish had said, rolling up the paper and thwacking it against her hip. "You could just go for a blind donation. I hear they're mostly from hot med students."

Meredith had read the full article on the train and had been moved by a comment piece written by a fertility specialist. He argued the case that the fetus has a "right to know." As a grown-up fetus herself, one who had been denied the facts about her father (even as a child, she had never believed her mother's pool-party story), Meredith could understand where the specialist was coming from. At the same time, she remained unwavering in her determination to have a baby on her own. The trick was to find out as much as she could about her biological partner before conceiving. Then she would have something to tell her baby when it grew up. Who knows, maybe she and the father could even keep in touch. At least she could get a photograph of the donor, which was more than she herself had ever had.

Meredith considered Barnaby. He was tall (check), with a full head of hair (check) and no evidence of skin problems or acne scarring (that she could see, anyway). He seemed bright enough (though maybe it was just the accent), and, perhaps most importantly, he had the right smell. Clean but not *too* clean. There was something about the way he'd put his jacket over her shoulders and guided her back to her seat that night. For all his initial fumbling, he knew what to do when doing something mattered. Meredith liked a man who knew how to move. True, his teeth were a bit snaggled, but nothing a bit of North American orthodontistry couldn't have fixed. Perhaps he drank a little too much, but that could be said about most people here. In short, he was promising. And Meredith was keen to kiss him again. That was a good sign.

The real question, of course (and the one Meredith had been studiously ignoring ever since she stepped on a transatlantic flight to seek her biological fortune), was whether Barnaby (or any other man, for that matter) would mind fathering a baby that was to be, in no uncertain terms, *her* baby. Above all, she wanted no interference—financial, emotional or otherwise—in her parenting project. She imagined an annual round of Christmas and birthday cards, perhaps with a bookstore gift certificate stuck inside, and maybe the odd visit (lunch on the day he happened to be passing through town on business), but that was absolutely it. Anything else verged dangerously on a *relationship*.

Barnaby met them at the train wearing a yellow mackintosh and matching boots, and looking, Meredith thought, exactly like an overgrown Christopher Robin. He kissed both Meredith and Mish lightly on their right cheeks and insisted on carrying their bags to his car, an ancient Austin Mini so encrusted with rust it was hard to tell the decay from the original ruddy paint job.

"Your train was only forty-five minutes late," he said, cramming their things into the non-existent trunk. "That's early for British rail."

Meredith smiled. Mish rubbed her face, still grumpy from sleep.

"So sorry, but I'm afraid you'll have to sit on top of each other in the front, as the back seat is full of dead things."

Meredith laughed and then saw, through the grimy back window, that it was true. On the back seat lay a tarpaulin with a pile of limp furry bodies, mostly rabbits, squirrels and a couple of small birds.

"Ghastly of me. So sorry. I'm afraid I didn't even notice they were there until after I'd arrived here at the station. I was planning to take them over to the publican the day before yesterday—he makes the most fantastic game pie—but I completely forgot, and now I suppose I'll have to bury them. But then the dogs will only dig them up, so that won't work either. Perhaps when we get back to the house you could help me put them down the garburator."

Mish made a gagging sound.

"I'm only kidding, of course. I don't have a garburator." Barnaby smiled. "I hope you won't hold it against me."

"We couldn't care less," Meredith lied. "We're from Canada. We grew up trapping our own food and living in ice huts."

"How fascinating," said Barnaby, getting into the driver's side.

Meredith couldn't tell if he thought she had been joking or not. His mind seemed to be somewhere else. Without discussion, Mish took the seat and Meredith perched as gracefully as she could on her friend's bony lap. Mish poked her angrily the entire way, and Meredith was feeling irritable and sore by the time they pulled into the gates at Hawkpen Manor.

The village of Stow-on-the-Wold was located in the damp heart of the Cotswolds, just down the road from Shipston-on-Stour, and halfway between Morton-in-Marsh and Bourton-on-the-Water. Hawkpen Manor was a fifteen-minute drive west of Stow, along a winding series of country roads with towering cedar hedges that rose up impenetrable on either side of the road. The estate itself was composed of several hundred acres of uncultivated moorland. On the eastern border, about half a mile in from the road, sprawled the main house.

As they rounded the bend and it came into view, Meredith felt as though the air had been squashed out of her. A stadium heap of golden Cotswold brick, the house reclined across the lawn like a sleeping lion. A shameless grin beamed out from its bow-windowed front facade.

"You actually *live* there?"

"Oh, no," said Barnaby, keeping his eyes on the road in front of him. "My brother and his wife do. I'm down the road in one of the cottages in behind."

There was a confused silence.

"Second-son syndrome, you see."

"So your older brother got the house," said Meredith.

"And the title, and the land. And I got the aviary—otherwise known as the unpolished jewel in the

Shakespeare crown." Barnaby winked. "He lets me live in the cottage, but technically speaking, Nigel is my landlord. Law of the land. We've been invited there for dinner tonight, by the way."

Barnaby Shakespeare lived in Pear Cottage, a shabby outbuilding to the south. He pulled the car onto a grassy knoll beside a little yellow-brick cottage with a moss-shingled roof. They climbed out of the car and Mish and Meredith wandered inside while Barnaby unloaded the trunk.

For a minute or two they were alone in the cottage. Mish looked around the main room, making goofy faces over the dilapidated furnishings and dirty dishes, while Meredith sniffed the air.

"I think we should go," Mish said in a flat, robotic tone.

Meredith started. "Why?"

Without taking her eyes off her friend, Mish pointed at the butcher's block. On the block was a blood-splattered meat cleaver and four black-and-yellow king cans of Double Diamond—one standing, three squashed.

"So what?" Meredith shrugged.

"So what if he's a serial killer is what," Mish hissed. "Think about it. All the signs are here. Lives alone. Socially isolated. Has a predilection for murdering small animals—"

"He just happens to have outside interests, okay? It's called a hobby. Which is more than I can say for you."

"I have outside interests."

"Such as?"

"Such as—" Mish searched, twirling a piece of hair between her thumb and forefinger. "Shopping."

"That *so* doesn't count."

"Skiing."

"One trip to Whistler with an ex-boyfriend six winters ago? Come on."

Mish looked at the ceiling and bit her lip. "I read."

"Being able to read is different from actually reading."

Mish opened her mouth.

"And magazines don't count."

She closed it.

"Well, I give him points for the family spread," said Mish. "I just wish you were dating his brother instead."

"Mish, could you please not—"

Barnaby walked in carrying their bags and a few paper grocery bags and caught Meredith mid-hiss.

"Am I interrupting?" he asked, setting down their duffle bags and the groceries and removing a can of beer.

"Of course not," Mish chirped.

Meredith shot her a poison look.

"We were just saying what a lovely place you have here. When exactly was it built?"

"The main cottage was constructed in the mid-1700s, and then the kitchen and bathroom were added

184

on about a century later. I'm afraid it's rather a mess."
He reached down and tried to push a bit of polyester
stuffing back into a slash in the sofa cushion, but it
kept popping out the other side. Finally he gave up
and walked over to the stove.

"Would you like a cup of tea?"

Mish and Meredith accepted, and once they had
drunk it, Barnaby showed them to their separate rooms.

When she was alone Meredith lay down on her
thin army-issue cot and looked around. The room was
bare but bright, and sparsely furnished in the way she
had always imagined a room in a Swiss sanatorium
would be. Apart from the bed, the only furniture was
a rickety wooden dresser and an oval-shaped mirror,
glass permanently fogged with age. On top of the
dresser was a curious thing: a yellowed bone inside a
glass jar with a cork in the top.

There was a soft knock.

"Yes?" Meredith said, without moving from the
bed.

Barnaby pushed open the door. He'd changed
his jacket for a muddy brown oilskin, and a leather
sack hung from his hip in a Robin Hoodish manner.
Seeing Meredith on the bed, he began to stutter.

"I—I was wondering if—that is, if you're not
already—" He paused and quickly rubbed a hand
over his face. "Perhaps you'd rather just nap. So sorry
to have bothered you." He began to withdraw from the
doorway and pull the door shut.

Meredith laughed and called him back.

"Wait a minute," she said. He let the door open a crack, so that now only his head was poking through.

"What's that?" She pointed to the bone in the jar.

"It's a ham bone."

"Why are you keeping a ham bone in a jar on the dresser of your guest bedroom?"

"It's *more* than a ham bone. It's a family heirloom. My grandfather found it on the front lawn during the war. It was dropped by a German bomber with a note attached mocking the 'starving English.'"

"How awful! Were they starving at the time? Your family?"

"Hardly. But they did have orphans sleeping on the tennis courts and an infirmary set up in one of the barns."

"That's nice of your grandfather."

"I suppose it was the least he could do." Barnaby shrugged. "Listen, I know your friend is having a nap, but I was just going out to see the birds, and seeing as you're awake I thought perhaps you'd . . ."

Meredith hopped off the bed. As she did, a shiny black nose pushed itself between Barnaby's legs and into the room.

"Portia, rude girl, get back." He squeezed the space between his legs shut and the dog snuffled back into the hall.

"I'd love to meet the birds. And your dog. Hey, pooch."

Barnaby stepped aside to reveal a squat black Lab with grey whiskers around her muzzle. The dog waddled into the room, wagging her tail so hard it made her entire body curl up one way and then the other like a sausage squirming in a frying pan.

"Portia's my flying retriever. More of a beggar than a retriever really, but she likes a walk, so I take her along."

"Would you take me?" Meredith dug her fingernails into the spot just above Portia's tail where dogs most love to be scratched. "I'm a talented fetcher and I take direction very well."

Barnaby nodded, beaming.

A little later, they were outside on the path. Barnaby reached out and took Meredith's hand. She had been in the middle of explaining to him the plot of the film she was working on and had just got to the part where the spinster pathologist is ravished by the inspector on the morgue table. Meredith lost track of what she was saying and trailed off, embarrassed. Barnaby stopped walking. They were standing just outside the aviary, so close Meredith could hear cooing from the pen. Rain was spitting and the wind was blowing, and Barnaby reached over to push Meredith's hair out of her eyes. He was leaning down to kiss her, when there was a noise from inside the pen that sounded to Meredith like a burping contest. *Brack! Brack!*

Barnaby laughed. He took her arm and guided her over to the first pen in the aviary, where two of the meanest-looking birds she had ever seen sat on wooden perches. Whatever dispute they had been having a moment before, they now abandoned, united in dark suspicion.

"Vultures always fight when they mate," said Barnaby, unlocking the door of the pen with a key he drew out of his battered leather hip bag. He reached in and pulled out a large handful of dead mice, and dropped the tiny bodies into an empty margarine container on the floor in the corner. The birds watched him with canny interest. Meredith found it hard to swallow.

"But I thought your birds were for hunting," Meredith said. "Don't vultures just eat dead things?"

"They are mainly scavengers, yes. But they're still lovely birds to breed and train. Falconry isn't only a blood sport, you know." He drew two slivers of steak out of his pouch and fed one to each of the vultures, who took their treats with greedy gulps. "Many people think of them as unpleasant, but they're actually rather beautiful once you get to know them." Barnaby reached out and stroked their blue-black feathers. "This is the female, Martha. And the male is George." Their heads were covered with matching bonnets of grey down, which gave them the appearance of stern pilgrims. They eyed first Barnaby and then Meredith, and then glanced at each other, nodding their hooked beaks and gathering their shawls around them.

In the next cage was an enormous bird Barnaby introduced as Waverly, a European eagle owl. Pale flotsam covered his body—as though he'd just flown through a cloud of ash—apparently part of the bird's annual moulting process. He had a queer, knowing face that rose from his body in a hump and he swivelled it all the way around to observe his visitors with insomniac eyes. Meredith made a clucking sound like the kind she had heard people produce when trying to soothe horses, and the owl widened his eyes and gave his wings a restrained half-flap that blew her bangs off her forehead. She raised her hand toward him and Waverly cracked his beak and hissed, wagging a grumpy black tongue.

"Don't mind him," said Barnaby, running a finger along the chicken wire and eliciting an emphatic *hoot* from the owl. "Waverly's been in a bad mood ever since I retired him from breeding last season."

"Too old?"

"No, no," Barnaby chuckled gently, keeping his eyes on the bird. "Too rough. Poor devil fractured the neck of his last pen-mate. Eagle owls are the largest of all British owls and Waverly here is quite powerful when he gets excited. Don't quite know your own strength, do you, old boy."

Meredith pushed her hands into her coat pockets and walked farther down the aviary.

In the corner pen at the end of the row was the peregrine. A brass plate screwed into the base of the cage bore the name HARRIET. Harriet seemed extremely serious and dressed up, like someone about to attend an important business dinner. Her chest was white and the feathers swept up, decorating her throat. Meredith admired her in silence.

"*Falco peregrinus minor*," said Barnaby, unlatching the cage door and stepping inside.

The hawk swooped from her perch with a swift double-flap and landed upon his gauntlet. She dug one claw into the leather and stamped with the other to steady herself. There was a magical tinkling sound when she moved. It came from the jingle bell attached to her fine yellow ankle by a leather strap, and from another bell sewn into her tail feathers. Glancing coolly at Meredith, the female smoothed her feathers back into place with a haughty backward shoulder roll, in profile, and looked at her master with a single black eye.

"Meredith, I would like you to meet Miss Harriet Helena Horatio Shakespeare the Fourth, Lady of Pear Cottage, and, thus far anyway, the single all-consuming love of my life."

He reached into his falconer's pouch, pulled out a dead chick and offered it to the peregrine. Harriet snapped off the fuzzy yellow head, pulling out several thin, spaghetti-like strands of tendons along with it, and then swallowed the rest of the body, bones and all, in three jerking gulps. Barnaby explained that her stomach would sort out all the bones and feathers from the flesh and a few hours later regurgitate a pellet containing all the undigestible materials. The idea was to get down as much food as she could before her competitors stole it.

"And day-old cockerels are Harriet's favourite—aren't they, darling?" Barnaby stroked the bird's back with his ungloved hand.

Meredith watched his fingers, fascinated, surprised at herself. "She's awfully hungry."

"Yes, virtually always. Especially if you fly them every day, which I try to with this one. There's no workout like it. For her, I mean." Barnaby reached into his bag again, and for a split second Meredith was afraid he was going to perform some terrible trick—a twisted magician pulling a dead rabbit from his top hat. Instead, he revealed a tiny leather hood with a tassel on top. With his free hand he pulled the hood over the bird's head so that her eyes were covered.

"Hoodwinked," said Barnaby, and he stepped out of the pen with the bird perched on his glove. Attached to her ankle was a short braided leather leash, which he wrapped around his arm. "Tricks her into thinking it's nighttime. That's where the term comes from, you know."

As Portia circled their legs, huffing with anticipation, Barnaby let them through the gate behind the barn and into the open country, or what he called "the quarry." Walking and brandishing the peregrine on his arm like he was some sort of ancient woodsman, he seemed more at ease than Meredith had seen him yet. She worried aloud that Mish (who was napping)

might wake up and not know where they were, but
Barnaby insisted they carry on. Mauve pouches were
gathering above the horizon, making the sky seem
unnaturally close to dark. Meredith looked at her
watch and was surprised to note that it was only four
o'clock in the afternoon.

As they walked the moor, climbing over the uneven
knobs of soft grey grass, a landslide of trivia poured
from Barnaby, and Meredith found herself wondering whether on a day-to-day basis he had much company—of the human variety at least.

"Peregrines like Harriet are the second-fastest birds
of prey in the world," he said, "the fastest being the
Gyrfalcon—latin name *Falco rusticolus*—which are
terribly expensive and nearly impossible to breed.
I saw one once while visiting my cousin in New
Mexico. Amazing creatures. But Harriet here is one
of the fastest birds in Britain. With the right wind
conditions, I reckon, she can get up to one hundred
and fifty kilos an hour."

"There, there, lovely," Barnaby soothed, running
two fingers down her tail feathers, before continuing.
"Peregrines are commonly known as the king—or in
Harriet's case, queen—of all raptors. Which, of course, is
another name for birds of prey—as well as being a bas-
ketball team in Toronto, or so I've noted on the Internet.
At any rate, the problem for most British falconers is that
in order to fly a peregrine properly, you need true open
country. And to that extent, I've been blessed."

They climbed up the slope to the edge of a cliff. A gentle incline of rubble and wild grass sloped down before them, opening onto a vast expanse of countryside. Only a few unkempt cedar hedgerows and crumbling fieldstones delineated one meadow from the next. It was like an oil painting you might find at a small-town art fair.

Near the horizon was a small stone cottage that Meredith would not even have noticed if not for its smoking chimney, which cast an interrogative yellow swirl in the sky above it. She wondered what portion of this tiny island Barnaby's family actually owned. One percent? (Something told her it would be rude to ask.) The amount of uninhabited countryside before her seemed impossible, particularly after the frenetic crush of London. For an agoraphobic moment she envied Harriet, who perched calmly on Barnaby's gloved thumb, safe in the dark shelter of her hood.

Without warning, Barnaby pulled off the bird's headgear. The bird flapped her wings twice and pushed off her master's glove, bearing down with her claws to gain momentum and then springing up. In a blink Harriet was airborne. The higher she rose, the less energy she appeared to use, resting on air currents that carried her up and up as though on a rising tide.

"Will she come back?"

"Of course. She's well trained."

"Who trained her?"

"I did, of course. It's an awful lot of work, but rather rewarding in the end. I have the time after all."

"So that's mainly what you do with your days?"

"Training the birds? No. I also feed them and breed them, which is like another job in itself. Well, not a *job* exactly. To tell you the truth I've never really had one of those, so I wouldn't know."

"Never?" Meredith asked. "That's amazing."

"Really?" Barnaby looked pleased, and then frowned. "Is that a good thing or a bad thing?"

Meredith shrugged. "Neither really. It's just unusual."

He stooped down slightly and kissed her on the mouth. His lips were thin, but dry and soft. He touched her waist and increased the pressure of his kiss. As their faces drew apart, she could feel Barnaby tilting his head up slightly to keep an eye on Harriet.

"We'd better tramp down the hill a bit, if you don't mind. She's moving east."

Once they got off the path, the terrain was harder going. He took her hand again as they climbed down the hill, guiding her over every fallen log and hole.

Meredith felt she could get used to this man, with his soft skin and old-fashioned manners. She looked at the back of the hand that held hers. Strong, full of blood. She felt her spine unfurling at its base.

Yes, she could get used to him. Not as a boy-friend, of course—but to his characteristics, genetically speaking.

"So you follow the bird—and then what?" The spitting rain had started to soak through Meredith's tweed coat (why had she not bought something waterproof instead?). Her knees ached. They had been out for over an hour.

"Eventually she spies something she wants for tea."

"Then she dive-bombs it."

"In a manner of speaking, yes. When she sees something tasty-looking in the grass—sometimes a rabbit, or a snake, or maybe a grouse—she swoops down and grabs it with her talons. If the prey isn't killed instantly by the speed of the stoop—that's what it's called when she, what did you call it?—when she 'dive-bombs' it—she has a special tooth on her beak called a tomial tooth, which she uses to break the neck of her quarry."

"Do you let her keep it?"

"God, no. What would be the point of training her to kill her own food? The point is for her to hunt down food for *us* and then we feed her, thus ensuring her dependence. They aren't stupid, these birds, and they're not particularly social animals either. Birds don't get attached the way dogs do." He glanced down at Portia, who flicked her tail from side to side and gazed back at him with dumbstruck love. "The thing is, it's not possible ever to entirely tame a raptor. You can only convince them, through training, that you are the best and most efficient food source around. Even then you're only appealing to their survival instinct."

Barnaby shaded his eyes from the glare, watching Harriet wing her way towards the crest of the hill and curve back again like a self-propelled boomerang.

"The main point is, no matter how devoted you are, a bird of prey will never love you back. She'll work for you, certainly. But there has to be something in it for her." Barnaby reached into his hip satchel and pulled out a furry swatch that looked to Meredith like a shred of fur coat. "Once she's caught something, then we chase her down and make the trade with this."

"What is that?"

"It's called a dummy-bunny. You wrap some raw beef inside when you call in the bird, and then take the quarry from her."

Meredith didn't think that sounded fair at all.

In the sky, Harriet began a leisurely loop back towards the slope they had just descended.

"That's odd."

"What?" Meredith wiped the damp from her eyes.

"She seems to be circling back to the field we just came from, which is unusual."

"Maybe she just wants to go home and have a hot bath before dinner," Meredith hinted, but Barnaby and Portia were already halfway up the hill, following the bird, which had flown out of sight. Meredith mucked along, cursing herself for not bringing rubber boots. Not that she owned any.

Harriet was still out of sight when they heard the scream.

"What the devil . . ." Barnaby gasped.

By the time they reached the crest of the hill, the shrieks had stopped and there was Mish, standing in the middle of the moor dressed in a long oilskin coat and knee-high leather riding boots, holding her head and moaning. Meredith, who had thought she was too exhausted to go on, broke into a sprint and ran ahead of Barnaby. When she got close enough she threw her arms around her friend.

"Are you okay?" she asked, prying Mish's hands away from her face and checking her eyes.

"I'm *fine*," Mish said in a manner that suggested she was anything but. "This insane bird appeared out of nowhere and stole my hat. I was just coming out to find you guys and I was wearing my new beaver hat I got at the January sale at Holt's in Montreal—*Aaah!*" She began flapping her hands around her head and whirling around. "Is it back? It's back?"

Meredith looked up but saw nothing but sky. By this time Barnaby had made it beside them. Portia greeted Mish with a push of her snout, but her efforts, or maybe something about the proximity of fur, only amplified Mish's hysteria. Meredith pulled the dog out of the way by her collar and tried to calm her friend down while explaining the situation to Barnaby.

"Extraordinary behaviour for a falcon," he said, pulling at his hair. "Certain larger owls—particularly the Great Horned and the Snowy—have been known to be aggressive to the point of attacking humans, but not—"

"Oh, will you shut the fuck up?" said Mish.

Meredith winced and continued to soothe her friend by stroking her back. She gave Barnaby a look as if to say, *Don't take it personally,* but he didn't see it. His head was thrown back, eyes searching the sky. Without looking down, he pulled from his pouch a fan of black feathers attached to a string, and whistled twice. Tossing the fan in the air, he swung it around, where it caught the breeze and sailed for a few moments like a small kite. Seeing the wings, Mish dove face-down into a patch of longer grass, covered her head with her hands and began screaming all over again.

"What the hell are you doing?" Meredith demanded. "Can't you see she's terrified?"

"Oh God, of course. Terribly sorry." Barnaby reeled in the feathers. "Magpie wings—to lure her back." He slipped them back into his bag, looking like a chastised dog.

Meredith looked down at Mish, who was now flat on the ground, her face pressed into a patch of wet heather.

"Perhaps it's best if you two go back and have a drink at the cottage," Barnaby said after a silence. "I'll call Harriet in and meet you there before we carry on to the main house for dinner. Again, I'm awfully sorry. This sort of thing never happens."

And with that he set off across the moors, leaving Mish and Meredith to return to the cottage on their own.

**

Two hours later Barnaby stood with his guests on the front step of Hawkpen Manor. At the third rap the door swung in with an anguished *creak*. Meredith shivered. Was it possible the door had opened itself? Before she could process the thought, a thin, formally dressed man with a receding widow's peak slipped out from behind the door and welcomed them in with a sweep of his hand.

"Master Barnaby," he said, taking in their damp clothes with an expression of unconcealed disdain.

"Didier," Barnaby said, pulling one can of Double Diamond off a plastic web and handing the man the remaining three.

Meredith raised her hand to be introduced and the Frenchman stepped back as though she had pulled a pistol on him. Then he sniffed the air and walked away without a word.

"Didier's our butler," said Barnaby. "He's French."

They were standing in an enormous foyer with wood-panelled walls and gleaming floors that reminded Meredith of a particularly grand government office. She fought the urge to take a number and wait for someone to stamp her form.

"Who was the architect?"

Barnaby shrugged, cracked open the can of beer and drank deeply. "I'll let my brother explain it all to you if you don't mind. He loves to bore new people with the history of the house, and I can never remember any of the relevant dates and architectural terms anyway."

Soon a pair of black high heels descended the staircase. Attached to them was an extremely pregnant woman wearing a smile so large and forced that Meredith was afraid her face might unhinge at the jaw.

"Darling!" She kissed Barnaby on each cheek but avoided touching his jacket, which was flecked with mud. The hostess then turned to Mish and Meredith. "How lovely you could come. I'm Chubby, Barnaby's sister-in-law. We so rarely have guests, this is such a treat. Now come into the drawing room and have a drink and then Nigel can take you on his tour. He absolutely lives to show off the house. It's appalling, really. You must stop him the minute you get bored. I'm afraid all we have is cream sherry for you ladies tonight—we're not really trendy vodka people—but the sherry *is* rather good."

Meredith was offered a seat beside Barnaby on a stiff-backed antique sofa covered in slippery upholstery. It was about the size and dimensions of the piece North Americans would call a loveseat, but there was nothing loving about the design. With back rests at opposite ends of the narrow seat, it ensured the bodies of its sitters were as far apart from each other as possible.

This was just as well, as Barnaby had fallen into a sulk upon entering the house. Meredith watched him suckle on his beer can, while Chubby interrogated Mish with the enthusiasm of a young police constable.

Judging by her hostess's interest level, Meredith could tell she assumed Mish was the one in whom Barnaby was interested, not herself. Maybe it was the mini-dress, she thought. Or the blond highlights ("buttery chunks," Mish called them). Either way, Meredith didn't mind. She was used to Mish getting more attention than she did. Not just from men, but from the world in general.

"So now, Trish," Chubby was saying, while pouring sherry from a cut-crystal decanter. It was the kind with a huge glass stopper, which Meredith had thought existed only in television adaptations of old murder mystery novels.

"Actually, it's Mish," she said, vanishing her sherry in one go.

"Oh gosh, terribly sorry. *Mish*. That's an interesting name, isn't it?"

"It's short for Michelle."

"Is your family French Canadian, then?"

"No. Just plain old Canadian Canadian. Jewish Canadian really."

"Really? I'd never have known you were Jewish." Chubby had an unnerving way of looking to the left and slightly above the head of whomever she was addressing.

"It's probably the nose job," said Mish. "I got it for my sixteenth birthday. Family tradition."

Barnaby doubled over and began to cough. Meredith pounded him on the back, even though she knew you weren't really supposed to. Across the room Chubby located a pair of large wrought-iron tongs.

"So tell me," Chubby went on, "what does your father do in Canada?"

"Mostly golf and fight with my mother. He's retired."

"And what did he do *before* retiring?" Chubby seemed to remember to smile and then forgot again just as quickly. She traded the tongs for a poker and began stabbing at the coals.

"He worked a lot. And golfed less. And fought with my mother."

Seeing she was getting nowhere, Chubby switched the line of questioning. "And so how do the two of you ladies know each other?"

"From school. We were both in the knitting club." Mish looked over and winked.

Meredith tensed. She could see the devil coming out in her friend.

"And what school was that?"

"Oh, just a school in Toronto—you wouldn't have heard of it."

"A public school?" Chubby gave up looking for whatever it was she wanted and began blowing into the fire to stoke the flames. It didn't do much good because she couldn't bend down properly.

"God, no," said Mish. "The public school system in Canada is terrible."

"Really?" Chubby righted herself and placed a hand at the small of her back.

"Oh, yes, total crap. Burgeoning class sizes, no extra-curricular activities, teachers who barely know how to read themselves. It's like crowd control."

"That's awful," said Chubby. "The English public school system is one of the only good things left in this country. That and the fact we still have our own currency—but who knows how long that will last with this EU nonsense. At this rate we won't have a monarchy in ten years. Organic lemons imported daily from Italy in every corner store? Not a problem. But the *Queen*? Ridiculous! It makes me miserable just to think of it. Now, Barnaby, would you please come over here and do something about the fire." She gave the face-splitting smile again. "We have central heating in the back wing where we spend most of our time, but I'm afraid my husband is dead set against it in the rest of the house. He's ridiculously old-fashioned in some ways. Well, speak of the devil."

Nigel Shakespeare appeared in a flying leap that landed him in the centre of the room on top of a large oriental rug that slid for a couple of feet before coming to a rest. Three Yorkshire terriers yipped at his ankles, and narrowly escaped being crushed beneath his dancing feet. "Hallo, foreign guests! Hallo, beautiful wife! Hallo, prodigal sib!" He went around the room shaking hands and telling everybody not to get up. The dogs, upon seeing Chubby, began yelping and squeaking and did a flea-circus performance of rolls and prances in exchange for handfuls of heart-shaped ginger snaps she pulled from a silver box on the mantel.

"Ooh, c'est très bien, mes petits poo-poo bijoux! Vous êtes très, très chouettes, n'est-ce pas? Maman vous aime, oui? Oui, oui, oui?"

When Nigel reached Barnaby he paused and ruffled his brother's hair. Barnaby neither flinched nor smiled; he stood stock-still like a wax figure of himself. "Marvellous to see you, old chap. Well then, how are the birds holding up?"

"Fine. Well, actually today there were some problems—"

But before Barnaby could finish, Nigel took Mish and Meredith each by the arm and proceeded to steer them towards the double doors. "I hope you don't mind if I steal your womenfolk for a tour of the house," he said. "It is so refreshing to have visitors. We so rarely do." And then, turning to Mish, he winked. "We've been busy restoring the frescoes in the ballroom and I was hoping I might have a dance."

Seeing the movement towards the door, the Yorkies abandoned their floor show and ran over to follow.

"Your dogs are so cute!" Mish loosened her arm from Nigel's grip, squatted down in her miniskirt and scooped up two of the terriers—one in each hand. The remaining creature began to whine pathetically.

Meredith, who wasn't keen on small dogs, bent down and picked it up. "What are their names?" she asked.

"John, Paul and George," Nigel said.

"What!" Mish laughed. "Why no Ringo?"

"I'm afraid only my wife can answer that particular question."

"Oh *God*," said Barnaby, who had clearly heard this particular tale before.

Chubby sighed as if under duress, then launched into the story. "When I was a small girl of six or seven, my oldest sister took me to London to meet the Beatles. It was my first trip to the city. She knew them through a cousin of ours who ran a famous gallery in Chelsea at the time. Anyway, we ended up back at the Savoy—where they were staying, of course—and . . . oh God, I remember it like it was yesterday." Chubby pressed a hand to her throat as her eyes fluttered to the ceiling.

"Go on," Mish prompted.

"You must understand I was a sheltered thing. Not at all like six-year-olds today."

"Her parents kept her locked up in the nursery with a German nanny," said Nigel, squeezing Meredith around the waist and pinching a bit of back fat between his thumb and fingers.

"Yes, they essentially did." Chubby took a slow sip of sherry.

Mish stamped her foot. "And then what?"

"I was eventually sent to boarding school. Then to Cambridge for art history."

"No, I mean with *the Beatles*."

"Oh right, the Beatles. Well, there we were at the Savoy, just the band and my sister and I, when

Nancy—my sister—announces to the entire room that she's a virgin."

"How old was she?" asked Mish.

Meredith kicked her sideways.

"Let's see." Chubby counted on her fingers. "If I was six, she would have been, oh, eighteen. She seemed a lifetime older than me at the time. I'm not sure what she was thinking, bringing me along. But anyway, after a few more drinks and whatnot, they all decided to draw straws. To decide—you know." Chubby opened her eyes very wide.

Nigel took over. "And guess who Nancy got?"

"Who?" Mish's whole head quivered.

"Ringo."

"No!"

Chubby lowered her head and shook it miserably. "The truth is . . . I don't really want to discuss it any further. It's too difficult."

Mish nodded.

"Well, that's enough of that," Nigel sang, clapping Mish and Meredith around the hips. "Come along, girls. Bring the dogs if you like. I want you to see what we've been doing to the maids' old quarters."

***

By the time they returned to the sitting room, the fire had gone out and Barnaby was sitting alone on the loveseat, his long legs stretched out and crossed at the ankles, chin on his chest, gently snoring. Meredith thought he looked like someone trying to sleep on an airplane. Chubby was nowhere to be seen.

Meredith sat down beside Barnaby and squeezed his arm.

Barnaby started. "I'm so sorry," he said.

The look on his face was so confused, Meredith felt the urge to pull him onto her lap and rock him back to sleep.

"No, no, it's fine. Nigel just took us on a tour of the house. You were only asleep for a little while. Not even an hour."

"Oh." Barnaby slumped, then pulled himself up and made a serious face. "I couldn't find Harriet. I called and called but she wouldn't come."

"She'll turn up."

"I hope so. It's highly unusual behaviour. I so rarely have guests. Certainly not women. I think she may have been jealous."

Meredith looked across the room to where Nigel was pouring Mish more sherry from the crystal decanter. "Surely birds don't get jealous," she said.

"I don't know." Barnaby motioned to Didier for another Double Diamond. "They might."

There was a commotion in the corridor, the double doors swung open and two little girls in white cotton nightgowns trotted into the room. The smaller child ran up and wrapped her arms around Barnaby's knees. A plastic comb was snared in her hair.

"Little Miss Titty," he said.

"Uncle Barnaby, I'm so glad you've come. Tatia pulls my hair so hard after my bath it makes me cry, even when I'm not at all sad." She lowered her voice and looked back at her older sister, who hung by the door looking bored. "And Petsy's been *beastly* all evening."

"Really?" said Barnaby, eyes widening. "Well, you know what you must do to older siblings who torment you?" And he bent down and began to whisper in the little girl's ear, sending her into shrieks of laughter—which stopped when a red-haired woman walked into the room hoisting a fat infant on her hip.

"Girls," she said, in a steely, East European accent. "Say hello to the guests."

Petsy and Titty had begun a reluctant but well-mannered round of limp handshaking when Chubby returned, looking like a tired work pony—all swollen belly, knobby knees and coarse, dry mane. She clopped across the room and placed her girth squarely between her husband and Mish, who was receiving an involved lecture on the history of the sixteenth-century Florentine door frames. Nigel's hand had been resting on Mish's upper arm, just inches from the side of her left breast, when his wife appeared. He let it flutter gradually to his trouser pocket, skimming the edge of Mish's buttock in the process.

"Darling," Chubby interrupted in a louder-than-necessary voice. "Dinner should be ready in a few minutes. Would you like to show the guests to the dining room?"

Nigel smiled at his wife. "Of course, my love."

The Yorkies reappeared from under one of the sofas, where they had been devouring a forgotten piece of lint-covered liver pâté. They began to yap furiously and pull at the hems of the girls' nightgowns. The children squealed in delight.

"Girls!" Chubby shouted, "How many times must I tell you—use your French when speaking to the dogs!"

Tatia held out the baby to be kissed while the other girls took turns saying good night to the adults. Petsy, the sullen older one (who looked about twenty-two but was actually eleven), seemed suddenly reluctant to go to bed. Having to make small talk with strangers was a bore, her expression said, but being sent to bed at nine-thirty on a Saturday night was downright humiliating.

"Mummy, do you mind if I take the dogs out for a walk around the garden before I go to bed? I think they might need to pee."

Chubby looked suspicious for a moment, then sighed. The late stages of pregnancy seemed to have pushed her beyond argument. "Just make sure you put your boots on and mind you don't get your nightgown wet." Petsy glowered and sauntered out of the room with John, Paul and George in tow.

Soon enough, dinner was served. The guests advanced to the dining room, a drafty, music-free chamber dominated by a blazing electric chandelier.

A woman in a starched apron distributed wedges of mysterious-looking game pie.

The table was a large walnut oval, polished to a reflective gloss. Meredith checked her lipstick while pretending to admire the china pattern. They were seated in an even spread around the table, so conversation had to be shouted, creating an echo off the ceiling. Apart from the blazing chandelier, the enormous walk-in fireplace, and the oil paintings of plump, unsmiling ancestors, Meredith was reminded of her loft back in Canada. Something about the cold rectangularity of the room. She reached for her napkin but found there wasn't one.

At the other end of the table, Chubby watched her husband talk to Mish. For a pregnant woman, Meredith noticed, she wasn't eating much.

"Your children are so polite," said Meredith, hoping her words wouldn't sound disingenuous (they weren't).

"Oh, thank you." Chubby seemed to soften a bit, took a sip of her wine. "I'm sorry you didn't really get to talk to them. Petsy's going through a snarky adolescent phase and Titty's so in love with Barnaby she can't bear to talk to anyone else when he's around."

"I thought they were sweet." She smiled at Chubby's tummy. "When are you due?"

"Any second now. Actually, not for a month. But it feels like any second."

"You must be an expert at it by now." Meredith shook her head, awed. "Four. I can't imagine."

"But that's just it. *Neither can I.*" Chubby fiddled with her earring and avoided looking down. "You think it's something you're going to *do*, and then in the end, it just sort of *happens* to you."

Meredith picked off a bit of gravy-soaked pastry with her fork and chewed it with her front teeth. It tasted like coat lining.

"Do you have any siblings?" asked Chubby.

"No, just me. My mother wasn't into being a mother."

"Ah." Chubby nodded deeply. "A careerist?"

"In a way. She was a poet. Still is, I guess."

"Ooh, really! I adore poetry. What's her name? Perhaps I know her."

"I'm sure you don't."

"Is she famous?"

"Not really. Her name's Irma Moore."

"Irma Moore! Of course. *Dirty Girls on Acid*, yes?"

"That's the one."

Chubby's jewellery began to jingle. "Why, Nigel!" she trilled across the table. "Did you know we have a daughter of a famous poet in our midst? Meredith is the daughter of Irma Moore."

Nigel removed his gaze from Mish. "Pardon me, darling, what was that?"

"You know Irma Moore? The famous poet?"

"Member at the Club, isn't she? Absolutely barking."

"What I was trying to *tell* you is that Meredith is her daughter."

"No!" Nigel narrowed his eyes as if he was seeing Meredith for the first time. "But you don't seem . . . anything like her. Are you absolutely *certain* she's your mother?"

"Oh, Nigel, don't be ridiculous. Of *course* she's sure. She does *look* like her." Chubby stood up, a process that involved much straining and hoisting. "I have one of her collections in my study and if I recall correctly, the author's photo looks just like you. It was taken in the sixties, of course, and her hair is bobbed just like yours. Except she's wearing something eccentric. An Indian sari?" She squinted at Meredith, who shrugged. "Your mother is *such* an original. I'll just ring Didier to pop over to the north wing and get it."

Chubby worked her way across the dining room and pressed the button on the wall beside the door frame, and just as she did, a loud, unmistakable *crack* of gunfire came from somewhere outside—but not far from—the house.

Barnaby, who had been silent for the entire meal, jumped up so quickly his chair flew backwards and narrowly missed smashing the glass door of the liquor cabinet.

"Do be careful, old chap," Nigel said in a shouty voice Meredith hadn't heard him use but she sensed it was close to his usual tone. He turned back to Mish. "That cabinet belonged to our cousin, the seventh Earl of Coventry—he brought it back from his honeymoon in Rome after marrying the daughter of Lord Pemberton.

Actually, speaking of Pemberton, did you know he was a great friend of Octavius Paisley, the cricketer?"

But before Nigel could take a breath and launch into the story, Barnaby shot from the room.

"What on earth do you suppose has gotten into him?" Chubby drawled, leaning back in her chair and rolling her head back and forth on her shoulders to release tension from her neck. "It's probably just some local schoolboys."

Nigel shrugged and returned to eating.

Then they heard the scream. A girl's. And then another shot.

Meredith rose from the table and rushed outside after Barnaby. The others followed.

The light from the sitting room flooded the topiary garden. And at the foot of a giant hedge in the shape of a chicken was Petsy, on her knees, her nightdress stained with something thick and dark. Barnaby was bent over, trying, it seemed, to get her to stand up.

"Paul is dead!" she wailed, yanking her arm away from her uncle and remaining on the ground. "That awful bird just dropped him on the ground!"

Barnaby stepped back. Meredith saw that Petsy was cupping a fuzzy bulk between her palms—the twitching body of a terrier.

"My God," said Chubby. But as she moved towards her daughter, there was another blast of gunfire, this time closer. The surviving terriers pranced in frantic little circles.

Barnaby sniffed the air. He charged over to a bush in the shape of a toadstool and pulled it aside to reveal Didier holding a shotgun high on his shoulder. The butler aimed and danced back on his feet.

"Move aside, *monsieur*," he said.

Just as Barnaby made a dive for his arm, Didier took aim and shot again. This time the noise was followed by a fluttering and a *thump*. Something had fallen out of the night sky. Barnaby walked over and sank to his knees. He sobbed once and went silent. The rest stood there struggling to grasp what had happened.

It was Chubby who broke the spell by wrenching the dead Yorkie from her daughter's hands. "Oh, for heaven's sake, darling, put poor Paul down, would you? You'll only dirty yourself more. You haven't been smoking, have you? You smell of smoke. Come inside. Didier is going to put away his gun and make us both hot toddies—aren't you, Didier?"

The butler blinked as if waking from a dream. He gave a small, deferential bow to no one in particular, handed the rifle over to Nigel and escorted Chubby and Petsy inside.

As soon as his wife and daughter had disappeared, Nigel turned to his brother, gun in hand.

"How many times have I told you those birds are a danger to everyone, including yourself? And now *look*." With his free hand Nigel gestured to the carnage on the gravel between the garden hedges. "Stop sniffling like a girl. If Father could see you now he'd . . ." Nigel paused and then finished his sentence with a disgusted guttural noise.

Mish tugged at Meredith's arm, indicating they should go back into the house, but Meredith stood still.

Barnaby lifted his head. His face was a coiled spring. At first Meredith was afraid he would scream. Nigel might shoot him if he did. Instead, Nigel walked over to his brother and held out the gun.

"What do you want me to do with that?"

"I expect you to go straight back to the aviary and promptly destroy and dispose of every last one of those blasted birds," Nigel directed. "After tonight, surely we can agree they're a danger to everyone. I simply won't allow it any longer."

"But—" Barnaby began in desperation but then stopped, defeated.

"Perhaps you could finally take up tennis," Nigel offered.

Barnaby got up and, as he did, grabbed Harriet's bleeding body by the throat. He snatched the rifle from Nigel and set off without a word, across the winding gravel path through the topiary garden towards Pear Cottage and the aviary.

Meredith followed, and when she finally caught up to Barnaby, he was sitting on a stump outside the aviary draining another tallboy. Beside him on the ground was a burning oil lamp. Without a word, he shoved over on the stump to give her room. She sat down beside him. He reached into his jacket pocket and offered her a can, which she took.

For a long time they sat and drank in silence. When Meredith began to shiver, Barnaby took off his blazer and wrapped it around her shoulders. She leaned her head on his arm.

"Shall we?" he asked perhaps five minutes later.

"What?"

He took her hand and they stood up. He began to walk toward the aviary, tugging her along behind him.

"Are you sure your brother meant it?" Now *she* was the one whining.

Meredith had never seen anything killed except in the movies and she had little desire to now. Why was he making her come with him? If only she could get away and run back to the cottage and find her earplugs and sateen sleeping mask . . . She tried to wrench her hand free but his grip only tightened around her wrist. He had put on his falconer's gauntlet, which made his grip inescapable.

He opened the door of the pen and stepped inside. When he raised his arm the owl swooped to meet him, eyes glittering like topaz in the dark.

"Well now, Waverly."

Barnaby laid the gun down on the floor of the pen and, grasping the leather leash attached to a bracelet on the bird's ankle, wrapped it around his arm twice. Then he stepped out of the pen. The owl was so large that while he was perched on Barnaby's arm his head stood higher than Meredith's.

"You take him," he said.

"I'm not taking him."

Barnaby shifted the owl over to his left arm, pulled off his glove and gauntlet with his teeth and handed it to Meredith. She took the glove and slipped it over her cardigan sleeve. Barnaby instructed her to whistle, and she did, the only way she knew how: feebly, through the tiny gap between her front teeth. The sound, though thin, seemed enough for Waverly, who with a great flapping leap transferred himself from Barnaby's arm to Meredith's and immediately began picking through her cardigan pockets for dead mice. Holding the bird, heavy on her arm and yet somehow floating in air at the same time, was like lifting a person under water.

"Now what?"

"This way."

Barnaby wrapped the leash around her bird arm, then took her free hand and led her away from the aviary. They stopped in the middle of the yard. From inside the house Portia gave a warning bark. Barnaby held the oil lamp above his head and stepped back. The lamp was swinging back and forth, and when the light fell on his face she saw his eyes were blazing. He made a call— a strange throaty *hoot*. Waverly took off, shaking himself free of the gauntlet and causing Meredith to stumble backwards. The bird was swallowed by darkness.

"Aren't you going to call him back?"

"No," said Barnaby.

For the next quarter hour Meredith and Barnaby set about freeing the birds. Some, like the peregrines, needed little more than an open door, while others, like the vultures, had to be coaxed out of captivity. Meredith did not ask about their chances of survival, or if they would come back. She didn't want to hear the answer, and she was sure Barnaby didn't want to talk about it.

When they were finished, they both returned to the stump and sat down. Meredith looked at Barnaby and noticed he had a small blob of shit-coated owl down stuck to his left cheek. She licked her thumb and wiped it off.

As soon as she touched him, Barnaby began to kiss her. She was excited, but not by the kissing so much as by the way he took her in his arms. *Gathering me up*, she thought.

He made a sound of surprise.

"Are you okay?" she asked.

"Oh, yes, fine. It's just that you are so *amazing*."

Meredith climbed on his lap and they fooled around some more. Meredith, as always, simply wanted the making-out part to go on and on.

But Barnaby was already looking around for another place. The lights had gone back on in Pear Cottage, which meant that Mish had returned.

"Come along," Barnaby said, taking Meredith by the arm. He led her back towards the aviary and, to her surprise, into the one pen that had been empty from the start: Harriet's. He set the oil lamp on the floor and the space—you could not call it a room—became apparent in streaks of light. In the middle of the pen was a piece of wood erected as a perch, and at the top, Meredith noticed a smallish feathered body slung over one of the upper branches. Harriet. Meredith looked at Barnaby, attempting to conceal her horrified cringe with an expression of curiosity.

"Is that . . . ?"

"It was her favourite perch. . . ." his voice trailed off.

And then, before she could make a comforting noise, he gathered her up again and they resumed kissing. After a while he eased her down on the hay bale in the corner. When she winced, he told her not to worry, that he had just cleaned the pen that morning. She didn't believe him.

She reclined and pretended to be Claudette Colbert in *It Happened One Night*. If sex outdoors was romantic, why not sex in a birdcage?

Barnaby coughed. He seemed to be having a problem with her stockings, so she helped him along and while she did, he unbuttoned his pants.

And then, out of nowhere, Meredith was struck. *This isn't right*. It was the only thing she knew.

"Barnaby, wait. There's something I've been meaning to tell you."

He had taken off his glasses and his eyes looked small and vulnerable.

"Really?" He retrieved his glasses from his jacket pocket and slipped them back on.

"The thing is, I like you very much—I don't want you to think it's anything to do with that because it isn't. But at the same time, I feel I should tell you that I have another, you might say *parallel*, agenda."

Barnaby blinked. A sacrificial goat encountering an altar.

"Go on."

"The thing is, I'm thirty-five."

"Are you really?"

"Yes."

"Goodness. I thought you were a good deal younger. More like twenty-eight or twenty-nine. Not that it matters in the least."

"Thanks," she said. "Anyway, my age in and of itself is not the point. The point is that I'm at a stage in my life where I want to have a child."

"Oh, me too," he said, beginning to smile. "I adore children."

"No. I mean *now*. Or as soon as possible, at any rate. And—" She paused.

"And?"

"And, in addition to other things in my life, I'm searching for the right father."

Barnaby rocked back on the hay bale beside her. He touched his chin and looked up, then touched his chin again.

"But we've not even had one night together—and

what we've had has been rather tumultuous at that,"
he started, his brain apparently steaming with the
effort of cutting through the grog. "Don't you think—I
mean, don't you honestly think that even a discussion
of marriage is a bit premature?"

"I wasn't discussing marriage."

"Well . . ." Barnaby shrugged. "C'mon."

"C'mon what?"

"I reckon it's six of one and half a dozen of the other,
isn't it? Having a child together is having a child
together, wouldn't you agree?"

"Not at all. I was the product of a very unorthodox
alliance myself, so I can personally attest to that. What
I'm trying to say to you is that while I'm deeply interested in having a child, I'm not particularly interested
in marriage or even a long-term relationship."

Barnaby grimaced in confusion. "Are you asking
me to be the father of your baby?" he said finally.

"Not exactly."

"Then why are you telling me all this?"

"Because I thought it only fair that I tell you the
whole truth at this point in our . . . liaison."

"*Liaison?*" Barnaby returned to kissing her on the
neck, this time more aggressively, while he fumbled
with his boxer shorts.

She extended her arm to help but he waved her off
as though she were a house guest offering to perform
some menial household chore.

Just when Meredith was getting fed up, he collapsed,

but not in the way she'd expected (with a gurgle of pleasure into the crook of her neck). Instead, he slid off her and down the hay bale onto his knees, where, to Meredith's bafflement, he began to weep.

"I—I—It's no use," he stammered, the words bottlenecking in his throat.

"You're . . . crying?" She was irritated.

Barnaby began to sob and as he did she sat up and pulled down her dress, brushing the clingy bits of hay off her thighs and bum. She looked down at him where he knelt in front of the oil lamp, choking on his grief. She felt the way she imagined a cad does when a conquest blubs for her lost virginity. Sorry, but not too sorry.

"Look, Barnaby, I hope you don't think it's callous of me to say it, but you can always get another bird."

"Not if I want to stay here I can't," he wailed.

Meredith watched, horrified, as his body began to convulse. It reminded her of the dying Yorkie.

She stroked his back and resolved to check the train schedule before she went to bed.

13

"I'm just not sure it's such a good idea."

"Oh, don't be ridiculous, darling. Not to mention hypocritical. You've always complained that I never take any interest in your life and then as soon as I do you get all up in arms about it."

"What are you talking about? I never complain. Not about *that* anyway."

"Haven't you? I was sure you had at some point. At any rate, I don't usually. Take an interest in your life, that is. And the point is that now that I am, I think you really ought to be more accommodating. I am your mother."

"Yes. You certainly are."

"Oh, come now, my duck, don't be so difficult." Irma patted Meredith's knee and produced a small plate bearing a piece of toast and two oily sardines plucked from the tin. "See? I made you dinner."

Meredith took a bite of toast (she loathed canned fish, while her mother lived off it) and swiped the crumbs from her chin. "Don't you have any napkins in this apartment?"

"It's called a flat, darling. And I already told you, no napkins. Such a useless expense."

"Well, could I at least have my butter ration for this toast, or did you already use up all your food coupons?"

Irma reached into the fridge, scooped a bit of butter on the end of a spoon and handed it to Meredith. She stood before her daughter, eyes bright, hands in prayer position, like an expectant child.

"So?"

"So, what?"

"So, may I come visit you on your movie set?"

"I have conditions."

"Fantastic! I can't wait. A piece of cinematic history in the making. Imagine. Perhaps I'll finally get *discovered*." Irma patted her own cheek appreciatively and laughed while Meredith stared at her in silence.

"Don't you want to know my conditions?"

"Yes, of course, darling. I'm absolutely dying to know, can't you tell?"

"One. No bugging the director. He's busy and, besides that, he's my boss. Two. No talking to the actors. At all, whatsoever. Unless they talk to you first, in which case, keep it brief. Three. You're not wearing that thing."

Irma's hands flew to her throat in panic. She fondled her pendant—a petrified tarantula she'd picked up on a trip to Australia two decades ago. (She wore it whenever she wanted to attract attention, which meant she took it off only once a week to bathe.) "But, darling!"

"Absolutely not. Those are my conditions. Take 'em or leave 'em."

Irma sank down onto the sofa beside Meredith, pouting. Meredith resumed reading her copy of *American Cinematographer*. There was an interesting article about the innovative lighting techniques used in Godard's *Contempt*.

"All right, I agree," Irma said after a sullen pause. "But don't blame me if disaster strikes. It's my *protective amulet*, you know."

Meredith opened her mouth to answer, but then reconsidered and closed it again. There really was no point.

**

Early the next morning Meredith and Irma took the tube together all the way up to Kewkesbury Park. Meredith had implored her mother to be silent as she went over her notes for the upcoming day. Irma read the ads and hummed to herself maddeningly the entire way. Meredith wondered why Irma hadn't thought ahead and brought a book. For all her mother's literary accolades, Meredith had rarely, if ever, seen her concentrate long enough to read anything more than the cutlines in the social pages of *Tatler*.

And speaking of concentration, Meredith had to focus on this script or she was going to be completely behind once the day started. It promised to be a long one. They had four scenes to get through, one of which was a closed-set love scene between Swain and her co-star, a supple, young, semi-closeted gay actor from New Zealand who played the inspector. She wouldn't be surprised if they went into overtime, which could mean being on set for as long as sixteen hours straight. She hoped against hope her mother wasn't planning to hang around all day, but didn't say so. Meredith couldn't handle an argument this early in the morning.

On set, it was the usual post-weekend chaos. Grips and sound technicians charged back and forth carrying spools of wire, dollies and crane weights. Meredith took Irma by the arm and gave her a cursory tour. She was careful to point out every mechanical obstacle on the floor in case Irma tripped and fell and broke her hip or something (which, Meredith thought darkly, would be just like her). When they reached the monitor station and the big black folding chair with the word DIRECTOR stitched across the back, Irma stopped.

"Is this where you sit, Moo?"

"No, Mother, that's where the director sits. I would have thought that would be obvious."

Her mother's face froze and then fell as if smacked. Meredith felt a familiar hand squeezing her guts.

"Well, it is obvious. I only meant, isn't this *near* where you sit? Since, isn't it your job to sit with the director all day?"

"Yes, Mother, sorry. It is near where I sit." Her irritation softened into a feeling of embarrassed gratitude for

Irma's interest in her job. How surprising her mother would remember something like that. Especially when she hadn't remembered Meredith's ninth birthday . . . or her twelfth. Or her twenty-fourth.

"Listen, Mum, I'm going to take you over to the tea cart and get you a cup of tea, and then I have to meet with the director and go over the day's schedule. Do you think you'll be okay on your own for a bit?"

"Of course, dear. You know I'm famously independent."

***

"I don't care if he doesn't have a tri-band connection. My question is, where the hell is he? Do you hear me, Andrea? This is completely un-fuckingacceptable. He was supposed to *be* here by now, and now they're saying we start shooting the first scene in half an hour, which means—and I know you know what it means but let me vent anyway, would you?—Dr. Shellman says it's good to let my emotions surface—which means I'll be busy all day long and won't have a free second until tonight, by which time I'll be completely exhausted and need a drink. Did you manage to find any of that organic French vodka I asked for, by the way? That was at least three days ago, you know. . . . No, I told you, I read about it in *Harpers & Queen* not *Harper's Bazaar*. Of course I don't know what issue. Do you think I write down every fucking issue number of every fucking magazine I happen to read something in? Anyway that is not the point. The point is, I am flying the man over here at my own expense and he isn't here yet. Do you know if he even got on the plane in—where was he flying from again? Right. Well, at least there's *that*. Have you made sure the plane didn't crash? Or get rerouted? Or—I don't fucking know—hijacked? Could the plane have been hijacked? Have you made absolutely sure? Well then, how can you be sure? How can you not know? He was supposed to be here OVER TWO HOURS AGO."

As she reached the pinnacle of her tantrum Swain's voice snagged and cracked into a sob. The makeup girl buried her face in her hands as Swain—half dressed in bloomers, sports bra and a petticoat—collapsed into a flood of tears that sent her eyeliner streaming down her face. Mish took a box of Kleenex from the shelf and placed it on Swain's lap, but the actress shook her head and pushed it to the floor.

"Silk hankies," whispered the makeup girl, producing one from her pocket and handing it to Swain. "Better for dry skin."

Mish settled into restitching a bit of lace on the bottom of the petticoat. Now that Swain would need her makeup redone there seemed no point in hurrying. Swain had stopped crying and was speaking into her cell in a hushed, girlish voice.

"I know, I know. It's just these hormones. I think they're making me really . . . I don't know . . . something like that. And this movie. I just feel so *lonely* all the time. I just want to go back to L.A. and see Joel and Evie. I miss them so much. Are you sure we can't get around those silly quarantine rules? Yeah, I know. Oh, thanks. Oh, honey, you're *too* sweet. Do you really think so? Really? I mean really *really* really?" Swain glanced up at Mish and the makeup artist and frowned. "Look, hon, I've got to go. They want me on set soon and we have some fiddling to do. Okay, I will. I promise. 'Kay, bye."

***

Two hours later the crew was still setting up for the first shot. It was a night scene, so all the windows had to be draped from the outside. The lighting crew was moving a cherry picker around in the outside garden attempting to nail blackout blankets into the stone facade of the house. This upset the owner, who threatened to shut down production should another nail penetrate his ancestral masonry.

"As the custodian for the next generation, I must insist you stop that immediately," he implored the technicians, who shrugged at him mutely as if their headsets prevented them from communicating with anyone other than one another.

Eventually, the crew were forced instead to take down the blankets and tape black plastic garbage bags over the windows. By this time the cherry picker was stuck in the mud and had to be towed out with the help of a van, which caused the old man to begin howling again, this time in defence of his historic perennial beds. Luckily Richard Glass was as smooth as his name. Within moments of chatting at the tea cart, the poor old earl was soothed.

"That fellow certainly has a way with people, doesn't he?" Irma said, sipping her tea, looking at Richard.

Meredith shot her mother a withering glance that was meant as a silent indicator that she really ought to stop talking about the director immediately in case anyone overheard her.

"So what's the story, then? Is he single? What's his relationship history?"

"I have no idea, Mother. All I know is he directed a couple of BBC literary adaptations."

"Ooh, really? I love those. He didn't direct anything by Jane Austen, did he?"

"Not that I know of."

"*Prime Suspect*?"

"I'm pretty sure not."

"*Love in a Cold Climate*?"

"I don't know."

"*The Forsyte Saga*?"

Meredith turned to her mother in a state of irritated disbelief. "If you're trying to make me lose my mind at work, you're doing a good job."

"Well, darling, I was just trying to—"

Thankfully Mish whizzed over to where they were standing. Her arms were filled with half a dozen pairs of lace-up vintage boots.

"Can you believe none of them fit her properly? Apparently the Victorians didn't make half sizes."

"Michelle, darling, how marvellous to see you again!" Irma cried, kissing Mish on each cheek.

"And you as well, Irma. Meredith mentioned you might come for a visit. You're looking fabulous. *Love* the hat."

Irma put a hand to her cheek and smiled. Not for the first time, Meredith noted that flattery worked on her like beef jerky on a golden retriever.

"So did you get that e-mail from Elle?"

"About what? I haven't checked mine for a couple of days."

"Her little sister is getting married."

"Nicky? You're kidding. To whom?"

"Some doctor guy named Michael she met at Elle's tennis club."

"She actually met someone there?"

"I think she actually knew him vaguely from high school or something. Or Elle did—it wasn't clear from the e-mail. But anyway, the cool thing is they're having a really big wedding in Italy in July and we're both invited."

"That's cool. Where in Italy?"

"Not sure. Apparently his family has a holiday place but they're having it at a hotel in Florence. So now it's a challenge."

"How so?"

"For us to find hot dates by then."

Meredith snorted. "Speak for yourself. I'm not actually dating, remember?"

"Oh, right, you're more like . . . genes shopping."

"Exactly." Meredith smacked her lips in a wicked way. "You might even say I'm *looking for the perfect fit.*" This cracked them up so badly they failed to notice that Irma had slipped away. But before long Meredith felt a creeping anxiety, as though she had forgotten something, and swivelled her head around to see her mother standing half concealed behind a huge rack of lights, deep in conversation with (who else?) Richard Glass.

"Oh God. I'd better go separate them before she decides to show him her scorpion tattoo."

"Your mother has a tattoo? Wicked."

Meredith started over, but Mish grabbed the sleeve of her cardigan and tugged her back. "Oh, just leave them. She's *fine*. She's hilarious. You're way more bothered by her than anyone else is."

Meredith emitted a closed-mouth growl.

"Which is perfectly natural, since you're her daughter and it's your job to be insanely irritated by every single thing about her. Besides, I want to talk about this wedding thing. Do you think I should invite the key grip?"

Meredith reached for a baby carrot on the snack cart but then decided against it. She had read somewhere recently that baby carrots were made from the shaved-down innards of blackened, rotting full-sized carrots. It made sense. How could they all be the same shape like that? She took a broccoli floret instead.

"Depends. Where do you stand at this point? Has he asked you out?"

"No. But he rubbed against me in the lunch line," said Mish.

Meredith sniffed the broccoli. It smelled like vegan fart. "So see how it goes. And try not to fast-forward." Fast-forwarding was their private term for the dangerous habit of fantasizing futuristic relationship utopias with a person you'd just met.

"Who me? Fast-forward? It's not like I've picked out our china pattern or anything." She shrugged. "I've always preferred stoneware anyway. It's more modern."

Meredith stared at her with half-amused disapproval.

"Oh, don't *worry*. I'm not getting my hopes up. It's been so long since I had hopes, I doubt I'd have the muscle to raise them if I did." Her cell phone rang. She flipped it open and looked at the screen. "Her highness calls. I better get back to the wardrobe trailer and start cramming the wench into her corset," she said, and rushed off.

Meredith could not believe her mother was *still* talking to Richard. He leaned down and whispered something in her ear and they erupted into laughter. What on earth could they be on about? She hoped beyond hope it had nothing to do with her, though she probably needn't have worried. Her mother almost never spoke about her to other people. Half the time when she met new acquaintances of her mother's they seemed surprised to find she had a daughter at all.

While it provided Meredith with some relief to know her mother didn't spend hours fretting over the dormant state of her personal life (the way so many other mothers with unmarried daughters did), it also filled her with childish resentment. As in all matters concerning her mother, Meredith felt she was on the receiving end of far too much or not nearly enough. With Irma there simply was no in-between.

She sat down, uncapped her pen, opened up her continuity log and began revising the day's schedule to account for the delay. But before she could make a single note, she was interrupted by Richard.

"Meredith! Put down that binder and come over here for a moment and explain yourself. Why on earth didn't you tell me your mother was a famous poet?"

***

They'd offered to put him up somewhere fancier—price, the movie star's assistant had said, was not an issue—but he had requested Hazlitt's, a small hotel on Frith Street just off Soho Square. He liked its cockeyed charm, and he had chosen to stay here again because it was located in one of the only areas of the city he knew his way around.

London had always seemed an impossible tangle of roundabouts and hidden alleyways and he needed all the help he could get. At least, that's what he had tried to tell himself. But as soon as he had opened the heavy blue-painted door and spoken to the tiny Scottish girl at the front desk, the past had charged into the present, bellowing like an uninvited drunk. This is where they had stayed on their honeymoon. Before she died. Before all of it.

It seemed like a lifetime ago when he had made the reservation, but as the girl led him up the ancient staircase to his fourth-floor room—the very same room he had stayed in before—he was overwhelmed by how little had changed. He tipped the girl and closed the door. Not a seam on the upholstery was different. This was one of the things he loved about the English: their inherent understanding of the comforts of permanence. It appealed to his sentimental side, the part of him that wanted everything to stay the same forever and ever. But as he looked at the crooked little room with its lopsided floor and canopy bed, he was only reminded of how astonishingly his life had changed since the last time he stayed here.

He picked up the phone and dialed home. Voice-mail picked up. It was a new message recorded by Livvy in her most serious voice. "Hello. You have reached the Veil household. Please leave a message at the sound of the tone."

He left a short message for Livvy saying he missed her, and asking her to remind Katia, the occasional housekeeper, that the roofers would be coming by on Wednesday afternoon. Then he unlaced his shoes and sank down on the bed. Fatigue overwhelmed him and he lay back, feet still on the floor, remembering the last time he was in this room.

He had spent the day at a conference at a hotel in Earls Court while she had wandered the Tate alone. He imagined her now, walking from white room to white room staring apprehensively at the Warhols and the Bacons. For all her type-A perfectionism as a doctor, she had never been particularly independent and resented having to do even the smallest things alone, often appealing to him to accompany her to the corner store to buy milk. When they met back at the hotel at the end of the day to dress for dinner she was shirty with him, asking about his day in a voice that suggested she was interested in anything but. It was all so transparent and predictable. He found himself irritated by her insecurity and childish resentment, but resisted accusing her of any of these things and turned the subject around to *her* day instead. At first she was shruggish and quiet, but once they were out, with an open bottle of wine on the table, she relaxed and described to him the inside of the main room of the gallery—an industrial space so inconceivably huge, she said, it was like being *in* TV. And he loved her again—just like that.

It had always been that way between them: jagged, never easy, but rewarding all the same. Like hopping across an ever-widening river on a series of wobbly rocks. But that didn't seem quite right. He would have to think of a better metaphor. Maybe if he had time on this trip he would take a notebook to a restaurant and write for an afternoon. It had been ages since he'd written a word—about anything other than fertility-related issues, that is—and the thought of attempting it again filled him with a kind of queasy longing. All through his wife's illness he had promised himself that when she died he would start writing again for pleasure, but somehow that hadn't happened.

Here, in this very room, he and Debra had first begun trying for a baby. Other people might have thought of it as newlywed sex, but Debra was far too pragmatic for that. Everything with her was an efficient means to a desired result. But making a baby, they soon found out, was not as easy or straightforward as other tangible, attainable things in life. When things did not transpire as planned in the first year of marriage, there were clinics to be visited and tests to be taken. At first Debra was convinced the problem was her own, and while Joe decried this suggestion out loud, privately he agreed. She hungered for a baby so badly, it seemed impossible that her state of wanting would ever end. Somehow her fears and frantic desire had conspired to make her infertile.

What a surprise it was, then, to find out the problem lay with him. A twenty-seven-year-old man (Debra was a few years older), just embarking on his graduate studies with a new wife, and yet he couldn't perform this most basic of marital chores. Something in the combination of them both proved toxic. Her womb, they had been told at the time, was a "hostile environment" for his sluggish sperm. The exact cause could not be determined, the doctors said. The only certainty seemed that pregnancy was impossible. He quit social smoking, beer and red meat, but after months of trying, nothing gave. He was, as they say, shooting blanks, a jaffa orange—for all intents and biological purposes, more gelding than stallion. Ashamed that he was unable to give his wife what she wanted so terribly, Joe agreed to adoption as soon as they could afford it.

A year and twenty thousand dollars of her parents' money later, they were flying home from Cambodia with Livvy, a serene, black-eyed Buddha of a baby. That was eighteen years ago. In the fall she would enter university and major in literature. It seemed incredible to Joe that he and Debra—two head-down scientists— could have raised such an artsy, free-spirited girl. All he could do now was offer guidance and refuge.

It was Livvy who had inspired Joe in choosing his specialty. While Debra was on maternity leave, Joe changed his major from oncology to fertility. If he couldn't get his own wife pregnant, the least he could do was help some other women achieve the pregnancies they so desperately desired.

What a bitter irony it had been when cancer killed Debra a decade and a half later. At the time he had felt like a failure not only as a husband, but as a doctor. But rather than sending him into a downward spiral, this blackness spurred him forward. When Debra died, Joe did the opposite of fall apart. Instead, he became a super-functioning baby-maker and miracle worker. He submerged himself in other work—research, papers, lectures, conferences, book contracts, office hours and a doubled patient load— and in the midst of it barely found time to spend an hour with Livvy (by this point an emotionally remote adolescent) in the evening before returning to the office. His life felt full to bursting and yet at the same time devoid of meaning. The thought of taking on another project seemed impossible. All his friends had expected him to collapse for a time after Debra died—that's what people were supposed to do after all, wasn't it? Retreat to the country and wound-lick for six months while keeping regular phone appointments with a psychologist who implored one to "not be afraid to let it all out." Friends had offered their cottages and Hawaiian time-shares, presuming that what he needed was an escape. But instead, he'd stayed in Toronto, in the same semi-detached Victorian in Parkdale they had bought with help from Debra's parents the year Livvy arrived. He had thrown himself into his research—something he had always been somewhat ambivalent about before, preferring instead the humane routine of the clinic.

But no more. The publication of *Baby Love* had catapulted him into a new strata. He was now part celebrity, part doctor, a role his agent described as "medical pundit." He cringed every time he heard the term.

Kathleen Swain was his first celebrity patient. Her personal assistant had been cagey about Swain's age on the phone, and he would have to get to the bottom of that mystery if they were going to proceed. The thought of this impending conversation made his stomach sink. He was due to meet her on the set of her movie at some point today and he had no idea how to get there. He reached into his pocket and pulled out a piece of paper with the name "Kooksbury Park" scrawled on it and a cell-phone number for Andrea, the cagey-yet-aggressive personal assistant. He was supposed to call her the moment he got in, so she could send someone to pick him up. He would call—but after he'd had a bath and a quick shave. In the meantime he thought he might close his eyes, just for a few minutes.

***

It was entirely predictable and yet Meredith could hardly believe it. Mish had taken Irma back to Wardrobe and was having her fitted and made up for a dinner party scene scheduled to be shot later in the afternoon. It was the climax of the second act and required a dozen or so extras to play small roles as guests. Meredith should have seen it coming. Richard had been bitching to the casting director for weeks now that the people coming in to read were too blandly attractive. "They don't look like *people*," Meredith had heard him complaining into his mobile phone earlier in the week. "They look like *actors*."

Irma Moore, apparently, did not look like an actor. She had *character*. She was a *delightful eccentric*. Just the sort of person everyone wants to have around, but no one wants to live with—let alone have for a mother. While Meredith had to concede her mother certainly didn't look like an actor, she also found it difficult to see her as entirely human. As she twirled her way toward the tea cart where Meredith sat on a folding chair quintuple-checking her script notes and waiting for the next set-up, Irma Moore in her Victorian layer skirts looked adorable—to everyone except her daughter. In Meredith's eyes she was a five-foot-two-inch velvet-swathed gorgon.

"Well, darling, what do you think?"

"S'fine." Meredith opened her eyes as wide as she could and nodded twice before dropping her face into her notes again.

"Don't tell me you're angry."

Meredith flipped a page and made a note reminding herself to speak to the props mistress about who would be filling the wine glasses for the party scene. It was imperative the liquid level remain consistent with the timeline. The axis must be consistent. She would have to speak to the director of photography.

"I couldn't very well say no, could I?"

Perhaps she could convince one of the production assistants to help her measure the liquid in each glass to make sure.

"Well, if you're going to be childish and refuse to speak to me, I'll just leave, then."

And she mustn't forget to call Ralph and tell him the lab would be printing off an extra take of the strangulation scene for Richard to watch in rushes. Where *was* her pocket-sized tape measure anyway?

"My makeup call is in a few minutes. I guess I should go, then."

Finally.

Meredith exhaled and watched her mother retreat, her bustle bouncing along behind her. *Maybe I'm being ridiculous*, she thought. *But at least I come by it naturally.*

***

A pelting ring tore Joe from his nap.

"Hello?" Years of being on call had trained him to answer the phone no matter how tired, disoriented or otherwise unconversational he might feel.

"*There* you are." The flat Californian squawk of the movie star's assistant. "What happened? We thought maybe your flight was hijacked or something."

Joe made a noise to explain, but it was immediately apparent Andrea Braxton wasn't the sort of person to waste her time listening to explanations.

"Okay, so here's the deal. We're sending around a

driver to pick you up right away. Kathleen finishes shooting around eight or nine tonight, maybe later, depending how things go. They're doing a big dinner party scene today as well as a love scene, so things are going to be a bit frantic. But we might be able to fit you in between scenes. You never know. What she's interested in is having a consultation to find out what you could offer to a woman in her situation." She paused for breath, and Joe took the opportunity to jump in.

"Actually, that's what I'm trying to find out myself."

"Pardon me?" There was an underlying defensiveness to everything she said.

"What hasn't been made clear to me is exactly what Ms. Swain's situation is."

"Well, obviously she would like to have a baby."

"Yes, but why does she need my help? What I mean is, I don't know anything about her history."

"I'm sorry but you'll have to speak to her privately about that."

"Of course."

"Now, there are a few things you're going to need to know before you meet Kathleen. Some will seem quite obvious but I'm going to have to brief you on them anyway just to be on the safe side."

"Go ahead."

"First off, no questions about her personal life. Kathleen won't ask you about yours and you shouldn't ask about hers. If you do, you'll be on a plane back to Toronto faster than you can say 'O Canada.' Got it?"

Joe looked out the window and noticed a pigeon pecking at its wingpits. "Naturally I respect her privacy, but I feel compelled to point out that it will be somewhat difficult to have a fertility consultation with someone without discussing their personal life. She is aware of physician–patient privilege?"

"I'm sure you'll find a way around it. You seem like a tactful man."

"You've never met me."

"I saw you on *Oprah*." She paused. "Finally, it would be very considerate of you to avoid mentioning the Academy Award nomination list or the Oscars generally. And don't bring up anything to do with marriage, politics, astrology, Scientology, jazz, cats, plastic surgery or the stock market. And please refrain from wearing the colour green. Kathleen has an aversion to it, particularly the deeper shades, but if I were you, I'd just stay away from green altogether."

Joe made an affirmative noise.

"I trust you've made notes on all this."

"I have a pretty reliable memory."

She hung up without saying goodbye—just like a personal assistant in the movies.

Act 3, Scene 6, Take 14
Master angle towards dining room
door. Kitchen Maid enters. Pan her
walk X-L-R to head of the table where
Lord Beckinsdale sits at a table

full of dinner guests. Hold Full 4/
should over Kitchen Maid L-should to
3 seated at table: Inspector, Miss
Hornby, Dinner Guests as Kitchen Maid
moves down the table serving soup.
Tite/4: Lady Beckinsdale begins to
eat.

                    LADY BECKINSDALE
    Medicine. Such an unusual profes-
    sion for a woman. Tell us, Miss
    Hornby, however did you decide to
    go into it in the first place?
            DINNER GUEST 1 (OFF-CAMERA)
    Yes, do tell.

Tite/5: Miss Hornby swallows a spoon-
ful of soup.

                    CELIA
    Well, I was always interested in
    science. And at school—
            LADY BECKINSDALE
    Was your father a doctor as well?
                    CELIA
    Actually my parents are dead. I
    grew up in an orphanage.
            DINNER GUEST 2
    How appalling!

Richard was halfway across the set before he'd called "Cut!"

Meredith clicked her stopwatch and drew a line through her notes, indicating the end of the take. She made a note of the time and watched as Richard removed his headphones and headed for the long polished table where the Victorian dinner party guests sat frozen in place—hands in the air holding cut crystal mid-sip, soup spoons lifted to mouths. Six sets of widened eyes moved as they watched him approach. As the object of his attention became clear they relaxed, the women fiddling with their corsetry while the men scratched beneath false moustaches. He stopped at Dinner Guest 2 and whispered something in her ear.

Irma Moore giggled, gave his arm a gentle push and rolled her shoulders back into place. The other actors pretended not to eavesdrop, but from where she sat, Meredith could see they were straining to listen. Meredith noticed an extra set of headphones hanging on the director's armrest and she slipped them over her ears. She dropped her head behind the monitor, where she could watch her mother talking to the director in grainy black-and-white pixels.

". . . be silly, darling, I'm twice your age."

Soowishsoowishsoowish as Richard whispered something in Irma's ear.

Laughter.

"You are a vile, nasty, disgusting man, aren't . . ."

More laughter and a rustling sound.

"Are we going to do another take or not? I need to make a call." Swain's voice, but in her put-on English accent. Flawless as a BBC news reader's.

Richard said something indecipherable to Swain.

In the monitor Meredith watched her stand up halfway and sit down again.

Irma's voice: "I do have one little question. About my character's background. Is she an *educated* woman? I mean in the classical sense, not in the contemporary sense, because as we all know, a Victorian woman of her upbringing—" At this point she was cut off by Kathleen, who had dropped her accent.

"Listen, honey, I'm not sure who you think you are, but I'd like to finish this scene so I can make a very important call."

Meredith gripped the monitor, unable to believe what she was hearing. Through the headset, her mother sniffed.

"In fact, I think you know quite well who I am, dear," she said haughtily. "We met through our mutual friend Osmond Crouch many years ago. My name is Irma Moore."

Meredith watched her extend her hand, which Kathleen refused to take. "I'm surprised you don't recall."

Kathleen's "What the fuck" followed by the diabolical music of Irma's laughter.

Meredith couldn't make out the words. Then something clipped and loud from Richard. A clap of the hands and he turned to the camera operator, looking directly into Meredith's eyes through the monitor. Panic rippled through her chest and she tore off the headphones.

Richard cupped his hands like a loudspeaker and called out to the crew, "All right, everyone! Romans! Countrymen! Unwashed Masses! We're going again."

Meredith pulled her binder to her chest and resumed her industrious scribbling—actually a list of her favourite boys' names in alphabetical order: Augustus, Angus, Cassius, Clayton, Hugo, Henry, Johnathan, Magnus. For some reason she couldn't think of any past the middle of the alphabet. Girls' names were easier. Still, she was hoping for a boy. Even today, boys had easier lives. Meredith was nothing if not pragmatic.

"Your mother is an extraordinary performer," Richard said. He was sitting in his chair again, waiting for one of the lights to be readjusted.

"She keeps sipping her wine at different times on her line. It's going to ruin the scene."

Richard laughed. "Oh, you script girls. How can you stand yourselves? What's that irritating little rhyme you have?"

"Which one?"

"Oh, come on, surely you know it."

Meredith averted her eyes and shrugged.

"You *do* know it."

"Maybe."

"Oh, come on, how does it go? Go on, say it. For me?"

Meredith sighed. "When I ask you to match your action / Why do you refuse it? / What's the good of a close-up / If the cutter cannot use it?"

Richard threw his head back and howled. A couple of nearby crew guys joined in. Her throat tingled.

"Brilliant!"

"Well, it's *true*, you know," Meredith began. Her voice teetered and for a second she felt like she might cry.

"Of course! Of *course* it's absolutely true," Richard said between hiccups of laughter. "Yes, you're absolutely correct, my dear." When he had stopped laughing he looked at her carefully and smiled. "Tell me, are you and your mother actually related?"

"I hope not—"

The sound of shattering glass interrupted them. At first Meredith was relieved simply to have escaped Richard's patronizing scrutiny—until she looked at the set.

All the actors had scattered except for Irma and Kathleen Swain, who appeared to be frozen in a strange embrace at the far corner of the dining room table. Glancing at the monitor, Meredith noticed Swain's hands clutching her mother's hair and her mother's hands tugging at Swain's high lace collar. They remained in this awkward stance for endless seconds before Swain gave an impressive teenager-in-a-slasher-movie shriek and twisted Irma onto the table.

Irma retaliated with a low kick that sent Swain and her skirts stumbling back into the waiting arms of the gaffer, who restrained her from going in for more.

"Get your fucking hands off me, you cunting *fuck*!" Swain smacked the backs of her hands at the gaffer's face and shoulders, but he was strong enough to hold her in place.

Irma smoothed her costume and looked around for Richard. When he appeared, she smiled as though she had conjured him from a hat.

"What seems to be the problem, ladies?"

"Richard, I can explain—" Irma began.

"Crazy old bitch," Swain cried, unleashing a torrent of hysterical slander against Irma that ran unabated for several seconds, until her personal assistant appeared. "She thinks she knows me, but she doesn't. I want her *out now*."

As soon as she saw Andrea, Swain went limp. The gaffer released his grip on her arm but stayed close. Andrea reached into her tote bag and pulled out a bottle of Evian water and a white silk hankie. She unfolded the cloth to reveal a round blue pill, which she handed to Swain before fastidiously folding up the hankie and placing it back in her handbag. Watching her assistant's face intently, Swain opened her mouth and dropped the pill on her tongue. She took a sip of water and swallowed.

"Shall we take a break?" Richard asked no one in particular.

Meredith looked at her schedule and saw that it was nearly time for lunch anyway. She checked her stopwatch and made a note of the exact time, down to the quarter of the second. As she did this she noticed her hand shaking slightly. In the monitor she watched Richard put an arm around Swain and usher her out of the room. Irma turned and began to come toward the camera, walking out of the frame and into her daughter's field of vision.

"The woman is completely barking, you know," she said after a while. "I read about it in *HEAT*. Apparently she has a history of violence. She once assaulted a photographer. Or her bodyguard did. I forget. Anyway, I'm sorry if you're angry at me, darling. I suppose you think I've ruined everything like I always do, but I really didn't aim for things to turn out this way. Honestly. It's just that things like this always happen to me. Or *around* me, at any rate." Her hand fluttered to her throat where her spider usually hung.

Meredith slid her pencil into her pencil case and closed her script binder, smoothing the Velcro protector flap shut with the heel of her hand.

Irma continued. "I can't imagine what set her off. I was only trying to make polite conversation. These Hollywood types behave like mad royalty from six centuries ago. You should have seen her, darling. She just lunged at me. And for no *reason*. No reason at all." Irma patted her head where Swain had grabbed her hair. "Tell me, darling, am I missing a spot? It's still numb from where she yanked it and I'm afraid she's pulled a chunk out. At my age it won't grow back, you know. I'll have to resort to wearing wigs. Oh . . ." She pulled a wadded square of toilet paper from the lace cuff of her dress and began to dab at her eyes.

Meredith's gaze fell upon Richard's headphones. She felt as if she was turning a dial in her brain, switching her mother's garble from English to Swahili. She popped the headphones over her ears. Irma continued to lip sync her teary monologue of woe, oblivious to Meredith's dead ears.

Inside the headphones there was silence, and then she heard a crackle followed by a sniffle and Swain's tearful wobble, now devoid of English accent. Swain sounded almost out of range. Probably back in her trailer, raising hell. But as Meredith listened, she was surprised to hear that the actress sounded not angry but plaintive.

"How could she have known?"

Pause. Static.

"Well, *she* brought it up. She *knew*. Somehow. It was like she knew him. Knew about the whole thing. The role. The abortion. Everything."

Heaving noise followed by the sound of something being brushed aside.

"I don't know. The question is, why is she even here? I shouldn't have to deal with this shit, especially not today, like this, when I'm in the middle—" The air went dead.

She must have taken the microphone off.

Meredith realized her eyes had been closed, and when she opened them Irma was standing there, her mouth, astonishingly, still opening and shutting. Meredith kept the headphones on until Irma stopped speaking.

After Irma moved off, Meredith stayed behind, going over the day's shot descriptions. A few minutes later her phone rang. It was Mish.

"Her Impossibleness is having a meltdown."

"Tell me about it."

"She ripped apart her entire trailer before I could stop her and now I'm fucking stuck here trying to get organic fucking blueberry juice stains off an original Victorian undergarment."

"Oh God."

"Anyway, I don't want to talk about it anymore. How's your mum? I helped her pick out her costume. Adorable."

"That's . . . one way of putting it."

"What's wrong?"

"I feel like my head is about to pop off."

"Come see me. I'm in her trailer. She's gone off for some appointment with one of her team of travelling specialists. Probably getting a new chin or something. She won't be back for hours."

"Are you sure?"

"Totally. I'm mixing martinis."

"*Mish!*"

"Golly gee, Meredith, don't be such a prude. It's the old world. Everybody here drinks at lunch."

"I'll come but I can't drink."

"Great. I'm making yours extra dirty."

***

The door of Kathleen Swain's trailer was open. The reassuring sound of Mish's Top 40 radio emanated from inside. Anywhere in the world one could hear the same rotation of musical lollipops interspersed with traffic reports and jokes about the weather. Meredith stepped in and paused. The trailer was in even worse condition than the first day she'd seen it. Piles of clothes everywhere. Stray bottles of hair goop, moisturizer and random cosmetics products on the floor. The flip-up folding table, half torn from its hinges, hanging on the wall like a loose tooth about to give.

An enormous cloud of lace and crinolines gushed through the bathroom door, and in the centre of it was Mish.

"*There* you are. I was just soaking all this shit in soda water." She held up a purple-splotched garment. "It's completely useless. Hope Herr Direktor doesn't want to show her knickers in the sex scene or I'm screwed. Oh!" She dropped the clothes in a heap, remembering something. "Liquid lunch. Almost forgot."

"Mish—" Meredith began to object, but it was too late. Mish had already opened the travelling velvet-lined bar kit, poured several ounces of vodka into a stainless steel shaker, and was popping heart-shaped ice cubes out of a tray from the mini freezer.

"Don't you love my bar set? I got it in one of those junk stores on Portobello. It's so James Bond. All I need now is poison lipstick."

Her phone rang and she flipped it open with one hand, shaking the cocktails with the other.

"Yeah? Oh. Uh-huh." She lowered the shaker. "Mmm. No problem. Sure. I'll be right there. No, I obviously won't forget." She closed the phone. "That was Andrea-the-Lackey. Turns out her highness is now too stressed for her appointment and has decided to spend the afternoon getting body makeup done for the love scene instead. I have to go and glue a patch over her pussy."

Meredith laughed. "Have fun."

"*Man.*" Mish began gathering her things together. "And I was just about to get you in trouble too. Hang out here and have a drink if you want." She gave Meredith a smooch on the ear and ran out without shutting the door behind her.

Meredith was about to follow when she thought— why bother? The star's trailer was by far the most comfortable place on set, not to mention the safest hiding place from her mother. She reached into her bag and pulled out her book—a ragged copy of *The Portrait of a Lady* she'd borrowed from the bookshelf at Coleville Terrace—and flopped down on a pile of costumes.

She was only a few paragraphs in, when she heard a tentative knock at the door. A Bryan Adams song played on the radio. She briefly considered pretending not to be there.

"Hello?" she said.

"Hi," said a man's voice from behind the threshold. "I was looking for—ow!" He'd stepped in and banged his head, and was now wincing and rubbing his skull. She didn't see his face. Meredith looked down and pretended to be absorbed by her book.

"Low ceilings in these things . . . Meredith?"

She glanced up. "Oh my God. Dr. . . . ?"

"Veil. What on earth? I mean. How incredible. Really. What a . . . what a pleasant surprise."

She dropped her book on her lap without marking the page. An eerie composure overtook her. "Listen," she said. "I'm not sure why you're here, but now that you are, would you by any chance care for a martini?"

"Sure," said Joe, setting down his bag.

"Seriously. What are you doing here?"

"I'm working. This is what I do."

"You're an actor?" he asked.

"God, no. I'm a script supervisor. I do continuity. In films. What about you? Have you become an on-set medic?"

Joe laughed—a low huff—and fell silent.

Meredith leaned back, arching her back, and stretched her arms in the air. Thoughts passed through her mind like sticks whooshing down a river. Why was he here? What could it possibly mean? Did it have anything to do with her? Did any of these questions really matter? She was filled with a strange elation. One sip of lunch-hour vodka had infused the moment with an illicit thrill. The trailer seemed to cup them in a aluminum cradle, and after a few minutes of chat their coincidental meeting seemed the most natural thing in the world.

"Seriously. Why are you here?"

Joe hesitated, remembering the assistant's not-so-veiled threats. He prided himself on his discretion, but the vodka and jet lag were disarming.

"Can I tell you something in confidence?"

Meredith threw up her arms and lowered an invisible dome over their heads. "Cone of Silence," she said.

"I'm here to examine Kathleen Swain."

"Shut *up*." Meredith found herself leaning over and gently slapping his shoulder. "That is too weird."

"Tell me about it."

"She flew you over from Toronto just for an appointment?"

Joe nodded.

"You must be a big deal. Are you ready for another martini? There's some left in the shaker."

He hesitated. Looked at his watch. Shrugged. "Why not?"

"So how did she hear about you anyway?"

"I wrote a book. I was on *Oprah*."

Meredith asked Joe about his book. He answered her questions politely but didn't seem overly keen to talk about himself, so she returned to the subject of Swain.

"And now she wants you to knock her up."

"In a roundabout way, yes. I'm here to run some tests. How do you know that?"

"She told me. That she wants a baby, I mean. Seems like the underlying theme of the making of this movie."

"What's the movie about anyway?"

Meredith shrugged. "It's a murder mystery."

"Who did it?"

"Either the lord of the manor or the parlourmaid. Depends what the test audience decides. We're shooting two different endings. Is your drink cold enough?"

Joe nodded. "Do you have a trailer?"

"I wish!" Meredith laughed a little too loud. She opened the mini- fridge door and stuck a hand inside, searching for ice. "Didn't you notice the big gold star on the door?"

"I did."

"Trailers are for important people," she said.

"Are you calling yourself unimportant?"

Meredith stuck out her lower lip and nodded. "Pretty much."

"You seem more confident than that." Joe smiled.

"Not really," she said. "The next thing you're going to say is that I seem 'pulled together,'" she said, referring to their exchange in Toronto.

He laughed. "I know, you're actually a mess, right?"

"Exactly. Like an egg. Smooth on the outside, runny and goopy on the inside."

"And delicious fried in butter."

"Just like everything else."

They laughed, delighted with this shared bit of nonsense. *Eggs*, Meredith thought, *shut up about eggs*.

She waited a moment then asked him, "So why did you call me that time, anyway?"

"You mean after you ran out in the middle of your appointment?"

"Was there any other time?"

He shot her a knowing look. "I was worried about you," he said. "I was following up."

"Oh." Meredith deflated. Whatever she'd been fishing for, she hadn't found it.

"I also kept thinking about that thing you said," he added.

"What thing?"

"About me not seeming like the sort of person who would take a leap of faith."

"Oh," Meredith said, waving a hand, "you shouldn't have listened to that. I was just freaking out about other things. I don't even know you. It was presumptuous."

"Yes," he said, "it was."

She held up the shaker and tipped it towards his glass. There was a bit of rust near the spout.

"Will that give us tetanus?" she asked, draining the

rest of the vodka into his glass, sloshing a bit on the sleeve of his sweater. Cashmere, she noticed.

"Only if you suck on it for ten thousand years," he said. "But you should probably clean it off to be on the safe side."

Meredith looked at the rust mark. "I wonder if they have CLR here," she said, more to herself than out loud.

"I love that stuff," Joe said, taking the shaker and rubbing at the spout with his thumb. "It's amazing. It would definitely get this off."

"I know!" said Meredith. "I use it on everything—faucets, tiles, countertops."

"Have you tried soaking used flower vases in it?" he asked. "Like magic."

"Seriously? I hate those stains at the bottom. The ones you can't even reach with a scrub brush? They drive me nuts."

He nodded. "All you do is pour in some water and a little CLR and let it sit over night. In the morning—gone."

"What does the name stand for again?"

"Something Lime Rust," he said.

"Clean Lime Rust?"

He shook his head. "No, it's something else."

They were silent for a moment, sipping their drinks.

"Calcium!" Meredith jumped to her feet. "Calcium Lime Rust!"

"That's it!" Joe offered her the high five, and she did a little victory dance. Then he coughed, remembering himself.

He looked at his martini glass and back at her.

"Are you sure we should be doing this?"

"Doing what?"

"Drinking. In the middle of the day. In a movie star's trailer. On a film set. Where you are employed."

Meredith made a fake snoring sound. All of sudden she was sick to death of being the responsible one. After several moments of shameless enjoyment, she stood up and sauntered over to the trailer door, pulled it shut with a cowgirl wink. She thought of what Mish would say in this situation.

"Don't sweat it. Kathleen won't be back here for ages. She's getting her body makeup done."

"Body makeup?"

"For the nude scene."

"Riiight."

"So I guess she bailed on your appointment."

Joe shrugged and nodded at the same time. "Looks that way. Fine with me really. Just means I get to spend another day in London."

"How long are you here for?"

"Just a couple of days. I have to get back. My daughter."

"Right. Of course."

For a moment they sat in silence. They sipped their drinks and tried not to stare at each other. It was hard. He *was* handsome. But in a slightly outdated, unfashionable way, as though he should be wearing a soldier's uniform and kissing a girl with braids in a Norman Rockwell painting. It really was too bad about the ring. She checked his left hand. Still there.

"How old are you?" she asked, suddenly curious.

"Forty-six."

"When did you get married?"

"A while ago. But my wife—"

"Never mind about your wife," Meredith said. The last thing she wanted to hear listed were the virtues of the underaged gazelle she'd seen him with in the drugstore. She wished she hadn't brought the marriage thing up.

"My wife," Joe began again, but Meredith chopped her hand in the air.

"Enough about *her*—I want to hear about *you*. Where did you go to medical school?"

"University of Toronto. But I studied literature first and switched to medicine later. Listen, Meredith, I've been wanting to ask you ever since we spoke on the phone that day . . ."

"Uh-huh."

"Did you ever end up seeing another doctor?"

"Well no, not exactly. I came over here and started working and things have been pretty crazy since then."

"Crazy how? If you don't mind me asking."

"I don't mind you asking but I'm surprised that you'd be interested."

"Of course I'm *interested*." He leaned forward slightly. "I've thought about you."

"What did you think?"

"I wondered how you were."

"Were you worried? I mean, about my ovaries shrivelling up inside me?"

"Not like that, no."

"Well, I've been dating. I guess you could call it that. I've been looking for, you know, The One. But not in the romantic sense. More in the biological sense."

"Can you separate the two?"

"My mother did."

Joe smiled. "You'd know more about that than I would."

She felt a hot stab of resentment. The smugness of married people! He probably drives a BMW sedan with leather interior. His wife was a former hospital candystriper—some innocent society flower who grew up in the suburbs surrounded by plush carpets and protective parents and now spends her days doing pilates and taking Tuscan cooking courses. Probably has season tickets to the symphony and a time-share in Arizona. Probably they call each other some silly equal-opportunity pet name like Snooger Booger. What can people like this know about life?

Meredith felt indignant. How could he have any idea what it was like to be single for years and years and worry about growing middle-aged alone in a condo with exposed ductwork and no walls? What it was like to long for the company of a cat but resist getting one for fear of becoming a single woman with a cat? She drained her martini in a gulp.

Discovering a candle nub on a plate with a packet of matches, she lit the wick and set it on the floor between them. After a jittering start it flamed high. The smell of lilac and sulphur filled the trailer.

"Tell me, Doc, what's in your bag?"

Joe looked down at his battered antique doctor's bag, a gift from his late father-in-law, a retired obstetrician.

"Oh, you know. The usual tools of the trade — potions and lotions and a lot of frightening stainless steel devices."

"Because I was thinking . . ."

Joe raised an eyebrow. "You want to reschedule your appointment?"

"I want"— Meredith lowered her head, covered her face and spoke into the warm fleshy mask of her hands—"I have no idea what I want."

Meredith uncovered her face and, dropping her arms clumsily, managed to send Mish's travelling mini-bar clattering the linoleum.

"Oh shit." She crouched down and began clutching at half-melted ice cubes that skittered out of her fingers like beetles.

"Meredith." Joe managed to sound calm and deeply alarmed at the same time.

"Relax, it's nothing—" But before she could finish, Meredith understood. Her skirt had managed to skim

the top of the candle and catch fire. She began to
jump up and down like a mad pogo stick while Joe
swatted her bottom with a rolled-up newspaper.

"Water!" she screamed. "Stop, drop and roll!"

"No," said Joe. "Get it off." And with a single yank
he ripped off her skirt, leaving her naked except for
her underwear.

The fire died as soon as it hit the soaking linoleum
and the charred skirt lay smouldering on the floor
between them.

Before they could say a word everything in the
room changed: a whine of hinge, a shift of light and a
gust of damp outside air.

Richard Glass was in the trailer.

"Excuse me, sir," Joe said, as indignantly as he could
manage. "Can't you see we're occupied here?"

"Of course," Richard said with a chilling politeness.
"I'll give you two a moment to straighten up." He
turned around and stepped out of the trailer, shutting
the door firmly behind him.

"Oh *God*," Meredith groaned.

Joe handed her a petticoat to put on. "Not again,"
she whispered.

"You've done this before?" Joe seemed slightly
amused.

"No," she snapped. "I've been fired before."

Joe laughed. "No one would fire you for this."

"Don't count on it." Meredith struggled miserably
with her shoelace. "That was my boss." Her hands

were shaking. Joe noticed and put a hand on her shoulder. "It's a long story."

After a minute Richard stepped back into the trailer. He didn't knock, but simply came in and began inspecting the place. He lifted a martini glass to his nose, sniffed it once and set it down again. He picked up Meredith's novel, opened it to a random page and read a line or two, and then set it down again.

"Well, Miss Moore," he said. "It's been quite a day."

"Look, Richard. I'm sorry. I know this looks terrible, but let me explain." Try as she might, Meredith could not staunch the gush of useless clichés pouring from her mouth. "It just sort of happened. It was an accident really. We were talking and then the bar fell over and I tried to clean it up but my skirt lit on fire so Joe here pulled it off and that's when . . ." She paused to inhale. "I know it's a mess. Just give me another chance."

Richard raked his hands through his hair in raffish mock-consideration. "Another chance? Do you think soldiers get second chances on the battlefield? Movie making is war, Meredith, and I am the general. If you can't toe the line, I'm afraid you'll have to be court-martialled. This behaviour is entirely unacceptable. What if Kathleen had walked in on this? It's inexcusable. And after the way your mother . . . Well, let's just say I can't take any more risks on this set. I'm sorry."

Joe had been standing beside Meredith with one hand half raised in a helpless gesture of emotional support, but he broke in. "Now look here," he began.

Now look here? Meredith thought. *Who actually says that?*

"I don't know who you are or what you do here, but you should know a few things before you make any rash decisions. Meredith is a respectable and hardworking young woman and I am entirely to blame for what went on here today, which I am prepared to admit was entirely inappropriate, and for that I apologize."

Richard cocked his head at Joe and then turned to Meredith. "Your Dudley Do-Right here is very gallant, but would you please ask him to leave?"

"He's not my Dudley Do-Right—he's my *gynecologist.*"

"My deepest apologies. Allow me to rephrase." Richard swivelled around to face Joe. "Who the fuck are you and what are you doing on my set?"

Joe took a step towards Richard just as Kathleen entered the trailer. She was dressed in a Chinese robe and trailed by Andrea and a thin man holding a flattening iron. When she saw Joe her hand flew immediately to her hair.

"Doctor—you're here!" She looked at Richard and the toppled mini-bar and paused. "What's going on?" Her pupils seemed to shrink when she laid eyes on Meredith. "What is *she* doing here?" She turned to Richard and spoke through clenched teeth. "I thought this was a closed set."

Richard picked up the continuity log and handed it to Meredith. "Naturally we'll need you for the rest of the day," he said.

She looked at him, eyes dry. After a moment she tucked the binder under one arm and the hem of her petticoat under the other and left.

14

Meredith was halfway out of a nap when the buzzer rang at the flat on Coleville Terrace. The low-pitched static made her teeth tingle. It was five in the afternoon on a Saturday, but she barely stirred. One eyelid opened and she took in the room. A stream of dust-seasoned light poured in through the window. Her face was smushed into the pillow. She could feel the seam pressing into her cheek, making a shallow indent there. Again with the bell. Her mother must be out. Probably attending some committee meeting or other. Meredith was pleasantly surprised to notice she did not feel remotely guilty for being in bed. This must be what depression was like, and upon reflection she decided, it did not seem so bad.

After being fired from the Crouch picture, she had retreated into the guest room of her mother's flat, first in an effort to avoid her mother and then in an effort to avoid everything else. She watched her cell phone squawk and beep until eventually the battery ran dry. Her laptop, similarly, languished unopened in the corner. She hadn't bothered to check her e-mail in over a week.

For the first couple of days she was restless, occasionally getting up and eating some toast from the kitchen or wandering over to the small, high-set window and looking down at the street below, wondering about the people walking by on their way to work or to see friends. People carrying umbrellas and pushing strollers and looking so purposefully blasé that it made her long for bed and sleep. Now all curiosity about the outside world had drained away. She felt safe in her little room with its stained yellow wall.

Again the buzzer. Meredith imagined someone putting a finger to the button and leaning in hard. This was followed by a staccato series of buzzes, an atonal rendition of "Jingle Bells." Meredith kicked off her quilt and stumbled down the stairs towards the door. She did not think of brushing her hair or putting anything on over the washed-out flannel nightgown she had been wearing for the past week and a half. She did not want to see the person on the other side of the door. The sound was irritating her and she simply wanted to make it stop.

"Finally!" said Mish. Meredith struggled to haul the door open.

Mish was wearing a clear plastic raincoat with yellow polka dots and holding a long, dangerous-looking umbrella.

"It's sunny," said Meredith.

"No shit, Sherlock. I've figured out that dressing for rain is the only way to ensure nice weather in this perverse fricking place." She pushed past Meredith and into the dim, soup-scented hallway. "What floor are you on?"

Meredith ignored the question and led the way upstairs with zombie steps. She didn't bother to turn on the timer light. It always went off before she made it to the top anyway. Once inside the flat she returned to her room, lay down on the bed and pulled the covers up to her chin.

"I was napping."

"I can see that." Mish bounced on the corner of Meredith's bed. She looked around the room and wrinkled her nose as though remembering something unpleasant. Pulling a Kleenex from her handbag, Mish spat on it, reached into her shirt and wiped under her armpits. "Raincoats make me sweat."

Meredith attempted a smile and found her mouth wouldn't seem to go that way.

"But I love them anyway. Hey, remember my Strawberry Shortcake poncho in school? The blue one with Strawberry Shortcake and her dog on it. What was her dog's name again?"

Meredith thought for a moment. "Huckleberry Pie?"

"No, I think that was her boyfriend."

"She didn't have a boyfriend."

"Sure she did."

Meredith sank deeper into the mattress and blinked once to refocus her eyes. The small talk was a kind of test. Bait dangled to see if she was up for the bite. She and Mish had been over the topic of her childhood rain poncho before, of course. That was the nice thing about girlfriends—you could have the same conversations over and over again without anyone ever getting bored. A good girlfriend was like a TV channel featuring all your favourite reruns. But not today.

Mish left the room and returned a few moments later with two glasses of tap water. "Your ma's not exactly Martha Stewart, eh?"

Meredith hadn't bothered to apologize about the mess because she had stopped noticing it herself. She felt a distant twinge of shame and closed her eyes.

"The show's really boring without you," Mish said. "I have no one to talk to on set except Courtney, that makeup girl from Essex or Sussex or wherever. Remember her? Anyway, I went out on a hen night with a bunch of her friends last weekend in Covent Garden. That's what they call bridal showers here. Hen nights. Except instead of having sandwiches and spritzers at somebody's aunt's house they all go out to a nightclub wearing schoolgirl outfits and get completely tanked and flash their boobs and make out with strangers. Craziest girls I've ever hung out with in my life. I mean *I* felt demure around them. *Me*. Which is obviously saying a lot. They were like . . .

like . . ." Mish searched for words, then banged her fist down on Meredith's knee, which caused Meredith's funny bone to vibrate. "They were like Roman soldiers in Topshop halter dresses. I've never seen so much exposed back fat in my life."

Mish tossed her head back and honked. Meredith made a neutral humming noise.

"Okay, I'm sorry but that was really funny," Mish said. "I've been saving that up for you all week. You okay? I left like three hundred messages."

"Sorry." Meredith had let the covers slip down a bit and now propped herself up on a stuffed corduroy reading rest she had found in the closet the day before. She motioned to her prone body and shrugged.

"So you've just been lying around all day? Are you sick? Have you just given up?"

"More the latter, I think. Though I may have a sore throat. I'm not sure."

"You look super skinny. Have you been eating?"

"Sometimes. Look, Mish, please don't get on my back. I'm just totally exhausted. I can't even tell you." Meredith felt something inside her chest split open like a walnut in a nut cracker.

"Exhausted from *what*?"

"By my own brain. From being alone."

"I thought you weren't interested in relationships."

"I'm not. Not romantic ones anyway. I just want a baby—a little friend. I don't care about meeting someone," Meredith said. "I'm done with searching."

"What about Barnaby? He was good. I liked him. And his family's loaded."

"Barnaby is a very nice guy who also happens to be an alcoholic falconer. I'm not sure I want to tell my child his father was an alcoholic falconer," Meredith said. "And money is beside the point. I'm not looking for a husband. I don't even want a boyfriend."

"I don't know, Mere. He was pretty cute. Anyway, it's not like you have to live with him or anything. You just have to get him to knock you up." She thought for a moment and added, "He's tall too."

Meredith put a corner of the duvet in her mouth and gently began to suck. "That's true," she admitted.

"And he's got it bad for you."

Meredith shook her head to one side. She hated it when Mish exaggerated.

"I'm serious. He *does*. Have you talked to him?"

"No. Why?" Meredith lowered the duvet corner from her mouth. It was warm and damp and the material was much darker where she had sucked it.

"I ran into him at some pub in Fulham the other night and he said he was trying to reach you. He wanted to invite us to a dinner at the club tonight."

Meredith shrank under the comforter and groaned. "I don't know. I'm not really feeling . . ." The rest of her excuse was lost in the moist polycotton stuffing.

"Oh, come on, it'll be fun. It's time you got out. We could get our hair done first. Toni and Guy takes walk-ins."

"I'm unemployed and broke."

"I'll pay."

"I'm in a bad mood."

"I'll cheer you up."

"I don't feel like talking to people."

"I'll do the talking."

"I want to be alone, okay?"

"Actually, no, it's *not*. Because if you don't come out to dinner with me tonight I'm going to sit here at the end of your bed and irritate you all night. So you won't get a chance to be alone one way or the other."

Meredith looked at the ceiling and pressed her lips together. They were dry and flaking off in little papery scales. She picked off a bit and was about to put it in her mouth and nibble on it to see if she was salty from dehydration when she remembered Mish was there and flicked it somewhere down the bed.

"Fine, then."

***

Two hours later Meredith stood in the club draining a glass of champagne behind a velvet window drape. The people here, she knew, would call it a curtain, not a drape. She would call it a curtain too, but in her head she would think of it as a drape. There were other rules like that: couches were sofas, bathrooms were loos. The reuse of jam jars was frowned upon as was taking off your shoes in public or any overt obsession with household cleanliness. All of these things, Meredith had learned since arriving in London, were telltale signs of being middle-class and provincial. Meredith had never thought of herself as either, but now that she considered it, she supposed she was probably both. She had never really thought about class or religion or race at all, in fact, because no one in Toronto ever seemed to bring it up. She had been raised in an institution that protected her from this strange minefield of rights and wrongs that went far beyond social etiquette and became an encoded language based on tiny signals that indicated your entire background and even, in certain eyes, your life's worth. In London, it was as if the sum of everything you had ever done or experienced could be tallied and measured by the way you pronounced the word "vase."

She rubbed her throat, hoping to dissolve the mysterious lump that was threatening to cut off her air. The club bar was far more crowded than it had been the last time she'd come with her mother and Mish for dinner. There was some sort of book launch being held. A biography of an eighteenth-century duchess. Barnaby had left their names at the door but was nowhere to be seen. Within seconds of arriving Mish had disappeared into the back garden to smoke a joint with a group of journalists whom she seemed to know from somewhere.

The room was packed with people Meredith neither knew nor trusted. They all seemed to adore one another. The air was full of the premature applause of greetings: lips smacking cheeks and palms patting backs, squeals of exaggerated delight. A haze of Turkish tobacco hung above the crowd. Free champagne circulated on filigreed silver trays but did not make it anywhere near Meredith's hiding spot at the far side of the room near the garden window. Her glass was empty. Meredith peeked through the curtains and looked across the bar to where rows of flute glasses brimmed with fizz, lined up for the taking. It was a terrible whatchamacallit. A catch-22. She wanted one of those glasses badly, but she was not brave enough to walk through the chattering throng to get it. The only thing that would give her the courage to get another glass of champagne was another glass of champagne.

The party guests were either very young or very old, with no one in between. Closest to her was a long thin woman in her late teens or twenties with bulbous eyes set so far apart she looked like an exotic insect. Meredith recognized her as a model. She was listening to a grizzled count who had, many years ago, been narrowly acquitted of murdering his wife. "It's just for show really," he said, holding up an ivory walking stick. "I use it for beating women. They love it, of course." The model laughed and wriggled as if she was being pinched all over.

Meredith recalled there had once been a movie about the count. About the story of his trial. It had been released years ago, and in it he'd come off looking very guilty, but sexy and clever. Meredith wondered how the count felt about the movie. She wasn't the sort of person to ask him, but wished she was. The count leaned over and whispered something in the girl's ear. The model pushed two fingers inside the old man's vest, pulled out a heavy gold pocket watch on a chain and looked at it. They kissed on both cheeks three times, and separated.

With no one to spy on, Meredith found herself suddenly exposed to the room. It made her feel naked and jumpy, like being on the subway without a book to read. She inched her body out from behind the drapes. She had lost weight. The lightness made her feel like a paper-doll version of herself.

Why was she being such an invalid? Why shouldn't she just stride across the room and take a glass and drink it? But each time Meredith lifted her shoe to move it forward, her lungs threatened to collapse. Her mouth was dry and her windpipe stuck to the inside of itself every time she inhaled. There were two strange horizontal black bars at the top and bottom of her vision and they began to slide towards each other like a letterboxed film on a plasma-TV screen. She watched them dispassionately, wondering when they would meet and leave her in darkness. Perhaps she was going blind. She had forgotten about champagne by this point and now thought only of water. Water and a gulp of outside air. Something to lift the sand-bag from her chest. If only someone would open a window. Or bring her a chair to sit on. But before she could ask for any of these things, the room faded.

After that, blurred light and distant noises. A woman's panicky hoot. A hand behind her head and another beneath her knees. The herbacious smell of Marlborough Lights.

"I'm fine," she tried to say, but it did not seem to come out that way. She tried to sit up but the hands that were holding her gently pushed her back down. She had been placed, horizontal, on some sort of daybed. The kind of sofa that existed only in *New Yorker* cartoon shrink's offices. Meredith thought this was funny and wanted to say so, but when she tried to make words they turned to porridge in her mouth.

"Look at her face," someone said. "She's white as a sheet."

"More of a puce," said another voice. "Poor thing."

Soon a cool bottle was being pressed against her cheek.

"Here," said a voice.

She lifted her head and began to wretch. Several convulsing contractions, like a humiliating reverse labour, except she had eaten nothing, so nothing came out but an acid drizzle that burned her throat and made her tongue feel numb. She sensed people watching her and felt terribly ashamed. Why wouldn't they go away? Everyone but the hands that carried her here and the voice. The voice saying, "Darling. My poor darling." Somewhere far away but coming closer. She took a sip of water, a slow breath and opened her eyes.

"Meredith, my poor sweet," Barnaby said. One of his hands cupped her head and the other dabbed her chin with a hankerchief. "Shall I take you up to my room so you can lie down in private?"

"Yeth," she said.

And he scooped her up in his arms and carried her upstairs to bed. She was safe.

***

The next morning she woke to the sound of a vacuum cleaner. *Why?* she wondered. It was as if the EU had passed a law stating that all hotel hallways must vacuumed by nine a.m. or proprietors would be fined. She saw that she had been sleeping in a narrow single bed with a metal tube frame that reminded her of ones in an orphanage.

A rickety wooden dresser stood cowering in the corner. The top of it was covered with small change. Thick shiny pounds and burnished pence pulled from someone's pockets. A frayed shirt cuff struggled to flee the top drawer.

Meredith was still fully dressed. She searched the room with her eyes and found the shoes on the floor, arranged neatly together under the windowsill. At some point between her passing out and the open bar closing at the book launch, she recalled, it had been decided she should stay the night at the club. She remembered Mish coming into the room, wobbling with drink and gushing apologetically for abandoning her, and then her mother, who turned up at the party as well, asking her if she wanted to go, as the last tube was leaving shortly.

Meredith didn't recall speaking to her. These recollections were followed by a sleep so deep she felt as if she had emerged from it into another dimension of reality.

Meredith closed her eyes again and pulled the pilly flannel sheet under her nose. It occurred to her that she felt better than she had in many days. Must be the change of scenery. Something about her mother's flat was making her crazy and depressed. She would look into that. That and what she was going to do now that she had no job and no real reason to be here. Her money was running low, and she could not bear the thought of asking her mother for a penny. Soon she would have to return to Toronto and her hamster-cage condo. She thought of the stainless steel appliances, the way they picked up every fingerprint and smudge of cooking oil no matter how often she wiped them down, and shuddered. She realized she didn't want to go back. Not because of her empty condo, but because of her empty life.

The years after she'd graduated from school and begun working seemed to slide together in her mind, each one indistinguishable from the next. For a long period she and Mish had roomed together in a big ground-floor apartment on Shaw Street. Then Mish had moved out to be with her boyfriend (a manic-depressive tabla drummer named Ned). Meredith had tried other women roommates but they drove her up the wall in various minor, yet unignorable ways—one was a hummer, another talked at her through the bathroom door, and the last one came with a pissing cat—until she decided to forget it and just buy a place on her own. She didn't care where, really, as long as it was clean, affordable, and she could be alone and in peace. But mostly just alone.

There had been guys. Guys who took her out to movies and dinner and showed up with half-wilted tulips from the grocery store. Guys who stayed overnight and made her scrambled eggs in the morning (which she loathed). There was one guy who even took her home to Sudbury to meet his retired schoolteacher parents. But never anyone she would have considered sharing a home with, let alone a future. The roommate thing had put her off the idea of living with other people. Other people who didn't share her DNA anyway. Maybe it was the result of growing up an only child at boarding school, but Meredith had never been particularly inclined towards the idea of sharing her life. She wanted a baby, yes, but that was more of a continuation of existence rather than a concession. She wanted a whole new reality, rather than a merged one. A part of her, rather than a partner. It was, she realized with a chill, probably the same way her mother had once felt.

She wondered what time it was. There was no clock on the wall and she had left her watch at Coleville Terrace. Meredith began to sit up, and as she did there was a soft knock on the door.

"Just a minute," she said in a higher than normal voice, and she looked around for her clothes before remembering she had slept in them.

She kicked at the covers and tried to hop out of bed but her feet got caught in the sheets and in her struggle to rise she fell off the bed and onto the floor with a humiliating *thump* on her right bum cheek. She grunted and the door opened at the sound. Barnaby was standing behind it holding a tray with plates and a small vase with a bit of holly. His hair was sticking up and his eyes were showing a lot of white.

"Are you all right, then?" He placed the tray on the threshold and stepped over it to where Meredith lay, stiff beneath her sheets. "Oh, poor you," he said.

"I'm fine, I'm fine. This time I mean it."

Barnaby helped her up and she shook his hand off her arm once she was standing, the sheets in a white cotton puddle around her stocking-clad feet. He didn't seem to notice this rebuke and went straight for the tray, picking it up and holding it out in front of him with stiff toy-soldier arms. His eyes were glazed but expectant.

"I brought you some breakfast," he said. "I hope you don't mind the intrusion."

Why was he being so nice? There was a small black comb on the dresser and she wanted to pull it through her hair, but not in front of him. Meredith smoothed her dress flat and picked some bits of lint that had attached themselves to the material during the night. The room seemed far too small for the two of them. She suddenly had the feeling of being on a steamer ship, heading across the ocean for the first time. Imagine, she thought, living like this for weeks on end.

Barnaby showed no sign of leaving. He sat down on a small chair across from the bed and placed the tray on the bedside table. The reading lamp had to be moved to the floor to make room. Meredith stole a glance in the mirror above the dresser and noticed a ruddy lipstick smudge on her chin. She licked her thumb and tried to rub it off.

"Please sit," Barnaby said, indicating the unmade bed.

Meredith did and felt immediately more comfortable.

"I guess I ought to say thank you," she said. Then, feeling bad, she rephrased it. "What I meant to say is, thank you."

"Nonsense." Barnaby closed his eyes and shook his head, snorting a little through his nose. "I just gave you a place to stay. You seemed so . . . unwell."

"I guess I have been lately. It's staying with my mother, I think. And the movie and everything . . ." She trailed off, realizing she couldn't possibly explain the story of how she had been fired. Not that Barnaby would have asked her to. He never did anything intentionally to make her uncomfortable.

"Mish told me you decided to leave your job."

She shrugged and smiled a little, and his expression brightened in a way that made her feel apprehensive. "Thanks for letting me stay here," she said, letting her face drop into seriousness. "I'll pay you back for the room."

"*God*, no," he almost shouted, and then caught himself and leaned back slightly. "I insist."

"Are you sure?"

"Yes, yes. Really."

"Okay. I mean, if you insist." Meredith was secretly relieved. She had no cash with her and her credit card was nudging its limit. "Where did you sleep, then?"

"Oh, well." He shook his head dismissively as though the matter of where he slept was trivial. "The club manager was very accommodating."

"They gave you another room?"

"No, actually they were entirely booked. I slept on the sofa in the lounge."

"Oh God, Barnaby, I'm so sorry."

"Don't be. Really. For once I had a good excuse to close the place down. And it certainly isn't as though it's the first time I've ever spent the night on a pub sofa."

Meredith laughed, and Barnaby's eyes seemed to dart out of his head. They smiled at each other for a long moment and blood began to thump in her ears. She coughed and searched for an excuse to change the subject, or, more specifically, she sought to ward off whatever subject she sensed he was about to bring up.

"Did you find your birds?"

"The owl and the vulture came back, yes. They're actually quite tame and old, so I knew they would. But I fear two of the young falcons are gone for good."

"Will they be able to survive?"

"I should think so. Better than you or I. It's just the loss of the time. All the training gone to waste. Anyway, I shall be leaving Pear Cottage shortly, so they wouldn't have me to return to even if they did."

"Why?"

"Things with my brother have degenerated and I think it's time I found somewhere else to live, at least for a little while. I'll still have the cottage for holidays, of course, but living there all the time was becoming . . . untenable."

Meredith touched the back of his hand.

"I'm actually thinking of getting a job."

"Really?" She squeezed his fingers and hoped he did not find the gesture gushy.

"There's a falconry centre down the road in Gloucestershire. They've got hundreds of birds and they're always short on trainers and people to do flying demonstrations, so I thought I might . . . help out."

"Barnaby, that's great. I mean, it really is. You're changing your life. That's amazing."

Her hand was still on top of his and he surprised her by placing his other hand over hers and pressing down.

"Meredith, I've been thinking about what you said. About our talk that weekend. Specifically it made me think that I want different things from the things I thought I wanted before. Not that I thought I really wanted anything in particular. The point was I didn't really know. I had no idea. Until now, that is."

Meredith waited.

"I was wondering if you would ever consider coming to Gloucestershire with me. To live. I mean to—to live as my wife."

Meredith pulled her hand out from between his so fast she accidentally slapped herself. Words began to pour. "Wow. That is huge. I mean, that is such a big *thing* you just asked me. I really don't know what to say. Hmm."

He put a finger to her lips to make the words stop.

"It's just that I know you want to have a baby— which I think is wonderful by the way—and I thought that, well, given that my brother seems to be having such a difficult time producing a son, maybe if we were to . . ."

"But what about Chubby?" Meredith said, touching her stomach.

"She gave birth last Thursday to a girl," Barnaby said. "Penelope. But everyone's taken to calling her Pud."

"Barnaby, look," Meredith said after a pause. "I just want to have a baby. I wouldn't make a good wife."

"To me you would."

"I know myself pretty well and I'm telling you now. I wouldn't."

He smiled, then reached out and caught her hand again. "You don't understand. If we are to have a son, we must get married."

"Why do you assume it would be a boy?"

"Of course I don't know that it would be a boy but I should obviously hope—"

"Why? Don't you like girls?"

Barnaby laughed. "Of *course* I like girls. And I should like to have a dozen daughters after we marry and have a son."

"Why does it matter?"

"Because I *told* you—a legal heir can only be produced within the bonds of wedlock. I could leave you alone entirely. You could even have your own house if you wanted. Your own life. And I could have mine. I know it might seem unusual to you, but such arrangements are not as uncommon as you might think."

The room got much quieter after that. Meredith said something to the effect that she would think about it, and then tried to eat some of the breakfast Barnaby had brought up to her. The coddled eggs were slimy and the toast was hard. She took a few sips of lukewarm coffee mixed with some kind of milk formula and then reached for her bag. "Do you mind if I check my messages?" she said.

"Not at all." Barnaby picked up the paper.

There were four messages on her cell phone. One from Mish and the other three from her mother. Though it was the first time she had turned on the phone in over a week, the voice-mail informed her that several unheard messages had been deleted from her mailbox, which annoyed her. A bit like the postal office writing to tell you it lost a package.

Barnaby read the *Sunday Telegraph* as she cupped her phone to her ear and listened.

"Heya." It was Mish. "Hope you're feeling better. God, I am so sorry I made you go out last night. Please don't hold it against me, okay? Okay? Anyway, I thought I'd leave one more message just in case you were returning calls. Wacky news. Remember that guy Benedict? The German banker dude we had naked sushi with? Well, he invited me to his place in Munich. Or Frankfurt. One of those places where they drink beer from giant mugs and dance around in suede overalls. Anyway, do you think I should go? I mean, I barely know him. But I guess you went to Barnaby's for the weekend. And look how that turned out. Although I must say he was looking pretty cute last night. The way he caught you as you fell and then carried you out of the room like Clark Gable in *Gone With the Wind*. Okay I'm gonna go now. *Call me*. Bye."

A beeping sound, and then her mother's voice in a mechanical tone.

"Meredith, it's your mother. Call me back."

Beep. Irma again.

"Moo, it's Mum. I'm calling about . . ." A loud mechanical thrumming noise drowned her out for a moment. "Sorry, darling. That was just my friend Philip practising his didgeridoo. Now, what am I calling about? I know there was a reason—" The noise grew into a roar. "OH, WOULD YOU KNOCK IT OFF FOR TWO SECONDS. YOU'RE GIVING ME A HEADACHE." A pause and then Irma's voice resumed its normal chirp. "Oh, yes. I wanted to ask you how your head felt. I meant to say last night that you shouldn't go to sleep if you've hit your head. You might have a concussion and go into a coma. Though I suppose it's a little late for that now. Anyway, if you haven't yet gone to sleep, don't. And if you are in a coma, that's terrible. Comas can be awful. Philip knows because he spent four years in one. Of course that was drug related. Oh, darling, you *must* meet him. He's terribly talented. I met him at the book launch last night. I *do* think you would approve. Call me. It's your mother. Did I already say that?"

Beep. Irma again.

"Isn't that funny? I completely forgot the reason why I called you in the first place. It was about this letter that came addressed to you, of all people. It looks intriguing. Philip and I both think you ought to open it as soon as possible. I wanted to open it but Philip said no. Wasn't that proper of him? Anyway, if you don't come home for it soon, curiosity may overcome my resolve. Bye, duck." *Click.*

Meredith looked at Barnaby, who had folded the paper into eighths, just like one of the old men in three-piece suits she saw travelling to work every day on the tube. It must be a skill particular to English men. The women never seemed to do it. He was completely absorbed in a column written by a well-known Tory pundit known for his ruminations on such topics as why-the-London-transport-poses-a-threat-to-the-city's-septic-management. How fascinated he seemed, when just a few moments ago he had been proposing his "arrangement" to her. She wasn't sure whether he thought she had turned him down or left it at maybe. None of it seemed clear.

She looked at Barnaby with his sandbox hair and his moth-eaten sweater (undoubtedly his father's) and she thought that maybe life with him would not be all that bad. And then for the squillionth time since she'd arrived in London, Meredith wished there was a book of rules on what to do depending on how you felt and where you were. She wished she could look up "Correct response to proposal from sweet but bumbling alcoholic falconers" on an index and follow the directions there.

As it was, she was on her own.

There were no seats on the train at Pisa, so Meredith sat on her suitcase in the aisle. Shortly after the train began jerking towards Florence, a man in a fitted blue uniform approached and said something disapproving in Italian. He pointed to the vestibule between the cars. She over-pronounced an apology and began to move, pulling her suitcase through the aisle behind her. It ricocheted off the seats on either side in a series of humiliating thuds. The other passengers yanked away their arms and legs as she passed, making their resentment apparent. There was no air conditioning on the train and people seemed to be allowed to smoke wherever they liked. Meredith could feel pin-pricks of sweat beneath her sweater. She wondered if she smelled bad.

The folding jump-seats were taken, so she pulled her suitcase to the centre of the space and sat down on top of it. Several men were standing around, all of them smoking or talking into cell phones or both. They looked at her through mirrored lenses. She could feel their eyes examining each breast and buttock with the critical judgment of a greengrocer. Meredith scrunched her knees to her chest and prayed silently that her moisturizer wouldn't explode inside her bag and stain all her clothes. She hardly had anything to wear as it was.

In a way, the invitation couldn't have come at a better time. There had been no question of her *not* going. Passing up the chance to attend a dinner at Osmond Crouch's villa was unthinkable. "Like a nun bailing on an audience with the Pope," her mother had said when she expressed her ambivalence about the prospect of travelling to Italy for a dinner party. The mysterious thing was why he had asked her in the first place. The invitation, Irma said, had been delivered by a uniformed man in a chauffeur-driven car. It came in an oversized envelope made of thick creamy paper that smelled as crisp and metallic as money and was sealed with a blob of red wax and stamped with the image of two stags, their antlers interlocked. *Miss Meredith Moore*, it said on the outside in bold, blue fountain pen. Inside was printed a date, time and address and nothing more. *The 21st of June at 19:00 hrs. Vogrie, Fiesole.* And then in the same fountain pen at the bottom, the words, *Meredith, Do come.* Followed by an illegible squiggle—the signature of a person who spent a lot of time signing things. If it hadn't been for her mother's interpreting powers, Meredith wouldn't have had a clue what the invitation was for.

She had to fold the invitation twice to fit it in her handbag.

Meredith was nervous, but Mish said she had a professional obligation to attend. Not that Meredith was actually a professional anything anymore. As a freelancer she'd long ago grown used to never knowing where her next paycheque might come from. "Who knows?" she used to laugh. "I may never work again!" But the thought of unemployment was no longer a dark joke. After walking off one set and being fired from another, she might well never work again. She cursed herself for ever having tempted fate out loud. Meredith had once read a statistic that after two months of unemployment a person's chances of re-entering the workforce within the next two years dropped dramatically, something like sixty percent. It stuck in her head in the same way all those terrifying fertility statistics about your ovaries drying up after the age of thirty-five did. She imagined herself in half a decade—living alone in a basement rental unit in a dilapidated government-subsidized high-rise on the outskirts of some anonymous mid-size city. She would have broken down from the loneliness and adopted a cat. Probably two or three. They would have grown very fat and sad sitting around her apartment all day watching her watch the DVD box set of Audrey Hepburn films. She would have grown fat by then too. Fat, alone, infertile and unemployed. *God*.

The train halted, pitching her face-forward into

the crotch of the man standing in front of her. Meredith righted herself and rubbed her face hard, wishing she was dead. But the man did not seem embarrassed in the slightest. Nor did he offer to help her up or even pause in the point he was explaining into his cell phone. He looked down at his trousers and smoothed away the crease beside his zipper made by Meredith's nose.

The men here looked different to her. They were extra-smooth, like their skin had been blended into a sweet paste before being applied to their bodies. Their eyes were thick-lashed like women's and even indoors they hid under sunglasses. She wondered what it would be like to have an Italian baby. She would definitely name it something swishy like Libero or Prudenzia. They would live together in a crumbly old farmhouse in an olive grove. Meredith tried to imagine her life with her Italian baby. Making pesto for lunch with a mortar and pestle. Doing her laundry by hand in the local stream and hanging it to dry outdoors. The fantasy went on until Meredith realized she had no idea what an olive tree looked like or if they even grew in this part of Italy. And the reality of doing laundry in a stream was probably a lot less lovely than the oil painting in her mind.

The train moved reluctantly towards Florence, jerking to a stop in every village along the way and pausing for several inexplicable siestas in between. The machinery felt sluggish, but inside it Meredith was wide awake. She had slept on the flight from London to Pisa and the nap had left her hyper-alert. Early summer fields swooshed by in an unending pan. Erratic borders were staked with cypress trees. A farmer stood outside a stone shed holding a cow tied to a rope. As the train passed he lifted his arm to touch his hat—he was gone before Meredith could see whether or not it came off in his hand.

The station in Florence was crammed with people pushing in different directions. It smelled like popcorn and damp cement.

She walked outside and stood in line for a taxi. The sun was blazing and the grass on the front lawn was bleached brown in spite of it being only the end of June. June twenty-first, to be exact. Meredith remembered the date because the dinner party she was going to was an annual event, held each year on the same date in honour of the summer solstice. Her mother had told her this.

Meredith wondered, not for the first time, how it was that Irma seemed to know so much about Osmond Crouch. She had wanted to ask but did not, out of a long-held habit of not asking her mother for more information than absolutely necessary. Irma's history was a remote island Meredith had no inclination to visit. The wild travels and arcane accomplishments, her various affairs and endless vague connections to people filled Meredith with a numbing sort of anti-curiosity. She didn't know and didn't ask. When her mother offered something up, Meredith ingested the information with a salt mine of skepticism.

A dusty Volkswagen pulled up in front of the queue. The driver, a compact man in pressed denim and a fisherman's vest, jumped out and hoisted her bag into the trunk without a word and then opened the back door and waved her in with a flicking motion of his hand. Meredith looked for a seat belt in the upholstery cracks but couldn't find one. Instead of attempting an exchange in her non-existent Italian she pulled the invitation out of her handbag and handed it to the driver, pointing to the location. *Vogrie, Fiesole.* The man nodded and turned back to look at her more closely this time. Meredith noticed he was very young.

"*Sì, sì, signorina,*" he said. "*Una bella villa.*" He winked. "*Andiamo!*"

***

Less than an hour later Meredith lay stiffly on a single bed in a round room attempting to sleep. It was hopeless. She opened her eyes and looked about, reflecting for a moment on the many different rooms she had slept in during the past couple of months. These were the sort of quarters that would have thrilled her as a girl. A turret. Like the one Rapunzel got locked up in. The walls were made of yellow stones that looked about a thousand years old and there were tiny rectangular windows facing north, south, east and west, out of which you could see all the surrounding countryside, the village of Fiesole and all the way to the Duomo in the city centre.

Despite the heat outside, the room was cool and damp. The floor was made of flagstones and there was nothing on the walls. On her bedside table was a candle in a simple holder for carrying, so that she could see her way down to the bathroom in the night. The room was dim, unwired and unplumbed and the only decoration in sight was a small cheap-looking brass vase with three wilted sunflowers. Even castles, Meredith realized, did not always live up to their glamorous reputation.

She slid into something close to sleep. After some minutes or hours (she could not be sure which) there was a knock on the door. A flat, accented female voice informed her that cocktails would be served in the library at seven. The messenger did not wait for confirmation but immediately retreated down the stairs with a series of shuffling footsteps. Meredith checked her wrist and realized she had forgotten her watch at her mother's flat—something she never did. She hated to be without a watch and had worn one day and night from the time she was a small child.

There was nothing to do, she supposed, but get up and dress for dinner. She wondered how large the party would be and whether all the guests would be staying overnight or returning to wherever it was they lived. She had no idea what to expect.

She took a pink cotton washcloth out of her terry-cloth bath bag and cleaned her face and armpits. She brushed her teeth and hair and applied fresh deodorant and moisturizer and a bit of mascara. Meredith did not usually wear much makeup, but she had noticed on the train that Italian women seemed much more (as her mother might say) "put together" than their British or North American counterparts. With this in mind she took the time to arrange her hair, and even applied a smidge of lipstick. After nearly fifteen minutes of frozen deliberation she pulled on a black sleeveless sheath dress and a pair of matching flats.

She climbed down the turret stairs slowly, running her fingers along the stone, feeling its natural coolness rising to meet her skin. It was terribly dark. When she got to the bottom she stood stock-still, holding the wall, waiting for her eyes to adjust. She heard footsteps, and the next moment she felt something warm on her throat. A hand. She jumped back against the wall with a squawk.

"Terribly sorry!" said an English voice. "Completely inexcusable. It's just my candle . . . It . . . It . . ." the voice stuttered a bit and then trailed off. A sizzle of sulphur was followed by an orangey glow. Within it was a man's face—bespectacled, indeterminately middle-aged, with a bald head as perfectly round and luminous as a cultured pearl. He squinted at Meredith and pushed his wire frames up his nose with his middle finger.

Meredith extended her hand. The man stared at it as though she were offering him something to eat he wasn't quite sure of. Then he handed her the candle. "Thank you for inviting me," she said.

He moved in for a handshake and then quickly reconsidered and slapped himself hard on the top of the skull.

"Good God, no." He lowered his voice to a staticky hiss. "Bless you. What a little flatterer you are. I'm positively buttered. But no. You're wrong. I'm not *him*. We won't see *him* until later on. After the first round of cocktails, anyway. He likes to make *entrances*, you know."

"Who?" Meredith was not going to risk making another assumption. "Well, *obviously*," he said, snorting and rubbing his nose with both hands in a way that reminded Meredith of a large gerbil. "The dishonourable Master Crouch. Tony Wickenhouse Shaftesbury." He pumped Meredith's hand. "All-purpose hack. You've probably seen my byline. It's an eyeful. So you can just call me Tony Two Names if you like. I'm afraid everybody does. Who can blame them really? Mmm?"

"Meredith Moore."

He snorted once more and the candle went out. Once again the corridor was black as a mine shaft.

"Oh bugger." He finally took Meredith's hand, the one without the candle in it. "Come along. I'll take you to the library and then you can tell me your whole story. I'm certain you have one or you wouldn't be here."

The library was a cavern with sky-high ceilings and leather-bound volumes stacked all the way up the walls. A wooden ladder on casters rolled along a track attached to the top of the shelves. In the centre of the space hung a wrought-iron fixture in the shape of a triple-masted tall ship in full sail. It swung gently from side to side, blazing with candles. Somewhere in the room a sad man gasped a ballad through tar-clogged lungs—Tom Waits? Meredith glanced around but could not detect a piece of stereo equipment anywhere.

Tony Two Names smiled, raised his hand and waved at two other male guests standing by the fire at the other end of the room. The hearth was so large the mantel seemed to be resting on their heads.

"Tell me then, Meredith, how is it that you know our host?"

"I don't really."

"Ooh." Tony adjusted his glasses by wrinkling his nose and opening his eyes wide in disingenuous alarm. "Isn't that curious. So what are *you* famous for?"

"What do you mean?"

"You don't have to pretend to be shy with me. I mean, what is it you've done?"

"Nothing," said Meredith. "At least nothing that would make me famous. Or do you mean famous in a smaller sense of the word?"

"I didn't. But now that we're on to the subject, what are you famous for in the smaller sense of the word?"

He shifted his shoulders and looked right at her as though he were truly curious.

Although she was certain she would never trust Tony, Meredith realized it was quite possible she would end up liking him. With this in mind she carefully considered her answer.

"I suppose I'm famous for being anal about things."

"What sorts of things?"

"Oh, you know, tiny things. The sort of stuff that other people don't usually notice."

"My God, you make yourself sound boring. I hope I don't have to sit beside you at dinner." He narrowed his eyes. "But you're not really boring at all, are you. You're having us all on. Perhaps you've got a secret plan—*that's* it. You're a double agent—"

"Are you drinking?" Meredith said, hoping to change the subject.

Tony raised an eyebrow. He was aiming for a gesture of practised raffishness, but instead his eyebrow hovered above his spectacles, an inchworm stopped mid-inch.

"Perhaps."

"I'm only asking because I was wondering where to get one."

Tony smiled and reached over to a long narrow tapestry hanging on the wall beside the door. At the bottom was a brass ring, which he pulled. Somewhere far away a buzzer sounded.

"Someone will be along shortly."

Meredith thanked him.

"Oh, you are a sassy little thing, aren't you? I should be careful of you." Tony took her by the elbow and guided her across the room towards the men by the fire. "Now, come meet our lucky fellow guests," he whispered in her ear.

She could feel the fine hair at her temple wilt with the moisture of his breath. It smelled like spearmint and propane fumes.

"Dennis and Phillipe. Phillipe is from Spain. A dancer. Dennis is some sort of art collector. Terrifically rich. No one knows *how*. They just got married. Isn't that charming? Not that I'm gay. Thank God. Are you?"

"No." Meredith frowned. She wasn't used to personal questions from complete strangers. Tony, she sensed, was the sort of person who blurted things out in order to set his conversation partner off balance. It worked.

He kept whispering in her ear until they were only a few feet from the other two. The older man spoke with an American accent and wore his hair in a swooping pompadour. He was impressively tall and sumptuously upholstered in velvet and silk. His husband stood shyly beside him, looking out under a dark fringe of eyelashes, lips perfectly bowed and rosy-plump. If not for the pepper grindings of stubble across his jaw and a protruding Adam's apple, Meredith would have mistaken him for a particularly muscular girl.

Tony threw his arms around both men and squeezed them until they stumbled together like children in a potato-sack race. "Look at the blushing brides, would you? I'd like you both to meet my lovely fiancé, Meredith, uh . . ." he looked at her questioningly.

"Moore," Meredith said.

"Of course. Meredith Moore. Isn't she just a pudding?"

Dennis and Phillipe seemed to understand this as a joke, for they shook her hand laughing and offered no congratulations. Then a gaunt man appeared holding a silver tray clamped in a pair of white cotton gloves. He was dressed in what appeared to be a militaristic uniform, complete with decorative gold ropes and epaulets. Meredith took a flute off the tray and sipped the orange liquid inside.

"Bellinis. Osmond harvests the peaches from his orchard and squeezes the juice himself," said Dennis, watching her reaction.

Meredith felt exposed, as though she had just been caught inspecting herself in the mirror. She heard herself giggle.

The music switched to an impossible fusion jazz composition and the gaunt military butler strode out of the library, his tray heavily loaded with used glassware. At Tony's prompting, Dennis began to tell the story of his and Phillipe's recent seaside wedding in Spain. Meredith's eyes began to wander over the objects in the room. Most of the furniture was Florentine gilt. Delicate wooden pieces full of curving angles and filigreed edges painted in a vulgar matte gold. Heavy silk curtains hung beside the windows. In the corner stood a harpsichord, the lid lifted to expose its web of strings and hammers. Apart from the leaking candle wax, the room was immaculate.

"A local fisherman caught the shellfish and then his wife made an enormous paella," Dennis was saying, "which we served with the local wine in these fantastic swinging wicker baskets. It was all very homey. I wanted to create a casual sort of peasants-on-the-seashore vibe. Phillipe didn't want flowers but I insisted he carry a single calla lily. Just the one. Didn't I, darling?"

Phillipe gave a sleepy smile. "Dennith wath wonderful. He do everything. I jeth show up," he said with an irresistible Spanish lisp.

With a couple more sips of her bellini, Meredith felt her spirits rising. Small talk, which had seemed an impossible chore only a moment before, was suddenly effortless. A pleasure. She chatted easily with Phillipe and Dennis as Tony went off to greet some other guests who'd just arrived—a short youngish bald man with a tall, striking older blond woman wearing an enormous diamond necklace. More bellinis came and the room began to fill with people of every age, size and description. Between kisses and introductions, Tony would scoot over and insert bits of delectable information in her ear. "See the social X-ray in the purple dress? Just got out of rehab for mainlining coke. Lost custody of her children in the process. That man feeding her the oyster? Her barrister. And the angelic young couple holding hands near the window? They're only the hottest actors in Sweden. About to co-star in a big action thriller financed by our host. Fraternal twins, but rumour has it they fuck. Or they're fucking and rumour has it they're twins. I forget which."

Several languages she recognized plus a couple she didn't floated through the air and up to the ceiling where they merged into a canopy soundtrack of party chatter. Meredith kept looking around for Osmond, but having no idea what he looked like, she wasn't sure what to watch for, or even what she would say if she did see him. The party surged forward like a rowboat on high seas.

***

The following afternoon Meredith lay in the garden beside the pool. A wet cloth was draped across her face and she moved it aside only to take pinched sips from a can of lemon soda. The tin, which had been ice cold when the butler offered it to her from his tray, was now blistered from condensation in the blazing summer heat. A dozen or so of her fellow guests lounged around the patio. Meredith recognized a few of them from last night's dinner, but the rest seemed to have materialized out of nowhere. She took her place under the partial shade of a particularly leafy potted lemon tree and smeared her body from tip to toe in expensive French SPF 60 block she'd found on one of the garden tables. Then, as a finishing touch, she draped a beach towel over herself for extra protection. Meredith did not tan. Which is not to say she was one of those people who *couldn't* tan—just that she *didn't*, never had, and because of that, didn't know whether she actually could or not. Still, she could hardly sit indoors on such a perfect day.

Every thirty minutes or so, she raised herself from where she lay and slipped soundlessly into the pool. The heat was breathtaking. For a moment her hangover symptoms would abate, but by the time she hoisted herself over the cement edge and resumed her place on the chaise, her hair would dry into hippie mats and the droplets on her skin would evaporate, leaving her hot and throbbing once again.

The party the night before swirled through her brain. Snippets of conversation slid into one another. She felt as though she had been plucked up by a tornado and set down somewhere else entirely.

Osmond Crouch had materialized just in time for dinner—a short rounded man in a black suit and T-shirt, with a face that looked like the full moon when he smiled. He sat flanked by the Swedish actors, appearing contented but somehow removed from the scene before him.

Meredith never did get to meet him.

After dinner she was so woozy with drink and travel that Tony offered to help her back up the stairs to her turret room. She had a vague memory of slapping his hand out from under the back of her skirt as they climbed the stairs, but decided to put it from her mind, along with the cartload of other cringe-worthy moments from the past several weeks. Now, she told herself, all she had to do was get through the next few hours, go to bed and get up and leave in the morning. Most of the guests were staying on for a long weekend. Meredith hadn't even intended to stay an extra night, but Tony had persuaded her not to leave when she ran into him at breakfast in the dining room. Over berries and pressed yogourt, he and Dennis cheerily invited her to come with them for a bike ride into Florence. Many of the party guests were going, though she couldn't properly imagine how, given that most of them had stayed up drinking for hours after she had gone to bed.

Underneath her washcloth veil and beach-towel tent, the full weight of the afternoon heat pressed itself upon her. The sun had shifted again and she would have to move her chaise out of its reach. She huffed, irritably considering the prospect of going back indoors to nap on her clammy bed in the turret. Maybe if she just moved the chaise one more time the sun would stay in place. Meredith threw off her covers and looked in surprise at the figure standing above her.

Osmond. He wore a short terry-cloth robe that hung open over a black Speedo bathing suit. A silver shag carpet covered his chest and belly. He was holding the leaves of the lemon tree aside and grinning.

"You must be a vampiress," he said, cocking his head teasingly. "Most women get annoyed when a man steps into their sun but with you it is the opposite." He spoke with the word-perfect formality of someone speaking a second language that has become, for all practical intents, their first.

"I'm not a big tanner."

"Smart girl. The sun is damaging."

"It's not that really. I just don't like the feeling of exposure."

Osmond let the branches go and they swished back into place between them. "Ridiculous," he said, picking a dead leaf from the tree and crumbling it between his fingers. "A lovely young woman like you should be shown to the world. If anything, you should spend more time in the sun. Figuratively speaking."

Meredith had nothing intelligent to add but she felt she should do something. She sat up to introduce herself, causing the beach towel to fall away and reveal her bare chest. Somehow her bikini top had come unstrung. She covered herself, cupping a palm over each tit like a starlet on the cover of a fashion glossy. Osmond smiled. He did not look away.

"God." She tried to laugh in a casual way. "How very, uh, *European* of me." She grabbed the bikini top with one hand and wrapped the other arm around her ribcage so it covered both nipples. She struggled one-handedly to yank the two tiny cotton triangles into place without revealing herself. Without a word, Osmond moved to the other side of the chaise, took the strings from her and tied them in a bow around her neck.

"Thanks."

"My pleasure." He was standing behind her, but she did not want to turn around and face him just yet.

"I am so pleased you accepted my invitation, Meredith. I wasn't entirely certain that you would."

She stood up and wrapped the beach towel around her waist. He was still smiling. Indulgent eyes dancing in the crags of his cheeks.

"I trust you have enjoyed yourself?"

"Yes, I have. Thank you, Mr. Crouch."

"Call me Ozzie."

The wind was cooler now. They were high up, half a mile or so above sea level at least. Meredith could see Florence from where she stood. Village roads lined by ancient fieldstone and cypress trees looped down the foothills and joined in the city. Thousands of orange-tiled rooftops and Medici-era battlements surrounded the great orb of the Duomo, its roof gleaming pinkish in the afternoon light. It looked close enough to touch, even though Meredith knew it was actually a half-hour drive away.

"Recognize it?"

"Florence?"

"The view."

It was not a question that demanded an answer. Meredith shook her head.

"It's the same one they used in *A Room With a View*. The director was an old friend of mine. I let him shoot a few exteriors from here. After the film came out they issued a new edition of the book and came up and photographed it again for the dust jacket. I'll show it to you one day."

The breeze came up. Meredith shivered. Ozzie slipped off his robe, revealing more of himself than she was entirely comfortable seeing, and threw it over a chair. She could sense the other guests around the pool stirring from their prostrate positions and taking notice of what was going on behind the potted lemon tree.

"I was just about to take my afternoon swim," said Ozzie. "Why don't you go back to your room and get changed for dinner and then meet me in the library around five? I have something I want to show you." He checked his wristwatch, a stainless steel mariner's model with more switches and dials and gauges than a submarine control panel.

"How did you know who I was?"

"I recognized you from the photographs."

"What photographs?"

"The ones your mother sent. When you were a little thing. Irma and I were once great friends, you know."

"She mentioned something."

"I've always taken an interest in your progress. And now I finally get the chance to meet you as an adult.

I understand you were working on my latest film in London."

Meredith dragged her bare toes across the edge of a large pink flagstone. "That didn't exactly work out."

That grin again. Like a hungry cat. For a moment she was afraid he might actually open his mouth and lick his chops.

"Do not worry, my dear. It was all for the best. I'd never let a good script girl go to waste. You are . . ." He hesitated, waved a finger around and let it fall to his chin with a professorial tap. "Far too important to the process."

Meredith gave a skeptical snort. "It's a craft. At best."

"Yes," said Osmond. "And there are too few craftspeople in our industry today. Too many auteurs, not enough craftspeople. Too much creativity, not enough continuity."

Osmond patted her cheek and strode off towards the diving board to take his afternoon swim.

16

Osmond and Meredith met in the library at the appointed time. He bowed slightly when she entered, and offered a bellini. A finger moved over his lips. Then he walked over to one of the bookcases and pulled it aside with a magician's flourish. Where the shelf had once stood was a small door, flat to the wall, with an arched top. He took a candle from the top of the piano and lit it. Without breaking the silence, he opened a troll-sized door and led Meredith down a long hallway, a tunnel really, with a crumbly clay floor and ceilings so low even a tall child would have had to stoop to get through.

"The monks built this place in the seventeenth century as an escape route," Osmond began in the solemn tone of a tour guide. "They never were attacked, although one of the subsequent owners, a French countess, was bludgeoned to death by her cook and left to die here. And of course the Nazis occupied the place during the war. God knows what nastiness they got up to."

At the end of the tunnel was a bolted doorway. A line of white light glowed in the space between the floor and the crooked wooden slats. Osmond handed Meredith the candle and withdrew a long rusted iron key from his pocket. He opened the door and Meredith stumbled behind him into the early evening glow. She inhaled as though she had not drawn breath for several minutes.

"Mmm," said Osmond, raising his hand to the twilight. "Shame we're not shooting today."

The garden was gloriously ill-tended, an open expanse contained by high stone walls and spilling over with roses in full bloom, their fleshy petals spread and vulgar with scent. Jasmine and ivy vines made stealthy progress over everything that was not alive or asleep, twining themselves over a birdbath, a sundial and a crumbling marble bench, even climbing up the warty trunks of a clutch of ancient trees. In the corner a fountain burbled, glugging bilious water from the mouth of a cement stag. The animal looked about to dash, frozen mid-leap and vomiting swamp water. Lily pads floated on the surface of the small pond. Beneath the surface Meredith saw a metallic flash. Goldfish.

"Welcome to my movie set," Osmond said with deliberate ostentation. "Come." He led her down the path, under a wrought-iron arch and behind a rose bush that looked and smelled like a rich lady's cheek. There, hidden to the uninitiated eye, was a crumbly stone outbuilding.

Osmond took another key from his pocket and winked. "Step into my trailer."

Inside, the building was filled to the rafters with film equipment, some of it state-of-the-art, some of it vintage, and everything in between. There were four cameras, a Steadicam holder, two dollies and a pile of slates. High canvas folding chairs were stacked up against the wall in a row beside a mahogany makeup vanity, salon chair and lighted mirror. Meredith saw dollies, standing lights, smoke machines and fans. In the corner stood a huge metal contraption she took to be a generator, and beyond that, Osmond indicated a door leading to a private editing suite. A rack of costumes lined the back wall. Silk dresses and men's summer suits dangled askew from satin-covered hangers. The place even had the carnival smell of a film set. Meredith turned to Osmond, astonished.

"What do you do here?"

"I make my movie."

"But where's your cast and crew?"

"You've met most of them already. Reno, the butler, he's my leading man, as well as my director of photography. And my first assistant. And Marcella, the woman who served your dinner, plays opposite him. She is my muse, an old-fashioned star. Knows how to find her light without being told. She's also the wardrobe stylist, the dolly grip, the second A.D. and the focus puller."

"So who operates the camera?"

"I do, of course. All proper directors do."

"And what about sound?"

"No need. It isn't a talkie."

Meredith snorted. "You. Osmond Crouch. Hollywood big-shot. Purveyor of box-office-record-breaking commercial entertainment. In the twenty-first century. Are making a *silent film*?"

"What is wrong with that?" His tone was wounded.

"I'm just surprised."

"You are?"

"Obviously."

"Obviously what?" He shut the door behind him. The room got darker. There was a defensive glint in his eye. "I don't see that there is anything obvious about it."

"No, no, of course not." Meredith said this in what she hoped was a reassuring tone. "That's just the thing. It's unusual. I mean it's *cool*. Very . . . ahead of the curve." She watched his shoulders, which had become pugilistically hunched, lower themselves an inch or so. "How long have you been working on it?"

"Including script development?" Osmond looked at his watch. "About fifteen years."

Meredith coughed to stop herself from smiling.

"And how long have you been shooting?"

"Let's see." Osmond walked over to the director's chair, reached into the canvas storage bag hanging off the back. He flipped the binder open and read from a dog-eared hunk of papers held together loosely by a dried-out elastic band that was about to break.

"Monday will be day eight hundred and forty-four."

"So you've been shooting for how many years, then?"

"Off and on, about twelve." The elastic band snapped and papers swirled to the floor. Osmond bent over to gather them and clutched his lower back on the way up. Restless tendons twitched in his jaw. "Ever since I moved here. The film was really why I bought Vogrie in the first place."

"What's it about?"

"What?"

"The movie."

"A man and a woman in love. And other things. The essential themes. Sex. Death. The primordial, pagan cycle of the seasons."

"And how many days do you have left?"

"In the shoot? God knows. We're a bit behind schedule actually."

"So eight hundred and forty-four days of . . . how many?"

Osmond grinned sheepishly and shrugged. "Of thirty. It was originally supposed to be a thirty-day shoot but we got a bit waylaid."

"I see."

He moved towards a window and pulled aside a curtain. Dust tore through the room. He pulled a rag from his pocket and began polishing the lens of one of the cameras. When he was finished he walked around and peered through the eyepiece. Meredith couldn't imagine what he saw. The room was dark and the camera hung its head.

"You think I'm mad," he said after a while.

Meredith decided to skip the question. "How do you know my mother?"

He took his eye away from the camera and faced her. "We were never in love, if that's what you're asking."

"I wasn't."

"Well, now you know."

"No, I don't. I don't know because nobody ever tells me anything."

"Perhaps that's because you don't ask."

"Maybe so. But I'm asking now. What's going on? Why did you give me a job? Why am I even here in the first place?"

"Meredith," he said, lifting her hand then releasing it. "I want to be nothing but perfectly honest with you. Complete honesty is the only thing I aspire to anymore, both in my life and in my work." He motioned around the room. "I have known your mother for many years. We met before you were born. We see very little of each other now, but the fact is, I see very little of anyone anymore. I have chosen to live apart from the world. I speak to my line producers and the people who work for me in Los Angeles and in London. Occasionally I am forced to endure a conference call with some illiterate executive or other. The rest of the time I spend on *Avalon*."

His grip on her tightened. She was torn between the idea of ripping herself away and acquiescing.

"Suffice to say I have known your mother for part of her life, but I have known you for all of yours. Even if you can't remember me, I was around."

Meredith stepped back. "What do you mean, 'around'?"

"In a metaphysical sense. I was with you. I wondered. I worried."

Meredith wanted to bring the moment to its crisis. "What exactly are you trying to say?"

Osmond smiled. Confrontation appeared to relax him. "What I'm trying to say exactly, my dear, is would you consider staying on at Vogrie for a few weeks to assist me in the making of *Avalon*? I am sure it will not surprise you to hear there are a few continuity problems that need to be worked out. On an eight-hundred-day shoot it is to be expected."

So he could make fun of himself after all.

"You'll be paid scale of course. Or better. And the accommodations are not so terrible."

Meredith looked around at the equipment. All of the mechanical contraptions and digitalized devices she had taken for granted all her working life sitting, ominous, expectant. She shook her head and laughed. Ozzie extended his hand and she took it in hers and squeezed once, firmly. It was then that she noticed the ring on his baby finger.

A thick gold band with the design of a scorpion etched in jade.

***

That night at dinner Meredith felt perked up. She was seated several spots down the table from Ozzie and to the left of Tony, who admitted to her he had snuck in before the bell and changed the place cards to be next to her for the second night in a row. Meredith didn't mind, however, as Ozzie didn't talk much at his own dinner table, preferring instead to sit at its head wearing a beneficent smile, and attacking his plate as he absorbed the chatter of his guests.

Many of the party-goers from the night before had left, but a dozen or so remained. Despite her impressive short-term memory, Meredith had given up trying to recall all of their names, and had instead come up with pet names for them according to the stories they had told her or what she had heard from Tony. They included the Swiss ex-junkie-model-turned-society-wife, the ancient Italian lady of vaguely noble birth (Medici? Borgias?) with distressed leather skin, the American war correspondent, the Swedish twin actors, a silent English couple and the complaining Mexican heiress. Throughout the soup Tony would indicate each one using military code ("American war correspondent. Three o'clock. Word is he faked his own hostage-taking to get away from his wife. An extremely *trying* woman.")

Dinner was plain but the service was not. Meredith had never witnessed anything like it. After the guests were seated, Reno and Marcella appeared to pour

Chianti from bottles in baskets. Then they came round with silver platters offering each guest a choice of reheated pizza slices, presumably the remains of lunch. Meredith had skipped the midday meal, opting to sweat off her hangover instead. It worked. She felt much better, but terribly hungry. When Marcella stood beside her with the platter, Meredith indicated the two largest slices available, which Marcella, a whippet of a woman, picked up with a pair of filigreed silver tongs and plopped unceremoniously on the plate. Meredith was not sure but thought she heard her utter the word *"porca"* under her breath as she moved down the table.

"Another bitter actress-turned-servant," Tony stage-whispered into her neck.

Meredith bit her lip and thwacked him hard on the leg without raising her arm from under the table.

Unabashed, Tony persisted. "I'll tell you what she needs to do. She needs to go back to theatre school and learn how to *act like a servant*."

Meredith released an embarrassing snort and the complaining Mexican heiress across the table fixed them with a haughty look. She glared at Tony to stop it, which only pushed him further. The pizza on Tony's plate was wilted and cold, but Meredith took a piece anyway. She had finished both of her slices in a few enthusiastic bites and was too afraid to ask Marcella for more.

"Go ahead," said Tony. "Have your fill, my greasy little *porca*. I'm not eating."

Meredith made a face and bit into the cold little sliver. She wondered if Tony was *on* something. He ate little, and couldn't—or at least made no effort to—stop talking.

Whatever drug he was on, it certainly didn't interfere with his ability to consume wine. Meredith watched him swill most of a jug himself throughout dinner, aggressively offering to pour her more every few minutes or so, and expressing frustration at the slow consumption rate of his companions. For Tony it was not enough that people drink at the same time as him, he demanded they also drink at the same pace. "It's like running a race while lapping your fellow competitors. You end up running a marathon while they manage nothing more than a fifty-metre sprint," he complained.

Meredith accepted his pours to be polite. Twice over the course of dinner she went to the bathroom and dumped her wine down the sink.

As the supper moved into a dessert of peaches and gelato, Meredith gazed around the table wondering if the future father of her baby was present without her knowing it. She measured every male face with the critical expertise of a Grand National jockey examining a stable of thoroughbreds. If you were going to choose the father of your child for any reason other than love, didn't you owe it to yourself to be as selective as possible? Apart from Tony (whom Meredith had already ruled out as a charming little weasel) the men at the table were disappointingly geriatric. She felt it would be a miracle if any of their sperm still had aquatic motility—although, she reminded herself crisply, Saul Bellow *and* Clint Eastwood had fathered babies in their seventies. The fact that women and men were on completely different clocks was the reason she was here in the first place. Like a French matron at a fruit stand, Meredith looked without touching. She checked features for evenness, muscle groups for signs of deterioration, and shoulders for signs of spinal curvature. On the whole she was disappointed. Meredith moved from man to man until she came to Ozzie, on whom she lingered.

For a bulldoggish man in his early old age, he was, Meredith noticed, almost daintily elegant. He sat dissecting a white peach with a spoon, smiling at some private joke. She looked away for what she judged to be an appropriate amount of time and then let her gaze slide back to Ozzie. Something about his hands—the way they moved, flicking with purpose while the rest of him remained perfectly still. He sliced the fruit three ways using a technique she had never seen before, and then spread the peach with his thumbs and plucked out the seed. Setting the pit down on the small china saucer before him, Ozzie raised a shiny sliver of fruit to his mouth with a spoon. Then he paused and looked up and directly into Meredith's eyes. He seemed to have been aware of her gaze the entire time. His expression showed no self-consciousness—only an amused curiosity.

She felt like a naughty child caught out, and tried to shrug off the moment, but when she looked back, Ozzie caught her again. He pulled on his moustache and winked. She giggled, and Tony swivelled around in his chair.

"What's so funny, then?"

"Nothing," she said, pushing her chin to her collarbone in a losing effort not to smile.

Tony glanced over at Ozzie. "Don't tell me our lugubrious host has ensnared you in his web."

"What makes you say that?"

"I imagine you've heard the stories."

"No."

"Bit of a stickman. Not all of us can have as uncheckered a past as you, my darling. And I don't blame you for falling in love with him, by the way. You wouldn't be the first. After all, a pretty young china doll like you, someone really ought to be digging down to tickle those warm tender bits beneath your icy crust."

Meredith frowned and made a motion to turn away. "You're drunk," she said, and searched for something worse. "And *mean*."

"Perhaps." Tony grinned. "But if you do decide to let him tickle your bits, just mind you don't get in the way of you-know-who."

"Who?"

"You may be Canadian, darling, but you won't fool me into thinking you're completely stupid."

"I honestly have no idea what or who you're talking about."

"His *main squeeze*." Tony, who never seemed to care who overheard him talking about what, lowered his head and his voice. "Kathleen Swain. The actress."

Meredith snapped upright. "I'm aware of Kathleen Swain, thanks." She sliced her peach with a knife and hit the stone with a *tunk*. "Are they . . . together?" She posed the question without looking up.

An observant sort of drunk, Tony could see she was pretending to not care, but was in fact desperately interested. Like all journalists, he was incapable of retaining sensitive information, particularly when presented with an audience.

"Not in the conventional sense. But in the universal sense, most definitely."

"*Universal sense?*"

"In that they are bound to each other forever. Their fates miserably and inevitably intertwined, no matter how much they may fight against it." Tony lowered his head again and pursed his lips. "I really shouldn't say."

"Oh, for God's sake."

And with that Tony set about telling her the story of Kathleen Swain and Osmond Crouch, whispering in a deep movie-trailer voice into the dark crevasse of Meredith's ear as the rest of the guests finished their espresso.

***

It all started in the early eighties in Los Angeles, when Kathleen Swain, an aspiring starlet, began having an affair with one of the regulars in the hotel cocktail bar where she worked nights. The word *affair*, in this case, must be used in the most generous sense of the word, as this particular cocktail bar was known for its openness to a certain more, shall we say, *old-fashioned* line of women's work than slinging Fuzzy Navels to industry hacks. Kathleen, like most of her nubile cocktailing colleagues, was known to be conducting a brisk little side business.

One of the regulars was Osmond Crouch (formerly Cruchinsky), an ambitious hustler from Montreal who had worked his way up to being one of the hottest producers in Hollywood. Osmond, it was said, took more than just a passing interest in Kathleen, a girl twenty years his junior. He fell in love, or as close to love as anyone could manage during the eighties in L.A. At first he showed up once a week, then twice, and as his fortunes rose (he had moved away from distributing European blue movies to making serious cinema), he began showing up almost every night. Osmond would sit at his private booth reading scripts, drinking Campari after Campari and waiting for his paramour to get off her shift. When she did, they would retire to his suite on the fifth floor (which he used so often that the staff kept a set of monogrammed sheets just for him).

The months passed and soon enough Osmond introduced Kathleen to a few people in the business.

She started picking up some modelling work—lingerie and catalogue mostly, but anything was better than refilling peanut bowls at the hotel. Osmond, lucky punk that he was, had lately managed to get hold of what everyone in Hollywood has been searching for since the motion picture was invented: a decent script. It was just what audiences wanted at the time, only they didn't know it yet. A big-budget Western epic—a sequel to the film that launched his career. Like the original, it had all the classic Hollywood ingredients—shooting, punching, chasing . . . and rescuing weeping women in dusty petticoats, slinging them over the haunches of sway-backed horses. A big studio signed on, as well as a name director and a bankable male lead, and Osmond's deal was sealed. The green light was lit. All he needed now was a love interest. Someone fresh, new and sexy as a Georgia peach. The studio preferred blondes. They decided to hold an open casting.

Knowing that Kathleen would kick up a fuss if she ever got wind of it, Osmond didn't tell her about the project. Besides, after the thing was out it would be time for him to move on. If he was going to be a serious producer, Osmond would have to quit shagging cheap lingerie-models-slash-cocktail-waitresses and date some real actresses.

But unbeknownst to Osmond, poor young Kathleen had just spent the night crying on the phone to her mother back on the farm in Minnesota. Seems the poor little lamb had gone and got herself knocked up. She'd been faithful to Osmond for several months now, so there was no question it was his. Kathleen might have been a tart, but she was also a good Catholic girl, and after a tearful consultation with Momma, she knew there was only one thing to do.

The night she told Osmond, he went predictably ballistic, letting loose for the first time what would later be known as his legendary temper. Trashed the hotel room, wept, slapped her around a bit—anything to convince her to get rid of the baby. In a state of utter hysteria, he even offered to marry her if she would only get an abortion (an out-and-out lie if ever there was one). Osmond knew that if Kathleen had this baby now, she would become his burden, and his whole future as a Hollywood heavyweight—which was opening up before him like a flower—could be thrown into jeopardy.

Unfortunately for him, Kathleen was smarter than she looked. Their bitter standoff continued, until one day Kathleen overheard two actresses at the hotel bar talking about auditioning for a plum role in a certain hot new picture being produced by Osmond Crouch. A sequel to his legendary Western. When they went to the bathroom to powder their noses (which they did several times during the night), they unwisely left the script on the table, and Kathleen took a quick peek. She loved the part. She *was* the part. The classic whore with a heart of gold. When she returned home to her roachy bachelor apartment that night, she sat for a long time considering her options.

At first she was incensed that he hadn't offered the part to her straightaway, but her ambition soon washed away her anger. The situation seemed hopeless. There was barely a chance she could get an audition, and even if she did, Osmond would try to sabotage her chances, given her current condition. And after all, who would want a pregnant love interest? She suddenly realized what she had to do. She picked up the phone, called Osmond and set out the terms of her deal: if he dropped off a signed offer for her to play the whore by six p.m. the following day, she would agree to an abortion.

A simple quid pro quo, really. One that marked the beginning of a long and fruitful friendship.

The movie was a hit, one that launched one career and cemented another. Osmond continued to cast Kathleen, who quickly became a bankable star, and she continued to work for him.

They were never known to be lovers again, though no one could actually be sure. . . .

***

"That explains . . . a lot." Meredith exhaled as slowly as she could.

Tony sat back in his chair and drained with a bull-fighter's flourish what must have been his seventeenth glass of Chianti. He poured Meredith more wine and this time she drank it, downing half her glass in a single gulp.

"How do you know all this stuff?"

"I have my sources," Tony said smugly.

"How do you know Osmond?"

"A more apt question would be, How am I useful to Osmond?"

"Fine," Meredith said, "how then?"

"A man in Osmond Crouch's position needs information, and I happen to be possessed of a great deal of information. I take care of him and he takes care of me."

It all sounded a bit ridiculous to Meredith. She could see Tony wanted to be pressed for details. She wouldn't give him the pleasure.

"The question is," Tony said, "what's *your* connection to all this?"

"I'm sure I don't have one," Meredith said.

"And I'm sure you do."

"Really?" (Meredith assured herself he was drunk.)

Tony drew his lips up to reveal a set of wine-stained upper teeth. "Let's start with your mother."

"What about her?" Meredith bristled.

"Why don't *you* tell *me*?" he said.

"I don't understand."

"You will." Tony effected a woozy smile and patted her on the shoulder. "One day."

After dinner Meredith had planned to sneak off to her room and read a magazine, but Ozzie, noticing her retreat, managed to intercept her as she was slipping down the main hallway towards the turret.

"And where do you think you are going, Miss Moore?"

The naughty-little-girl feeling from dinner seized her once again. Meredith looked at her feet and shrugged. Her toenail polish was chipped.

After a minimal amount of stilted small talk (as neither of them, Meredith recognized with relief, was particularly good at small talk), Ozzie asked Meredith to come to the library and look at some of the rushes from *Avalon*. Most of the guests were returning home the next day, which meant they could resume shooting, and Ozzie was eager to begin right away. Would she mind doing a bit of homework before they began?

Meredith was relieved at the chance to concentrate on something impersonal and work-related. As the rest of the guests tottered off for a tipsy moonlit skinny dip in the pool, Meredith and Ozzie retired to the library, where he rigged up a projector and set it in the middle of the room. Sinking deep into a pair of green velvet armchairs, the two of them began the process of watching reel after reel of old footage projected on the fresco-decorated library walls.

Meredith was impressed by Ozzie's eye. There was no disputing his ability to capture light, to compose and create moments between the actors. The narrative, however, was another story. Specifically, what narrative? After sitting through the nine-hour rough cut, Meredith could think of little to say. There was no story at all—just a series of pretty, painterly pictures of two young (and later quite middle-aged) people falling in love and frolicking about an Eden-like setting.

The entire picture was set in the back garden, which put forth a number of continuity problems in itself. In the earlier reels the garden was quite spare and well pruned (no doubt the work of the Italian monks, Meredith reflected), but in later scenes it looked far closer to its current gaudy, overgrown self. The two lovers (played in silent-movie fashion by Reno and Marcella) were similarly inconsistent in their appearance. The biggest problem, Meredith immediately observed, was the irreparable and unavoidable problem of their *aging on camera*. Their costumes, which appeared tidy and tailored in the earlier scenes, were rags by the later footage. And their faces followed suit: moving from the freshness of youth to the well-seasoned appearance of people who had spent the better part of their adult lives working outdoors. All of this would be fine, if the film had been shot in continuity, which of course it hadn't. Shot over the course of a dozen years, the film included scenes from the first act that had been shot only a few weeks ago. Impossibly, the actors became younger as the plot progressed and featured two actors who looked like the nieces and nephews of their characters at the beginning. Ozzie was amazingly blind to all of these inconsistencies. Meredith realized the poor man had completely lost perspective and that her job would be to alert him to it.

Considering the epic length of the shoot to date, there was not a huge amount of footage to go through. The entire work had been composed by natural light, during twilight—only fifteen minutes a day of which were worth shooting, according to Ozzie. It often took him weeks at a time to shoot a single scene, completing dozens of painstaking takes from various angles until he got the moment exactly right. Time, it was obvious, was not of the essence in Ozzie's gilded universe. Watching *Avalon*, Meredith began to wonder whether he actually wished to make something marketable or just while away the years of villa-ensconced hermitude. After the screening, she put this very question to him.

"You dislike it, then?" he said. "You think it is worthless? Shit? A complete waste of film?"

"That's not what I said *or* meant," Meredith replied firmly. She was used to holding her own with hot-headed directors. In this context Ozzie didn't frighten her—at least not in any way that she was willing to cop to.

"What do you mean, then?"

"Do you want me to be honest?"

Ozzie glowered. "No, in fact, I think it is obvious I want you to soothe me to sleep with a string of gentle falsehoods. That is why I showed you this."

Meredith studied a branch of bougainvillea that happened to be slapping against the window. Beyond it was the dawn.

"Obviously, Meredith, I want you to be honest," he said finally.

Meredith looked into his eyes and saw the aggression receding. She began to give him her notes.

Her comments were much like she was—bluntly simple in some ways and lavishly complicated in others. Even Ozzie knew to hold his temper long enough to let her get to the end of what she was trying to say (they were, after all, talking about *his work*—a subject he enjoyed). When she was finished, he buzzed Reno, who appeared shortly with a pitcher of espresso, which he served.

"*Salute*," Ozzie said, lifting a cup and clanking it against hers. "To the beginning of a beautiful and fruitful friendship."

***

Over the next two weeks Meredith rarely left the garden-shed editing suite, save for meals and the occasional restorative stretch of sleep. She worked on a Steenbeck, cutting and splicing in the old way, surrounded by trim bins overflowing with film. It was a laborious task, but rewardingly tactile. She was literally making a movie with her hands. The rest of the guests had long gone (save for Tony, who lurked about the villa all day, sweating off his hangovers). Meredith was pleased to be back at work. Based on the footage for *Avalon*, she agreed to work with Ozzie on the grounds that he allow her to edit her own rough cut, which she agreed to complete within a few weeks. It was absorbing work on a hasty schedule—the sort of labour Meredith, like most people in movies, was accustomed to anyway. She had ideas about how the film could work, but she needed to be given carte blanche to make it happen. Ozzie would just have to trust her, she said, and for some strange reason he seemed to.

As the cutting progressed, the bond between them was cemented by intergenerational mutual respect. They bickered constantly, but in a productive, good-humoured way. They grew close in the way that people working intensely together in dark confined spaces for days and nights on end, almost inevitably do. Meredith was surprised to find that in spite of his initial defensiveness, Ozzie quickly allowed her to have her head on the matter of the cut. (He could, after all, recut the thing any way he wanted once she was finished.) It became clear he had ground to a halt where *Avalon* was concerned, and was surprisingly receptive to Meredith's suggestions. The truth was, the film was a complete mess and Ozzie knew it and appreciated her help.

As it happened, a mess was just what Meredith needed to lift her spirits and fill her with a renewed sense of purpose, one that she had not felt since she was first seized by the Quest. For days and days she thought of nothing but work.

When Mish called her on her cell one evening, Meredith did not notice herself rattling on until

Mish said, sourly, "Wow, are you taking requests for Broadway show tunes?"

"What's wrong?"

"Nothing," she answered, in a manner that indicated Meredith would soon get an extended speech on the subject of exactly what was wrong. "Hey, aren't you going to ask me how my weekend with the German went?"

And before Meredith could apologize, Mish had begun a long litany of her weekend woes. Meredith listened and made dovish sounds into the receiver.

"And then"—Mish's voice had reached a semi-hysterical pitch—"*and then*, after acting all offended because I refused to eat it, he takes me upstairs to see his dead grandmother's shoe collection. I figured the guy was just some kind of dandy, but no. Oh, no. It's like this enormous walk-in closet filled with nothing but women's dress shoes, most of them used. How psycho is that?"

Meredith heard her light a cigarette and exhale smoke into the phone.

"God, Mere, when are you coming back? I miss you."

"I thought your gay husband was in town," Meredith said.

"Shane? Oh, yeah, but it's not the same as a girlfriend. He's out clubbing it up with the boys every night while I'm slaving away on set. I only see him for like half an hour a day if that. This movie is driving me nuts."

"Kathleen?"

"Funny you should ask, because now that I think of it, her ladyship hasn't been half bad for the last week of shooting. Which is pretty surprising considering the hours we were doing—night shoots. You know the scene where she slides down the cliff? Oh my God, it was like fifteen thousand takes later, with me having to change her into a clean corset and petticoat in between takes. And new makeup and hair every time. Total hell for everyone, especially for her. We all thought she was going to lose it, but she didn't. Actually she was weirdly cheerful about the whole thing."

"Funny, isn't it," Meredith said after a short pause, "the way people who manufacture crises can often function very well when confronted with a real one."

"I wouldn't say it was a crisis really . . ." Mish drifted off, trouble in her voice. "Listen, Mere, I wanted to ask you. . ."

"Mmm?"

"Actually, it's rather awkward."

"Well, you might jolly well get on with it, then," Meredith said, parroting her friend's British affectation. But Mish, preoccupied with what she was about to say, didn't notice.

"Well, here's the thing. A few nights ago your ma invited me to see the pageant she was in at her club, so I took Shane."

"That's nice. Wait. She wasn't naked, was she?"

"No. Well, just topless really. And that was only for a second at the end. Anyway, I wish you'd seen it. They did a rock-opera version of some weird French farce. Bizarre. Anyway, Barnaby was there and we ended up having dinner and we were talking—not about you, though, I promise—and then he sort of . . ."

"Seriously?" Meredith said. "You and Barnaby? I mean, that's cool. That's totally fine."

"No, not me. God, are you kidding? After what his fucking bird did to my hat? *Pas de chance*. It's him and Shane who hit it off. And I mean that in the *classical sense*."

"Are you serious?"

"I wouldn't joke about something like this."

Meredith began to hiccup uncontrollably. "It . . . it's kind of funny."

Of course. The "arrangement." Barnaby was gay.

"I wanted to tell you now because I'm thinking of bringing them both to the wedding."

"Oh fuck, Elle's sister. When is that again?"

"This Saturday. In Florence. Did you RSVP?"

"Yes, then I completely forgot about it. We were supposed to bring hot dates, weren't we?"

Mish made an embarrassed sound. There was a drumroll of mutual silence before they laughed again.

After hanging up the phone Meredith tried to picture Ozzie at a wedding.

It was impossible.

***

Avalon, meanwhile, was a whole new movie.

Meredith had solved the problem of the plot by beginning the film at the end and moving the narrative backwards, from the tragic end of the love affair towards its blissful inception. The result was a simple, dreamlike story that seemed to occur as much within the minds of the players as it did in the eyes of the audience. In this way she compensated for the discontinuous look of the film—the varying ages and stages of the actors and the changing texture and colour of the filmstock all fell into place as part of the heady universe of *Avalon*. For a silent art film, Meredith decided, rewinding the reel, it didn't suck at all.

Ozzie had not been this pleased since the Macedonian builders stripped the paint off the kitchen wall and found a seventeenth-century fresco. In a fit of excitement he woke Reno and Marcella from their beds (it was the wee hours of the morning by the time Meredith finished her cut) and showed them the film, projected outdoors on the side of the garden shed. The two actor–servants seemed immensely relieved. It was obvious to Meredith that they had long ago come to view the making of *Avalon* as merely another eccentric aspect of their duties as butler and housekeeper at the villa. The continuity girl's recut meant they might finally be able to imagine a future as actors outside of the crumbling Etruscan garden walls of Ozzie's obsessive imagination.

The following night, Ozzie assisted Marcella and Reno in the preparation of a celebratory feast. Slabs of decadently marbled Florentine-cut beef were served with simple white beans drizzled in the palest green olive oil Meredith had ever seen. Bottles of fine Tuscan Chianti were brought up from a secret cellar, and set out with platters of steamed asparagus, spaghetti tossed with caviar and unsalted bread. After dinner they retired to the library and Reno and Marcella exhorted giggles from Meredith by performing dirty stock sketches from *commedia dell'arte*. Ozzie brought out his harmonica and played sly overtures to their scenes. Just the sight of him holding the harmonica to his lips like a dreamy hobo made Meredith feel her rib-cage was a spun-sugar sculpture dissolving inside her chest. When Marcella offered her a choice of digestives, she yawned and took a thimble-sized glass of Limoncello, thinking she would go to bed straight afterwards.

When they were alone for a moment, Ozzie looked at Meredith.

"You are a fantastic girl, aren't you," he said, reaching over and ruffling her bangs.

"Depends who you ask," Meredith said with a mock-petulant shrug.

Ozzie leaned back into the library sofa. "God, I can't believe it's done. After all these years of shooting and shooting, labouring towards some invisible idea of perfection, and all I needed was a new set of eyes." He looked at her solemnly. "I hope you will be happy with an editor's credit."

Meredith shook her head hard. "Don't do that."

"I insist," Ozzie said, so insistently that she gave up arguing. "And after that I want you to direct."

"Direct!" Laughter bubbled up from her gut. "What would *I* direct?"

"Whatever you wanted to," Ozzie said, looking as serious as she'd ever seen him. "Within reason of course. Probably romantic comedies, or tragic love stories. The sort of thing young women seem to direct. If they ever do, which is a rare occurrence. You're very talented, Meredith. You're able to make sensible stories out of . . . other people's messes."

Meredith raised an eyebrow to object, but Ozzie silenced her by raising his hand.

"I will not see your gift wasted on note-taking and stopwatch clicking and whatever else it is you continuity girls do."

"Actually the official title is 'script supervisor,'" said Meredith, feeling suddenly quite defensive. "And we do much more than take notes. For instance there's back-matching of the action, which is very important, particularly when keeping track of the coverage for a scene shot on a range of different axes—"

"You can be a bit of a bore, can't you."

Meredith shut up to indicate she was not in the mood to be kidded. She wondered why the idea of his wanting her to direct bothered her so much. Ozzie placed a hand over hers.

"Tell me, Meredith, what is it you want, if not to direct?"

The feeling came over her again. A tingling in her ears followed by a deep belly yawn. The Quest. For a split second she considered telling Ozzie about it.

"What I really want," she said after a moment, "is to know exactly how you know my mother."

Ozzie exhaled. It was the sort of preparatory deflation that indicated a speech of heavy importance was on the horizon. But before he could speak, another voice interrupted him—this one rich, familiar and as American as the smell of brewed coffee.

"Mind if I join the party?"

Kathleen Swain, long back arched into tight jeans meant for a woman half her age, stood there. At her side swung a two-litre bottle of Evian water all but drained. She did not seem to register, let alone recognize, Meredith.

"Well, well. What have we here? Did you take the train?" asked Ozzie.

"Nah." Swain dumped herself into an armchair and threw one leg over the side. "Hitched a ride with my friend Fadi. He was flying over Italy on the way back to Saudi Arabia anyway."

Meredith watched Ozzie examine for the first time a small spot of red wine, or blood, that had appeared at some point just below the breast of his camel cashmere cardigan.

"And to what do we owe this pleasant surprise?" he said into his chest. "Shouldn't you be working on my movie? What are we calling it now?"

Swain looked extremely bored. "*Death Is for Martyrs*. My scenes were finished yesterday," she said, "and I just needed to get the hell out of London for a bit." She tossed her head back and shifted her hips in the chair so that a peach-curve of flesh appeared between the top of her jeans and the bottom of her T-shirt. She sighed and yawned, covering her mouth just at the end.

Meredith felt Ozzie should offer something to drink but he didn't. Nor did he get up from his place on the sofa. Instead he reclined deeper into the green satin, closed his eyes and breathed heavily through his nose. The air was thickening. Meredith felt slightly sick.

She remembered the story Tony had told her of Ozzie and Kathleen, and shuddered.

"Are you cold, darling?" Ozzie asked, placing his hand on Meredith's forearm.

Meredith shook her head. He had never called her "darling" before.

This was enough for Kathleen. "There's actually something I wanted to speak to you about," she said to Ozzie.

"And all the telephones in London were broken?"

Kathleen laughed ostentatiously. Meredith felt she should just leave, but Ozzie's hand on her forearm pressed down, indicating he wished her to stay.

"I wanted to come and see you as soon as I could," Kathleen began, her posture collapsing. "I've been seeing doctors. The ones you recommended and others. One in particular who was actually pretty good and, anyway, I thought it would be nice . . . Basically I thought it would be nice if . . . we could . . ." Her voice trailed off and she looked at Meredith as though she had only just noticed her in the room. She arranged her face in a wincing smile. "Do you mind if I have him to myself for a bit?" she said. "Thaaanks."

Before she made it out the library door and down the hall, Meredith heard Kathleen laugh. "Brunettes?" she said, in a voice that made no effort to conceal itself. "You aren't lowering the bar, are you?"

What could Meredith possibly do but eavesdrop?

Ozzie mumbled something gruff in response. Then Meredith heard Kathleen's voice, scandalized and disbelieving.

"No. You mean she's *that* girl? I had no idea. I mean, I guess I knew she was Irma's kid, but I didn't put it together until now. Jesus, Ozzie, have you *told* her?"

Told me what? Meredith wanted to scream. But Kathleen walked over and pushed the door shut with an audible click.

Meredith turned in the dark and stumbled into Tony. He was leaning in a door frame, holding a glass of red wine and wearing a bemused expression.

"How dare you spy on me?" she hissed.

"How dare you eavesdrop?"

She felt like scratching the stupid look off his stupid face. Instead, she started down the hall towards the stairwell.

"Meredith," Tony called after her in a singsong, "Meredith Matilda Moore."

She stopped at the sound of her middle name.

"Have you been going through my things?" she demanded, privately trying to locate her passport in her mind. (Black bag, inside pocket.)

Tony strolled up to her, sipping as he walked. "Why would I need to go through your things when I can find out everything about you through other, more obvious, sources?"

"I don't know what you're implying, but Ozzie and I are just friends." Meredith's face burned.

"Oh, you're rather more than that, my dear, whether you want to admit it to yourself or not. What I'm wondering is—" he put a finger to his lips and circled her as he spoke—"how you could be so blind to what is right under your pretty little nose."

"Stop talking in riddles," Meredith snapped. "This is real life, not some melodrama in your alcoholic imagination."

"That's precisely what I've been trying to tell you," Tony said, with a laugh. "Now run along to your room. Maybe there'll be a present waiting for you."

"What—" Meredith began, but Tony wandered away.

Odious little man, she thought, stomping up the stairs to her turret room. Creepy bald freak.

Stepping over the threshold, she felt a current travel through her body. The room was just as she had left it, except for one thing. On her pillow was a file folder labelled "M." She sat down on the bed and opened it. Inside was a tidy stack of documents. She observed with dread and fascination that the documents bore the letterhead of the girls' boarding school she had attended in Toronto from grades one through thirteen. *"Meredith is quiet in class and always completes her work on time; however, she occasionally has difficulty sharing"* was the handwritten comment on the first page.

The phrase *the universe reeled* flashed through her brain. Leafing through the folder—carefully at first and then faster and more wildly as her realization grew—she came across copies of all her old school reports, excellence awards (one for perfect attendance and another for winning a grade-six spelling bee she could barely remember), receipts for school fees in Osmond's name, plane ticket receipts for various flights to London, as well as photographs of her that had been stuffed into envelopes bearing her mother's handwriting, addressed to Vogrie. One showed her at the age of three, ribby and smirking on a Mediterranean beach. Meredith remembered the holiday, which had occurred during Irma's brief and passing fascination with naturism. On the back it said, in her mother's handwriting, *"Little Mere in Mallorca, Summer 1973. Isn't she lovely? Lots of love, Irm."*

Meredith felt ill. She put down the file, let her hands fall to her sides and stared straight ahead, her mouth filling with the sour taste of unwanted discovery. She remembered her flashback in Holland Park—her tiny hand held in a man's larger one. The scorpion.

Ozzie's ring.

But if he was her father, why had he never told her?

For a few minutes she sat on the bed, lost in a tornado of thoughts. Her gaze became fuzzy, then somehow fixed again upon a new object set on her bedside table. A photo in a cheap driftwood frame, the kind you might buy in a tropical-airport souvenir shop. She reached for it. The snapshot showed three people, two men and a woman, standing by a pool clutching drinks in highball glasses. They were hamming it up for the camera, red cheeks fortified, laughing and squinting out from a washed-out pastel landscape of palm trees and Tiki torches that Meredith recognized at once as California, the late sixties. In the background was a swimming pool in the shape of a vital organ. The woman looked as twitchy as a greyhound in her green string bikini. The men stood on either side, grinning for their lives. For every inch of her nakedness, they compensated with high wool vests, thick knotted ties and pointy, gleaming dress shoes. A smoother, more sharply focused version of Ozzie stood on the far left, slightly apart from the other two. The taller man, the one with his arm around her mother's waist, Meredith had never seen before. Not that it mattered.

So that explained it. Ozzie was her father. The American director was in fact a Canadian movie producer, and instead of drowning in a swimming pool, he had hidden himself away in a Tuscan villa. She was, in fact, the progeny of a sordid Hollywood pool-house quickie after all. But her father was not dead. Other than that, however, the story matched up. It explained everything in fact. Meredith's education, which her mother (it seemed so glaringly obvious now) could never have afforded on her own. The fact that she was sent away to Canada to school. (Ozzie was originally Canadian.) The job her mother "arranged" for her in London. Ozzie's surprise invitation, as well as the interest he had taken in her career. And her. All of it made a sick kind of sense.

She grabbed the photograph and slipped it inside her bag. Then she started packing.

***

Half an hour later she walked down the corridor to the library door. She was leaving, but first she had a question. In her hand was the file she intended to present to Ozzie.

She opened the door a crack, but Kathleen's voice stopped her dead.

"I'm not begging you," said the actress in a high-pitched vibrato (the unmistakable harbinger of tears). "There are plenty of other candidates. But I just thought you deserved, you know, what do they call it? Right of first refusal."

Meredith could not see them from where she stood. She held still.

"As I said, I am very flattered you would ask, but at this point in my life—"

"But it wouldn't be *yours*," she interrupted. "I mean, of course it would be yours, but no one would have to know. And naturally I wouldn't ask you for—for anything. Ever. You know I could care less about that."

"What about one of those anonymous places— Couldn't you . . . ?"

"Look, Ozzie, the whole point is—the reason why I came really, is that I just wanted it to be with someone I *know*. Not just someone I know but someone who I've known for a long time and who I trust. My doctor recommended that I come to someone I trust first before resorting to—you know . . ." Her voice trailed off.

"I know, I know. Poor sweet." There was a rustling sound of upholstery as Ozzie comforted her somehow with his body. "Who is this doctor? The American?"

"Canadian actually. You'd like him. If you want I can fly him over at a moment's notice and we can both meet with him. He can perform the procedure right here in Italy. I know you hate to travel. I've checked it all out. I've arranged everything, darling. All you have to do is—God, it's so embarrassing. . . ."

Ozzie's tone became more playful, one Meredith recognized all too well. "What are you saying? We can't try the old-fashioned . . . ?"

This, followed by a round of giggling admonishments from Kathleen and more giggles and slurpy half silence. Meredith shivered in disgust. They must be kissing.

After moving away from the door, Meredith paused. She slid the file under the door.

Her taxi was waiting outside.

The Savoy, where the wedding reception was being held, was booked solid. This was a relief to Meredith, as the cheapest room cost roughly the same as a mortgage payment on her condo in Toronto. She ended up staying at the Hotel Excelsior, a hostel near the central station where the room keys were attached to large wooden blocks and the windows rattled in the panes every time a train pulled out. At least she could make a quick getaway if she needed to.

The day of the wedding Meredith had arranged to meet Elle for lunch at an outdoor café near the Duomo. The city was so crammed with tourists she had to touch her Ativan bottle twice during the walk there. She looked around, trying to determine whether this was the correct street in the crazy cobblestone maze of central Florence, and to her amazement, spotted Elle through the throng across the street. Her friend was doing the same wild-eyed dance—squinting down at a map and then up for a sign. Down, up, down, up, as the crowd frothed about her.

Meredith called out and ran to her, and the two women embraced, revelling in the excitement of meeting up with a friend from home, halfway round the world. Once they had secured a table and ordered a carafe of cheap red, everything seemed much more hopeful. They chatted about the wedding, making fun of the overblown insanity of weddings in general without forgetting to pore over every detail of the ritual itself. What was the bride wearing? Who was in the party? What was on the menu, et cetera?

And then Elle took off her sunglasses. She'd been living in the netherworld of sleep deprivation since having Zoe five years ago, but this was different.

"Andrew's moving out," she said.

"No."

Meredith hoped this sounded like disbelief rather than what it was: a protest.

"He's rented an apartment near his office," she snorted, and pushed her sunglasses back on her face. "No more sleeping on the office couch."

"Where is he now?"

"Took the kids to visit his parents in Florida."

"What was the issue?"

"How can you even ask me that?"

"I just mean, was there . . . *something else*?"

Elle shrugged, and Meredith noticed her upper arms had grown thin. As if to emphasize this, Elle lit a cigarette.

"I guess there's always something else going on in

situations like this. The question is whether or not that something else is the symptom of the problem or the cause."

"But, Elle babe, listen, are you sure?"

"Sure about what?"

"That he was, you know, that there *was* someone else." The words felt thick in Meredith's mouth.

Elle fiddled with her sunglasses but did not take them off.

"Not him, Mere. Me."

* * *

Meredith often ducked out of wedding receptions, and this one was no exception.

Three hours into the party she found herself leaning against a pillar in a vacant banquet hall of the hotel, watching waiters set up folding chairs for an event the following morning. Her body throbbed pleasantly with the effects of dancing. She sipped a soda with lime.

She had to admit it had been the very best kind of wedding. The kind where the bride and groom were young, beautiful and flushed with good intentions. Now all they had to do was go forth and produce more people like themselves—handsome, well-loved children of privilege, who would in turn create more immaculately happy people just like their parents and so on for generations until the whole world was awash in thousands of clean-living, prosperous, symmetrically featured couples and their laughing blond children throwing Frisbees in parks and shopping for old-fashioned ice-cream makers at Williams-Sonoma. Meredith, who never wasted time fantasizing about her own wedding (after she turned thirty the thought of gauzy veils and seashell table centrepieces embarrassed her), was suddenly overtaken by sadness that she would never be a bride like the bride she had seen tonight—twenty-eight and beaming in the presence of her sane and married parents.

Meredith watched the opera singer who'd performed two arias earlier in the evening folding up her music stand. A fastidious-looking switch of a woman, she wore her hair coiled on top of her head with ribbons like a demigoddess. Just before she left the room she gave Meredith a nod good night. Something about the exchange reminded Meredith of that fundamental rule of humanity: that no matter how impenetrable and well-appointed people might seem on the surface, beneath the waxed brows and bleached teeth they were just like you. A total mess.

"A perfect wedding," said a man's voice.

She turned to see him—Dr. Joe, standing with his hands shoved deep into the pockets of his trousers, smiling as if it were the most normal thing in the world for her to keep bumping into her gynecologist in different countries. For some inexplicable reason, she was not surprised.

"You know it's rude to read people's minds."

"Really?" he said.

"Yes. It's like any other super-power. There are rules. Manners." She looked at his cufflinks. They were silver. A very silvery silver.

"Like what?"

"Like . . . for example, Superman. He had X-ray vision but he never would have let Lois know that he knew, you know, what she looked like . . . underneath . . ." Oh God, what was she trying to say? This was ridiculous. What was he doing here anyway?

Joe stepped forward and slipped his hand under her elbow. "Why are you avoiding me?" he said.

"Avoiding you? Last time I checked it was a good idea for single girls to stay away from married men."

"My wife died over two years ago."

Meredith was momentarily abashed. "What's with the ring, then?"

Joe looked at his hand as if he had just noticed the narrow white-gold band he wore on his third finger. "She died of cancer two and a half years ago and my daughter gets upset if I take it off. She wears her mother's engagement ring. It's sort of symbolic, I guess. Half the time I just forget it's there."

Meredith paused, coughed, examined the rounded toes of her sensible black pumps. "Your daughter. How old is she?"

"Livvy is eighteen. She goes to university in the fall."

He reached into his breast pocket, pulled a photo from his wallet and handed it to Meredith. It was a school portrait of a dark-haired girl with a secret smile. Her hair was brushed forward in front of her shoulders, like a curtain. The girl from the drugstore.

"We adopted her when she was six months old," Joe explained. "She's not smiling there because she still had her braces on. They make them in rainbow colours now. It's supposed to be fun, but it just makes kids even more self-conscious. I keep meaning to get a more recent photo."

His face relaxed into a smile. He bent down and removed a piece of confetti from her forehead. He smelled deliciously clean, like cotton bedsheets and lemon balm.

"Don't you want to know how I found you here?" he said.

Her face turned hot and prickly. *Found?* Did he really say, *found?* Found implied he had *looked*, which implied that he liked her. Not just liked her but *like*-liked her.

"How?"

"I had to fly here to treat a patient. A mutual acquaintance," he said, with the look of someone trying to say something without actually saying it. "And when your mother told me you were going to be in Florence at a wedding at the Savoy, I decided to drop by."

"You talked to my mother?"

"I thought that's where you were living. I got her number through the production office on the film set."

"They just gave it out to you?"

"Not exactly. I had to pretend to be your brother."

"Oh. Weird."

"Sorry. It just seemed at the time to be the least, uh, lascivious-sounding of all the possible excuses I could give. And I was getting a bit worried after you didn't return any of my messages."

"You left me messages? When?"

"Dozens!" He coughed. "Well, several anyway. Certainly a few. A few sounds better, doesn't it? Let's say I left you a few messages. After that . . . altercation on the movie set, and you losing your job . . ." He rubbed a hand over his face. "Meredith, I felt terrible. I really did."

"So did I."

"I bet you did."

"Uh-huh. So bad I didn't leave the flat or check my messages for more than a week."

"That explains it. I'm so sorry."

"Has anyone ever told you that you apologize a lot for a man?"

He laughed. "Really, Meredith, I just can't stand the thought of making you suffer."

"I wasn't suffering too badly. I just needed to be alone. Sometimes I just sort of need to be on my own. It's an only-child thing."

"Like now?"

"No," she said, reaching out and touching his sleeve. "Not now. I'm glad you came."

"I'm glad, too. It's a bit out of character for me. I don't usually . . ." he said, searching.

"Chase girls around Europe?"

"Not usually, no."

"Would you like to be my date for the rest of the wedding?" she asked.

"I'd be delighted." He leaned over and kissed her on both cheeks.

Mish broke the spell by rushing into the room with Barnaby and Shane in tow. "*There* you are," Mish sparkled, flinging her arms around Meredith and hugging her so that the lavender sequins on her floor-length siren gown imprinted themselves on Meredith's cheek.

From the tilt and sway of her friend's lankiness, Meredith could tell she'd made a trip or two to the punch bowl that evening. Meredith started to squirm, but Mish was not letting her go. In the background, Barnaby and Shane quietly examined their manicures, having both visited the hotel spa earlier that day. Meredith took the high ground.

"Hello, boys," she said.

Shane quivered. Meredith gave him a small smile and he threw his arms around her. He kissed her sloppily and whispered in her ear, "Oh, honey, you're not mad at me, are you? I couldn't bear it if you were. I know it's a bit strange and everything, but you know how pathetic and weak I am."

Meredith pulled out of Shane's embrace but kept

hold of his hand. Without letting go she reached over for Barnaby's, which seemed to startle him.

"I think you're an adorable couple," she said, eliciting a sheepish smile from Barnaby.

Joe extracted himself to get everyone more drinks. As soon as he left Mish was upon her.

"Okay, spill," she hissed, pulling Meredith behind a potted palm.

"What?" Meredith sipped her soda water and smoothed her dress.

"Whaddya think—I want to know about what you had for breakfast this morning? Christ. Who is *he*?"

"Who?"

Mish pulled back and glared at Meredith to see if she was being had.

"*Heaven*—that's who. The one you were talking to a second ago."

Meredith tried to look casual. "Whatever. He's that gynecologist. The one we saw in the drugstore that day. And from Kathleen's trailer in London. Remember?"

Mish nodded furiously. "The one married to the model."

"Right. Except she's not a model, she's his teenage daughter, and his wife is dead." Meredith said this darkly, as if offering evidence against Joe's character.

"So?" Mish teetered back on her heels. "What's wrong with that?"

Meredith shrugged—she would *not* get her hopes up again—then faced her friend. "It's just that things are all screwed up for me right now. I can't even think about it. Between the baby thing and Ozzie . . . it's just kind of fucked. I'll explain it all later. What's the deal with you and the groom's little brother?"

Mish shrugged and let her head wobble in the air, her smile goofy. "He's in love with me," she said. "And I'm torturing him for all of womankind. It's a retribution thing."

Meredith laughed. Mish pressed her arm and looked serious.

"You really don't mind about Barnaby and Shane?"

"Not at all. I swear."

"Thank God." She grabbed Meredith's hand. "Enough blabbing. Let's dance."

***

After the reception Meredith and Joe went for a walk, first along the Arno and then over the Ponte Vecchio past the closed-up jewellery stands. They wandered through the Latin Quarter, along cobbled alleys and through darkened piazzas and all the way to the city outskirts, where they found a medieval church at the end of a crooked road. The night was warm and they sat down to rest. From the top of the church steps they could see an olive grove in the hills that cupped the city. The leaves shimmered in the half-light and Meredith said she thought she could smell the olives. (She would one day look back on the evening and realize that this was impossible as olives on the branch haven't yet been cured and as such give off no scent. Joe hadn't said a word, although he must have noticed her mistake.)

He asked about her mother and her job and her father and every major decision she had made in her life so far. She told him every important thing she could think of, and many unimportant things too, just so he wouldn't think the texture of her life comprised only big things. He asked her, with genuine curiosity, what was the biggest risk she had ever taken? (Leaving her job in Toronto and going to London.) What was the most triumphant moment in her life? (Winning the long-distance race at the district finals in grade nine.) Who was her favourite teacher? (Mrs. Stevens, a grade-five teacher who let her adapt Roald Dahl stories into plays instead of practising her multiplication tables.) What was her favourite pet? (She had never had a pet.) And where had she never been that she most wanted to travel? (India—though she was afraid of getting sick.) After a while she began to feel like she was being interviewed, and sensing this, he told her a bit about himself.

He recounted the time he sailed a boat from Bermuda to Halifax, and about the first car he'd ever owned (a brown Grand Marquis with mustard-velour interior) and about a yellow Labrador retriever called Boner he'd had when he was seven who was attacked one summer by a porcupine. He recalled how his father, a small-town pharmacist, had laid the dog out on the kitchen table and extracted the quills from his muzzle one by one with pliers. Joe was given the job of restraining the dog, but Boner was so trusting he didn't even struggle — just flinched when a quill came out and then sighed and laid his head back down as if he knew exactly what was going on.

He did not tell her about his dead wife, but Meredith felt he would if she asked him to. And she thought that someday she might.

They talked this way for almost two hours. Sitting on the church steps, the air cooling around them but the stone still holding enough of the heat of the day to warm their bums. Heads facing shyly forward as if adding eye contact to the intimacy of the conversation might overwhelm them. Occasionally they heard a Vespa backfiring in the streets below, but other than that the city was quiet.

Out of nowhere, Meredith asked him a question. "Who," she wondered, "do you think are more romantic by nature — men or women?"

Joe tilted his head one way and then the other. He was obviously the sort of person who rolled questions around in his brain before he answered them.

"Men," he said finally.

"Really?" Meredith was surprised. "Why would you say that?"

"Because I think men are more prone to idealistic fantasies about how things could be, whereas women tend to be more pragmatic. They look at how things actually are, and go from there."

"But if that's true, why are women always the ones who seem to be complaining about a lack of romance? You know, not enough candles and bubble baths and walks along the beach?"

"Or moonlit strolls through Italian cities?"

Meredith smiled. "You know what I mean."

"I think," Joe began, measuring his words, "that women complain when men disappear. Not physically, but psychically. And they do. We do. We just vanish. Many men—most men—have the ability to escape into this fantasy world, the same one romance comes from."

"Where is it?" Meredith asked. "What's it like?"

Joe laughed but took her question seriously. "Well, it's no place in particular, because it's everywhere. And it's filled with all sorts of ridiculous things. Baseball statistics and porn and monster trucks and submarine sandwiches as long as your leg, and important things too—symphonies and screenplays and the whole history of civilization. Some men just visit occasionally, but others live there full time. Don Quixote, for instance. Or Tom Cruise. Permanent residents. Anyway, the point is, women don't really want candles and bubble baths—they want men to be present. They want to get on with the business of living in the world. Lasting contentment and home, rather than temporary bliss and escape."

He looked at Meredith. "I know it's a gross generalization," he said.

"You're right," she said.

"About men or gross generalizations?"

"Both."

Then Joe's cell phone rang. It was his daughter. She could tell by the way he stood up and lowered his head as soon as he picked up the call.

"I know, sweetheart."

From where she sat Meredith could hear a wail of complaint through the receiver. Father and daughter wrangled for several minutes as Meredith scratched her initials into the steps with a stone and pretended not to listen.

"Livvy, I can't do anything about that. I'm halfway across the world. . . . On Sunday . . . Yes, I promise." Joe made some soothing noises into the phone before finally hanging up.

He looked up and Meredith thought he seemed very tired.

"She's having a problem with her course registration. I'd better go back to the hotel and make some calls," he said. "Sorry to bother you with all this. It must be pretty boring on your end."

"Not really," said Meredith. "You should go. I'll get a taxi."

"No, no, I'll walk you," he said, jamming the phone into his jacket pocket. "But before we go . . . listen."

He was stooped over a few steps down from her so that they were now eye to eye. Meredith hugged her knees and looked at him, waiting.

"Okay," he said finally. "I know things between us have been kind of strange up until now. It's understandable, especially given the circumstances of our first meeting."

"I'll say."

"But I was wondering if I could try to make it up to you. Since we're over here and everything, and I have a couple of days to kill, I thought maybe . . ." His voice drifted off. He looked at her. Looked away. Took one step down and a second step up. "Maybe we could hang out."

"What did you have in mind?" Meredith asked.

"I don't know." He shrugged and smiled. "Rent a Vespa. Hang around the piazza. Smoke. Learn to swear in Italian."

***

Later that night she lay in the cast-iron bath in her tiny room at the Hotel Excelsior. She slid down the tub and bent her knees so her head could dip back and under the surface of the water. She blew a noisy stream of bubbles through her nose and brought her head up for air, then submerged herself again and blew some more. She lingered long after soaping and rinsing her skin, allowing the pleasantly tepid bathwater to cool her blood. Something was different, as if somewhere along her walk through the streets of Florence with Joe she had passed through a membrane that allowed her to enjoy things she normally wouldn't. Earthy things, like taking off her shoes and walking barefoot along the smooth, hot cobblestones. Or taking a late-night bath in the sulphur-stained tub at the Hotel Excelsior. (Why was it, anyway, that all cheap European hotels were called either Bristol or Excelsior?)

The soap looked like it might have been used once and refolded into its waxed paper packaging, and the roll of paper beside the toilet was not new, nor was its end folded into a little point—all things that would have bothered her enormously before, but the new Meredith was like . . . whatever. It wasn't that she didn't care about these little things anymore, just that she suddenly felt unwilling to let them overcome her and prevent her from caring about the things that really did matter. Things like . . . like . . . *oh God.*

Meredith surged up suddenly in the bath. Water sloshed out of the tub onto the floor. *She wasn't beginning to . . . was she?* She got out of the bath and stood dripping on the cement. Reaching for a towel, she knocked her toiletry kit from its perch beside the sink. Tiny bottles of perfume, lotion and hair conditioner scattered everywhere. Something large landed between her feet with a *thud*. The ovulation-measuring device that Mish had given her back in London. Meredith bent down and picked it up. The screen was blank. She turned it on to see if the batteries still worked. It beeped twice and a little pink light flashed. She began to raise the thing to her ear to take her temperature, but then she had a stronger impulse. She held out her arm and dropped the device in the bath. It beeped again—a pathetic digital cry for help—and sank to its death. Water splashed over the side of the tub, soaking the mat and slinking off in rivulets. She felt giggles bubbling up inside her. *Uh-oh*, she thought, throwing a threadbare towel over her wet head. *This was not the plan.*

***

"You're smitten. It's pathetic. I can totally tell from the dopey look on your face."

"Excuse me. *You* should talk. I'm not the one who spent the night with a horny twenty-year-old."

"Actually if you must know he happens to be a very mature nineteen." Mish took a bite of her pastry and regurgitated it into a napkin. "Bleh! Gross. Why do the Italians do that? It's like a perfectly normal-looking croissant from the outside and then the inside is filled with, like, the most disgusting *spooge*."

"I think it's actually called marzipan."

"Whatever. It's fucking sick." Mish picked up the pastry with two fingers. "Wannit?"

"No, thanks." Meredith sipped her cappuccino. She couldn't eat. Not with the organ grinder in her stomach.

Mish tossed her head back and honked. "Oh my *God*, it's so obvious—you're in love. I'm sorry, honey, but it is."

Old friends were overrated. Meredith made a back-off face, but before she could control it her features had morphed from hostility to a goofy smile. *Fuck.*

"So c'mon, tell me. Is he The One?"

"How should I know?"

"Can't you just tell? I mean, Mere, he seems perfect—tall, good skin, lots of hair. He's a doctor so he can't be dumb."

Meredith began to object but Mish held up her hand.

"Wait. Did you check out his family history? Any alcoholism? Abuse? Mental illness? Because you know those things are genetic. A kid might look totally normal until the age of twenty and then—*pow!*—they turn into a hallucinating alcoholic. Think about it."

Meredith was shaking her head. "No. I'm off that."

"Off what? The Quest?" Mish was incredulous. "But I thought you were looking for The Donor, not a husband."

"I'm not looking for a husband," Meredith snapped. "I'm just sick of being a sperm bandit."

"But I liked you as a sperm bandit!"

"Really? I thought the whole thing actually bothered you. Because of what happened," Meredith said, referring to the miscarriage.

Mish paused, suddenly serious. "It did at first, a little. It just seemed like everywhere I looked, women were trying to get pregnant. But then I remembered that's actually just the way of the world. People are born, they make some other people, then they die."

"It's not the only thing," said Meredith.

"No, it's not. And it's not for everyone." Mish cupped her chin. "Much as I wanted it, it wasn't for me."

Meredith reached for her hand but Mish waved her away.

"The point is, I'm not going to be one of those childless women who spends the rest of her life feeling like a tragic failure because she never got to clean banana barf off the sofa. There's more to life than having babies." She stuck a finger in her pastry so the goo spurted out. "Having said that, I'm sorry you've abandoned your plot—quest—whatever."

"Yeah, well, it wasn't exactly working out."

Mish licked her finger, dipped it in the icing sugar on the plate and tasted it thoughtfully.

"No, I guess it wasn't. But you still want to have a baby, right? I have to be Auntie Mish to somebody."

"Yes! I mean, no. I mean, yes, but just for different reasons."

"Did you tell Joe?"

"Tell him what?"

"That you're no longer out to commandeer his jizz?"

"Oh God." Meredith wrinkled her nose.

"Well, have you?"

"It didn't exactly come up."

"Do you think it will?"

Meredith tried to answer but she felt too confused, so she changed the subject to Elle. Her affair with a single father she had met in her neighbourhood play group was now an open secret.

"They're in love." Mish shrugged. "She hasn't spent more than a few hours at a stretch with Andrew since law school. The guy's a total workaholic. Who can blame her?"

"They just seemed so perfect," Meredith said.

"*Seemed* being the operative word."

Then she made Mish tell her all about how things were going with Barnaby and Shane—well as it turned out.

Barnaby's brother, under a certain amount of financial duress, had consented to open up the grounds of Hawkpen Manor to the public and Barnaby was going to start a falconry breeding and demonstration centre as a tourist draw. He'd asked Shane to come and stay for a while and help him set up shop, and he was brimming with dozens of half-cocked ideas about setting up his own little gift shop on the grounds or becoming a milliner. Mish was planning to stay on and work with him too.

"He has this idea that he could use feathers from the birds. He wouldn't kill them, just collect the ones they dropped on the ground. Or if one died then he could stuff it and put it on a hat. Unless it was too big and then he could just stuff it and sell it as a decoration. Actually he's thinking of becoming a taxidermist. I told him I doubt they even have courses in taxidermy anymore, but you know how he is when he gets an idea in his head. I had a phone session with my shrink and she thinks it would be a great opportunity for me to get over my bird phobia."

As Mish prattled, Meredith felt something expand

inside her chest. It may just have been the espresso, but she felt more hopeful than she had in months.

"I said maybe I could help him teach the falcons tricks—they're super smart you know, and I took that dog training diploma. Then he could have like a travelling circus. We could hire gypsies to run it. Real gypsies. They have them over here. I've always wanted to hang with the gypsies. Or maybe Barnaby could learn magic and pull owls out of hats instead of doves, or maybe . . ."

Meredith considered for the first time the possibility that it was better not to decide on the outcome of your own story in advance. That maybe there was something to be said for serendipity. Much as it frightened her, perhaps letting the narrative play out on its own, without imposing outside controls and strictures, was the wisest course of action.

She tried the theory out on Mish.

"Didn't you know?" Mish said. She tapped Meredith lightly on the head. "That's what happens in the end anyway."

"What do you mean?"

"Life has its way with *you*—not the other way around."

18

Meredith set down her bag and stood on the landing, fiddling with the key to the flat on Coleville Terrace. Cracking open the door, she gave the place a pre-emptive sniff: book dust and caked lipstick. Not home exactly, but a whiff of something close.

She abandoned her suitcase in the little guest bedroom and mounted the steep, narrow stairs to the sitting room. As she climbed, her thighs complained. There was a dull throb between her legs. Rough rashy dry patches covered her skin at the knees and elbows, and her hair was still tangled in a damp mat at the nape of her neck that she hadn't been able to get out with the hair pik that lived in the side pocket of her bag. The last time she'd glanced in a mirror (at the Savoy in Florence earlier that day) she'd noticed her face looked sunburnt—a pinkish flush spreading from the tip of her nose over her cheeks, mouth and chin. She never exposed herself to the sun.

"Kissy rash!" Mish had shrieked at the sight of her when they'd met at the station to catch the train to Pisa, the first leg of the journey back to London. Despite the adolescent horror of being caught, Meredith could do nothing but grin like a simpleton. She felt as though all of the blood had been drained from her body in the night and replaced with slow-pouring cognac. The lobotomizing power of sex.

She hadn't expected her mother to be in, but here she was at the top of the stairs, a dishcloth in one hand and a teacup in the other. Her small head was wrapped in a large silk turban and pinned with an amber brooch. Meredith felt a stab of affection.

"What on earth have *you* been up to?" Irma said.

"Mum. I didn't think you'd be home."

"Why not? I live here."

"Well, I thought . . . I don't know. I figured you'd be out."

Irma moved behind the kitchenette counter and began scrubbing the oven. Her hands were hidden in rubber gloves.

Glancing around, Meredith couldn't help but notice a marked improvement in the place. You wouldn't call it tidy, but it was as if a few years' worth of dirt and clutter had been scrubbed off the surface.

"You didn't have to clean."

"Well, I thought I would. The place needed a little sprucing." Irma scratched the side of her nose with her shoulder to avoid contact with the glove and attempted to pry the top of a stove element off with the blunt end of the toilet brush.

"How did you know I was even coming?" Meredith asked.

"I didn't." Irma laughed, and as she did a flicker of realization passed over her face. "Oh, darling, you thought I was cleaning for you. No, no. Never make a fuss for *family*. I'm having a guest over tomorrow evening. Nothing fancy, just a cocktail before the party. Of course you'll join us. I assume that's why you came back."

"What party?" Meredith felt very tired.

"The *wrap* party, Moo. For the movie. Your movie. What's it called? *Death Matters*? Anyway, it's tomorrow night, just around the corner at a new club on Portobello Road. You're coming of course."

"First of all it's not *my* movie. I was fired. So no, that's not the reason I came back and I'm not going to any wrap party either. Frankly I'm not sure why *you* would, Mother, given the nature of your involvement with the project."

Her mother crossed the room and gave Meredith a dry peck on the cheek.

"If you must know, I was invited. Actually it's a date."

"A date?"

"Yes, and why not?" She picked up a straw broom and handed it to Meredith. "If you're going to just pop in like this unannounced, the least you could do is pitch in and help me get ready. The party is in twenty-four hours and there's ever so much to do."

Meredith sighed. She'd been hoping to come home and flop. Take a nap. Order in a Som Tam salad from that place on Askew Road. Maybe watch a movie.

Instead Meredith began to sweep. They worked for the better part of the hour, listening to pop songs on the radio. No talking. She watched her mother with a new curiosity. This jittery little woman, with her strange appetites and off-kilter vanity, represented more than she ever had before. For the first time in her life Meredith grasped the fact that her mother had lived a full existence before she herself was even around. But where and what had Meredith been? Just a couple of random cell clusters in separate bodies waiting to smack into each other and glom on, like strangers at a bar. Here before her, plunging a vase into a murky sink, was half of the equation that added up to herself. The other half was woven into every fibre of Meredith's being, and yet she could never know for certain who he was unless she asked.

The conversation had to be had. Meredith decided to start it subtly, in a manner conducive to opening lines of communication with her mother. She asked Irma about herself.

"So who is this guy? He worked on the movie?" Meredith said.

"In a way," Irma said, with a coquettish roll of her shoulders. "He was involved."

While she could often be astonishingly indiscreet, at other times her mother couldn't resist the impulse to withhold basic information—particularly if her audience was curious. Meredith continued sweeping. They cleaned in industrious silence for a few more minutes until Irma interrupted their labour with a sneezing fit.

"Woo!" she said when she was finished. "That was better than sex!"

Meredith threw her a disgusted look, but in her current state of mind not even her mother talking about sex could get to her. She felt protected by her own haze of remembered pleasure. She couldn't wait to go to bed and relive the past seventy-two hours in her mind's eye.

"How was Ozzie's, then?" Irma said.

"Fine." Meredith looked up, but her mother's face was hidden behind a cupboard door.

"He's quite a character," Meredith said.

"Ozzie? Oh, yes. Extremely strange. But not in a bad way, I hope."

"No, not in a bad way."

Silence. Meredith carried on sweeping but kept her eyes on the cupboard door that hid her mother's upper half. Slowly, apprehensively, the silk hump of her mother's turban appeared, then the brooch, followed by a tuft of hair, a furrowed forehead and, finally, a pair of startled eyes. For a moment Meredith and her mother stared at each other like this, each waiting for the other to speak.

Meredith broke the silence. "You lied."

"No, I didn't." Irma stepped off the stool she'd been balancing on and faced her daughter. She looked at Meredith but did not move towards her.

"Why didn't you tell me about Ozzie?" Meredith's voice skipped up an octave and then managed to steady itself again.

"You didn't ask."

"How could I have known to ask?"

"What exactly was I supposed to tell you?" Irma refastened the tie on her Madame Butterfly dressing gown.

"Uh, for starters, maybe the fact that he's my father."

"But he's not."

"Oh, Mother . . ."

"No, really, he's not. He's a friend of your father's. And he took care of you—I only mean *financially* took care of you—when you were little. He helped us out all along. I honestly don't know what I would have done without him."

"So Ozzie's not my father?"

"I'm afraid not."

"Who is, then?"

"I told you the story, darling. He was a director. I met him in Los Angeles. We had a romp in the pool house and he drowned in his pool the next day."

"Did he have a moustache?"

"He did. How did you know?"

Meredith shrugged. She remembered the picture. The man with the grin so big it looked like he was going to take a bite of the camera lens. "Lucky guess."

Irma resumed wiping down the stove, but Meredith wasn't finished with her. "Why didn't you tell me about the money, then? And why would Ozzie take care of me like that?"

"Let me tell you, young lady, when you were a baby I was in no position to look gift horses in the mouth. And besides, the money was none of your business."

Meredith considered the outlandish possibility that for once, her mother was right. As a child it had been none of her business where her school tuition or living allowance came from. She'd never thought to ask and consequently her mother had never mentioned it. She'd been a *kid* after all, and what was her mother supposed to say? *Your father was married to someone else and unfortunately he drowned in his own swimming pool a few hours after your conception, but don't worry, sweetie, because his ex-business partner is determined to take care of you out of his own mysterious sense of guilt and responsibility?*

Meredith took a step towards her mother and held out her hand. Irma seemed afraid to move. She hugged herself and pushed her hands under her armpits to try to stop them shaking.

"Mum, don't worry." Meredith put her arms around her mother. She was shocked at how breakable the old woman felt. "I'm not mad," she said. For once, she felt it was true.

"You're not?"

"No."

378

With this, Irma relaxed slightly. Her breath slowed. She seemed to gain weight in Meredith's arms.

"I want you to tell me the whole story."

"Right. The story. The *story*."

Irma produced two small glasses in the shape of tulip blossoms and handed one of them to Meredith. She poured a bit of sticky yellow fluid into each.

"Where do you want me to start, then?"

"At the beginning."

***

Florence came back to Meredith in flashes. Not recollections so much as relived moments—complete with smells, sounds and the aching texture of immediate physical experience. There was the smell of his breath and the taste of his mouth—savoury as gin-soaked olives. His second toe, a hammertoe, half broken and doubled over on itself. She'd lain end to end with him and taken that toe in her hand and tried to smooth it out with her fingers but it wouldn't stay flat. No matter how she rubbed it the toe snapped back to its crooked self. He said it was good luck—the toe. She couldn't believe it. Her luck, that is.

For three days Meredith and Joe stayed in his suite at the Savoy. Outside, the city felt like it was baking in a brick oven. Inside, their room was cool and clean. Every few hours they sent down for room service, ordering anything on the menu, no matter how ridiculous or oddly matched—cherry cheesecake with the Japanese businessman's breakfast, pink champagne and lasagna, oysters with mint sauce and apple cider, Tuscan bread soup followed by a whole lobster, cracked and dressed. Nothing seemed too silly or decadent. What they didn't eat they left on trays in the hall. What they didn't drink they spilled on each other.

At one point he leapt up on the bed, kneeled over her and began filming with the super-8 camera he'd brought along to record the wedding. At first Meredith covered her face with a pillow, but after some gentle coaxing she found herself vamping for the lens like the star of a French blue movie. She pouted her lips and lifted her bum in the air, waggling a pair of lacy knickers. *What had gotten into her?*

On the bedside table was a small bottle of Jack Daniels stripped from the now-nearly-empty mini-bar the night before. She picked it up and began running its hard cold surface over her abdomen, encouraging every mammalian hair on her body to rise. Joe began crawling towards her, across the bed. She took a slug of whisky and passed the bottle back to him but he waved it away, encouraging her to keep playing. She felt a little silly, but aroused all the same, so she began to experiment: taking the neck of the bottle in her mouth and moving her lips over it suggestively, taking a too-large swig and letting it run out the side of her mouth, dipping her fingers in and rubbing the bour-bon on her nipples—the astringent liquid buzzing on her flesh. Feeling sly and sexy, Meredith inclined the bottle between her legs. She slipped a finger into her panties. (Yes, *panties*, that was the word for them. She was now a woman who could say the word *panties* without cracking up.) She teased and taunted, fingering the lace and sliding the neck of the bottle nearer to the spot. Joe lowered his head slightly and opened his mouth, but before he could say a word, she raised her eyebrows and—*uh-oh*—poured whisky between her legs.

The pain! Before she knew it she was up and running around the room, clutching her crotch and howling like a woman on fire (which, in a sense, she was). Joe flew into action and before she knew it he was on top of her again, pinning her to the bed like a wriggling insect specimen and pressing a cold, wet facecloth to her crotch.

"You okay?"

He said this very seriously. So seriously she wanted to cry, before she noticed her cheeks were already streaked with salt.

"Mmm." She nodded, trying to imitate his seriousness in the hope of drawing out the moment of rescue. It was so nice to be taken care of. She pressed her face into the crook of his shoulder and started to laugh—a slow, rocking laugh so much like a sob that he comforted her for a moment by stroking the hair at the nape of her neck before he realized his mistake.

He could be a bit serious—it was his one flaw. She loved him for it.

***

The day of the wrap party Meredith booked a ticket back to Toronto. She didn't fly for a week, which gave her plenty of time to tie up loose ends in London, mainly in the form of actually getting to know her mother for the first time. Their relationship, which had never been particularly comfortable, now appeared to be on the verge of reaching an uneasy truce. At moments, they seemed almost related.

They went to the movies and saw a play—a bad translation of an even worse French farce—and Meredith cooked a proper dinner of roast lamb and potatoes.

She was feeling unusually flush (Ozzie had sent her a big fat cheque for her work on *Avalon*—enough to tide her over for the next few months at least), so she took her mother out for lunch.

They never mentioned the story Irma had told Meredith the afternoon she came home from Florence, but it sat between them like an armrest—providing a comfortable distance as well as a point of contact. For the first time, their shared history became their emotional buffer.

***

Before the wrap party Irma's date arrived for a drink. He was an old man, the sort you'd call a "chap." He turned up on the front stoop wearing a corduroy day suit with a bright yellow ascot. Meredith stuck out her hand, which he took and kissed in a dry, unprovocative way. He introduced himself as Jeffrey. There was something familiar about his face.

"Irma has told me ever so much about you," he said.

Meredith gave a skeptical smile. "Oh, sure."

"No, really, I tell you, she has. Quiz me."

"Pardon me?" Meredith was removing his jacket at this point and taking the champagne from him. Her mother had yet to appear.

"Really, do ask me. Anything you like. I know almost everything about you. When Irma told me she had a daughter, I made her tell me everything so I could get to know you in a sense before I met you. So now, you see, I feel like I already do."

Meredith laughed. "Okay, then, what's my shoe size?"

"Seven and a half. Narrow."

"Okay, you win. Can I get you something to drink? Unless she's converted you to the vile yellow stuff as well."

"No, no. Not yet. Scotch on the rocks for me, please."

He settled into the squashiest chair in the room and crossed his legs at the knee. Meredith saw he was wearing yellow socks to match his neckerchief.

The apartment had been scrubbed, purged and generally made over. Boxes of old junk disposed of and eons of grime and dust wiped off walls and shaken from the curtains and upholstery. Instead of looking like an overused landfill, the small flat now had a shabby coziness about it. Underneath all the detritus Meredith had been pleased to find her mother had quite a few "nice pieces," as Irma called them. One was the inlaid mother-of-pearl coffee table on which she placed Jeffrey's Scotch. Jeffrey had picked up an ancient copy of the *Canadian Literary Review*, which contained a rave review of one of Irma's books of poems from the late sixties. (Meredith was planning to take it back to Toronto and have it framed and sent to her mother at Christmas.)

Irma appeared, swathed in brown velvet, at the top of the stairs.

"Darling!" Jeffrey leapt to his feet and ran over to her on his tiptoes like a ballerina dashing across the stage.

Meredith half expected him to pick up her mother and twirl her around, but instead he placed a gentle kiss on each of her rouge-smeared cheeks. They murmured stuff to each other for a while and Meredith tried not to watch or listen. She'd never seen her mother in such a state.

"I see you've re-acquainted yourself with my daughter." Irma turned and smiled. "Meredith, you remember Jeffrey." She completed this sentence with one of her unsubtle wide-eyed looks that said, *And even if you don't, you'd better pretend you do.*

"Sorry," said Meredith. "Mother tells me you were involved with the movie."

"Ah, yes." Jeffrey coughed. More of a pause than a cough. "My house, more than I was."

"Oh my God, of course. You're the Earl of Dorgi!" Meredith clapped her hands in recognition.

"*Meredith*," Irma warned.

"No, no, that's quite all right, Irma, really. Is that what they called me on set, then? I think it's a rather becoming name. I'm not actually an earl, you know. Not that it matters where pet names are concerned."

Irma took a sip of her Limoncello, which had magically appeared in her hand (she was rarely without it) and placed a hand on Jeffrey's knee. "And how are the dear dorgies, then, darling?"

"Much better now that they have their house back. Now, my duck, we'd better hurry if we're to make our dinner reservation. Meredith, I do hope you'll come with, and then on to the party afterwards?"

"I wasn't invited," Meredith said.

"Nonsense, darling." Irma jumped up and began running around the room opening drawers. "Now where did I put that damn thing anyway?" She pulled open the refrigerator, flipped open the butter tray and took out an envelope. "Ah, yes, here it is. Now, look, you're most certainly invited. Sorry I hadn't made it clear earlier."

She handed the invitation to Meredith, who scanned down past the "You and a guest are cordially invited" part to an ink scrawl at the bottom. Ozzie's handwriting. "*Dearest Irm*," it read. "*Do come. And bring Mere as well.*"

She looked up. "Ozzie's coming?"

"One of his rare public appearances," said her mother.

"Who is this mysterious Osmond Crouch anyway? I've been hearing about him for years and look forward to finally meeting him." Jeffrey said, draining his Scotch. "Are we off then?"

Meredith shrugged. She hadn't planned on it, but then, what *had* she planned on lately?

***

Ozzie stepped into the booth, pulled the curtain shut and sighed as he contemplated the still-life laid out before him. On the small Formica counter sat a stack of plastic specimen bottles, a bottle of generic-brand water-based lubricant, a box of Kleenex and a pile of dog-eared smut mags—Brit porn, he noted sourly. The sort of publications that featured naughty schoolboy cartoons involving bishops and pictures of girls with thin lips in cheap lingerie. Figures that after a lifetime of mild disdain for the English, he would end up conceiving his only child in a London fertility clinic after an imaginary encounter with a fake-titted page-three poppet named Shirlee. But if he was going to do it, he might as well do it right. The Canadian fertility doctor Kathleen had in for a consultation at Vogrie said the procedure would benefit enormously if the specialists in London had a "full range of specimen" to work with, so here he was: offering up whatever he could.

He took his bifocals out of his jacket pocket and peered at the title topping the pile. *Tits 'n Bits*. He shook his head. Too depressing for words.

The truth was, he couldn't believe he was even here. After all those years of evading the bonds of fatherhood—all the girlfriends he had escorted to abortion clinics (including Kathleen), the countless tearful break-ups, the condoms, the last-second withdrawals, the paranoid nightstand searches for evidence of birth control pills, the secret stockpiles of morning-after antidotes—after all that, here he was, jerking off into a cup.

He chose a magazine from the middle of the pile and opened it to a random page. There was a photograph of a topless redhead in suede miniskirt and cowboy boots. She sat on some sort of countertop, cupping her breasts and looking down in surprise as if she had only just discovered them for the first time. Like most former pornographers, Ozzie was fairly inured to the sight of naked women, but something about this girl moved him.

It was the skirt. Kathleen had worn one exactly like it the night he first saw her. He remembered it like it was five minutes ago. Him sitting at his regular bar stool scarfing free salted nuts. Her leaning over the bar in a low-cut chiffon blouse, reaching for a glass, which she (thinking no one was watching) spit into and polished with a white cloth napkin. God, she'd been gorgeous. Still was. As fierce and exciting a creature as he'd ever known (and he'd known many). And while his feeling towards her was not exactly love, it was something far more certain: a belief that no matter what happened, their fates were linked. He owed her this baby, but that was not the only reason he was here in this phoneless phone booth, cock in hand, pumping away (well, okay, more squeezing and pulling, at this point), trying to draft a few million able-bodied DNA servicemen. No, the truth was, he wanted a child as much as she did, but for entirely different reasons. Not for the cutesy clothes and puréed carrot stuff, which was as frightening as it was a turn-off, but for the continuation of the larger narrative.

Seeing Meredith again had convinced him of the importance of leaving a legacy. Frank may have died the night of her conception, but a part of him lived on through the daughter he never even knew existed. Now that *Avalon* was finally finished Ozzie felt emptied out, his imagination overfished. He was overcome with the need for someone else to take over the story. Perhaps it was vain and sentimental, but he wanted a child with the hooded Cruchinsky eyes, whom he could set on his knee and to whom he could tell the story of his own tormented boyhood, of his mother's ceaseless toil in the sweatshops, of his father's flight from the pogroms of Europe and know that this small someone was a living, breathing continuation of . . . oh Christ. Fucking hell. This was not the right mental track at all.

Ozzie squeezed another daub of lube into his right palm and began again. He closed his eyes and ran through a series of mental photographs from his past. Two Kenyan airline stewardesses rolling around in a four-poster hotel bed . . . nothing. Okay, *next*. A grubby young hitchhiker whose name and age he forgot to ask. Nah. Too dirty. He began to flip through the mental picture book faster and faster, searching for something on which his brain could alight and find purchase. Kathleen—yes, it was appropriate he thought about Kathleen.

In his mind's eye he opened the photo album with her name written across the cover in girlish gold cursive. Kathleen in a hot tub, drunk, squeezing together her breasts and smiling up at him. Kathleen prancing down a runway in a transparent teddy and high-heeled slippers. Kathleen getting mock-fucked from behind on set by a large black man. Were these the right thoughts for a conception? He thought of that crazy night more than thirty-five years ago. The night Meredith had been conceived. The night Frank died. The same night Ozzie got the script that made his career. The script he didn't write but took the credit for anyway. Frank's legacy and Ozzie's darkest secret.

He remembered the party in snapshots, and the one that came to him most reappeared nearly every day. Even now, in mid-wank, it winged its way from the back of his brain to the front.

His old friend Frank—on the brink of death and about to father his only child but oblivious to either possibility—answered the door to his house. He, Ozzie, jumped out from behind a laurel bush holding six bottles of champagne wedged between his fingers like bowling pins. They embraced, Frank delivering several hearty back-slaps that nearly knocked the wind out of him.

"Ozzie! You shouldn't have. Come in, come in." Frank ushered him in, led him past the sunken living room done in the citrus and brown of the day (Ozzie recalled the strong presence of macramé wall hangings and varnished twig furniture) and into the kitchen, replete with state-of-the-art avocado-hued appliances.

Once he had poured them each a Scotch, Frank sat down in front of Ozzie and regarded him seriously.

"What's up?" Ozzie asked, feeling suddenly apprehensive.

Frank dropped his head into his hands, rubbed his face and looked up. "Look, buddy, I invited you here early—before the other guests arrive—because I wanted to give you something. It's real important."

Ozzie raised his eyebrows and cocked his head. "I'm all ears."

Frank crossed his legs and nervously wiped a bit of sand off the pointed toe of his snakeskin dress shoe. He had always been fastidious, both in appearance and surroundings. Hated the thought of a hair out of place, let alone a shot. He lit a cigarette, drew in hard and then got up and began pacing the kitchen.

"So ever since Annabel and I got married I've been thinking. She wants to have kids soon and this directing thing's not so stable. It's fine for now, but there's no way I'm raising a family doing soft porn, right? I need to make some cash. Regular, clean, nine-to-five-type cash." He paused to suck his smoke. "The truth is, I've been thinking of getting in on the other side. Maybe becoming an agent. Or even taking a job with Annabel's father's company—oil filtration."

Ozzie opened his mouth but Frank stopped pacing and raised his hand. "Wait. Hear me out. So basically I'm at the end of my rope. I figure it's make-or-break time and I'm giving myself one year."

Frank took a breath and before he had a chance to exhale, turned around and pulled open a kitchen drawer. It was the sort of drawer you'd expect to contain a can opener, a corkscrew or maybe a Danish butter-cookie tin filled with rubber bands. Instead he pulled out a thick file folder and tossed it in Ozzie's lap.

Ozzie didn't touch it. He raised his hands in the air, palms up. "What's this crap about 'one year'? You're talking about abandoning everything we ever worked for. You were born with a gift, my friend, a gift—"

Frank cut him off. He'd heard this speech before. "Just shut up and look in the folder, Oz."

"What's this?"

"It's a script. A script I wrote."

"Yeah, I got that, but how come I didn't hear about it until now? I thought we were friends."

"We *are* friends, Oz, and that's why you're the first person to see it. I haven't even shown it to Annabel yet. No one even knows I was working on it. For three years I got up every morning at dawn and went out to the garage and typed my fucking heart out and didn't tell a soul." He looked at the script with pained affection. "It's my last chance, man. This is it. Either it goes or I go. You know?"

Ozzie nodded, convinced. Slipped the script back inside its folder. Sipped his Scotch. Drummed five stout fingers on the folder.

"What's it about?"

"It's a Western."

"A *Western*."

"Yeah. I want you to read it. Tell me what you think. I'm talking dead honesty here. No dressing it up."

"As soon as I get home tonight. It'll be my pleasure."

Frank sat down at the table, visibly relaxed. He smiled and held up his tumbler. They toasted and drank. Through the kitchen window they would have looked like two friends celebrating an old sports victory or reliving past sexual triumphs. The fact that within twelve hours one man would be dead by accident never would have occurred to an onlooker.

He hadn't planned on stealing the script. But after Frank died so suddenly, things went crazy. Ozzie showed the script around, planning to give Frank a writing credit if the movie got made. But by the time production started so many people assumed it was his that he started to feel the same way. Credits got traded around all the time in the business, he told himself. Frank was dead. What difference did it make? Annabel's family had tons of dough. Frank wrote it—but he would have wanted it to get made, right? Even if that meant someone else—his closest friend—taking the credit.

This is what Ozzie told himself.

That night they poured more drinks and resumed their usual talk, a gregarious bluster of references to movies, mysterious business interests and actresses they'd like to screw. When the doorbell rang, Frank jumped up to get it. Just before he left the kitchen he paused, hands spread on the door frame.

"One more thing, Oz." He spoke very slowly, looking not at the script but straight into his friend's eyes. "Be careful with that. It's the only copy."

Jesus fuck!

Ozzie stood in the booth and shook his head— once, twice, hard, like a person trying to get rid of water trapped in his inner ear. Goddamn memory. It's like you spend the first two-thirds of your life as a walking, talking hard-on—sex constantly on the brain, all other thoughts a sideshow—then the last third you can't even concentrate long enough to get it up for a decent wank.

He resolved to start from scratch. The lube bottle farted out another dollop of goo. Ozzie picked up the magazine and looked more closely at the girl in the brown suede skirt. "When Dana isn't playing for the camera, she likes fast cars and even faster men," read the text. "'I lost my virginity to my driving instructor when I was sixteen,' says the Mancunian hottie, 'and since then I always get turned on when I'm in the driver's seat.'" Ozzie felt his mind lock in and begin to creep forward. He put himself in the passenger's seat, reaching over and slipping his hand under the brown suede skirt. Ah, yes . . . hello, Dana.

***

She couldn't wait to see him. Could. Not. Wait. Another. Second. Meredith wished she could commandeer the plane and fly it over the ocean herself. And now, of course, because of her impatience, the flight was delayed. And not just a few minutes but an hour. Another whole hour to add to the thirty-five years she had already spent without him. Which was fine before she knew him—but not anymore. Now there was no time to waste. Meredith had never felt so insanely impatient to see someone in her life.

The best of it was this: since Joe had seen her off in Florence she had not felt The Quest even once. Her sperm bandit days were over. Cured (dare she think it?) by love.

"Look at you!" her mother had said when seeing her off with Jeffrey at airport security several minutes before. "You're positively twitterpated." She had squeezed Meredith's cheeks and tousled her hair. "Mind you, don't get too happy and start eating everything in sight," she added, patting Meredith's left hip. "That always used to happen to me when I fell in love. My bottom would grow to twice its natural size."

Meredith prepared to say something caustic, but before she could, her mother let out a theatrical whoop and slapped Jeffrey's hand away from her nether regions.

"Darling! I told you, *not in public.*"

"Just checking to see if you care for me."

"Ooh, my little poopsie-woopsie." Irma began nuzzling his ear and tickling him around the middle.

Meredith rolled her eyes and took her place in the security line.

Nearly an hour had passed since then and she was still no geographically closer to her own poopsie-woopsie.

Why, she wondered, did infatuation turn people into such idiots? It was like Christmas—excruciatingly tacky unless you were in the middle of it, in which case there was nothing lovelier. She thought of Mish, staying behind with Barnaby and Shane to tend to the birds of prey in that wonky cottage in the Cotswolds. Life, she decided, was inexplicably weird.

And of course there was Ozzie. Surprisingly he had made more than a token appearance at the wrap party.

He was there when Meredith arrived with her mother and Jeffrey. The place—a new club near Irma's flat specializing in film types (there was a retrofitted movie theatre decked out with great leather armchairs and footrests)—was packed with people Meredith recognized from the shoot. Still smarting from the way she'd been fired, Meredith ducked Richard Glass and huddled at a corner table with Mish, sending Barnaby back and forth to the bar for more vodka-tonics.

"Your mother is in fine form," Mish observed, and Meredith saw she was right.

Irma swept among the clumps of people with the Earl of Dorgi in tow. Everywhere she stopped she seemed to cause a little scene of hilarity—uproarious laughter and spontaneous dancing broke out in her wake. Meredith smiled and, for the first time she could remember, took pleasure in the effects of her mother's charm. Then Ozzie came into view. He and Irma air-kissed and then Kathleen took a turn. The actress leaned down and whispered something into Irma's wig. From her vantage point Meredith could see something between them—either a bond had been formed or a blockage had been removed, or both. Ozzie had somehow facilitated a truce.

He smiled and scanned the room with his eyes. Meredith froze, waiting to be spotted.

"Is that him?" Mish gripped her forearm.

"Who?"

"Oh, fuck off. You know who. Whatshisface. The

Wizard of Oz. Hugh Hefner. Donald Trump. Alpha-boy. Mister Fuck-Off Producer guy. The Italian mystery man."

"He's not Italian, he just happens to live in Italy."

Just then his eyes fell on her. He began to push through the crowd like an unpenned bull.

"Whatever. Oh my God, look, he's totally coming over here."

"Ow!" Meredith yanked her arm away and examined it to see if Mish's fingernails had broken the skin.

"Hello, ladies."

Before Meredith knew it, Mish was having her hand kissed and giggling like a small-town deb at a Texas swan ball. Mish *lived* to have her hand kissed.

"Ozzie."

"May I steal you for a moment?" he said.

Outside on the roof deck he sipped his Campari and regarded her jealously. It was almost raining.

"That was quite a dramatic exit."

Meredith shrugged. "I had to go."

"You might have left a note."

"Yeah. I might have. I wish I could tell you I was sorry."

They stood for a moment in the drizzly silence. The conversation limped on.

"I suppose you think I should have told you earlier."

"Really?" Meredith felt her blood begin to rise. "Because I don't suppose you should suppose to know what I'm supposedly thinking at all."

"Oh, no?"

"Actually *no*."

"Look." Ozzie put a hand out towards her and then thought better of it and shoved it back into his pocket. He sighed, rubbed his eyes with his other hand, searching for better words. "Look, I should have told you earlier. About your father and my connection . . . to your past." He choked a little, and she saw it was difficult for him to get out the next few words. "I'm sorry."

"Don't apologize!" Meredith half shouted and then glanced around and lowered her voice. Ozzie looked as if he wished she'd spared him the trouble of saying he was sorry in the first place.

"The point is you bankrolled my entire childhood." She felt a blockage in her throat. "I mean, what am I going to . . . How am I supposed to ever pay you back for that?"

He shook his head vigorously. "But you shouldn't think that, darling. That's never what I expected. I never wanted for you or your mother to feel the least bit indebted to me. Not for one second."

"Why?" Meredith's voice began to quaver—she *would not cry*. "Why would you do that?"

"For your father."

"But *why*?"

"Because . . ." Ozzie looked down at his shoes and up again. "Because I owed him."

"For what?"

"For everything."

"What's that supposed to mean?"

"It doesn't matter. It's ancient history now. Just believe me when I tell you that I owed him. I still owe him."

"I just don't understand."

"In this case trust me when I tell you it's not necessary. You don't need to back-match the past, my dear." Ozzie stepped back and looked at her. "You're just like him, you know."

"Really?" She softened.

"Mmm. In looks, but also in your talents. You have his eye for detail. And his dramatic timing."

Meredith laughed, and emboldened by the moment, blurted out a question she'd been longing to ask. "How come you never had any kids of your own?"

His eyes shimmered. "I didn't need to. I had you."

***

Remembering the scene a week later brought on a tingling in Meredith's breasts. They still hurt from the man who had jostled her in the security lineup. She pushed all thoughts of Ozzie from her mind and concentrated on what lay ahead. A fresh start in Toronto. A romance. Maybe even (she could barely even think the word) *a boyfriend*.

The message on the screen changed again. BA flight 92 to Toronto delayed to 12:00. She growled. Another precious fleeting hour of her youth to be wasted in the airport. Why was nothing ever on time anymore? Meredith tapped her foot, fumed, tapped the other foot. The rest of the world may have decided punctuality was a virtue of the bored, but *she* was always on time. She was like clockwork.

Meredith froze.

She checked the date on her boarding pass and confirmed it.

She was four days late.

19

Joe stood at the Pearson arrivals gate wishing he were somewhere else.

Not that he didn't want to see her—just the opposite. He was afraid of precisely how much he did. That and the news he had to deliver.

It had been over a week since her train pulled out of the station in Florence. He warmed, remembering the hanky she'd waved out the window in an attempt to make light of the European romantic melodrama of the moment. After she'd gone he felt scooped out, but in a good way, as if he'd been emptied of all distractions and could finally appreciate his life for what it was. Joe had wandered around Florence for another day, sloping through galleries until his vision blurred and taking his espresso and panino standing up at the bar the way he noticed Italian men did. In the end he flew home a few days early. He had work he wanted to finish up before Meredith returned. And he needed time to think.

How did you tell a woman you'd just fallen for that you couldn't ever hope to make her pregnant? Joe wondered darkly if Meredith would break up with him immediately or put it off until after dinner (he'd booked a table at a little trattoria near his house, in honour of their Florentine adventure). Surely there was no way she would stay with him given his biological limitations. How could he reasonably expect her to, knowing so well the relentless, inexhaustible female drive to reproduce? He could make all the arguments he wanted about adoption and the joys of stepmotherhood and pet ownership, but in the end, physiology would triumph over psychology—Meredith's body would find a way to leave him.

He had to tell her that children were out of the question—and tell her sooner rather than later. Joe couldn't begin to count the number of desperate women who had come to him during his career, having frittered away their window of fertility on some lunkhead who had, in their words, been "wasting their time." Joe might have less than Olympian sperm motility, but he was still a gentleman. He wanted Meredith to have what she wanted (and arguably, needed) most, even if it meant being without her. He would not—much as he longed to—be the guy who wasted her time.

People clustered around the metal barricades, waiting for familiar faces to emerge from behind the frosted glass partition. Beside him stood a bald man with three small children. They squealed with happiness when they saw their mother swooping around the corner in a canary-yellow sari. She stooped to kiss them on their heads and then stood and looked at her husband and placed a hand on his cheek. In some ways, Joe thought, the gesture showed more affection than a kiss.

It took ages for Meredith to appear. A river of people poured past, each one identified in Joe's eyes only as *not her*. By the time she materialized his entire body was pricked with anticipation. The sight of her—*his* Meredith. (He had already begun to think of her, slightly guiltily, in this way.) Hair tucked neatly behind her ears, a blue raincoat he had never seen before skimming the tops of her pretty bare knees. She lugged an enormous black suitcase that looked like it must weigh twice what she did. He wished he could jump the gate and help her, and tried to call out, but although she paused and looked around with a curious expression (those cute little furrows on her forehead!) she didn't appear to have seen or heard him.

Joe pushed back into the crowd, determined to meet her when she emerged, but people crammed in front blocking his way. He kept pausing and scanning for a glimpse of blue raincoat. He should have warned her he was coming instead of making it a surprise. Surprises were emotionally risky. They only put people off balance, particularly people like Meredith. For all he knew, someone else was meeting her. Maybe he should just go home and call from there. As he was considering his options Joe felt a tap on his shoulder and turned to find her standing behind him, cocking her head.

"I came," he said, the words backfiring out of him, "and then I couldn't find— I was afraid you'd gone off on your own or that maybe you'd even seen me and didn't want—" He stopped himself blathering by reaching down and taking her into his arms. She pulled away first, just as he was placing a kiss on the hollowed-out part between her collarbone and her shoulder.

"Lovely to see you," she said, in an oddly remote voice.

He felt suddenly self-conscious and wished they could be alone together. "My car's two levels down."

"Thanks."

"What for?"

"Picking me up."

"My pleasure. How was your flight?"

"Fine. A bit exhausting. How was yours?"

"Mine?"

"When you came back. From Florence."

"Oh, fine. I guess. I slept most of the way."

They were silent until they got into his car. When he turned the key in the ignition the stereo blared to life. He'd been listening to Bruce Springsteen's *Nebraska* on the drive up and then had forgotten to take it out of the tape deck of the Jetta. The chorus that had seemed so soulful just a dozen or so minutes ago now embarrassed him. He banged his hand on the volume knob a little too hard and the whole stereo came loose and hung from its hinges. They both stared at it for a moment.

"Is everything okay?" she asked.

"Of course," he said, starting the car. "With you?"

"Mmm-hmm."

He glanced over to meet her eyes but her head was turned towards the window. He signalled to pull into the passing lane. Meredith inhaled quickly, as if she was about to say something. She turned to him, but as she did he flicked his head the opposite way to check his blindspot. She exhaled and stared straight ahead.

Joe shifted in his seat, keeping both hands on the wheel. "So what is it?"

"There's something we need to discuss."

"I agree."

"You do?" She swung her head and looked at him.

He wrapped his hands so tightly around the wheel that his fingernails dug into the heels of his palms. "I think so."

"What is it, then?" A slight challenge in her tone.

"The baby . . . thing." Joe glanced over. "Right?" She chewed her thumbnail. Faced forwards. He took her silence as a grim invitation. "Look, maybe we should talk about this later."

"No. It's fine. Let's talk about it now," she said.

"All right. Okay, well, I've been . . . This is hard. I don't know if I've experienced anything harder."

"Than what?"

"Than what I'm about to say to you. But the truth . . . the *fact* is, things are complicated for me." Joe exhaled and counted to three. "I could go into the whole story but I'm not sure the reasons even matter and it probably wouldn't be much of a consolation to you anyway so I won't, but the upshot is"—he paused—"babies are not in the picture for me at this point. I'm not going to have any more kids. I mean, I'm almost completely certain I won't. I've known that for a long time now. I've come to terms with it. I think in some ways, for Livvy and everything, it's probably actually better."

A ragged sound from the passenger seat. From the corner of his eye he saw her hands cover her face.

"This is exactly what I was afraid of."

"I know. *Fuck*." He banged one hand on the wheel and his foot stamped down on the gas. The car accelerated roughly. "I'm sorry."

"I hope," she said, "you don't mind. But I need to go straight home. I need to not be around you right now."

"Of course," Joe answered in his even, practitioner's voice. "Of course you do."

***

Meredith cried and she cried, and when she was done crying, she poured herself a bath but the smell of the lavender salts when they hit the water reminded her of their suite at the Savoy so she slid into the bath and cried some more. After a while she began to feel like a tragic amphibian. She had wept so much she could not tell the tears from the bathwater. The pads of her fingers, she noticed, were shrivelled up like albino raisins and it occurred to her that she might just die here, pickled in her own brine. Eventually the weeping exhausted itself. But she *wanted* to cry. When the current of tears began to slow, all she had to do was return to the source—the thought of losing him forever—and the floods would begin again, smashing through all the dikes in her chest and whooshing out over the landscape of her future—without him. It had been years since she had truly broken down and the force of it overwhelmed her. She had always secretly worried about her inability to cry as an adult and now it seemed she was making up for years of stoicism. She was secretly proud of herself, and of course she was also miserable.

She badly wanted a drink but knew she shouldn't.

Getting out of the bath and drying herself off, she sneezed from the dust that had collected in the towels during her absence. The condo felt even grimmer and emptier than usual, as if it resented her return. The purple terry bathrobe hung limp on the hook where she had left it and she wrapped herself inside it. She was afraid to put on clothes in case she might have expanded suddenly somewhere over the ocean. After months of yearning, now that she might have gotten what she wanted Meredith felt alarmingly ambivalent at the prospect. It wasn't supposed to have worked out this way. She and Joe had used a condom (at the crucial moments) and as far as she knew she hadn't even been ovulating at the time. But as Joe had laughingly pointed out to her before any of this, that was the bitter irony of biology: the more you tried to control your body the more your body controlled you.

Meredith dug into her makeup kit and found the rectangular cardboard box: the last of three she had bought in a panic at the Boots at Heathrow. The package said it was ninety-seven percent correct at predicting the outcome. There was always a chance. She lifted her bathrobe and crouched over the toilet holding the stick between her legs in what was now an awkwardly familiar posture.

***

She'd completed the first two tests on the plane. There was turbulence and a lineup of people waiting outside so she'd decided to economize and do two at once. With one hand she held the sticks under herself and then stood waiting for two minutes for the result. After an agonizing period, during which Meredith felt as though her stomach was crawling up her windpipe, her answer emerged: one stick had two blue lines and the other had one. A contradiction. She must have done it wrong—peed too much on one and not enough on the other. She tried to think which was more common, a false positive or a false negative.

If only she could phone Joe. But no, she couldn't

phone Joe. Not now on this plane and maybe not ever again. If it turned out she was pregnant, he would think she was a conniving sperm bandit who had tricked him and never want to speak to her again. Probably he would think she just wanted his DNA, or worse (and this was too horrible even to contemplate), the security of a husband. Under the circumstances of their first meeting, how could she possibly explain to him that it had just been an accident, a complete fluke, if that was in fact what it was? He would never want to talk to her again, that much was certain. She looked in the mirror and made a silent promise to herself. If in fact she was carrying his child, he could never know. She couldn't bear the thought of him thinking ill of her, even if it meant never seeing him again.

Just as she was about to do the third test on the plane there was a knock on the door and an attendant's voice asking her if she was "all right in there." People must have been complaining. She wrapped the sticks in toilet paper, shoved them back into her purse and returned to her seat.

Meredith had spent the rest of the flight trying to decide whether she was feeling nauseated or not and, if she was, whether that nausea was caused by turbulence, anxiety or a subtle hormonal shift that would mark the beginning of the rest of everything. She didn't sleep, clutching her bag on her lap, anxious for the plane to land so she could run to the first airport washroom she saw and do the last test—find out the deciding vote. She had planned to wait until after she got through customs, but then Joe had turned up. She hadn't known what to say or do. How do you tell a man you've just fallen for that you're sort of pregnant? And then his terrible admission that he didn't want any more children. So the whole thing was a moot point. She could have one love or the other, but not both. Meredith felt tricked—the victim of a wicked genie who grants your fondest wishes but only in a way that leaves you miserable and trapped.

When he dropped her off at her building he made her promise to call to say good night before she went to sleep—he didn't want to run the risk of waking her up when she was jet-lagged. Meredith knew the request was something of a test. A toe in the water to determine the depth of this strange new chill. She was blinking back the first of her tears as he pulled her suitcase from her trunk. She didn't look at him or wait to see his reaction.

"I can't promise anything," she said, quietly. "I just want to be alone right now."

***

Meredith waited for the final results balled up on the sofa in her condo. After a few minutes she reached into the pocket of her bathrobe. The stick was fuzzy, covered in bits of toilet paper and lavender lint. The light was fading fast, but Meredith didn't need glasses to read the result: two lines. Positive.

Days passed. Joe called several times and eventually gave up. Meredith set about tidying her life. She did not think—she merely functioned, made lists of tasks and methodically set about completing them, one by one, in the order in which they had been written.

She did her laundry and cleaned the apartment, made an appointment with her hairdresser, her eyebrow waxer, her therapist, her dermatologist, and finally repainted the kitchen cabinets.

One day she decided to drop her things off at the cleaner's. She carried a large net bag of soiled party dresses down the elevator and onto the street—the clothes she'd worn out in London and Florence now a damp burden hanging limply from her shoulder. It was a blank sort of day. Toronto weather: pallid cloud cover, empty streets, the sidewalks the same vapid non-colour as the sky. Meredith headed for the closest major intersection to her building. She had always found it a slightly disappointing corner, perfectly serviceable but devoid of excitement or life in the real sense of the word. Nothing about its angles made particular sense. On one corner was an upscale sushi restaurant in a redone national bank building, on the other was a divey old tavern with a wind-whipped patio with tables of off-hour bicycle couriers and aged, leather-faced drunks who never seemed to mix. Across from that was a McDonald's and a new wrapped-sandwich franchise she had never seen before. Meredith dropped her clothes off at her dry cleaner's, as always, amazed at the high-tech efficiency of the place—the young man who took her dirty laundry wore a tiny wire headset phone and typed her phone number into a thin laptop computer. He counted her garments with latex-gloved fingers and typed out a receipt with a date for pickup. They exchanged maybe seven words and Meredith's throat felt clogged when she smiled to thank him. She realized it was the first face-to-face conversation she'd had in three days.

Back in the vacuum of her condo, she found she had reached the bottom of her list. There was only one more thing to do. She picked up the phone and made an appointment to see Dr. Stein. All she needed now was official confirmation and a referral to an ob-gyn. Nature would take care of the rest.

She slept fitfully that night, and in the morning she felt sick. Not throwing-up sick, but greenish, as though she'd drunk a great deal the night before, when in fact all she'd done was eat half a roast chicken in front of the television. She was heavier too, but not in a fat way. It was more like an added density, as if her body was hoarding its resources, concentrating its efforts, in preparation for some monumental event, which she supposed it was.

During the months she'd been away Meredith had fallen uncharacteristically behind in her bill payments. Before her doctor's appointment she went to the bank and settled all her accounts. She paid bills in full, with interest, not questioning the amounts, using the money Ozzie had paid her for editing *Avalon*. She knew she ought to consider what she was going to do for money once her current funds ran out, but she found the future impossible to think about. Should she look for a new agent? Return to script supervising? Strike out on her own and make something new as Ozzie had encouraged? Maybe try another line of work altogether? And if so, what? Whenever these questions popped into her mind she felt her brain close tight. A boulder across the entrance of a cave.

Meredith wondered why she hadn't made an appointment with another gynecologist, at a different office, in a more anonymous part of the city, or just gone straight to an ob-gyn. But something pulled her back to that uptown office—the place where it had all started. Besides, Dr. Stein had long since returned from her stress leave, so Meredith had no reason to worry about running into Joe. And why shouldn't she go to her own doctor? Surely now more than ever was a time to consult someone she knew and trusted.

Nothing in the clinic had changed. The plastic flowers were still in their vase and Hyacinth was still jotting down notes to the same rotation of soft-rock hits. The magazines were the same bedraggled issues that had been in the wire standing rack for months, even years. Meredith selected an ancient *Maclean's* magazine and pretended to read.

Within minutes she had fallen asleep—something that had been happening to her with alarming regularity lately; she would just drift off in the middle of the day. She awoke to the sound of her name being called.

Once inside the small windowless room with the stainless steel desk and the reclining examination table, she realized she had not rehearsed what she was going to say to Dr. Stein. What if she asks me who the father is? Meredith wondered. But the doctor wouldn't dare, would she? Doctors weren't supposed to ask such things, and besides, even if she did there was no reason for shock. Having children out of wedlock was practically as common as divorce these days, and certainly better for kids than enduring some horrible drawn-out custody battle. Right? Meredith realized she was going to have to become very comfortable very quickly with the social aspects of being a solitary pregnant woman—something she had hardly considered before. All she'd thought about was babies. Having one inside her. And then the outside stuff: the feedings, the gurgles, the teeny-weeny shoes. Shopping for things called "singlets." She didn't care if it was uncool—her heart warmed at the thought. But now that the fantasy was finally coming into focus she saw that there was far more to it than she had first imagined.

Dr. Stein stepped into the room and smiled, closing the door behind her.

Twenty minutes later Meredith sat two floors down in the lab, waiting for the results of an on-site blood test that would determine the course of the rest of her life. She tried hard not to think about this, which was, of course, nearly impossible.

The waiting room was full of anxious, nauseated-looking people like herself, so she stepped out into the hall for some air. It was there, while pacing the barren corridor, that she saw him get off the elevator. Street clothes. No white coat. His features sharper than before. She realized he must have lost weight. He was searching through a courier bag as he stepped off the elevator and didn't see her right away.

"Joe," she said.

He looked up, and a series of expressions passed over his face. Delight followed by relief, then a downshift into dismay and anger, which was replaced, finally, with a cool distance.

"Hi," he said.

"Hi."

"I was just here picking up some things. I didn't think . . ."

"Me neither," she said.

They stood around for a moment looking at the floor.

"You didn't call," he said. "To say good night, the night I dropped you off. You said you would."

"I know. I'm sorry."

"You wanted to, but you stopped yourself."

415

"That's right."

"Because you figured . . . what? That things wouldn't work out in the end anyway, so you might as well cut it off now, before we got in any deeper?"

"I guess." Meredith exhaled heavily. "It's more complicated than that."

"I agree," said Joe. He set down his bag and composed himself. "It is a lot more complicated than that. I know you have a picture in your head of how your life is supposed to work out, but take it from me, that picture doesn't always match up. I'm not trying to convince you to be with me forever. I'm not saying I'm perfect for you. I know you'd rather be with someone who could make you pregnant. I'm just saying, you could have given it a chance."

"But you did make me pregnant," Meredith said quietly.

"And just because you grew up without stability," he continued, "doesn't mean you have to overcompensate by controlling everything around you as an adult. I know you don't want to end up like your mother, but don't you see that by trying to keep a grip on everything she let go, you're in danger of accidentally repeating all the same mistakes?"

"Joe?" Meredith said. "You did make me pregnant."

He shook his head. "That's impossible. I have a condition. . . ."

"I don't think you understand." She looked right at him. "I. Am. Pregnant."

"You are?" He staggered back.

"Yes."

"For sure?"

"Yes. I mean, according to those pee stick things. I'm just waiting for the results of my real test, but . . ."

"The pee sticks are pretty reliable." He rubbed his face with both hands. "Can I ask you something?"

"Of course."

"You're sure . . . it was me?"

"Oh fuck off." Meredith glared at him. "I can't believe—"

"No, Mere, I'm asking you for a reason. I have a condition. I tried to tell you that day in the car, but it came out all screwed up."

"I thought you didn't want to," she said. Her eyes burned. They still hadn't touched.

"No," he said. "I was trying to tell you, I can't. The chances of me . . . it's like one in ten thousand."

"Well, this is the one in ten thousand," she said.

They stood there in stunned silence.

A woman in pink scrubs opened the waiting-room door and stuck her head into the hall.

"Meredith Moore? Your test results are ready."

They looked at each other—Meredith, Joe and the woman in pink scrubs—waiting for the next part to begin.

Epilogue

Sperm Bandits: The New Battle for
Motherhood
A Documentary Written and Directed by
Meredith Moore

Produced By Meredith Moore and Osmond
Crouch

Act 1, Scene 1

The picture opens with a microscopic
close-up shot of a human sperm swimming fast along a Fallopian tube,
selecting an egg and then struggling
to fertilize it. The fifties song
"Baby Love" plays overtop.

    VOICE-OVER (A WOMAN'S VOICE)
   Every year in North America
   millions of women become pregnant

outside of wedlock or long-term,
stable heterosexual relationships.
For many, the situation is acci-
dental, an inopportune failing or
absence of birth control coincid-
ing with ovulation. For others
the conception is intended, even
planned, a consensual act between
two well-intentioned adults. But
for a growing minority of unen-
cumbered single women, the hope
of pregnancy is a private quest—
an independent goal that they are
more than willing to lie, cheat,
and, yes—even steal—in order to
achieve.

Close-up on the sperm successfully
wiggling its way into the egg and
coming to rest as the fertilized ovum
begins to travel in quick-time down
the Fallopian tube towards the uterus.

V.O.

One in five single mothers who
are without a partner at birth
say that their pregnancy was
planned—the question is, planned
by whom?

As the bearers of children, women
have for centuries carried the
bulk of the reproductive responsibility for the human race.
While a man may bear dozens of
children and never even know it,
a woman's existence is forever
altered by the decision to produce offspring. Does this justify
a woman's decision to help herself to male sperm for the purposes of pregnancy without the
explicit permission of her sexual
partner? What if a woman wants
nothing more from a man than his
DNA? Is she obligated to reveal
her intentions to the male, or
does nature oblige her to do what
she can to satisfy an urge that
many women describe as a biological hunger as strong as the need
for food or water?

Cut to Marissa, a financial analyst,
age forty-two, breast-feeding her
infant son Connor on her living room
sofa in a Madonna-and-child-style
pose.

V.O. (MARISSA)

The year I turned forty I decided
I was going to do everything in
my power—financially, socially,
medically and otherwise—to get
pregnant. I'd always wanted to
have children but the right relationship just hadn't come along
in time, or at the right time
anyway, and now here I was, staring the possibility of infertility straight in the face. It was
terrifying and to be honest, in
many ways I couldn't believe it.
How could I end up not accom-
plishing the thing I wanted most
in the world simply because the
timing was off? I was determined
not to become one of those women
who just "forgets," you know?

Cut to a shot of Marissa tenderly
bathing her gurgling son.

V.O.

My son was conceived while I was
on holiday at a five-star resort
on a Caribbean island. I had

arranged to arrive the week I
was ovulating and I'd been taking large doses of folic acid for
months before. His father was a
handsome guy, a successful lawyer
from Paris. We hung out for a few
days so I had a chance to ask him
all about his family background
and his own medical history. I
didn't do it in an overt way, but
just kind of made sure those topics came up. I doubt he ever suspected a thing. We never kept in
touch and I'm sure he has no idea
I became pregnant. He didn't ask
about birth control and I never
brought it up, so there was no
lying involved. Still, I'm sure
he had no idea of my plan. I
guess you could call me a sperm
bandit (*she laughs*). It sounds
pretty awful, but I don't regret
a thing. Having Connor is the
best thing I've ever done in my
life. . . .

Meredith felt her handbag vibrate beside her foot in
the dark. She stepped out of the editing suite into the
dazzling winter afternoon glare. She blinked, letting

her eyes adjust after several hours of tunnel vision in the small dark room. It was one of those cloudless winter days when the snow is so bright and dry the whole world seems like a frozen desert landscape. She walked towards the sandwich shop in a pair of Kodiaks, choosing each step with care. Pulling open the door she nearly lost her balance, but managed to right herself as the door chimes tinkled.

"Afternoon," said the shopkeeper, a weedy little fellow in a white paper hat like the kind people in 1950s fast-food restaurants used to wear. "The usual?"

Meredith nodded enthusiastically. "Please." As the man sliced off four pieces of sharp cheddar, she began the surprisingly arduous task of unwrapping the scarf from around her neck and getting her coat unbuttoned. She settled down on the wooden chair and watched the man melt butter for her grilled cheese with bacon. She'd had the same lunch every day for the past forty-four working days and amazingly, she still wasn't remotely sick of it.

Meredith pressed some buttons on her phone. Mish's voice came crackling over the line in a stern East European accent.

"Hallo, Ms. Moore. Zis eez your new doula, Olga. Vee are certain you haf been steeking to your streect diet of ze organic mung beans and doing your Kegel exercises regularly. Ozerwise ze bebbe vill be born visout a moral core. Understood? Yes? Zat is good." This was followed by some unexplained bumps that may have been Mish dropping the phone and retrieving it from the floor. Then her normal voice. "Hey, Mama. You dropped the brat yet or what? I'm hopping on a plane as soon as you do, so call me the minute your water breaks. Unless of course it happens in public in which case you might want to take a minute to clean up first. Ha ha. Just kidding. Actually, no, I'm not kidding at all. I'm being extremely serious. Anyway call me. Things are nuts around here. It's rained for the past eight hundred days straight. I swear to God. Barnaby and Shane say hi and"—muffled background noises—"what was that? Oh, they want me to say you might consider the name Barnaby-Shane if it's a boy. How's that for asshole narcissism? Anyway, later."

Beep. Next.

"Moo, it's your mother. Would you be a dear and call me as soon as you get a chance? These North American toasters are quite beyond me." A screeching smoke alarm in the background. An irritated guttural sound, then Irma raised her voice above it as though nothing remotely out of the ordinary was happening. "Ucchh. As I was saying, they don't make any sense *at all*. Could you call me? It's your mother. I can't believe you're *still* working. Could you please call me? Thank you, dear. Goodbye."

Meredith was about to call back when an automated voice informed her that an extra message had been added to her mailbox. She pressed one, and a smile crept across her face as Joe's voice filled the receiver.

"Hey, it's me. Just wanted to let you know that everything's, uh, under control with your mother. She just had a little mini-emergency in the kitchen but one fire extinguisher later and everything is completely under control. She's a funny one. You *sure* you two are related? Anyway, I was thinking we could order in roti or something tonight. Hope things are going well with the doc. Call me when you get a sec."

Meredith's grilled cheese arrived just as she was hanging up the phone and she resolved to eat before returning her calls. Eating had become a whole new priority for her over the past several months. The crumbs didn't even make it to her lap now, so she spread her napkin across her belly. The pregnant part of her was sturdier than she had imagined it would be, kind of like a giant inverted oil drum attached to her middle. She could feel the baby's foot nudging under her ribcage. Any day now, Joe said. She felt absurdly fat. Meredith looked around for something to read and the shopkeeper tossed the latest *Us* magazine on the table in front of her. She thanked him and flipped to a random page.

On one page was a trend story about male celebrities growing beards. Below that was a large photo of Kathleen Swain in a wraparound sundress walking down a city street with two small dogs. The editors had circled her swollen middle in red, highlighted by a large cartoonish arrow. KATHLEEN SWAIN'S MYSTERY BUMP! screamed the headline in eighteen-point font.

"Kathleen Swain, forty-five, is showing signs of pregnancy after a long difficult battle with infertility," read the text. "The aging starlet (who plays the lead in an upcoming as-yet-untitled Victorian costume drama) has been desperate for a baby for years. According to one friend, 'It had become an obsession that ruled her life. We were very relieved to find out that things had finally worked out for her. She's beyond happy.' Swain was recently seen shopping for pink and blue singlets at Barney's in L.A. and chowing down on an organic tempeh dog (and fries!) at her local greasy spoon. No word yet on who the father is, but a spokesperson for the actress confirms it's someone she knows and trusts. 'Kathleen would never have a baby with a stranger. At this point she's decided to keep the identity of the father a family secret. She's a very private person.'"

Meredith closed the magazine and finished her sandwich. Thank God for cheese. She leaned back in her chair and closed her eyes to rest—just for a moment—before returning to work.

Inside her, someone stirred.

Acknowledgments

Thanks to my agent, Anne McDermid, and to her fantastic gang of girls—Rebecca Weinfeld, Jane Warren and Martha Magor.

Thanks to my editor, Iris Tupholme, who took a chance on me, and to the eagle-eyed Kate Cassaday for narrowly preventing this book from being renamed The Discontinuity Girl. Thanks also to the patient friends who read earlier drafts: Liz Hodgson, Patrick Sisam, Stuart McLean, Sheree Lee Olson and especially Andrew Pyper, who devoted many selfless hours to improving this book.

Thanks to *The Globe and Mail* for granting me a leave, and also to Bruce Bailey, Clayton Ruby and Robert Hardman for providing me with places to write.

Thanks to Patrick Sisam for explaining about film and for teaching me to live in the moment. I feel so blessed. It's true!

Finally, thanks to my family for providing all the fodder—and love—in the world.